GRAND
TRAVERSE

A NOVEL BY
MICHAEL BERES

Platinum Imprint
Medallion Press, Inc.
Florida, USA

Dedication:

To KB and DMB.

Published 2005 by Medallion Press, Inc.
225 Seabreeze Ave.
Palm Beach, FL 33480

The **MEDALLION PRESS LOGO**
is a registered tradmark of Medallion Press, Inc.

Printed in the United States of America

Library of Congress Cataloging-in-Publication Data

Beres, Michael.
  Grand traverse / Michael Beres.
     p. cm.
  ISBN 1-932815-34-1
  1. Hazardous substances--Accidents--Fiction. 2. Class actions (Civil procedure)--Fiction. 3. Fathers and daughters--Fiction. 4. Women politicians--Fiction. 5. Chemical industry--Fiction. 6. Environmentalists--Fiction. 7. Revenge--Fiction. I. Title.
  PS3602.E7516G73 2005
  813'.6--dc22
                          2005016310

GRAND
TRAVERSE

A NOVEL BY
MICHAEL BERES

CHAPTER 1

A DEPARTMENT OF NATURAL RESOURCES sign at the public access ramp slop-
ing down into the water announces that Wylie Lake is two-hundred acres in size
and only electric motors are allowed. Other DNR signs, some of which are quite
weathered, warn of various species contamination, including zebra mussels.
Ripples from two boats in the center of the lake on this sunny, windless morning
distort autumn leaves in the lake's mirror, creating a kaleidoscope of color.

A young man in his 30s rows an aluminum rowboat similar to dozens
flipped upside down along the shore. The man wears a jacket and wide-brimmed
hat that shades his light complexion as he bends at the oars. An old woman
— well into her 90s — maneuvers a pedal boat that lists to one side because
of the lack of a second passenger. Rather than using the electric trolling motor
mounted on the stern of the boat, and despite her age, the old woman pedals the
boat. The woman has dark complexion and wears a brightly colored shawl over
an ankle-length frock. The pedal boat's solar cell canopy is designed to shade
two passengers, but the sun is low and it shines orange on its single occupant.
The woman's dark complexion is accented by a coif of thinning gray hair through

1

which her scalp is prominent.

As the bright morning sun rises above the tree line on the Michigan hillside, the ancestry of the two boaters is obvious: The old woman in the pedal boat is of African descent; the young man in the rowboat is of European descent.

The man stops rowing, picks up a fishing pole and casts a bobbered line as the rowboat's momentum diminishes. The woman stops pedaling and also picks up a fishing pole and casts. The two boats drift closer as if the center of the lake has a gravitational pull. Eventually the woman and the man are close enough to speak to one another.

"Lots of ashes in this lake," says the woman, her voice strong despite her age.

The young man answers. "Ashes? Is that some kind of fish?"

"People's ashes. They live down there. When they go fishing the bottoms of their bobbers are the tops of our bobbers."

The young man peers into the dark water for a moment, then looks back out to his bobber. A short stubble of thick facial hair is obvious on his white skin. Given a couple of weeks the man could have a fine beard.

The woman continues. "A lady friend of mine is down there." She chuckles. "When she died, I married her husband. Their daughter — my step-daughter — has skin as white as yours."

A high-pitched whine in the distance interrupts their conversation. Something hidden by the brightly colored trees approaches the lake from the northwest, skirts the northern shore. It sounds like a winged insect with a tiny jet engine. Although they can see nothing but trees, cabins, docks, and upturned boats, the young man and old woman follow the sound, watching the shoreline attentively. Eventually the road nears the shore at a clearing and an electric cycle races past. Because of a wind-breaker suit, gloves, helmet, and face shield, it is impossible to determine the rider's sex or skin color. The whine of the cycle lowers in pitch as it climbs a hill where the road turns away from the lake. Once over the hill the whine diminishes and it is quiet again.

The old woman has one hand to her throat. "At first I thought it was a siren. Sirens used to scare my second husband to death."

"Why was he frightened of sirens?" asks the young man.

The old woman continues looking to where the electric cycle had disappeared. "You'd think it would be because of the terrorist attacks back then. But it wasn't. Nightmares did it, sirens coming down a lonely road. He used to sleep with his hand resting on the switch to the reading lamp. Said the energy waiting upstream from the switch calmed him. He used to call out his first wife's name — Jude — my best friend. Short for Judy. When I married him, sometimes he'd call out my name, sometimes he'd call out Jude's name. The nightmare was always the same. His daughter—my stepdaughter—and another girl playing in one of those backyard swimming pools. Both girls little and the other one wearing a big old sun hat like yours."

The young man tugs at the brim of his hat, suddenly realizing he's imitating a cowboy tipping his hat to a lady without removing it. As he does this he thinks perhaps the terrorists who started all the craziness at the beginning of the century should have worn cowboy hats during their attacks. Crazy cowboys because, after all, one of the definitions of cowboy is a reckless person who ignores risks and consequences.

The old woman leans to the side and looks down into the water. "Funny thing is, before my first husband died, he was in the dream, too. Who would've guessed one day I'd be sleeping in the same bed with a white man who had dreams about my first husband. Two little girls climbing into a backyard pool on a wobbly ladder, and my husband — a one-armed chemical waste troll who lives in backyard pools . . . See, my first husband was a veteran, got his arm blown off in Vietnam when he was just a boy. The chemical thing was because of a chemical waste dump . . . "

3

The old woman looks up toward the young man. "None of this is making sense. I already got a mess of bluegills. I should let you alone."

The young man begins reeling in his line. "That's all right. I'm not using bait. Fishing's simply an excuse to come out here in the morning." He holds his line up by the bobber and shows her the bare hook. "I also left my phone in the cabin so no one can interrupt me."

"I've interrupted you," she says.

"No. My uncle, whose cabin I'm staying at, told me about you. He's dead now, but the family still owns the cabin. Anyway, when I saw you out here . . . "

She looks at him a little warily. "You're not recording, are you?"

He puts down his pole, holds up both hands. "Absolutely not."

She nods. "Well, even if you were, what the hell difference would it make now? Want some breakfast?"

"Sure."

The old woman reaches over the side of her pedal boat and holds up a stringer full of bluegills. "Nothing like fried fish for breakfast. The DNR's been stocking the lake with genetically pure pan fish for a couple years now. Catch them while they're young they're just fine."

She lowers the stringer back over the side and begins reeling in her line, staring down into the dark water once again. "When I look back over the years it's hard to believe how much has happened. I never talked about it much back then. But now that there's not much time left for me, it seems all I do is talk. If you weren't here I'd be talking to the water, or singing to it."

She looks toward the horizon. "And now with another winter coming . . . " She hums a few bars of a song, then turns back to the young man. "My second husband used to play The Beatles singing "Hey Jude" when he and Judy made love. They recorded songs on tape back then. You've probably never used a tape machine."

"I've seen them," says the young man.

The old woman continues. "Anyway, my second husband played "Hey Jude" for him and Judy. Not for me. Not when we made love. It was my first husband who told me about my second husband playing "Hey Jude." See, way back then we lived in the same neighborhood and the boys went for walks in the morning. Anyway, you know the song, don't you?"

As the young man rows and she pedals, the old woman's voice cracks the quiet of dawn. She hums "Hey Jude" and even tries to sing a few words of the song. But the only part that comes out clearly is the chorus and the repeat of the song title.

When the old woman gives up on the song she coughs to clear her throat, wipes her nose with her sleeve, and as the young man rows slowly alongside her pedal boat toward a dock in the distance, she begins telling him about, of all things, a freight train crossing Illinois farmland.

Three Decades Earlier

The track was seamless, welded atop a recently refurbished track bed. It was dawn, patches of ground fog lingering in ditches. The railroad right-of-way, whose shoulders in days gone by carried steam-pulled troop trains, then diesel-pulled vista cars, then freights, now carried a train the media had dubbed the Dawn Patrol because it conveyed its cargo only at dawn when winds were calm and overhead aircraft were banned.

The Dawn Patrol headed east on its sparkling seamless rails toward the imminent sunrise. It was forty miles south of Chicago and would soon cross the state line into Indiana. So far that morning it had traveled eighty miles since leaving the Iroquois Nuclear Power Plant in northern Illinois. After crossing the state line it would turn north-east and travel another eighty miles to the Tri-State Nuclear Waste Disposal Facility near the Michigan state line. As usual it had left the Iroquois plant at one in the morning and would not arrive at the Tri-State facility until nine in the morning. The reason it took eight hours to cover the one-hundred sixty miles was because the Dawn Patrol traveled at exactly twenty miles per hour, no more, no less. The reason for shipping nuclear waste from Iroquois was because plants throughout the Midwest had shipped waste to Iroquois for many years while waiting for the Tri-State facility to be completed.

Thunderstorms were predicted for later that night, many hours away. By then the Dawn Patrol's radioactive cargo for the day would be safely put to bed.

☢ ☢ ☢

Two men — one black, one white — out for a morning run, white man lagging behind. Black man shouts back to the white man.

"Here she comes, Paul. Where're the lazy bastard protesters who used to be out here?" Hiram's single arm swung in wide arcs as he made his way along the asphalt walkway.

"In bed," said Paul.

"Not very dedicated environmentalists."

Hiram's mention of environmentalists reminded Paul of his youth, back during the Reagan administration protesting when James Watt came to town. Environmental activism that introduced him to Judy and eventually led to their marriage. Environmental activism that turned out to be pretty damned ironic years later when their neighborhood in Easthaven was contaminated by Ducain Chemical. His daughter only two years old when it happened, his daughter who would later be called Chemical Jamie in grade school when legal appeals ran out for the chemical company and they finally put the senior Ducain on trial.

As Hiram set the pace in the wet-tipped dawn, his single arm twisting his stride out of balance as if sidestepping land mines, Paul wondered what Hiram would say when he told him about the dream. In the distant clearing, around a bend in the path, the Dawn Patrol moaned.

"Come on, Paul!" shouted Hiram. "Got a train to meet!"

The track curved, giving the iron-clad cars the look of a thick snake. The train growled on its seamless rails, its flanks glistening in dawn light.

At the crossing, Hiram ran in place, massaging his stump with his right hand, while Paul stood still, rubbing a tender spot beneath his left rib. The vibration of the earth caused by the train reminded Paul of an acid trip years earlier when Marty Kaatz spiked his beer at a Sigma-Alpha-whatever house party. As the cars rolled past, Paul noticed that each set of wheel trucks gave off a slightly different pitch. He stared at the wheels imagining he had X-ray vision and could see the inner workings of machinery. See inside where a roller bearing, overlooked during final inspection, has flat-spotted and is, every few turns, pausing and heating up.

But the train passed without incident, the whisper of morning returned, and the two men jogged across the tracks, exchanging waves with a state trooper parked on the far side of the road where the path came out of the woods. Once off the asphalt path they boarded the sidewalk and began walking the final leg back to showers and break-fast tables and good-bye kisses as both their wives left for work and both of them did a few morning chores before leaving for their own jobs. They slowed, cooling down.

"I had a dream about you last night," said Paul.

"How romantic," said Hiram. "I thought you only dreamed about chemical dumps."

"The dream was about the chemical dump."

"What was I doing at the dump?"

"You were outside the dump. A neighborhood pervert exposing yourself in a backyard swimming pool."

Hiram wiped his brow in an exaggerated way. "Lordy, for a second I thought you'd made me into a chemical company president. What was his name? I keep forgetting it."

"Harold Ducain."

"Yeah, Ducain. Your ace of spades. But back to the dream. What was I doing in a backyard swimming pool?"

"You were trying to grab Jamie and another little girl who was sitting with Jamie on the pool ladder. But the dream, the whole point of it, still had to do with Harold Ducain."

"Really."

As they continued walking, the silence of morning became eerie. The cadence of the clickity-clack of the Dawn Patrol on that partic-ular morning had triggered a feeling of déjà vu in Paul that he could not shake. He'd been here before, about to tell Hiram the whole story, only this time he really would tell the story. Why, after all the years they'd known one another — but why not? He had to tell Hiram about Ducain's daughter eventually. It was in the cards. It was déjà vu. The pressure to confess that morning was a technicolor pressure, insides exploding out, glistening in the morning sun if he didn't talk. *Just talk.*

"Anyway," said Paul, "in the past when I told you about Ducain I kind of left something out."

"Look, Paul, if you're trying to unload something, don't bullshit around. We're almost to my house and it's a work day."

"Okay, okay. See, Ducain's daughter's been in my dreams a lot lately and it's brought back memories. The trial never bothered me. What bothered me was Ducain's suicide. I always had the feeling he took the fall for someone else. It's not like he hauled those drums of shit out into that field on his back."

"How old was Ducain's daughter during the trial?"

"Eleven or twelve. Same as Jamie."

"And how old was Jamie when they chased you out of Easthaven?"

"Two."

"So, how can little girls two years old be sitting on a pool ladder?"

"In the dream Jamie and Ducain's daughter are the age they were at the trial. Ducain's daughter was a redhead and . . . anyway, it's just a dream."

"So you said. How many years has it been now?"

"Since the trial?"

"Since they chased you out of Easthaven."

"1989, that makes it twenty-three years."

"And so far everyone's still doing okay?"

"Everyone?"

"You, Judy, and Jamie. That's who you should be thinking about. Not a dead guy. A dead guy's a dead guy and you can't do a goddamn thing about him. What's important now is how your family's doing. So, the three of you, no new health problems?"

"Not since Judy's mastectomy."

"How long has that been?"

"Five years."

"If you can beat cancer for five years, the prognosis is damn good."

"Is this your Vietnam vet time-heals-all-wounds speech?"

Hiram stopped walking, turned toward Paul. "No," he said, sounding somewhat angry. "It's my dreams-are-bullshit speech. Best way to handle them is to get pissed enough to drive 'em the hell out. Think about what the chemical dump did to you and your neighbors. Ducain and his daughter didn't live next to his dump. You did!"

Paul turned to face Hiram, stared into his dark eyes. "How about slapping me around some?"

Hiram laughed and they continued walking.

"Yeah," said Hiram, "that's what Bianca used to do with me. When I'd wake up nights screaming about my arm, there'd be Bianca, who goes to Sunday church meetings with her girlfriends, slapping me around some, then holding me like a baby, saying over and over, 'It's all bullshit. It's all bullshit.'"

"Judy holds me when I wake up," said Paul.

As they walked into their neighborhood the sun was up and it was already hot. As if nudged from bed by the heat, the rest of the world had come alive. Doors slammed, cars backed out of driveways, the faint odor of coffee was in the air. But there was also the smell of decay, a smell Hiram sometimes commented on when reminiscing about his boyhood in the projects or his stint in Vietnam. It was garbage day, trash containers and recycling bins lining both sides of the street. As they neared Hiram's house, Paul thought about death and the shortness of life and remembered the invitation he and Judy had discussed but kept putting off, an invitation they had discussed again the previous night.

"Damn, I almost forgot."

"What?"

"We're going up to the cottage two weeks from Friday and we wondered if you and Bianca would come with us."

"Walden Pond, huh?"

"I don't think Thoreau ever made it to Michigan."

"Still planning to retire up there?"

"Judy wants to keep working a couple more years. I'd do it tomorrow."

"I'm with you, man. Tired of sitting in front of a computer all day. I'll ask Bianca about Michigan, let you know. And if there's any more of this chemical company lawsuit business you're holding back . . ."

"No, that's it, just some nightmares."

"Sounds like enough. See you tomorrow, man."

As he walked the last block to his house, Paul recalled the evening twenty-three years earlier when sirens sounded and lights flashed and squad car loudspeakers told everyone to leave as quickly as possible because of the mix of toxic chemicals that had been discovered seething in the field of drums behind the chainlink fence at the end of the block. The next day was to have been garbage day and he had been a younger, stronger man heaving the containers out to the curb in one trip. But the garbage wasn't picked up the next day because, by midnight, every man, woman, and child had been evacuated from the small town of Easthaven, Illinois, which, by the end of the century, had become a ghost town fifty miles from Chicago. A ghost town Rand McNally had long since taken off its maps.

Paul climbed the front porch steps and went into the house to get the garbage container and recycle bin. As he passed the downstairs bath on his way to the garage, he heard Judy singing "Angel of the Morning." It was a song Judy always sang in the shower, a song that had come out years earlier, long before she'd had her double mastectomy. A song she began singing in the shower back when they lived in Easthaven where, during that summer of 1989, she sang in the shower following a long swim in the backyard pool.

As always, the song brought tears to Paul's eyes. When he tried to wipe the tears away with the back of his hand, perspiration poisoned the tears and made his eyes sting like hell.

CHAPTER 2

At the University of Illinois, in the twin cities of Champaign and Urbana, a weather system heading east funneled intense heat north ahead of storms that were due to arrive by evening. It was so hot and windy a campus station weather forecaster, minoring in environmental studies, made a botched attempt at a joke to the effect that perhaps the expansion of the Sahara would jump the rising ocean and head for Illinois.

If it had been spring, near the end of classes, a few students suffering spring fever and ignoring melanoma warnings might have been out on the Quad soaking up some sun. But it was not spring. It was the end of August and the Midwest was experiencing another record breaking day in the hundreds followed by a night of storms. Because the fall semester had just begun, perhaps an initial surge of study also kept students indoors. Many students had chosen the library and the Krannert Center and the Illini Union where new high efficiency air-conditioning units had been installed the previous year.

Jamie Carter sat in a wingback chair in one of the quieter lounges in the Union. Spread about her, on the arms of the chair and on a side table, was the required reading for two of her classes — Public Opinion Formation and Dynamics, and Middle-Eastern Political Systems.

The reason Jamie studied at the Union was not because her room at the graduate house was un-air-conditioned. In fact it was air-conditioned and probably a lot quieter than here. No, the reason she'd come here was to hide from Heather whose room was across the hall. Now, as she sat staring at her book open to an article on the methodology of political polling, she felt foolish and a little guilty. If her fellow Senate pages could see her now they'd say she was dodging confrontation. If Senator Hansen were here he'd remind her of the need to be diplomatic, especially when dealing with a broadcast journalism major. But feeling foolish was one thing. It was the guilt that got to her.

Heather had gravitated to Jamie several years earlier, when they were both undergrads. Jamie's guilt in trying to avoid Heather was rooted in the fact that, while Heather had apparently confided in Jamie, confessing personal fears and desires, Jamie had not responded in kind. Heather admitted she was volatile, speaking about death and even suicide. And although Jamie thought she had done her best to help Heather, the fact that she hadn't leveled with Heather made her have her doubts. And Jamie's excuse to herself? She figured some day she'd use the story of Easthaven as a way of getting really close to Heather. Then she'd help her. Right. She'd told Heather her father had wanted a boy so he could name him Jimmy and he would have been Jimmy Carter. She told Heather that although she had the short brown hair and freckles, she didn't have the name. Jamie Carter would have to do. But she'd never told Heather about Easthaven, and Heather never hinted that she'd seen a documentary or read newspaper archives about a family named Carter being from Easthaven. But then Carter was a pretty common name.

As Jamie stared at her book, not reading, simply staring, she thought again, as she often did when she was feeling guilty, about the quote from Thoreau's *Walden*. "The mass of men lead lives of quiet desperation." It was an appropriate quote these days because of her father's *Walden* ideas. Of course the last time she asked her father about these *Walden* ideas of his, he had become critical, saying the world was crawling with people and that the flood of information flowing all over the place made his ideas ridiculous. Sometimes her father sounded so hopeless. And sometimes Jamie saw the world as being a hopeless place. Right after getting her bachelor's degree there had even been a time when she considered suicide. Her justification at the time for having these thoughts was, or course, Easthaven. Would she wait for cancer to come? Or would it be justifiable to take herself out? And although she'd beaten back thoughts of suicide, now she goes and makes friends with a guy who, like her, is lined up in the cancer queue because of Chernobyl when he was a kid. So, how in the hell is she supposed to help Heather deal with life?

As if on cue, as if Heather could read her mind, Jamie lowered her book, glanced up, and saw Heather heading her way, smiling. But instead of regretting the interruption, in that strange way that one cannot immediately grasp, Jamie welcomed the interruption.

15

No more quiet desperation, at least for a little while.

Heather picked up the Middle-Eastern Political Systems text from the arm of Jamie's chair and sat as if the chair arm were a hobby horse and she were a child. Heather wore shorts and a blouse tied up tight beneath her breasts. Although most considered Heather a redhead, Jamie thought of Heather's hair as amber. Heather's amber curls cascaded onto her shoulders. Jamie noticed two male undergrads on a scrolled-arm sofa across the room nudge one another like Norman Rockwell school chums. One of the boys was also a redhead, just like Norman Rockwell would have drawn him.

Heather flipped through the Middle-Eastern Political Systems text, then handed it back to Jamie. "Pretty dry stuff. Some day they'll have a text on extraterrestrial political systems and I suppose that'll be just as dry. The Area Fifty-One people insist on depicting aliens having huge bald heads. I bet they have heads just like us because computers take care of the extra brain power even for them. In fact most probably have neat, short brown hair like you. And freckles, too. Wouldn't that be a kick?"

"What are you talking about?"

"Didn't you hear? It was on *The Today Show*. A professor from MIT has been analyzing static from another galaxy that he says isn't static at all. Says he's found patterns based on mathematical formulae. Says it'll take years to analyze, but that he's sure it's our first contact. Should make for some damn good news stories."

"I didn't hear about it," said Jamie. "Has anyone verified the professor's findings?"

"I doubt it," said Heather. "But even if it's not verified, even if there's only one source, it's still a great story. It's what people want to hear. The kind of thing I'll be handling when I get myself on the air. Much better than your terrorist political system crap."

Heather tilted her head back and shook her curls. She stretched out one leg to maintain her balance on the arm of Jamie's chair. On the far side of the room the number of males watching Heather had multiplied and the term "built like a brick shithouse" came into Jamie's mind. Heather, with amber hair and green eyes and perfect nose and ample breasts and not-too-big-but-not-too-small hips, would be a great anchorperson some day. A sexy anchorperson to scrutinize while being given details about a terrorist attack or the latest global warming statistics or a food riot somewhere or the latest political sex scandal. Heather West. She even had the right name for a media figure.

"I guess extraterrestrial communication does make a great story," said Jamie. "In science fiction films they avoid alarming the public, but I suppose we're beyond that. If it's going to happen, it'll be like this. Bits and pieces here and there as it's interpreted after the hundreds of light years it takes to get here."

"You're so damned analytical," said Heather, turning and smiling down at her. "Speaking of being analytical, did you finish the reading for Public Opinion?"

"Just started."

"Any ideas for the paper?"

"Maybe I should do it on extraterrestrial messages from space."

"Right" said Heather, glancing across the room toward the two Norman Rockwell school chums, then turning back to Jamie. "But I thought you'd have yours picked by now. Something on urban poverty or the environment. Or something like in English Comp back in the Middle Ages when you wrote about that town in California. Had a name like cologne."

"Casmalia. It was near a toxic waste dump."

"Right, Casmalia. Drexel said your paper was good but a bit long for a freshman paper."

"And too opinionated," said Jamie.

"Anyway," said Heather, "your social and environmental concerns inspire me. I'll change my name to Oprah, spend some time in a tanning booth, and announce that I want to *gain* a few pounds. Then, when I'm having trouble gaining the weight, the tabloids'll dig up those shots of me topless at the Sigma-Alpha-Epsilon bed race and I'll be on my way to fame, anorexia nervosa and all. Of course I've never had anorexia nervosa, but it's one of those gimmicky things tabloids love."

"You'll be a great influence on public opinion, Heather."

"I know. And like you, I'll do my part to keep the environment in the limelight. I'm writing my paper on the effects of disasters on public opinion. My case study is that Easthaven chemical disaster back in the 90s that screwed . . . what was his name? . . . Senator Bill Moore. The spill that screwed Bill. Great title for a paper, huh?"

Jamie suddenly felt very cold and rubbed her arms to take away the chill. She looked up at Heather who smiled absent-mindedly as if she'd just mentioned a sitcom instead of the worst chemical spill in Illinois history.

"It didn't happen in the 90s, Heather. The Easthaven spill was in 1989."

"Okay, 1989. Anyway, I remember seeing news about it on TV when I was a kid." Heather laughed. "Even back then I knew TV had been invented for me."

But Jamie did not feel like laughing. "What made you think of writing about Easthaven?"

Heather shrugged. "Because I knew there'd be plenty of source material in the library. Is something wrong? You look . . . I don't know. You okay?"

"I'm fine."

"What is it then?"

"Easthaven."

"What about it?"

"I lived there."

The story came out in a rush. Not in the semi-quiet lounge, but downstairs in the noisy basement cafeteria.

She told Heather all of it — the night the police made them leave; the discovery of ruptured steel drums that had been leaking for some time; the news that the runoff from the drums had contaminated the topsoil and storm sewers and basements of houses in almost the entire town; the discovery of high levels of toxins — including DBCP, a known carcinogen — in their backyard pool where it was theorized a boy named Ricky Wade — now dead — had jumped in wearing heavily contaminated shoes; the realization that everyone in her old neighborhood had been exposed for at least an entire summer; the class action suit filed against the owner of Ducain Chemical for negligence; the appearance of her father on television as spokesman for the group; the accusation that racism was behind the lawsuit because her father had hired an African-American attorney and Ducain Chemical had once won a controversial civil rights case.

After that was the winning of the lawsuit; Harold Ducain's suicide; the removal of Easthaven from Illinois maps; the move to a new town and a desire for anonymity; the prognosis that, like Jamie's mother, cancer would most likely show up in her some day, especially after further testing of water taken from the swimming pool in which her mother had decided that particular summer to use for exercise. A long circular swim every morning before her shower. And then in the afternoon, if it was warm enough, a more leisurely swim with two-year-old Jamie.

"Sometimes my mother took me with her in the pool," said Jamie, sipping the iced tea Heather had bought her. "I'm considered a long-term experiment. They've got samples of water from the backyard pool and they've got me to keep an eye on. I report back to the University of Chicago Medical Center every three months. Hell, I'm better for research than a goddamn cadaver, and I've got my own built-in health care system. Eventually I'll get some kind of cancer, like Mom did, and boy, oh, boy, will the researchers be clicking their heels then."

Heather stared down at her iced tea, stirring it slowly with her straw. "What kind of cancer does your mom have?"

"Both breasts. It's been five years and so far she's okay."

"Have they linked it to the chemicals?"

"We won't be sure until enough of the people from the neighborhood are statistics."

Heather continued staring at her iced tea. Jamie reached out and touched Heather's hand. At first Heather drew back. But then she held Jamie's hand and smiled.

"Quite a story," said Heather.

"Thanks for listening," said Jamie. "Most of it's second hand because I was too young to remember all that happened. But I do remember a lot of it. I guess because I was aware of how it affected my parents."

"How come you never told me about this before?"

"I don't like to talk about it, even though I know I should. The counselors the state sent in after moving us out said it would be best to unburden ourselves once in a while. But I'd prefer you didn't tell anyone."

"That guy you were seeing a while back, did you tell him about it?" asked Heather.

"You mean Brian Jones?"

"Yes, him."

"I did tell Brian."

"Is that the reason you broke up?"

"No, Brian's still a good friend."

"What about the new guy I've seen you with?"

Jamie hesitated, then said, "His name's Arkady. He's from the Ukraine doing a one-year foreign study stint. At first I figured I'd introduce myself so I'd have someone to practice with for my Russian class. But when I found out he and his family had gotten a pretty heavy dose of radiation at Chernobyl back in 1986, I realized we had a lot in common. Yes, I've also told Arkady about Easthaven."

"I saw you with him in the lobby," said Heather. "Does he live in our building?"

"Yes."

Heather shook her head sadly. "I didn't mean to bring this all out. I feel like shit about it."

"Don't."

When Heather stood to leave she said, "See you tomorrow morning in class."

As Heather walked out of the cafeteria, under the close scrutiny of many undergraduate male eyes bloodshot from the first weekend of drinking parties at good old U of I, Jamie clutched the handles of her two canvas bags full of books and trudged out of the Illini Union and into the hot sun like — as Arkady said last night after they'd made love — "a peasant woman from the Ukrainian steppes looking for a new homeland."

CHAPTER 3

THE DOOR TO HEATHER'S ROOM made a sucking sound when it closed, its weather-stripping preventing the escape of air-conditioned air into the hot hallway. Heather turned, walked to the center of the room, glanced toward the bathroom. It was a small bath, no tub. But the absence of a tub did not suppress the image of bathtub as coffin the day she saw him there, hands folded across his chest, not because he has been arranged by an undertaker, but because the tub is narrow for his large frame, forcing arms and hands into a coffin-like pose, his eyes down and open in astonishment at the blood on his shirt front, the absence of movement causing her to move closer until she sees the pistol down at his side in the bottom of the tub, until she sees the river of blood running toward the drain at his feet.

Heather turned from the bathroom with its image of death. As she walked across the room she could hear his voice. The concern of her father was obvious as he stared at her grade school report card. He'd been drinking as usual. She could hear it in his voice. "See you got 'nother D in science, honey. In this world you've got to be real, even at your age. You'd be better off switching this D in science with the A you got in English 'cause a white gal can't make it any-where in English. I know you want to be a journalist. I seen your papers and they're pretty good. But they got too many slots already picked for coloreds and chinks, honey."

The drinking started after Easthaven. After the media blitz put the blame on her father and gave him no way out. The media right there in the bathroom pulling the trigger. The media not satisfied to wait until the millennium, but instead taking him in 1999 when she had just turned thirteen.

Heather realized that, as her father spoke from the grave with advice she ignored, she had walked to the window. Below, a thin, dark-haired young man with a prominent nose wearing a backpack paused at the bike rack. The man touched the seat of a bicycle, then shook his hand and blew on it, glancing up toward the vicious after-noon sun. The young man had recently been pointed out to her as an exchange student named Arkady from the Ukraine. When he began walking away from the building, Heather went to her dresser, picked up her hairbrush and ran it through her hair a few times. Then she hurried out of the room and down the hall to the elevator.

☢ ☢ ☢

"Jamie has classes tomorrow. Why would she go home for the weekend?"

"I don't know."

"How could you tell she was leaving for the weekend?"

"She was carrying two bags."

"She always carries two bags. She told me once that carrying two bags balances the weight of the law books so she will not contract a spinal curvature."

"She's way too health conscious."

"Don't you think it's good to be health conscious?"

"Of course, but when one carries it to an extreme and imagines potential dangers around every corner and inside every candy wrapper . . . "

"I don't blame her for being cautious. I, too, feel that way."

"I've heard about you being a Chernobyl survivor. I'm also a survivor. When the extraterrestrials attack Earth I'll run away and prove I can survive without help from anyone. Or maybe I'll become a miniature extraterrestrial and get inside *you*. That way I can watch everything you do, stay hidden and strike when you least expect it. When I was a little girl I loved to hide. Sometimes when I hid, I'd pretend I was with a man, a man with very thick eyebrows."

They sat in the shade of an old maple tree being watered by the trickle from a soaking sprinkler. They were on the west side of the Quad. The concrete bench on which they sat was still warm from the sun it had received that morning. Heather moved closer to Arkady. They both wore shorts and she could feel the brush of his hairy leg against hers as she turned toward him.

Heather placed her hand on Arkady's arm. "The Chernobyl disaster must have been horrible for you and your family. Would you like to talk about it?"

"Everyone has tragedy they must deal with. Mine is no worse."

Heather moved her hand from Arkady's arm to his thigh. "How

can you say that after all those people lost their homes, then were told their life expectancy was shortened? I know there've been tragedies in which many more were killed, but Chernobyl was a once-in-a-lifetime thing."

"I hope so," said Arkady, glancing at her hand resting on his thigh.

"How old were you when it happened?"

"I had just been born."

"Did your family have to move?"

"Yes. We all lived on the same collective — my mother and father, my brother and two sisters, grandparents, uncles, aunts, cousins. I learned about Chernobyl as I grew up. Chernobyl became second nature to me."

"Where did your family go after it happened?"

"For almost a year my family lived in tents and other temporary housing in collectives around Kiev. Then they moved into one of the villages the government had constructed just north of Kiev. But it wasn't the same. Families had been split up and young people who had always longed to leave the farm could not sit still. Those who were old enough moved to Kiev or Moscow or any other city where they could find work. They'd had enough of the farm and didn't feel like sitting on a manure pile waiting for the cancer to come. Somehow, there, on the manure pile, it seemed the cancer would come sooner, as if it knew where it could find them. I was considered the lucky one, young enough to be sent away to live with relatives during the initial time shortly after the accident. But more than likely I stayed on longer than I should have."

Arkady looked off into the distance. Heather took her hand from his thigh and grasped his hand. "Come on. Let's walk somewhere."

Arkady looked at his watch. "I have a class in half an hour."

"What class is it?"

"Social Gerontology."

"Old people?"

"Yes. I chose it in case I'm not around long enough to learn about being old first hand."

"You're a morose guy."

"I know."

"Are all men from the Ukraine that way?"

"No."

Heather walked with Arkady to the Social Sciences building on the other side of the Quad. Several times along the way she touched his arm and tried to hold his hand, but he seemed determined to avoid contact. On the stairway in front of the building she asked him to wait.

"What is it?"

"Aren't you going to say good-bye?"

"Of course. I wasn't sure how far you were going."

Heather knew an opening when she heard one. She was standing a step below Arkady and leaned toward him, her breasts pressing against his belt. She looked up at him and said, "I'm a vampire. I don't go far during the day, but at night . . ."

Arkady smiled down at her, his dark eyebrows larger when viewed from below.

"Would you like to come to my room later?" she asked.

"I don't think so."

"You don't think so?"

"No. I've a lot of work to do. Perhaps another time."

"Perhaps another time."

When she said this, Heather wasn't sure if she had mimicked Arkady's voice, sounding like what he'd probably call a boot-licking whore. So she added, "Yes, perhaps some other time would be best. I'm also quite busy."

At the bottom of the stairs she turned and saw Arkady still standing there, staring at her. Farther along the sidewalk she looked again and saw that he was gone, pulled from the entrance of the building like a scab pulled from a wound.

She remembered overhearing her father tell the joke when attorneys were with him to discuss his defense. They'd been in the bar downstairs and she'd hid on the landing. The horrible joke about an aging diseased whore and the pleasure to the customer being enhanced after her scabs are pulled off. And then, of course, the image of the skinless whore's body shrunk as it always did and became the fetus they took from her when she was thirteen. Peter the fetus, whom she and Mom and even her older brother blamed on the high school kid named Pete who did it to her in the park pavilion.

Of course nobody really knew if Pete was the father or not. And nobody talked about the other possibility. Not with voices. With eyes, yes. But not with voices. Better to let it fester until there's nothing left to do but tear off the scab.

Although it was brutally hot, she ran back to the grad house. She often ran when she was angry. Running not only kept the weight off, but helped her deal with anger.

In her room she stripped and stepped into the shower, leaning against the wall as the cool water poured over her. Although she tried not to think about it, the image of her father lying in the tub with blood from his head running in a river toward the drain kept coming back. And then there was another image. Daddy with Jennifer on his knee. Daddy calling Jennifer his "precious bundle of molecules." At one point she felt dizzy as if the shower stall had been tilted on its side, ready to be carried off, a shiny white coffin for Heather West, renowned newscaster and television personality struck down suddenly in the prime of life.

When she finished showering, Heather dressed in sweatpants and sweatshirt, spread the books from her classes on the bed, then sat cross-legged amongst the books and began — as she often did when the past became more vivid — a night-long binge of study. As she studied, she could see storm clouds building on the horizon outside her window.

She loved storms, especially at night. Violent storms that could race through neighborhoods and suck everyone — Mom, Dad, the kids, the cat and dog, even terrorists plotting their next move — right out the goddamn windows.

Maybe she should have chosen the name Storm instead of West when she changed her name. No, that would have been too burlesque. Heather West was fine. West, the direction from which storms appear. Vicious storms capable of reeking havoc, and vengeance.

CHAPTER 4

Phone ringing. Jamie looked at the clock radio, saw it was only eight o'clock, wondered why it was already dark, then heard a distant roll of thunder.

"Hello?"

"Hi, hon. You sound tired."

"Hi, Mom. I was napping. Fell asleep studying for tomorrow's classes."

"How's the weather? They're forecasting storms there tonight."

"I should have known. You always call when storms are brewing."

"A mom can't help it. Especially with the crazy weather we're having. Why can't we have simple rain showers like in the old days instead of these violent storms?"

"Mom?"

"Yes?"

"Tell me how you're doing. I'd rather talk about you than the weather."

"I'm doing fine. Had another follow-up today. So far, so good."

"How's the new prosthesis?"

"Better than the old one, except it bounces when I walk."

"Maybe you should tighten it, or not walk so fast."

"I've got to walk fast to keep up with your father."

"Are you going out with him for morning walks now?"

"No. He and Hiram walk mornings. They leave when it's dark, like thieves. We take a more leisurely walk in the evenings. I tell your father he's a fanatic. He tells me about studies showing there's no such thing as too much walking. We repeat this litany to one another while we walk."

"You'll be neighborhood legends when you leave for the cottage."

"Yes, the cottage, living on our savings, down-to-earth simplicity. He's turning into Henry David Thoreau or B. F. Skinner, I don't know which. Talking about model communities for retired folks, using less resources, making social statements." Her mother had spoken more loudly, an indication that her father was listening in.

"Are you and Dad going this weekend?"

"Next weekend. Hiram and Bianca are going with us. Just a minute. What? Oh, Dad wants me to ask if you'd like to bring a friend to the cottage one of these weekends."

"I'll come, but I don't know about a friend."

"There was someone you mentioned . . . Heather?"

"Not such a good friend."

"Dirty politics starting already?"

"Nothing like that. Just not a very close friend."

"Well, if there's anyone else, she — or he — is invited."

"He?"

31

"It's the twenty-first century, Jamie. Besides, I trust your judgment."

"Thanks, Mom. That's a nice thing to say."

"Some day a lot of people will be depending on your judgment."

"I'm not Sandra Day O'Connor yet. There's still these things called law school and the Bar to get through."

"I wasn't referring to law school. I meant your judgment will be valuable whatever you do."

"Thanks again."

"Let us know a week or so ahead when you and your friend can come up to the cottage. Not much warm weather left and Dad wants someone to go sailing and fishing with him."

"I'll let you know as soon as I can. Say hi to Dad. Love you both."

"I will. Love you, hon."

After she hung up the phone, Jamie turned toward the darkness of the room, reached across the bed, touched a hairy chest.

"You're invited to the *dacha*."

Arkady sat up, a dark shadow hovering above her. "I thought the *dacha* was only for immediate family."

Jamie reached up and touched Arkady's nose. "We make exceptions in America when the visitor has a honker like yours."

Arkady's face came close to hers and he kissed her lightly on the forehead. "This nose does not honk." He bent lower, kissed her breasts. "On the other hand, perhaps my nose will begin honking."

"Why?"

"Because of these; they are as ripe as plums."

"Guys in this country would probably say melons, not plums."

"Melons are large and unwieldy like my nose, whereas plums are just right."

"Is that why Heather couldn't tempt you?"

"She has Chernobyl plums," said Arkady, tickling her ribs and starting a tickling contest that ended with him falling off the bed with a thud.

Jamie turned on the lamp and leaned over the side of the bed. "You're more ticklish than me. You shouldn't have started it."

Arkady lay in the narrow space between the bed and wall. He stared at the ceiling, his hands folded across his chest. "Practicing my coffin pose."

"Is that supposed to be funny?"

"Yes. Northern Ukraine humor is very dark. Tell me, where is this *dacha* to which I'm being invited."

"In Michigan, a small lake south of Traverse City."

"What does 'traverse' mean?" asked Arkady.

"A passage or a crossing-over from one place or state of being to another. The county up there is Grand Traverse. I've always liked the name."

"A grand passage from one state of being to another sounds impressive."

"Maybe the extraterrestrials will come to Earth and give us a machine that'll suck the radiation out of all the Chernobyl victims. Did you hear about the MIT professor who contends he's deciphered messages from extraterrestrials?"

"Yes," said Arkady, "no panic in the streets or anything like in the old science fiction films." He smiled an evil smile. "By the way, I'm very interested in that part about sucking out the radiation."

As Jamie stared down at Arkady, still lying on the floor between the bed and wall, thunder, much closer than before, shook the walls of the grad house and made Arkady wince. He reached up and she took his hand. Back in bed, lying side by side on their backs, they could hear the storm approaching. When she turned off the lamp, lightning flashes of varying intensity made their bodies and the room dance before her.

"Your friend Heather is quite strange," said Arkady.

"She was strange when I first met her. When we were freshmen she wrote a comp paper about a survivalist group in which she obviously identified with the survivalists. She went on about their right to destroy *anyone* who came near their compound. I said I didn't understand why she picked me, of all people, to critique her paper. After that she avoided me for a while."

"Strange," said Arkady. "When she spoke with me this afternoon, she mentioned being a survivor and said when she was a little girl she used to hide from others. She wanted to hide with me."

"For a quickie?"

"I don't know how quick it would have been."

"Are you sorry you didn't take time to find out?"

Arkady smiled. "No. Danger would have awaited me."

"What kind of danger?"

"A man-eating chastity belt."

"Very funny."

"That depends which side of the chastity belt one is on. Nevertheless, I've never come across a girl or a woman like her during all my travels throughout the irradiated Ukraine where plums grow to the size of melons and break the branches off their own trees."

"You're nuts."

"Here, give me your hand. Nuts have also been known to grow

larger in the Ukraine."

"You've got the worst come-ons . . . "

"But clever. You've got to admit they're clever."

"Tell me more about Chernobyl."

"What more is there to tell?"

"Tell me how your family first found out."

"According to the story, one day they were doing spring planting, the next day they — we — were on buses speeding south. Of course I don't remember any of it because I'd just been born. But I'm told the critical twenty-four hours — the time during which we received the heaviest dose — seemed like it never happened. My family spoke about it for many years afterward. My older sister said it was ironic — everyone running about asking what's happened and what's going to happen, when the critical part — the irradiation — was happening as they spoke. My older brother, who's dead now, had a psychological approach. He said the day during which we were silently bombarded was blanked out in our collective memories because we wished the day out of existence. Even the religious felt this way. *Please, God, if I can give back one day, just one.*

"It was a Saturday. My mother was walking between rows of radishes with me in her arms. She remembers one of the collective's trucks speeding down the road. Vasily the joker was driving and she thought she'd hear some gossip about Gorbachev. What happened instead was that my mother was told of the cause of the explosion she'd heard during the night.

"My family and I were ten kilometers from the plant. Since many lived much closer, my parents assumed we were safe. Unfortunately they were unaware of the trick the wind was playing as they

35

stood speculating like farmers in any remote district tended to do. I remember my father saying years later that we'd been no better in protecting ourselves than cackling hens.

"The next day, so I'm told, masked army men herded us onto buses and we were unaware that everything we'd left behind was gone forever."

After a pause, Arkady cupped Jamie's head in his hand and turned her toward him. "Now, tell me more about the Easthaven chemical disaster."

For the second time that day, Jamie told about the sirens and the loudspeakers, the discovery of ruptured steel drums behind the chainlink fence, the contamination found in their backyard swimming pool, the subsequent death of Ricky Wade who had contaminated the pool weeks earlier by simply jumping into it with his shoes on. She told about the class action suit years later and the publicity of the trial and how hard the trial and its publicity was on her father, especially after the suicide of the owner of Ducain Chemical. Finally, she told about the prognosis of the doctors that the probability of cancer was significant, and it was only a matter of time.

As Jamie relived the Easthaven disaster, she remembered telling it to Brian when they first met and recalled how Brian had listened patiently and had not reacted until the following day when he railed against an establishment that allowed the chemical company to get away with it for so long. It had been a sunny day on a bus ride across the Illinois prairie when she told Brian. Now, as she told the story to Arkady, it was dark outside except for occasional lightning in the distance. Back when she told the story to Brian he had been silent, no reaction until the following day when they were on their bicycles,

Brian pedaling uphill ahead of her, panting as he took out his anger on local and federal officials.

Although Arkady also remained silent during the telling of the story, she was accompanied by the background music of the approaching storm building to its own crescendo. All during the telling she wondered how Arkady would react. Appropriately, at the climax of her story, when she revealed the dire verdict of the doctors concerning her future, the loudest crash of thunder so far shook the building.

Arkady held her close, had held her more and more tightly as the storm approached and the story unwound. When she finished her story she closed her eyes and recalled Brian listening patiently and holding her hand as she told him about Easthaven. Perhaps it was meant to be. She'd find someone to protect her, to hold her, and this was how she'd spend the rest of her life. But if so, why had she let go of Brian? He was not the one who had let go. She was. Her education and future career taking over, tearing her away from Brian. And now here was Arkady holding her.

Outside, after the reverberations of yet another climactic clap of thunder had subsided, Arkady said, "Disaster has brought us together."

"Hell of a reason," said Jamie.

The announcement came then, the building's public address system, that was rarely used, clattering to life as someone clicked on the overly-sensitive microphone, manhandled it for a while, then said, in a whiny voice that was unrecognizable as male or female, that a tornado had been sighted in the area and everyone should go to the shelter in the basement.

☢ ☢ ☢

The grad house basement had an exercise room, men's and women's locker rooms and showers, a lounge with tables, chairs, and vending machines, and a laundry room. When Jamie and Arkady arrived, the lounge was already crowded, so they opted for the exercise room where several groups sat in circles and a few loners sat against the walls studying. One of the loners was Heather, who sat in a corner behind a weight machine, wedged in a narrow space between racks that held extra weights for the machine, her shoulders hunched forward so she could fit between the racks.

Heather wore a loose-fitting black sweatsuit. Her hair was limp and lack of makeup made her face look strangely pale and colorless. She sat with her knees up and a book propped in front of her. When Jamie and Arkady walked in, she glanced up but looked quickly back to her book.

After Jamie and Arkady sat on a weight bench just inside the door, the lights dimmed and a clap of thunder sounded, muted by the floors above.

"Notice how everyone looks to the ceiling?" said Arkady. "We're on a movie set following the director's instructions."

"Heather didn't look up. I'm surprised she hasn't come over."

"She's a little girl," said Arkady. "Hiding from monsters."

"Us?"

Arkady nodded. "She seems frightened of us in a unique way, as if she is the last of an endangered species and we are predators."

"We should talk to her," said Jamie, standing up.

As they started walking across the exercise room — a round-

38

about route between circles of other students — an extremely loud crack of thunder shook the floor and the lights went out.

Arkady held Jamie's hand. "We'd better not move or we'll step on someone."

As Jamie's eyes grew accustomed to the darkness, she turned and could see students silhouetted at the entrance where emergency lights flooded the hallway. Some students started whistling and shouting.

"Just like a student senate meeting," said Jamie.

"You've been on the student senate how long?" asked Arkady.

"The last two years. I'll probably run again this year."

"You certainly act the part of a politician."

"What do you mean by that?"

"You can't say no to a challenge. We observe our friend hiding in the corner and you suggest mediation."

"I inherited activism from my parents."

"Is activism what brought your parents together?" asked Arkady.

"You mean the way the two of us being victims of disaster brought us together?"

A loud crack of thunder shook the building. Arkady held her, and the way he held on she thought he might be weeping. But when the lights finally came on, he made a face at her, his eyes crossed.

"You're nuts," she said, laughing.

He clutched her hand more tightly, uncrossed his eyes and opened them wide. "Please, not the nuts again. At least wait until the lights go back out."

"You're crazy," she said, turning toward the corner of the room.

But the corner between the stacks of weights was empty.

"She's gone."

"Yes," said Arkady.

"I'll talk to her in class tomorrow, find out what's wrong."

"You'll make a fine politician."

"Why?"

Arkady smiled. "Trying to please everyone."

CHAPTER 5

WHEN SUMMER ENDED, CAMPUS LIFE at the University of Illinois turned inward, not so much because the weather was cooler, but because the fall semester workload had caught up with students. And then with winter came semester finals and term papers to be completed. Everyone on campus agreed that Christmas break went by much too quickly.

Although Jamie Carter went home for Christmas, it seemed less like a home. For one thing, her parents had made the decision to retire early and make what her father referred to as their "grand traverse" to the cottage life. The house was full of packed boxes and absent of furniture that had been donated to the Salvation Army. Jamie's father had even given away his most recently purchased computer to a local school saying he had been a computer programmer all his life and now he was done with bits and bytes. He would become a tinkerer, work with his hands, do whatever he wanted hour after hour, day after day, year after year.

Although Jamie's father was only fifty-six, retirement obsessed him. He was full of stories about Wylie Lake not being an ordinary retirement community. No golf or bingo for them. However, he did admit he might do some fishing. He had tried to get a coworker named Eric Shaw to retire with him, but said that Eric and his wife wanted warmth for the arthritis they insisted was coming, and moved to Florida instead. He was working on Hiram now, feeling certain he could convince Hiram and his wife Bianca to join them.

And so, with all the excitement in her parents' home — excitement concerned with leaving — Jamie felt as if the last threads of the apron strings had been cut. Another reason it seemed less like home that Christmas was because throughout the first semester she had imagined Arkady coming home with her. Unfortunately, at the final hour, he had received a ticket for a flight to Kiev from his grandmother who was near death and wanted the entire family at her bedside for what she considered her last holiday season on Earth.

☢ ☢ ☢

Heather also went home for the holidays. But the large house in Olympia Fields, Illinois, where she had spent her childhood, contained the second floor bathroom where, in 1999, she'd found her father's body, and also the basement wine cellar where she'd hidden for an entire day and night until the police searched the house. Not much of a home now because her older brother--who had retained the family name as well as ownership of the family business — lived there with his family, making Heather the unwelcome guest.

Heather felt more at home during visits to the St. Anne home for the mentally ill. Heather's mother was not judged severely ill, but had proven dangerous to a grandchild during the previous year in a bizarre incident involving the depth of bathtub water. To Heather, her mother seemed happier at St. Anne, and that's what counted. Perhaps this happiness was a sign that her mother had finally driven from her mind the looming possibility that the aborted fetus named Peter might have actually been the result of one of those afternoons in the bathtub with dear old Dad in the house in Olympia Fields.

☢ ☢ ☢

When the second semester began at the University of Illinois, Jamie and Heather spent more time together, the incidents of the first week of the first semester seemingly forgotten. By an unspoken agreement neither mentioned their personal relationships, but instead focused on the present and on the future.

Although Jamie's dual major was law and political science, while Heather's was broadcast journalism, and although they no longer shared a class, Heather often came to Jamie's room to discuss current events. Heather said that playing devil's advocate to Jamie's concerns for urban problems and poverty and the environment was good practice for a broadcast journalism major. Jamie said that being forced to answer difficult questions and having charges thrown at her by Heather was good practice for a law major specializing in political science. If overheard by someone passing in the hall, some of the discussions might have even been mistaken for bitter arguments.

"You're obviously trying to capitalize on your past, Jamie."

"It's the only past I have."

"Being at Easthaven doesn't mean you have anything in common with the urban poor."

"I didn't say it did."

"You implied it. You said something about poverty and referred to your own past. You begged the question."

"All I said was we have to figure out a better way to get people out of poverty. You're the one who begged the question when you suggested moving them around like game pieces. All I said was that I knew a bit about being moved around."

"So, how the hell are you going to avoid kicking people out of their apartments who don't want to work? Another tax-and-spend handout?"

"No, a program in which social workers' benefits are tied to how many people they get *out* of the system, *not* how many they process."

"Okay, fine. Now, what about this global warming scare you like to use?"

"Great transition. But I don't think I'm *using* global warming."

"I heard recently that the Earth actually dropped in average temperature a few years back because of that volcano in the Philippines."

"A slight variation. But considering climate data over the last three decades, and the increase in violent storms, the upward trend in global temperature is obvious. We can't expect the Earth to get us out of this one. And I don't think anyone will breathe easier if volcanoes on Earth blow enough dust into the atmosphere in order to reflect the sunlight before it gets into our manmade greenhouse."

"Speaking of green, how do you justify to the American people the fact that you don't attend church?"

"What's that got to do with green?"

"Never mind, I'll think of something later. Maybe I'll accuse you of being a malevolent alien or something. Anyway, answer the question."

"All right. Religions are founded in part on the idea that no one can be turned away . . . wait, let me finish. If a religion turns anyone away or fails to preach acceptance of all human beings, then it's not a religion, but a sect. My religion, rather than being founded on dogma, is founded on the principle of deciding, moment by moment, what is ethical, then acting upon it. I invite others to take this view whether they belong to a formal religious institution or not. So you see, I'm a very religious person."

And so it went during the first part of that semester in the grad house when two friends got together, one to sharpen her interviewing skills, the other to practice presenting her views to a sometimes hostile public.

Arkady was also back in Illinois for his final semester of two in his study abroad. When he knocked on Jamie's door at the grad house the afternoon the shuttle arrived from Chicago, his first words were, "Hello. I am Ukrainian student. I come to study *a* broad."

They studied like enthusiastic, career-minded citizens of market economy countries that second semester. When not answering Heather's barbs, Jamie studied comparative politics and international law and terrorist threat litigation and participated in research seminars in international relations and political theory. Arkady studied social structures and population and participated in seminars in medical sociology and cultural change. Of course, high on both of their lists of study was the study of one another — mentally, physically, and emotionally.

Heather, when not practicing tabloid talk show host with Jamie, studied communication in politics and advanced oral interpretation, participated in a seminar in mass communication and held an internship at the university television station where she broadcast news and weather, occasionally glancing at her image in the monitor, an experience much more satisfying than staring at her face in the bathroom mirror and recalling events of the previous millennium.

And so, life went on at the University of Illinois and in the rest of the world. This, despite the continued menace from various terrorist organizations, continued problems in the world economy and its effect on the third world, and continued threats to the environment because of the recklessness of the twentieth century.

One environmental threat traveled by rail three times a week all that winter on its one-hundred sixty mile trip from the Iroquois Nuclear Power Plant in Illinois to the Tri-State Nuclear Waste Facility in northern Indiana. Engineers at the Iroquois plant estimated that at three trips a week, it would take several decades to safely move all of the nuclear material. But this estimate, which told of the immense volume of nuclear waste at one of the oldest plants and temporary storage sites in the country, was kept quiet and appeared only in scientific journals. Therefore, with no other solution at hand for the disposal problem, the Dawn Patrol rolled on.

In March of that year, an incident involving one of the specially constructed cars of the Dawn Patrol caused concern among citizens who lived along the route. During an empty return run to Iroquois — at greater speed than its usual twenty miles-per-hour — a wheel bearing on one of the cars locked up and started a minor wheel fire. That evening at the University of Illinois television station, a news spot about the incident was among the items given Heather West to read. The news spot that Heather read — while assuming a serious pose in which simulated worry lines appear on her forehead beneath her styled amber hairdo — went like this:

"Today, in the small town of Beecher, about forty miles south of Chicago, a nuclear waste disposal transport train called the Dawn Patrol had a problem on one of its cars. Apparently a wheel bearing froze and the resulting friction caused grease in the bearing to catch fire before the wheel locked up. A spokesperson for the Tri-State Nuclear Waste Facility in northern Indiana said the problem posed no danger to the public not only because the train was running empty on its return run, but because, if the train were full, its speed would have been low enough that the overheating would not have occurred. 'It shows,' said the spokesperson, 'that the system works. We run back at high speed to put every nut and bolt to the test.'"

At this point, Heather smiled to show that the potential danger that might have been read into the earlier "hook" for the spot was for naught. Then she continued. "In Beecher, here's our own Jason Lewis from the Chicago campus link."

The image switched from Heather's face to an elevated railroad track bed in a farm field. The camera panned left from the track bed until two men were on the screen. Both were African-American, a young man wearing an overcoat, and an older one-armed man wearing a sweatsuit.

"This is Jason Lewis in Beecher talking to Mr. Hiram Davis.

Mr. Davis, tell us what you saw this afternoon."

"Well, I was out on my afternoon walk when I saw the Dawn Patrol highballing on its return run, smoke coming from one of the wheels, then flames. It was squeaking God-awful. I thought the thing would jump track."

"You mentioned earlier that you used to walk in the morning and would see the Dawn Patrol on its eastbound run."

"Yeah, used to walk with a friend, but he retired and moved away."

"You said your friend had a bad feeling about the Dawn Patrol."

"Who wouldn't with the shit it carries."

The intern looked a bit upset, but he was graded on field interviews, and he'd been told there was time to kill, so he continued.

"Mr. Davis, you said when the Dawn Patrol first started running there were protesters here in the mornings. You said they reminded you of anti-war demonstrators in the '60s. I wonder if you could comment on that."

"Well, yeah, they reminded me of the '60s only because of the signs and things. But the resemblance ends there. In 1968 I was in Vietnam. I wasn't even twenty years old and when I watched the protests on the news it was like the protesters were angry with me personally. A lot of guys in 'Nam felt that way. Here, with the train, you could tell protesters had something more specific to be pissed about than a war nobody wanted."

"Is that where you lost your arm? In Vietnam?"

"Yeah, Tet offensive, 1968. Ancient history to you."

There was an uncomfortable silence during which the one-armed, gray-haired Vietnam veteran stared at the nervous young man with a look of *You-don't-know-shit* on his face. Then the young man glanced at a slip of paper in his hand and continued yet again.

"Mr. Davis, getting back to this friend of yours who felt uncomfortable about the Dawn Patrol . . . "

"Yeah, he said the chance of a bearing going out on the train made his ass pucker."

At this point the older man smiled and the intern looked more upset than ever. Finally, after it was obvious the interview was over, the camera panned away from the older man and closed on the younger man who said, "Well, that's it from here, Heather. Back to you."

Heather's reply to this, before moving on to the next story, was a stylized retort meant for the audience to hear. "Next time, Heather, don't assume the Chicago staff has edited their feed, because if you assume . . . " Her smile was full of dimples, her cheeks rosy. Later, in the control room when she reviewed the recording of the broadcast, she had to smile again because her reaction to the playing of the unedited link from Chicago seemed, at the same time, down to earth and professional.

Things were going well for Heather at the station, so well that when other students went home for spring break in April, Heather stayed on. As the station manager said to her one night in bed after they'd made love, "Running a TV news show is like sex. You've got to be smooth and you've got to use your imagination. I think you've got those pluses down pat."

☢ ☢ ☢

Jamie and Arkady did not stay on campus during spring break.

They went to Michigan where her mother and father now lived. In phone calls and letters before summer, her father had insisted on referring to their new home as Walden Pond. But it was really called Wylie Lake, in the small town of Heritage in the county of Grand Traverse. Jamie's mother, who had finally been convinced to quit her job and move there, called it simply, "the cottage."

CHAPTER 6

IN EARLY MARCH, A MONTH after Hiram's news interview about the wheel fire on the Dawn Patrol, Hiram and Bianca made their move. They bought a small cottage that had gone up for sale on the far side of the lake and became residents of Heritage, Michigan, population three-hundred. But after only two weeks at the cottage, and only a few morning walks around the lake with Paul, Hiram died suddenly in his sleep on a Friday night. The Heritage paramedics — one of whom wore a T-shirt advertising the Friday night fish fry and Saturday night barbecue feast at the Heritage Inn — said the cause of death seemed to be a massive heart attack. The doctor who examined the body in Traverse City agreed.

On a late April morning, four weeks after Hiram's death, Paul walked alone around the lake. As he neared the halfway point on his five-mile walk around the lake, Paul again saw the light in the window of the cottage Hiram and Bianca had bought. The light had been there every morning since Hiram's death. Although Bianca was not home, the light remained on all night, every night.

But this morning on his walk, for the first time since their parting at the cemetery, Paul saw Bianca. After Hiram's funeral Bianca had come back to Wylie Lake only long enough to put Hiram's ashes into the lake, then she'd gone to stay with her sister on the west coast. Now, Bianca was back. Paul did not speak to her. He simply saw her standing next to the lamp at the window. She was wearing a white gown. As he neared the cottage along the path on the shoreline, he could see the deep brown color of her skin where it defined the vee at the opening of the gown below her neck. Her hair formed a halo darker than the skin about her face. He could not see her eyes in the shadows and was reminded of a black power poster from his youth.

Seeing Bianca in the window at that distance in her white gown reminded Paul of the infatuation he'd felt when he first met Judy. Two young innocents protesting at a downtown Chicago environmental rally, then the next day marching with blacks on the south side at an anti-segregation rally. He recalled telling Hiram about the anti-segregation rally, how he and Judy must have really stood out being that they were the only white people there.

"Gives you just a small taste how a black man feels," said Hiram. "Any time a black man goes out in the white man's world he might as well have a sign hanging on his shoulders saying, 'Be careful. Just you be careful 'cause this dude's out to get something don't belong to him.' That's the look a black man gets."

Then Paul remembered how Hiram ended the conversation, Hiram always telling a joke to make anyone he was with comfortable. Hiram said, "Of course now, being older, I carry my sign lower, in my gut. Right now it says, 'Nothin' to worry about here, just an old fart making wind.' "

When Paul passed the front of the cottage facing the lake, there was a hint of dawn light in the sky. He waved toward the cottage and, after a pause, Bianca waved back. Shortly after Bianca waved to him, just after the path curved away from the lake and into the woods, Paul saw a doe. During that instant, as the doe stared at him before disappearing into the underbrush off the path, Paul was certain he'd seen Hiram's eyes there ahead of him, beckoning him to follow.

But Hiram was not there beckoning him toward the path to death, and the sun came out as it always does, putting life into another day, and when Paul arrived home he felt glad to be alive as he showered, shaved, and brewed coffee.

Paul sat on the porch facing the lake where two men fished. One was a man he did not recognize in an aluminum boat, the other was Joe Siebert who never missed a day of fishing in his green wooden boat. Joe had already bought an aluminum boat for his grandchildren and nieces and nephews to use, but insisted on using the old wooden boat that he had to bail out every few minutes.

Behind him in the house, Paul could hear the whine of water in the plumbing. And soon, as she always did during her morning shower, Judy began singing "Angel of the Morning." The song seemed livelier than it had in the last few days, and Paul knew this was because today was the day Jamie and her friend Arkady would arrive to spend their spring break at the cottage.

As he sat staring out at the serenity of the lake, at its glistening surface alive with water bugs, thoughts of genital contact and sexually transmitted diseases invaded his mind. But then he knew Jamie was a big girl, a smart girl. And he also felt strongly that he was not the only father who feared such things and had such thoughts at the beginning of a new day when everything can seem fresh and innocent and benign.

☢ ☢ ☢

The trip to Heritage, Michigan, took all day. First was the short bicycle ride to the train station in Champaign, then the train trip through flat Illinois farmland to Chicago, then a bus to Milwaukee — with barely enough room in the luggage compartment for the bicycles—then the new ferry service from Milwaukee northeast across Lake Michigan to the port of Frankfort, and finally the bicycle ride inland to the cottage on Wylie Lake. Jamie took her time during the ride from the ferry dock to the cottage, not wanting to pressure Arkady to ride faster. She'd had practice going on long rides when she dated Brian, and she could tell Arkady would sometimes become winded after very little exertion.

Jamie and Arkady received the grand tour before dinner — cottage, garage, storage sheds, wood pile, trees, rowboat ride on the lake with glasses of wine in hand — while Jamie's mother insisted on staying behind to prepare dinner.

Arkady sat forward on the bow seat while Jamie sat at the stern facing her father who insisted on rowing. She held her glass of wine in one hand and her father's glass in her other hand. The setting sun made sparkles of orange flicker on the lake, in the wine, and in her father's eyes.

"I've been anxious for you to see why we moved here, Jamie."

"It's beautiful, Dad. And this is the perfect time of day. I love the way the sun sets behind the trees."

"You should see it from that hill there, behind the cottage. We get a double sunset from there — one when the sun drops below the treetops, the second when it drops below ground level." Her father glanced back toward the setting sun. "By the way, Arkady, I'm also glad you came."

"Thank you. I'm glad I could meet Jamie's parents."

"Paul and Judy. You can call us Paul and Judy."

"I will," said Arkady, staring at the sunset. "Paul is a good name. Judy is a good name. I like them both."

When Arkady said this, Jamie's father paused in his rowing and raised his eyebrows at Jamie, making her smile.

After the last sliver of sun slipped below the treetops, Jamie's father put the oars up on the gunwale and pointed out how the sun still shown on the hill behind the cottage on the eastern shore. They sat still for several minutes this way, no one speaking as the oar blades dripped water behind the transom on either side of Jamie.

Now that the sun had set, the silence on the lake intensified as if the previous silence had substance and this silence did not. Then, when her father began rowing again, Jamie could feel the cool of night touch her face as the oar tips gurgled in the dark blackness of the water. Around the lake several lights appeared in cottage windows. There were a few other boats on the lake — pedal boats and rowboats, one with a small fishing motor that the fisherman used to reposition himself before casting in his line. When Jamie's father turned, his profile seemed to Jamie cold and sharp as stone. He seemed to brood and she wondered what was on his mind. His straight gray hair was tinted orange-purple by the remaining light in the sky.

"Mom phoned you about Hiram, I guess," said her father.

"Yes. I was sorry to hear about it."

"Maybe you'll get a chance to see Bianca. We'll invite her over one night while you're here. The company will do her good."

"Is she going to stay here by herself?"

"I don't know. They didn't have children. Might have been the Agent Orange. That's what Hiram always said."

Up at the bow Arkady turned toward them. "In this world I believe more lives have been affected by manmade chemicals and radiation than anyone would ever have guessed. Some day they'll discover that even AIDS is a manmade affliction. Not in a laboratory, but in our inability to appropriately relate to an environment in which everything is related." Arkady turned back toward the sunset. "I'm sorry if I seem cynical. The sky is beautiful. It reminds me of sunsets on the Ukrainian steppes when I was a boy."

"Red sky at night, sailor's delight," said Jamie's father. "Have you ever gone fishing, Arkady?"

"Yes. An uncle of mine took me to the Pripyat River. We caught trout."

"What did you use for bait?"

"Smaller fishes."

"Would you like to go fishing with me tomorrow morning?"

"I don't have any . . . equipment."

"I have extras of everything. We'll run into town for a license."

Jamie's father had come out of a gloom that had descended following the sunset. Jamie leaned to the side and saw Arkady looking back toward her.

"Go ahead, Arkady. That's why I brought you along, remember? So Dad can pretend he had a son instead of a daughter."

"You can come, too," said her father. "Here at Wylie Lake we're completely non-sexist."

"Thanks," said Jamie. "I'll keep Mom company."

"Hell, yes," said her father, stroking with one oar to turn them about. "Let's do it. And in the afternoon when it gets windy, we'll go out in the sailboat. Jamie's mother doesn't like boats. Lives on a lake and she'd rather *watch* the boats. See, there she is on the dock watching us."

Jamie turned. There were trees along the shoreline behind the dock with their trunks lit dimly by the orange sky to the west. Any one of them could have been her mother. But then an arm raised and her mother waved to them.

"Would you like me to row back?" asked Arkady.

"Why not?" said Jamie's father.

Before they switched seats, Arkady drank down his wine and found a safe place for the empty glass on a coil of bow line. Then Jamie's father took his wine from Jamie, stood carefully near the bow seat and held up his glass.

"Land ho!" said Jamie's father. "I think I see one of the *natives* now."

The way her father said *natives* recalled bronze-skinned girls going topless in a south seas film. But this reminded Jamie of her mother's mastectomy, of the colored scars etched into the white skin of her mother's chest. As Arkady rowed in, she felt tears in her eyes and hoped the rest of the week would not be as melancholy as this first night.

☢ ☢ ☢

While her father and Arkady went into town to get a fishing license before the general store closed, Jamie helped her mother set the table and make salads. Her mother seemed less on edge than she had been when she and Arkady first arrived. She remembered that her mother had actually taken a step backward when Arkady approached open-armed to give her a two-cheeked kiss and a hug. She also remembered her mother straightening her prosthesis after the hug. And now that Arkady and her father were gone, Jamie's mother adjusted the prosthesis every few seconds.

"New parts don't fit so hot?" asked Jamie.

"Not since Arkady's bear hug. Did you tell him I have a phony chest?"

"I told him you'd had a mastectomy. It came up after one of our mutual conversations about us getting zapped by chemicals and his family getting zapped by gamma and X-rays."

"Well, since he knows about my chest, I guess I could go back to wearing a sweatshirt if I want and get rid of this thing."

"Do whatever makes you comfortable, Mom."

"What would make me comfortable would be to grow a beard and pretend your dad and I are old fishing buddies. With Hiram gone he needs a buddy."

After they set the table, Jamie and her mother sat on the porch waiting for her father and Arkady to return. The sky was dark now and several lights across the lake glistened in the water.

"It's funny," said her mother. "As a younger woman I never dreamed I'd be in this situation when I reached fifty-five."

"What situation did you think you'd be in?" asked Jamie.

"I thought I'd still be working. I imagined myself somewhere about halfway up the corporate ladder building up my 401K for a retirement that wouldn't come until sixty-five. Hell, I'd made it into the middle class and I figured I'd live until ninety or so with all of my organs intact. The reason I'm telling you this, Jamie, is because I feel bad for you. At least I was allowed to have those kinds of dreams when I was your age. What I'm trying to say — and not doing a very good job — is that I wish you didn't have this thing hanging over your head."

"I try not to think about it because there's nothing I can do for it except get my checkup every three months."

"Does Arkady have a place he goes for regular checkups?"

"Yes, but not as often. While he's here he visits the campus clinic."

"Crazy world. Terrorists, war . . . a terrible place to bring up kids. And now kids are having sex, politicians are having sex, sex all over the place . . . and you two have this. I suppose it was destiny you should meet Arkady. But I have to say I don't like the idea of you being hurt any more than you have been. I remember last year when you and Brian were on the student senate together. I remember the talk we had back then. Most of all, I remember feeling sad at the time that you'd chosen to go alone to Washington that summer to work instead of going with Brian on his Sierra Club outing. I remember feeling you deserved Brian's devotion and the life the Jones family money could give you. Mothers are selfish that way, wanting nothing but the best for their kids."

"We all do what we have to do, Mom. Going to Washington was what I had to do. Brian and I are still friends. I see him on campus."

"But he's not a disaster victim."

Jamie turned to her mother who continued staring out at the lake. "You're right. Brian's not a disaster victim. He said almost those exact words to me. I felt like hell when he said that. I felt like . . . like I didn't deserve him. You know what I mean, Mom?"

"Yes, I know what you mean."

"Do you think my becoming involved with Arkady will eventually cause pain?"

"Yes."

"Keeping busy will save us."

"You'll save the world, Jamie."

"Come on, Mom."

"I mean it. You've got beliefs and brains and nothing can stop you."

"Nothing?"

"I'm sorry I said what I said before. We all have to make the best with what we have. You'll make the best of your life in law and helping good old Mother Earth and seeing to it that children everywhere have food to eat."

"You sure there's nothing else I'm going to do? In my spare time?"

They both laughed at this and sat close, Jamie leaning her head on her mother's shoulder. Out on the lake a shadow passed right to left, then the vibrations of the reflections marked the boat's wake.

"I see a boat out there," said Jamie. "Shouldn't it have lights on?"

"Yes," said her mother. "Since it's passing right to left it should be showing red and white. Probably fishermen heading in and their battery is going dead."

"Mom, I have something I need to tell you and Dad and I thought I'd tell you first. I might be going to Moscow University next year. I've applied for a study grant from the College of International Legal Studies and it looks like I might get it."

"That sounds like a fantastic opportunity, Jamie."

"It is. You thought I was going to say Arkady and I were planning to get married, didn't you?"

"Yes, that's what I thought."

"I fooled you."

"Will he be back over there while you're there?"

"Yes, but he'll be in the Ukraine, in Kiev, and I'll be five-hundred miles away in Moscow. I might be able to travel to Kiev but I can't be sure until I find out more about the program. I admit I tried for the university in Kiev, but they weren't offering grants."

"Do you love him?"

Jamie thought for a moment about Arkady and Brian and honesty and what was important during her short stay on this old Earth. If her mother had asked if she loved Brian, would she be able to deny it? Wasn't it possible to love two men? Finally, she lifted her head from her mother's shoulder, stared into her mother's eyes, and said, "Yes, I love Arkady."

Jamie's mother stood and took Jamie by the hand. "Come on. Let's put your things and Arkady's things into the guest room now so we don't have to go through an uncomfortable conversation later. I'm afraid your father will feel obliged to mention the availability of the sofa bed in the living room if your bicycle bags are still out when they get back."

☢ ☢ ☢

There were four bicycle bags, each a matched pair of panniers designed to hang on either side of a bicycle's rear wheel. Arkady's panniers were old and faded, emblazoned with 1982 patches commemorating Kiev's 1500th anniversary. The patches showed a representation of the old stone gate to the city. That afternoon, as they rode their bicycles from the ferry to Wylie Lake, Arkady told Jamie that he'd purchased the panniers to do his part for Ukrainian literature. He'd gotten them at a fundraiser for the old museum dedicated to the life and work of Taras Shevchenko, the famous Ukrainian poet. Arkady said the gate shown on the patch was a thousand years old and was built by Yaroslav the Wise to protect the city. He said that it might have been wiser if old Yaroslav had built his gate a bit further north, like at the future site of the Chernobyl reactor.

Jamie's panniers, on the other hand, were much newer, dark green and emblazoned with Sierra Club patches showing a hiker with backpack and hiking stick on the move in a green valley with a mountainous backdrop. The panniers, which, when removed from her bicycle unsnapped to become a pair of small backpacks, had been given to her by Brian.

After her mother helped carry the panniers into the room, she left Jamie alone to unpack and get ready for dinner. Jamie sat on the edge of the bed facing the small dresser, unpacking the two bags and putting her clothes into drawers. Although she'd had the panniers for some time, this was the first time she had used them on a bicycle trip.

The panniers were a gift from Brian. He'd given them to her

after they'd gone on a bicycle trip together the previous summer. A Sierra Club sponsored weekend trip on the Great River Road along the Mississippi River between Moline, Illinois, and Hannibal, Missouri. During the afternoon bus ride from U of I to Moline with their bicycles packed into the lower luggage compartment of the bus, Brian's hair blows in the wind coming into the bus window. Fine hair, the color of sand, fluttering in the wind as she tells him the story of Easthaven. Brian staring at her with blue eyes the color of the sea.

The movement of the bus across the Illinois prairie was gentle, no hills until they neared the Mississippi. They'd held hands. It seemed the natural thing to do on a bus ride while she told the story of Easthaven — the ruptured steel drums, the evacuation, the analysis that uncovered toxins like DBCP, the death of Ricky Wade who'd gone for a swim in their backyard pool, her mother swimming in the contaminated pool, the class action suit filed against the owner of Ducain Chemical. It had been the first time she'd told the entire story to anyone. When she was younger she avoided talking about it. Even when kids in high school who knew about Easthaven asked questions, she'd refused to answer despite taunts about her being, as Brenda "Loose Hips" Wilson said one day in the locker room, "A fucking Barbie Doll snob."

Maybe Brian was the first one to hear the story of Easthaven from her because he held her hand. The story bouncing around inside her all those years, even the dentist complaining to her parents about her grinding her teeth and making her wear a mouthpiece at night. The story hunting for a way out until Brian came along and gave her time to tell it the way it needed to be told. Not rushing her to talk about her past. Not cutting off the story before she really got into it because, surely their must be something else to talk about.

In the bus that afternoon she simply rested her hand on her thigh and, as she stared out the window at fields of corn, she'd felt Brian's hand on hers. Not that they hadn't held hands before. She remembered Brian grasping both her hands as they made love the night before in his dorm room. Not that he hadn't listened before. He was always a good listener. Perhaps it was the bus ride across the prairie that had triggered it. For whatever reason, the story had finally found its way out. And once out, it was easier to talk about to others. Arkady, a couple of her professors, and even Heather in the Student Union at the beginning of the previous semester.

On a bus ride from U of I to Moline the story spilled out the way the chemicals had spilled out of their rusted drums. No comment from Brian until later. Instead he let the story fester.

In Moline they spent the night at the YMCA. Everyone on the bus piling in through a side door that led to the gym. The riders wheeled their bicycles inside, leaned them against the walls of the gym, took exercise mats from piles against the walls and claimed spots on the floor. Soon the gym floor looked like a giant manila envelope with stamps applied from end to end.

Brian had marked their territory with his panniers. She didn't have panniers yet, and Brian insisted that since he'd had more experience cycling, he'd carry her things in one of his panniers. After the overhead lights were dimmed, Jamie and Brian lay on their backs and held hands. They'd tried using Brian's panniers for pillows, but they were too bulky. Instead, they unpacked sweatshirts and used these as pillows.

"I thought they would've given us rooms at the ol' Y instead of this here gym floor," whispered Brian in the faked southern drawl he sometimes used.

"One big-assed room," whispered Jamie, also trying out a southern drawl.

"Not much privacy."

"Who needs privacy?"

Brian, up on his elbow. "You mean . . .?"

"Lie down."

"I just thought . . . "

"Don't think so much."

"I like thinking."

"About the past, or the future?"

"Both."

"Speaking of the past, how did you lose your drawl?"

"The Birmingham educational system. And I have to confess, sometimes it feels good to put it back on."

"Speaking of confessions, what did you think of mine?"

"Yours?"

"Easthaven."

"Why should telling me that be considered a confession?"

"Because of my health concerns."

Brian, up on his elbow again, staring at her in the semi-darkness. "I don't care about your past. Do you care about mine?"

"I don't know that much about you."

"My parents are part of the Birmingham, Alabama, elite," said Brian, his voice echoing in the gym. "They're loaded."

"You mean they drink a lot?" she asked, as she poked him in the side.

"Shh," came from nearby.

"We're trying to sleep," said someone else.

Brian came closer. She could see the red of an Exit sign above a nearby doorway reflected in the moisture of his eyes. He hovered above her for a moment, then lay back down and she could just make out his profile as he stared up at the ceiling.

"I'm sorry," she whispered.

"I'm sorry, too," he whispered.

"For what?"

"Being an ass."

"That makes us a couple of sorry asses," she whispered.

"I'll kiss yours and make it better."

"Go to sleep."

During the bicycle ride in the hot sun the next morning, Brian insisted she ride ahead of him. "I need an incentive to keep up the pace," he said. "Just make sure you don't order chili when we stop for lunch."

Later that afternoon she rode behind Brian. "It's much easier back here," she said.

"The old incentive?"

"No, drafting you makes it easier."

"Most outings aren't this hard. I didn't realize there'd be so many hills. Next time we'll stick to hiking. That's what I'm used to. My dad and I hiked a lot when I was a kid."

The road leveled out ahead and there was no traffic. She pedaled up next to Brian and they slowed.

"Did you and your dad go on hikes before or after the divorce?"

"Both. My mom never went along. Dad's second wife goes hiking with him, but I've never gone with the two of them."

"By chance, or choice?"

"A little of both."

"Your dad's second wife is a lot younger?"

"You bet."

"How old were you when your parents divorced?"

"A very immature twelve."

"Why immature?"

"Because, at the time I was into video games and hung out in my room a lot. I was so divorced from reality I fantasized about a game in which I had access to a magic gun that, when pointed at any situation, would put things back the way they'd been at a previous point in time."

"That doesn't sound immature," said Jamie. "Especially to me."

As they approached a steep hill, Brian stood on his pedals to move ahead and looked back to make certain she slid in behind so she could draft him up the hill and take the edge off the climb. As she followed Brian up the hill he shouted back to her.

"I can't believe how the federal government, and even local governments with all the codes they must have had in place, let a chemical company get away with it for so long! Why didn't the goddamn bureaucrats simply wait until you'd all turned yellow with jaundice? Much too busy rubber stamping dumping permits to do their goddamn jobs! And what about the local doctors? Couldn't they see there was a pattern? Much too busy checking the chemical and pharmaceutical portions of their portfolios to even think along those lines! In some ways I'm all for global warming! It may be the only way to wake the damn bureaucrats up to the fact that everything we do has consequences!"

After crossing over the crest of the hill, she coasted alongside Brian.

"So, what did you think of my diatribe?" he asked.

"My leg muscles were burning too much for me to think about it."

They stayed in YMCAs again the next two nights, sleeping in gyms on exercise mats, the high ceilings echoing whispers and snores and laughter. On one of the nights, a couple not far from them made love. During this, Brian moved close and held her, pushing his hand into her sleeping bag and touching her gently. She recalled thinking of her mother while Brian touched her breasts. She recalled thinking of prosthetics and wondering how one would feel. She hoped it felt natural, the way Brian cupping one of her breasts as he slept felt natural.

The final day of the ride took them across the river into Hannibal, Missouri. While sitting on the bus that would take them back to U of I, and watching as the bicycles were packed into the luggage compartment, Brian said he felt like Tom Sawyer.

"In what way?" she asked, touching Brian's hand.

"At the beginning of *Tom Sawyer Abroad*, Huck Finn says that his and Tom's and Jim's adventures on the river poisoned Tom for more adventure and travel. Thus, another book."

"You'd like to travel and write books?"

"I'd like to travel," said Brian. "Who wouldn't?"

"Is that why you're in the Sierra Club?"

"It's one reason." Brian turned to her. "Another reason is that being in a club in which there's some activity every weekend gives me built-in excuses."

"Excuses?"

"Yeah. When Dad wants me to visit or wants to meet some-where, I've always got a damn good reason to turn him down."

During the bus ride back to U of I, Brian mentioned other up-coming Sierra Club trips. Working trips clearing walking trails somewhere out west, or cleaning riverbanks somewhere out east. Hiking trips in the Rockies and Appalachians. Trips to the tropics, trips to the Arctic Circle. Trips to Washington — the state, not the nation's capital.

During the bus ride back to U of I, she told Brian about her plans to go to Washington — the capital, not the state — where Senator Hansen of Illinois wanted her to work not only as a page that summer, but as a personal aide. She'd already made her plans. She'd leave campus as soon as classes were over and find a place to live in Washington.

Brian tried to convince her to come back after she found a place and travel with him for a week or two until the Senate was back in session. She told him she'd planned to do research in the archives. He told her she could tie her research in with the trip, do some en-vironmental research that would be helpful during the summer session. She told him her plans were already made. As they spoke, Brian stared at her, his blue eyes open wide as if he could read her mind. He also stared at her when he said she had to do what she thought was best, and that he understood.

That's how it happened. Just like that. And then at the end of the semester, Brian showing up on the morning she was due to leave for Washington with the two bags. "You can use them both together for luggage, or one as a backpack, or both as panniers when we go on a long bike ride across the country some day."

She and Brian were still friends, they agreed to always be there for one another, but on the bus ride back to U of I from Hannibal, Missouri, she had drawn a line in the sand. Her career took precedence. Her future was in politics. She recalled the look on Brian's face as the bus turned onto Lincoln Avenue and the sun flashed through the trees. He had stared straight ahead, squinting as if he were watching a film depicting their lives, lives that had to be lived in another world

Jamie sat on the bed in the guest room with both panniers in her lap. The panniers were lighter, emptied of their contents, empty except for a side pocket in one of the bags where she kept her student ID and credit card, and something else. She reached deep down into the side pocket, tearing a hangnail as she did so. As soon as she pulled the tattered photograph out and looked at Brian's face smiling back at her she recalled the moment she'd tucked the photograph into the side pocket. She'd been alone like now, sitting on her dorm bed, pulling her clothes out of the dresser to prepare for her summer move to Washington. The photograph of Brian was from the previous year when he ran for student senate, his hair longer back then. She'd cut the photograph out of a flyer for his senate run. She'd taken the photograph from the top of her dresser and tucked it into the bag, not only for safe-keeping, but thinking, at the time, that the photograph tucked into the bag would be a reminder of where she'd gotten the bag.

It was a black-and-white photograph. Brian smiling as seriously as he could for his student senate run. Not at all like the smile during the bus ride. No blue eyes. His light sandy hair appearing gray in the photograph, making him look older. She tucked the photograph back into a side pocket, tearing her cuticle again. Then, as she clutched the panniers to her, she looked up and saw a light flash brightly on the thin curtain over the window to the guest room and heard her mother call from the kitchen.

"They're finally back! I bet Old Man Rybicki at the general store talked their ears off! You can't just go there and get a fishing license! You have to tell your life story!"

☢ ☢ ☢

"It is very quiet here. If I were an American I believe I would say you can hear a pin drop."

"The door's closed. We're all adults. Don't feel uncomfortable."

"I shouldn't. When I was a boy our entire family slept in one room. But did you notice how loudly the bed squeaked when we got into it?"

"If we lie very, very still no one will know we're here."

In the brief silence that followed Jamie knew that this might have sounded like what her mother used to call a "poor me." A thinly veiled allusion to Easthaven. And when Arkady finally spoke, she knew he had picked up on this.

"Tell me, Jamie, how did it feel growing up in America after what happened to you?"

"When I was little I imagined myself as a pimple. A blemish to be squeezed out, something that could be made to disappear."

"That is very depressing."

"It was a childish way of looking at things. Sometimes I enjoyed watching peoples' reactions when they heard about Easthaven. Sometimes I'd pretend they had scientific instruments to get an exact measurement of my chemical makeup."

"In my country Chernobyl survivors say they identify with the Gypsies," said Arkady. "The Gypsies live on the outskirts of villages and cities in camps built from scraps. In Russia before the end of the century many people were made into Gypsies by the economic situation. You'll see Gypsies all around Moscow when you are there. Perhaps some of them will need legal assistance."

"I'm a pimple, remember? I've never felt strong or outgoing."

"Then, you must become outgoing."

"It scares the hell out of me."

"Of course it does. That's part of what makes it necessary for you to do this."

"You mean this?"

"Please, Jamie, how can I lie still when you do that?"

"Don't you like it?"

"Of course I like it. And soon, as they say in Siberia, I'll be as hard as a fence post in a blizzard . . . Shh. Don't laugh. Great, first they hear laughter, now they hear the springs. If you're not careful I'll have to cover your mouth."

"How?"

"Like this."

Then Arkady kissed her.

☢ ☢ ☢

"Spring is here."

"Yes, that's true. What made you say that now?"

"I hear the springs squeaking in the guest room."

"We have guests."

"I know."

"And he's not here to tutor our daughter in Ukrainian or Russian."

"I should have known when she took that first Russian class in high school. Of course who would have guessed she'd end up with a Russian-speaking Ukrainian. They did say Gorbachev's velvet revolution would eventually touch everyone on Earth."

"Let's get back to spring being here."

"What about it?"

"A time for rebirth, a time for growth. Maybe I'll grow a new pair."

"You're not an earthworm."

"I'm shaped like one."

"I meant that earthworms grow back parts when you cut off parts."

"Very funny."

It was silent again. The squeaking from the next room had stopped.

"Paul?"

"Yes."

"Why do you always pay so much attention to me there?"

"Because I don't want you to think I love you any less. And why do you always ask me?"

"Because I like to hear you say it."

CHAPTER 7

"IT IS VERY QUIET HERE."

"Compared to the university?"

"Yes. Many students have motor scooters that buzz like over-sized insects. It was the same at university in Kiev, except the scooters there were old black market jobs that took a hundred kicks to start, and smoked terribly when they did."

It was past dawn. Paul and Arkady were fishing the shaded waters on the eastern shore near a stand of dead birches, some of which had fallen long ago and lay waterlogged on the bottom like fallen pillars. Across the lake, Paul could see Joe Siebert bailing out his green boat, and beyond Joe he could see Hiram's and Bianca's cottage on the sunlit western shore.

They fished with yellow- and white-skirted jigs, their casts alternating, one reeling in while the other cast toward the sunken birches. They had been out an hour and had not had a single strike. Paul suggested they switch to the crawlers they'd bought the night before when they went into town for Arkady's license. But switching from the activity of casting and reeling to the passivity of staring at a bobber was delayed because of that universal optimism fishermen throughout the world share — that the next cast will find the perfect fish.

As Paul made another cast and sat on the stern seat of the rowboat to reel in, he glanced back toward his cottage about a quarter mile along the shore around a bend. Every time he looked at the cottage this morning he recalled knocking softly and opening the guest room door before dawn to awaken Arkady. Normally the guest room remained open and attained the same temperature as the rest of the cottage. But this morning, after he'd dressed and walked through the cool kitchen and living room, the air of the guest room had been warm and moist with a faint odor of bed linen. The room had seemed a living thing when he leaned in and whispered Arkady's name. Then, from the darkness, he had heard rustling, the squeak of bedsprings, and Arkady had appeared before him in the dim light wearing undershorts. For some reason, not seeing Jamie, yet knowing she was there, had upset him. Perhaps because of his dreams of impending doom surrounding the chemical spill, perhaps that.

Arkady had reeled in his line and cast out again without standing. Paul reeled in slowly, barely fast enough to keep the jig off bottom.

"I suppose it's hard to recall because you were so young," said Paul. "But I wondered if you sensed a loss of cooperation and community that existed on the collectives after the Soviet Union broke up."

"An unusual question from an American," said Arkady. "Most of the time when Americans think back to times before the Middle East they seem . . . I'm thinking of a word meaning self-congratulating."

"Smug."

"Yes, Americans often seem smug when they recall the fall of the Union. Perhaps they feel they invented the changes, or that they personally sowed the seeds that toppled the Union from within."

"Americans — or the west — had an effect, didn't they?"

"Of course," said Arkady. "But sometimes westerners think they were the only effect, as if our people had little to do with it. At least that's what my old Trotskyite uncle always said."

"Is your uncle still alive?"

"Yes," said Arkady, casting out again. "He lives in the village of Svyezhl north of Kiev with the rest of my family."

"One of the new villages built after the Chernobyl disaster?"

"Yes. *Svyezhl* is Russian for fresh, as in fresh-start, I suppose. The name was a sick joke. We moved there in 1989 when I was three-years old, the same year your Easthaven disaster occurred. Anyway, after independence, villagers tried to change the name to the Ukrainian word with the same meaning. Finally everyone agreed to leave the Russian name stand, probably because it contained more irony. Ukrainians are fascinated with irony. It helps us push onward despite our lot in life."

"I always wondered," said Paul, casting out his line, "if independence made people in the villages more cooperative or less cooperative."

"Much less cooperative than before," said Arkady. "In the past we had stability, or at least we thought so. Despite changes in the country and in the world and even at the local committee level, we had our land. Then, in 1986 when so much land was irradiated and lost forever . . . " Arkady cast his line out again. "Anyway, when we settled in the new villages the land meant nothing. The land and the boxes they built on it called houses were simply places to exist until the next catastrophe arrives."

"Is that why you decided to study sociology? Because of Chernobyl and the way you were forced to live?"

Arkady shrugged. "That . . . and guilt."

"Why should you feel guilty when you were one of those most affected?"

"Guilt is a strange thing," said Arkady, staring at the water. "A professor of mine theorized it is strongly related to the sense of generativity within all of us. The sense that each of us must have meaning for future generations even if we do not create offspring."

"You mean you feel guilt because you can't procreate?"

"No," said Arkady, smiling. "I don't feel guilt because I'm sterile, which I am by the way. The generativity I have in mind is one in which the individual feels a sense of responsibility for future generations. My professor's theory was that guilt in humans evolved when we realized life goes on after we are gone, that what we do in the here and now can, and will, have an effect we will never be able to experience."

After a few more casts, they switched to fishing with bobbers and thick wriggly crawlers pink as baby's butts for bait. A slight breeze from the south had come up and they slowly drifted north along the shore watching their bobbers jump slightly as fish too small for the hooks nibbled.

They fished in silence for a minute or two, then Arkady pointed to shore and asked, "Are those solar panels on that house over there?"

"Yes. My friend Bill Cochran lives there. He says solar isn't as efficient here because of the cloud cover off Lake Michigan, but he keeps trying. Your mention of generativity reminds me of conversations Bill and I have had about self-sufficiency and how we might set something up here at the lake. Solar power and making compost and not allowing high-speed boating on the lake — things like that. That's why I asked earlier about the collectives in the old Soviet Union. I'm fascinated with this idea of self-sufficiency, maybe a community of retired folks proving you don't need to rape the planet in order to scrape out a life."

A dragonfly landed on the tip of Paul's bobber. He gave his line a tug to make the bobber jump before continuing. "There's a fish that became extinct in the lakes around here a few years ago. No big deal, some would say. But the way it went extinct really got to me. I looked up test results at the Department of Natural Resources office in Traverse City. The reason the fish is extinct now is because in the 1980s, due to the chemical runoffs of previous decades, every fish of that species tested had liver cancer. Every one."

Arkady stared at him without speaking and Paul suddenly felt foolish. "This model community bullshit sounds like goddamn Shangri-la, doesn't it?"

"No, it doesn't" said Arkady, looking out across the lake toward Bill's house. "Perhaps I could meet Bill while I'm here."

"What?"

"I'd like to meet Bill. Not only because of his solar panels, but because he is a friend of yours."

78

The south wind stiffened during the day and by afternoon it was warm and gusty. Although small craft advisories had been issued for Lake Michigan, and the weather report had warned of April showers later that afternoon, it was a perfect day for sailing on Wylie Lake where waves were measured in inches and a shoreline was never more than a half-mile away.

At first Jamie's father took both her and Arkady out. But the sailboat was only twelve feet long and the only place Arkady could fit was at the bow. Because the lake was small, they had to come about quite often, and each time they did, Arkady was forced to unhook the jib sail from the stem fitting so he could duck beneath it as Jamie pulled the sail over him. At her father's insistence they all wore life vests and the bulk of Arkady's vest did not help when it came time for him to duck beneath the sail.

Jamie's father wore a blue baseball cap with the word *Captain* embroidered on it in gold. Although the temperature was only in the 60s — warm for April — they wore bathing suits. Jamie's father had insisted on this in case the boat capsized. To keep warm they wore sweatshirts beneath their life vests.

As the wind stiffened they had to shift their weight more rigorously to trim the boat. The tacking came more often because of their speed in traversing the lake, and finally, as they passed near the cottage where Jamie's mother sat in a lounge chair, Arkady jumped overboard, screamed that the water was like ice and swam ashore.

As she and her father skimmed away in the sailboat, hiking out on the grab rails to keep the boat from heeling over too far, Jamie saw Arkady run up onto shore, strip away the vest and wet sweatshirt, and take the beach towel offered him by her mother.

Jamie's mother wore blue jeans and a loose-fitting sweatshirt. From this distance, because of the folds in the bulky sweatshirt, and because she had chosen to discard the prosthesis, she looked like a very thin woman with very small breasts. And when she stood with one hand on her hip and the other shading her eyes, her mother seemed elegant and proud, a woman spying them across a wind-swept expanse of uncharted seas. As her father shouted the order to come about once again and Jamie grabbed at the jib sheets, she made a point to remember to tell her mother how good she looked.

The wind grew stronger and the sky darker as they reached the far side of the lake. Instead of coming about, Jamie's father put the boat into the wind. He had to shout to be heard because of the snapping of the sails.

"Take the tiller, Jamie! We'll switch places and head back in!" He patted his belly. "More weight here to lean out and keep us from going over!"

But as they started back, gusts of wind heeled the boat over violently, this despite the fact that Jamie's father was leaning out as far as he could with his toes hooked beneath the hiking straps. About half-way across the lake, an especially violent gust to the windward side caught both Jamie and her father off guard and the boat went over.

"This water's like ice!" screamed Jamie.

"Haven't had enough warm weather yet!" shouted her father from the other side of the laid-over boat.

Jamie floated between the mainsail and the laid-over hull. Luck-ily, the momentum of going over had not completely upended the boat mast-down and the sails lay submerged only a few inches below the choppy water. Around her in the water were spare lines and the jib sheets.

The water was so cold she thought of hypothermia, imagined a chart of numbers in a medical book giving water temperature versus exposure time. She turned toward the stern of the boat, lifted the tiller and swam beneath it. When she swam around the boat she saw her father already hanging on the daggerboard keel where it stuck out the bottom of the boat. He was hatless, his gray hair matted to his scalp, his cap floating away, pushed by the wind.

"My weight's not enough!" shouted her father.

Jamie reached up, grabbed onto the daggerboard with both hands. But despite their combined weight they could not pull the boat upright.

Her father turned to her, his face close enough so he did not have to shout. "Water's just rough enough to keep the sails under. I'll swim around and lower the sails."

The wind had increased, the sky growing darker, and she remembered her mother and Arkady on shore. She swam back from the boat a little to wave that they were all right. But instead of her mother and Arkady waving from shore, she saw her mother sitting in the rowboat putting on a life vest as Arkady rowed like mad toward them. It would have been funny, not an emergency at all, if the water were not so cold and if the wind had not gotten so strong. She could hear the wind now, hissing on the tops of small whitecaps that had begun to form. And then there was a flash of lightning followed by a clap of thunder as the storm came on.

The rain started as her mother and Arkady arrived in the rowboat. Jamie wanted to stay in the water and help put the sailboat upright, but Arkady insisted she climb into the rowboat. The chop on the lake rocked the rowboat from side to side. On a larger lake the rowboat would have gone over. Once Jamie was on board she took the oars and steadied the rowboat while Arkady jumped in to help her father.

"Put all your weight on the daggerboard!" shouted her father from the far side of the sailboat. "I'll lift the mast out of the water!"

When they did this, the boat came up like a cork and Arkady scrambled on board pulling in the lowered sails that lay in the water.

Jamie's father swam toward the rowboat. "We'll tow it in!"

Jamie threw a line to Arkady who went forward to tie it to the bow eye.

To get her father into the rowboat, Jamie had her mother sit on the far side to trim the boat while she grasped her father's life vest and pulled. As soon as her father was on board he went to the oars. Then, when Jamie turned back to the sailboat to see about Arkady, a white-hot door opened in the sky and lightning struck the mast of the sailboat. Arkady, seated below the boom, was thrown into the bottom of the boat near the steaming mast.

☢ ☢ ☢

After Jamie dove into the water and went on board the sailboat, it took only a few minutes for Paul to row back to shore. But they were long minutes during which Paul rowed as fast as he could and felt Judy's hand on his shoulder as he watched Jamie cradling Arkady's head. Just before they got to shore it began raining hard. But through the sheets of rain Paul could see Arkady sit up and wave to them.

The inside of the cottage never felt warmer or cozier. Paul built a fire in the wood stove and had everyone put on dry clothes. Although Arkady seemed unaffected by the lightning bolt, Paul insisted they take him to the doctor in town for a checkup. And so they all piled into Paul's car as the rain and wind continued.

☢ ☢ ☢

It was cool and clear at the cottage the day after the storm. Except for an excursion along the shore to retrieve Paul's cap where it had lodged in reeds, they sat within the enclosed porch all that day snacking, playing Scrabble, working puzzles, and repeating the story of the capsize, the rescue, the lightning strike, and how lucky it was that the boom and mast were made of wood instead of aluminum. They acted like any survivors of near disaster.

The following day Bianca came over for lunch and seemed cheered by the diversion. Bianca spoke of Hiram, saying it was the first time she had been able to do so since his death. Bianca said she enjoyed listening to Arkady talk because of his accent. When she said this, Arkady began speaking rapidly, joking that the electrical shock had sped up his metabolism. He raised his eyebrows toward Jamie, making her laugh. Everyone else laughed, too, even Paul who knew that the joke must have been a carryover from the night before when he heard Jamie and Arkady laughing in the middle of the night as the bedsprings squeaked.

Bianca stayed until evening and joined them for dinner. After dinner they had brandy and sat on the cool porch talking about Paul's dream to create a Walden-like community of self-sufficient retirees around the lake.

Several brandies later, Paul and Judy began recalling their college days at U of I. They told about a brief encounter with the police
at a protest march. They told about a bus trip to Hanford in Washington state as environmental activist newlyweds. Judy told about
trying pot and going braless. Paul told about his episode with acid at
a fraternity party that put him into the hospital and made him think
he had X-ray vision.

During a break in the laughter of reminiscence, Bianca began
speaking about Hiram again. She spoke in detail about a tough,
streetwise kid from Chicago's south side, about Hiram arriving home
from Vietnam missing his arm, about Hiram joining other veterans
demonstrating against the war, about Hiram going into computers
and learning to type with one hand, about Hiram wanting children
but finding out he couldn't have any of his own, and finally, about
Hiram saying only a year earlier that he wished he would have given
in to Bianca's desire to adopt.

At the end of the evening, after the "dead soldier" brandy bottle
was tossed into the recycle bin, Bianca said goodnight and went to
the door to walk home. But Arkady and Paul would not let her
walk around the lake alone at night and both accompanied her.
While they were gone, Jamie remembered that she had wanted to
tell her mother how good she had looked on the lakeshore without
her prosthesis. When she did, her mother hugged her tightly and the
feel of the bones of her mother's chest against her reminded Jamie
of how it was to hug Arkady.

When Jamie told this to Arkady that night in bed, Arkady held
her and stroked her breasts gently.

The next day Paul took Arkady to visit Bill Cochran. Bill showed Arkady his solar cells and batteries and the 12-volt lighting system he had wired in the house. He showed Arkady the solar water heater and plans for a wind generator.

During this tour of the house, Bill's wife followed closely behind, light-heartedly commenting in her drawl — she was originally from Texas — about the cloudy days and the dimness of 12-volt bulbs and the icy cold of the bath water. Bill took the ribbing with humor and Bill's wife's true colors came out when Arkady mentioned Paul's self-sufficient community idea and she showed great interest.

"It'll be like *Walden II*," she said. "We'll be pioneers and folks'll come from every which way to see how we do it."

The remainder of the week went by quickly and soon it was the last full day before Jamie and Arkady had to return to U of I. Paul had mentioned earlier in the week that he wanted to take them on a bicycle ride to the state park beach on Lake Michigan. Jamie said they should stay home the last day with her mother, but Judy insisted they go.

The day was sunny and dry and in the 50s. The trip to the state park beach was ten miles--the first five miles on secondary roads, the last five miles on an old railroad right-of-way that had been blacktopped for bicycling in summer and cross-country skiing in winter.

Paul's bicycle was old, not as easy to ride as Jamie's and Arkady's bicycles. Half way to the beach, Arkady insisted he and Paul switch bicycles.

"Is this a Russian bicycle?"

Arkady laughed. "No. I used to have an Hungarian bicycle but I sold it before I left and bought this bicycle from another student. It wasn't until I'd bought it that I found out this one was also made in Hungary. My old bicycle had fenders and was a different color and had different markings. But everything else is the same."

"Are you glad you came to America?" asked Paul.

"Of course he is," said Jamie who was riding a little ahead and had heard the question and coasted back. "If he hadn't come here he never would have met me." After her comment, Jamie smiled and rode farther ahead, apparently to allow them to speak without her overhearing.

"Yes," said Arkady, "I'm glad I came here. It gives me what you call a new horizon on things."

"You mean a new perspective?" asked Paul.

"Yes."

"Would you ever consider moving here?"

"Of course I would consider it. But I don't think I will, as least not for several years."

"Why not?"

"Because there is work to do back home."

"What will you do when you get back?"

"Finish one more year of school."

"Then what?"

"I've been taking classes in social issues and specializing in gerontology. I suppose what I dream of doing is very similar to the idea you expressed to me this week. I'm disturbed by the fact that the elderly in my country are becoming castaways. It's been happening since families have gotten smaller due to the harsh economic conditions. Instead of having grandchildren to care for and keep them occupied, the elderly are becoming purposeless. But they still love children. I'm fascinated by the idea that there might be a way to focus that love of children. Your idea of a model community of elderly who attempt to give back to the Earth what they've taken from it inspires me." Arkady turned to Paul and smiled. "The only problem with your idea is that you are not yet elderly."

"Maybe the model community should be middle-aged," said Paul. "We spend the first half of our lives working for the system — business, government, corporation — and spend the last half working for future generations."

"Now I know where Jamie gets many of her ideas," said Arkady.

Paul glanced up as he rode. "Did you ever notice the sky isn't as blue as it used to be?"

"Yes," said Arkady. "All the more reason the world needs people like your daughter."

☢ ☢ ☢

There was a class of sweatshirt-clad kindergarten children at the beach for a spring outing. While the two women and one man who chaperoned the outing sat on the sand watching the children, Jamie joined two little girls and a little boy who were making a sand castle.

The little girls and Jamie formed the walls and towers and turrets and bastions; the little boy brought bucket after bucket of lake water to keep the moat around the castle filled. They built the castle several feet up from the waves of Lake Michigan whose waters were even colder than the water in Wylie Lake had been.

The little boy reminded Paul of the little boy named Ricky Wade who, one day years earlier, had climbed a low spot in the Ducain Chemical fence and played in the dump, then, that same afternoon, had climbed their backyard fence and jumped into Jamie's backyard pool with his cloths on. No one knew about the toxicity of the dump then. The leaking chemicals hadn't been discovered until later that summer after the damage was done. Ricky Wade had been six years old. Jamie had been only two. Now Jamie was a woman, and in a year or so would probably have her degree and be off to Washington lobbying for the environment.

One of the little girls building the sand castle was black and Paul was reminded of Hiram and Bianca and the child they never had. The other little girl had a freckled complexion and brown hair, short and curly like Judy had cut Jamie's hair when she was little. Although the boy with the bucket who had reminded Paul of Ricky Wade was only five or six, the boy had a look about him like boys sometimes do when they are planning something evil. Eventually the plan emerged when the boy dumped a bucket of water on a turret, washing it away.

Paul turned to Arkady who sat next to him on the warm sand. "Did Jamie tell you the details about the Easthaven disaster?"

"It seemed quite detailed."

"Did she tell you about the trial?"

"Yes."

"Did she tell you about Harold Ducain's suicide?"

"Yes. It must have been upsetting for you."

"Everything about the Easthaven disaster was upsetting. And still is. I've never stopped having nightmares about it. I suppose it's a lot like the Chernobyl disaster, on a smaller scale of course."

"Nothing is on a small scale when it comes to human tragedy," said Arkady.

☢ ☢ ☢

The ride home from the beach was pleasant and cheerful until they were almost back at the cottage. Jamie sang golden oldies she could remember, Paul and Arkady sometimes joining in after hearing a verse or two. They sang "Hotel California" and "Elvira" and "Bette Davis Eyes" and "We Are the World." Then, just before arriving at the cottage, Jamie sang "Angel of the Morning."

Perhaps because of the mood set by the song Judy always sang in the shower since her mastectomy, or perhaps because Jamie and Arkady had to leave early the following morning, or perhaps because of the realization that Jamie was no longer a little girl — for whatever reason, it was a tearful reunion as they rode up the driveway lined with hundred-year-old trees and Paul saw Judy standing there in a sagging and faded sweatshirt.

CHAPTER 8

THE STATION MANAGER AT CHANNEL 10, the ABC affiliate in Champaign, Illinois, was named Leslie Gale. Leslie's family name, Galinski, had been shortened to Gale for her media career. She'd told this to Heather at their first meeting when Heather, being interviewed for the position of part-time newscaster, asserted that West was indeed her real family name.

Leslie Gale was Heather's second boss. Heather's first boss had been the station manager at the University of Illinois campus station. His name was Professor Martin Jackson. Martin might have gone places in commercial television, especially being an up-and-coming, well-groomed black broadcaster back in the 1980s when black broadcasters were needed to even things out. But Martin had been lured into academia by what Heather claimed was his need to associate with young people as he grew older.

The conversation about Martin's so-called need to associate with young people took place near the end of the first semester during

Martin's last visit to Heather's room in the graduate house.

"Heather, honey, you asleep?"

"Can't sleep. Resting up for round two."

"No round two tonight, babe. Family business."

"Kid's choir recital?"

"Doesn't matter, simply family business."

"I thought you'd stay tonight. I had something I wanted to tell you."

"We got time. Tell me."

"I got an offer from Channel 10."

"No shit, in the newsroom?"

"Yes."

"You going to take it?"

"I already did."

"I didn't know you went both ways."

"What?"

"Both ways. Station manager at 10's a dyke."

"And you're a fuckin' son of a bitch!"

"Take it easy, babe."

"I mean it, Martin! You and your goddamn academic life! You're here instead of going commercial so you can stick it to a different intern every semester. You've probably used the same ancient-history Anita Hill-Clarence Thomas line a hundred times. Maybe I should call that new talk show host on FOX, have her do a show on coeds who've been seduced with quotes from those way-back-when Hill-Thomas hearings. Or maybe the next one'll be a male intern who'll spread 'em wide for you. Is that it, Martin? Is that why you like Greek? Because it don't make no goddamn difference from that end?"

Martin had slapped her then. After the slap he apologized, saying he didn't blame her for taking the position at Channel 10, that it was a damn good opportunity. After that, contrary to what Martin had said earlier, and despite his so-called family business, Heather and Martin did have a round two that night. But it was their last night together. She had learned a lot from Martin, and it was time to move on.

And so, Heather West became a part-time broadcaster at Channel 10 where she co-anchored the news every evening at five. It was a *coup* for Heather. She was the first full-time broadcast journalism graduate student at the university to land a non-intern commercial spot before graduating. Heather was featured in the campus newspaper, in the Champaign-Urbana press, and even made a guest appearance on a Chicago station. Heather's career was well on its way before she graduated, and Heather had Leslie Gale to thank for it.

Despite Professor Martin Jackson's claim, Leslie Gale was not a dyke. She was, in fact, married to a local attorney who enjoyed hunting and fishing, and they had a five-year-old son. The reason Leslie had decided to nurture Heather's career had nothing to do with what she might get in return. Leslie was one of those true believers in talent, like a dedicated agent who helps clients because their skill and hard work make them deserving of help. Leslie knew Heather had broadcast talent and a face and body to match. Indeed, Leslie viewed Heather as a kind of alter ego who would break the ground Leslie might have broken if she had not made the decision to have a family. Although she did not reveal this to Heather, Leslie dreamed of the day Heather West would be hailed as one of the most influential broadcast journalists of the twenty-first century.

☢ ☢ ☢

Because it was Sunday evening and the clerical staff was not there, the offices of Channel 10 in Champaign were quiet. Instead of going into Leslie's office to speak, Heather and Leslie sat outside the office, Leslie behind her secretary's desk and Heather in a side chair. The reason both Leslie and Heather had stayed on after the early evening Sunday news broadcast was because this was Heather's first night doing a live opinion commentary on the news from campus and they wanted to review the recording of the broadcast. They had watched the recording in the control room and come here to discuss it.

"I like the way you compared last week's environmental protests to the protests of the 1960s, Heather."

"Are you sure it worked?"

"Yes, especially the repeated references to taking full responsibility for one's actions. You made it clear to viewers that this particular group of activists had better put their ethics where their mouths are if they're ever going to succeed."

"I hope it didn't come off like I'm against environmental concern."

"Not at all, Heather. You came off like someone of their generation who has the same concerns but is searching for reasonable solutions."

"So, you don't think the Sequoia Power Plant should be shut down?"

"That's not the point, Heather. Actually I *do* think it should be shut down. The beauty of your commentary is that even though I didn't agree with the fundamental direction of the argument, I do agree with bringing all ideas out for discussion."

"I didn't sound ultra-conservative or old-fashioned?"

"Not at all."

"Good. After taking the side of the survivalists who are against sending messages back to extraterrestrials, and now this, I was concerned about being labeled before I even get out of school."

"Don't worry, Heather. You've got the talent to avoid a label. Down-home good looks and professional presentation are a hell of a combination. That's why I want you here after you graduate."

"Here?"

"Yes. If you want it, I'll save a full-time spot for you."

"I don't know what to say."

"Don't say anything. You've got time to think about it. We don't have a huge local audience, but we're affiliated and it's a good jumping off point for someone who eventually wants to go national. It doesn't happen often, but once in a while I spot someone who deserves a jump start."

Before Heather left the station, Leslie got a phone call from New York. The nightly network news was also doing a spot on the controversy surrounding the Sequoia Power Plant and a friend of Leslie's had called to say that a portion of Heather's commentary from Channel 10 would be used.

☢ ☢ ☢

Instead of making her national network debut later in her career on an affiliate in one of the major cities, Heather was going nationwide while still a student working part time at Channel 10. Thinking about this as she left the studio that night made her laugh out loud and think in clichés like, "being on cloud nine" and "the cat that swallowed the canary."

But, damn it, sometimes clichés say it all. Like, suddenly everything was going right for her. Breaking off with Martin had helped, she was getting good grades in her classes, she was the first student anchor on Channel 10, or maybe the first on any network affiliate. And now this — her face on televisions across the nation, her voice echoing in living rooms and family rooms in every corner of the country. For the first time in a long time she had something to celebrate. She had made it on her own, made it without bedding down with someone. As she considered her future from this new position of strength, she decided the best thing to do would be to keep up the momentum. Go back to her room, study for tomorrow's classes, pile success upon success, make a difference in the world instead of simply existing and marking time. She'd make news instead of waiting for it.

Of course there must be time for celebration. She'd watch the broadcast "live" tonight. Not only that, but she had a station disk of the broadcast with her and, if she wanted, she could play it over and over in private and no one would laugh at her vanity. She deserved a little vanity. Everyone deserved to feel this way sometimes.

It was a pleasant night. Earlier in the week, while most students were away on spring break, there had been storms, but now it was calm and windless, the smells of spring in the air. The students were back after being gone for the week, and the fast food palaces, pizza joints, and bars were busy again.

As she approached the front entrance of the grad house, Heather saw two bicycle riders coasting toward her in the dark. The bicycles were heavily laden with bulging rear bags, and as the pair coasted beneath the overhead lights she could see it was Jamie and Arkady. She paused at the bike racks while they unloaded their bicycles.

"Hope you had a good time. How are your parents, Jamie?" While she said this she felt as if she would explode.

"Fine."

"How was the American version of the *dacha*, Arkady?" Any minute they would guess, ask what was really on her mind.

"You can no longer call it a *dacha*," said Arkady. "*Dacha* implies a second home in the country. Jamie's parents have moved there permanently."

"Where is it again?" Who cared where it was? What mattered was her news, her debut tonight at ten.

"Michigan," said Jamie, looking at her with a puzzled expression.

"You didn't ride all that way, did you?"

"We took the train and a ferry," said Jamie, still staring at her.

"That's spelled f-e-r-r-y," said Arkady.

They laughed at this, Jamie and Arkady seeming to become almost as giddy as her. Heather couldn't stand it, and the news about her success came out in a rush. Her voice full of clichés and up an octave describing how her first commentary at the station had somehow grown into an appearance on the network. The news spilled out into the night very un-anchor-like, as if from a child.

"What was the commentary about?" asked Arkady.

"The demonstration in the Quad before spring break," said Heather.

"Did you take the conservative side?" asked Jamie.

"That depends how you look at it."

"I mean did you speak out for keeping the plant open?"

Heather stared at Jamie for a moment. "Yes, I did. But even a bleeding-heart liberal like you would have been proud of me. I said the demonstrators should take responsibility for their actions the way civil rights marchers did, the way your parents did."

"You didn't mention my parents by name, did you?"

"No, but I guess your telling me about how they got arrested during a demonstration inspired me."

"I'd rather not have my parents' private lives spread all over the place," said Jamie.

"I said I didn't use their names. What if I had? People make choices they have to live with all the time and your parents are no different. They got married and had you, didn't they?"

Jamie stared at Heather without answering.

"Anyway," said Heather, waving her hand. "Don't be such a prude about Mommy and Daddy. I simply use specific details for focus. Thinking about your parents' roles as activists gave me something to hold on to. Besides, what difference would it make if anyone knew about something that happened so long ago?"

"I guess it doesn't matter," said Jamie. "When you first mentioned it I was concerned my parents might be in for a surprise when they tuned in the news tonight. Anyway, congratulations on your break into the big time."

Heather helped Jamie by carrying one of her bags up the front steps of the grad house. "God, this thing's heavy. Your parents grow a kilo of pot up there and pack it into bricks for you?"

When neither Jamie nor Arkady replied to this, Heather said, "Sorry, just kidding."

On the elevator Arkady took the extra bag from Heather. "I can manage it."

When they got off the elevator, Arkady went with Jamie into her room while Heather went alone into her own room across the hall.

☢ ☢ ☢

It was a night like no other. As she watched the recording of her broadcast over and over while waiting for the evening network news on which it would be played, Heather felt there was nothing she could not do. She was in control. She'd tasted power and the taste lingered. By simply expressing an opinion using appropriate words and just the right facial expressions and pauses . . . yes, as long as she worked hard and never expressed true emotions or feelings, she'd have it made. And with success would come more power. And with power she'd be able to do anything she wanted to do. Maybe move out of the grad house to an apartment.

She was on the sofa. She had changed out of the skirt and blouse she had worn during the broadcast and now wore only a robe. The recording of her broadcast, which she had played at least a dozen times, had just ended. She pushed the display button on the remote control and saw that only an hour remained before the news. She switched to Channel 10, which was showing a situation comedy involving a New York family and a Moscow family who have traded places and keep in touch via video conferencing. The show was called *East Meets West* and was quite popular. Millions of viewers would be watching this program and many, perhaps all, would soon see Heather West, a bitchin' redheaded commentator from central Illinois. She muted the sound on the television, put the remote control unit down and went into the bathroom.

In the bathroom she closed the door and took off her robe. She turned on the shower to warm it up and stood looking at herself in the full-length mirror she had recently mounted to the back of the bathroom door to make it easier to get her clothes and appearance just right for her broadcasts. She smiled at herself. It seemed a friendly, honest, sincere smile, the more so because she was naked, her arms at her sides, nothing hidden.

As she stared at herself, at that saintly goddamn smile, she tilted her head to the side slightly, a movement she had used during a pause in the broadcast to convey a sense of objectivity at a key moment. When she tilted her head, something dark became visible behind her. Something dark on the white of the shower curtain.

She felt a sudden chill and began to turn slowly about. She half expected to see him there inside the shower, her father there standing in the shower, bleeding in the shower the way he had bled in the bathtub at home. She closed her eyes as she turned, imagining his image blurred by the semi-opaque shower curtain. But when she opened her eyes, she saw that the darkened area on the curtain at eye level was simply a fold in the curtain caused by the battering of the water from the shower head.

She opened the curtain, felt the temperature of the water, lowered it slightly, then stepped into the steam as if stepping into another world, a world in which Daddy was there bouncing little Jennifer on his knee and laughing with joy because of the success of his precious bundle of molecules.

As she showered, she closed her eyes and imagined lovers somewhere else in the grad house. The boy lover large for his age, swollen more by altered DNA than by arousal. The girl lover, just off Daddy's knee, so tight and priggish she's torn open and bleeds profusely, the blood washed down the building's plumbing system, flowing down where all waters ultimately meet.

She opened her mouth and looked up, taking the warm blast from the shower head full on her face. The water had a metallic taste. Or perhaps this was the taste of fetuses flushed down toilets.

With this thought she hurried through the rest of her shower, stepping out into cool, dry air where the evening news and the admiration of classmates and the power to be heard awaited her.

CHAPTER 9

THE OLD WOMAN STOPS PEDALING her pedal boat and the young man stops rowing his aluminum rowboat as they arrive at a dock made of composite materials resembling painted boards. It is quiet enough to hear the rustle of leaves in the birches lining the shore. Some of the leaves fall in the morning breeze, a few landing in shallows on either side of the dock where they float out onto the lake like galleons beginning a voyage.

The young man climbs onto the dock, ties up his rowboat and the pedal boat, then offers to help the old woman. Instead of clasping his hand, she unwraps her shawl and hands it to the man. Next she puts a seat cushion out onto the dock and crawls out from under the canopy of the pedal boat and onto the dock, kneeling like a penitent. Only then does she take the man's hand in order to help her stand.

Up close the man can better see her age in the mottled colors of her skin. To the man it seems age has changed her skin from that of a black woman into a sampling of the skins of all women. This, and the dignified movements as she takes back her shawl and uses it to cover her thinning hair, adds an aura of wisdom and knowledge.

She begins walking toward the end of the dock, then stops suddenly. "The fish. We can't fry fish without the fish."

The young man reluctantly leaves the old woman standing unassisted on the narrow dock, retrieves the stringer of bluegills and goes back to her.

"I can usually make it to the end of the dock without falling off," she says. "But if I'm specially teetery, sometimes I'll take the cushion with and sit myself down half way to shore. Making do with what I've got."

Once on shore the old woman pauses, looking toward her cottage. When she moves forward, into the shade of larger trees surrounding the cottage, she pauses again, this time hanging onto a birch tree. The young man sees that the white bark is shiny where the old woman rests her hand.

"My first husband helped my second husband plant this tree," she says, looking forlornly toward the cottage. "Then, the very next day, he died. And now their ashes are washed up here feeding the tree. Funny how things outlive people."

She turns to the young man, smiles. "Come on, let's get to those fish. And while they're frying I'll tell you more about the lake and its people."

As they walk slowly up the gradual incline to the cottage, the old woman speaks of children, how they leave home and make lives for themselves. She says that although she never had children of her own, she has come to think of her best friend's little girl as her own. The old woman is back in the past again, speaking of two girl babies born in the late 1980s, the two girl babies growing up, getting an education, becoming young women and starting out in the world. One of the young women starts with a bang in television, the other begins a trip to the other side of the world.

☢ ☢ ☢

In June, Heather West, who was becoming recognized in households throughout the Champaign-Urbana area as a quick-witted, up-and-coming commentator, finished her classes with high grades, despite the workload at Channel 10, and graduated in the class of 2014 with her masters in broadcast journalism. The week before she graduated, Heather got to do an interview with the MIT professor who claimed to have interpreted messages from extraterrestrials. The professor, who was attending a conference at U of I, said that the extraterrestrials would most likely send new messages at regular intervals, but that he did not know exactly what those intervals would be. He said one way to determine the intervals would be to find where the messages originated and to study the planetary cycles in that solar system. He also stated that our solar system was most likely among billions of other targets of these messages, changing the age-old supposition from "We are not alone," to "It's awfully crowded out there." The professor was a talkative and newsworthy interviewee who seemed to take quite a liking to Heather.

Heather celebrated her graduation with coworkers at Channel 10 and with classmates, including Jamie Carter and Arkady Lyashko, at a party given for her at the home of Leslie Gale, general manager at Channel 10. No one from Heather's family attended the party and after graduation Heather did not visit the estate in Olympia Fields where her brother lived.

In July, Heather visited her mother at the St. Anne home for the mentally ill. Her mother showed no reaction to the details of success Heather tried to explain. It was a disappointing visit, her mother seeming to stare through her.

One of Heather's projects that summer was to rewrite her family history in order to have a concise and consistent fictional past at her disposal. Among the details of her fictional life was the story that her father was a high school science teacher who died of lung cancer when she was a little girl. And her mother? Her mother married a younger man shortly after Heather entered college. They ran away together and she hadn't heard from her mother since. To put her change of identity in cement, Heather was able to go into university records prior to graduation, eliminate all ties to her family and even change her Social Security number.

That summer, while working full time at Channel 10 as the evening and late night co-anchor, Heather mentioned that her father had died of smoking-related lung cancer. She did this after reading a story about a statistical decrease in the incidence of lung cancer in the United States due to the decreased popularity of smoking in recent decades.

Because she was no longer a student at U of I, Heather no longer did her campus commentary spot. But the following winter, after having worked full time at Channel 10 only six months, Heather was given the opportunity to do commentaries on local and state politics and proved quite successful at it. She was even able to use the byline she had dreamed up while still in school. At the end of each commentary she would say, "I'm Heather West with news that makes a difference." Then, after staring at the camera a moment longer for effect, she would turn it over to the weather person with a joke about the latest blizzard in this winter of blizzards amidst all the warnings about global warming.

☢ ☢ ☢

Although Heather filled the airwaves in and around Champaign-Urbana with her smile that winter, Jamie did not see Heather on television.

Jamie was in Russia at Moscow University doing two semesters of study specializing in foreign affairs. Although her application to the foreign study position had been accepted before the end of the previous school year, the position had been further enhanced by a glowing recommendation from Illinois United States Senator Jim Hansen that Jamie be a student ambassador for certain matters of interest to the senator and other members of both the Senate Foreign Relations Committee and the Environment and Public Works Committee.

Senator Hansen wanted to bolster Jamie's political career, even though it hadn't really begun, because the previous summer she'd worked as his aide in Washington and he made it clear that he admired her work. Initially, the stint in Washington was to have been a clerical job with some hands-on experience in the capital while Congress was in recess. But that summer, economic issues stirred by public opinion kept many senators in Washington where they were determined to hammer out new budget cutting and tax proposals to present to the President prior to the drafting of his budget.

Perhaps it was partially fate, perhaps partially skill, perhaps simply being in the right place at the right time. Whatever the underlying reasons, Jamie became involved with Senator Hansen's assigned task of writing the text of the Senate proposal. In the process of editing drafts of the proposal for the senator, Jamie made several recommendations concerning the Social Security program and the issue of the growing elderly population. These recommendations, which centered around her father's recent ideas about senior citizen service to society, seemed good political sense at the time, and the recommendations were written into the proposal given to the President.

And so, after working as an aide on domestic affairs for Senator Jim Hansen during the summer, Jamie was off to Moscow University to take courses in foreign relations and political theory and to gain valuable exposure to Euro-Asian governments.

One of the first special assignments given Jamie in the student ambassador role defined by Senator Hansen was to coordinate between Russian and American students interested in international environmental issues. But shortly after her arrival in Moscow, scientists anxious to work with American counterparts to stem the pollution of new Russian business, contacted Jamie and began communicating to the United States Congress through her. During her role as liaison she mentioned a concept her father used. It was a common concept which had many names. Her father had given his version of it the name "random thinking." Jamie told one of the Russian scientists that environmental researchers needed to be less critical during the creative phase of a project. She said researchers needed to imagine solutions without the usual intervening negative thoughts so common in human nature. She said researchers must strive to think like science fiction writers instead of being buried in the details of their disciplines. After all, wasn't the current work being done to unravel the mystery of the extraterrestrial message proof that one should think like this? The comment caught on, spread among researchers at Moscow University and another scientist, in repeating the story to a reporter, used the term "random thinking" and it ended up in a story in a story on the front page of *Pravda*.

While in Russia, Jamie hoped to travel south to Kiev to see Arkady. The last time she saw him was at the beginning of summer when she was off to Washington and he was returning home. Her original plan to visit Arkady during the Christmas season did not work out because she was at a critical point in the work on her dissertation. She and Arkady kept in touch writing one another weekly and, in January, agreed that she would travel to Kiev in February when they could both get time off from their studies. The plan was to spend a few days with Arkady in Kiev, then go with him to the village of Svyezhl to visit his family.

During the four months she'd spent in Russia, Jamie had met with local committees in and around Moscow, had interviewed various ministers and members of government, and had even interviewed the Russian President. Part of the reason for her having been able to meet all of these officials was because Senator Hansen and several other senators and even a leading Russian scientist had sent letters of introduction for her. The officials seemed genuinely interested in her ideas concerning an environmental plan for the future of the world, a plan in which world citizens of middle age and older help improve the environment while, at the same time, help to ensure economic stability. This young woman from America had captured many hearts and minds in old Russia.

The most successful of Jamie's meetings was one with the Chairman of the Committee for Labor and Social Affairs. During the meeting Jamie expressed some basic ideas her father had recently expressed to her. The ideas involved details for setting up voluntary communities of middle-aged and elderly retired and semi-retired people. The purpose of these communities was not simply self-suffi-ciency, but to perform various community services for the rest of the population. A week after the meeting, Jamie received an invitation to join the chairman on a tour of retirement homes for pensioners in and around Moscow. The tour was covered by the Moscow press and media. As a result, Jamie was called later that evening by the United States Embassy and invited to meet with the ambassador the next day.

The ambassador's name was George Denison, a tall Californian in his mid-50s. His hair was completely gray and this premature grayness reminded Jamie of her father. After walking through the snow in the embassy courtyard and into a large reception area that felt unheated, the ambassador's office was warm and cozy.

"How do you like our weather here in Moscow?" Denison's handshake was enthusiastic.

"Seems to have snowed every day since Christmas," said Jamie.

"No," said the ambassador. "It *has* snowed every day since Christmas. The staff has a pool going and they're keeping track. Not for money, mind you. The person who has the misfortune of having picked the first day that completes its entire twenty-four hours without one flake of snow falling out in our courtyard has to go to the nearby Moscow MacDonald's the next day and bring back lunch for everyone. We pay, of course. But the poor soul who loses has to stand in line."

The secretary came in and offered coffee. Both Jamie and the ambassador decided on tea.

"Please don't think I'm overly anxious, Mr. Ambassador, but it's not every day I get called into an embassy."

"Yes, I should have told you right off, perhaps included the fact that this is a social invitation with no particular concern in mind. You can call me George by the way, as long as I can call you Jamie."

The tea came. The ambassador picked up a lemon wedge from a plate on the tray. "California lemons. But not shipped to us. We bought them at a local market, part of the new import-export program."

After they had prepared their tea and each had taken a few sips, the ambassador continued.

"I asked you here because of a call I received from the President."

"Our President?"

"Yes. It seems the media coverage of your tour yesterday with the Labor and Social Affairs Chairman was picked up by the networks back home. You may not realize it, but overnight, so to speak, you've become a celebrity."

"I had no idea."

"In fact there are reports from the networks saying they've received a lot of calls asking if you're related to ex-President Jimmy Carter."

"Why would people think that? Carter's a common name . . . "

Denison smiled. "I assume the humanitarian concerns you've expressed in ideas you gave to a Senate subcommittee, and ideas you repeated here in Moscow, were reminiscent of Jimmy Carter. Carter and his wife did a lot of work in equal housing, and since he's viewed as one of our great humanitarians, and because of the name — even your full name has the same down home ring to it. Jamie Carter, Jimmy Carter — they sound alike."

Jamie could feel the heat of a blush. "Wow. I never expected this."

"You should take advantage of it."

"Advantage?"

"Yes. If I were you I'd forget about school and get into public life where you've obviously already got a following. Foreign service isn't bad, especially now with the obvious relationship foreign policy has with your concern for the environment. You have life experience the world needs these days. I don't mean a backlash against polluters or anything like that. But a woman with your background in world politics today has a certain ambiance. The world moves in cycles. Perhaps it's time for new blood. Our Russian ambassador even said something to the effect that if and when we send a message back to the extraterrestrials, you should compose it. So, what do you think? Can you see your way to leaving your formal education behind and getting into the fray?"

Jamie turned, looked out the window at the heavy snow that was falling. She thought of Arkady and his work in the Ukraine. Important work. Work that should be recognized. She thought of Brian and his work in the Sierra Club and other environmental organizations. Also important work. Why her? Why not Brian or Arkady? Then she turned back to the ambassador. "No."

"Why not?"

"Because when things happen too fast they tend to get out of control. The time's not right and I don't like the idea of being created overnight by a media that can just as quickly throw you out with the bath water." She caught herself laughing. "I know I probably sound like a baby, but I've got to finish school. It's a commitment. Don't get me wrong. I *am* a law student and a political career is my dream. But if I quit school now with only a few months to go and my dissertation to finish and the Bar to pass . . . "

"You don't want to be labeled a quitter."

"I don't want to *be* a quitter. I know what instant world communication can do, and part of me wants to take advantage of it. But the power of sound bytes and the tendency to act too quickly scares the hell out of me. I feel at this point I've got to be careful not to act too quickly."

"Then, I admire you. No specific predictions, but some day I think I'll be telling the story of this meeting whenever I get the chance."

Before she left the office, Denison offered Jamie the possibility of a foreign service position following graduation. "Since I just got my appointment, I'll probably still be around," he said, shaking her hand.

Outside the embassy it was snowing even harder than when she had arrived. The wind had increased and Muscovites bent their heads into the wind and looked very, very cold. But to Jamie, the cold was nothing. She felt warm all over as if it were a hot August afternoon in the middle of the Illinois prairie.

☢ ☢ ☢

But it was not August in Illinois. It was January there, too, and the entire Midwest, including Illinois, was being ravaged by a wet blizzard, the type of blizzard usually reserved for early or late winter.

While it was late afternoon in Moscow, it was early morning in Champaign. The snow came down so heavily that news broadcasts had already begun announcing school closings and closings of certain functions at the University. In her apartment in central Champaign, Heather sat at her kitchen table sipping a cup of strong black coffee. She had just received a call from the station and was told she would be needed mid-morning rather than in the afternoon because of the extended storm-related coverage that was anticipated. While the coffee was brewing she had taken a hot shower. Her head ached from a hangover.

It was the first time in months she had gotten drunk, and she hated to admit the cause of it. Last night after work, unable to vent her true feelings while in the studio at Channel 10 reading news of the success of her "close friend" in Moscow, Heather had changed into jeans, a U of I sweatshirt and parka, and gone to a local bar.

The bar catered to students over twenty-one who wanted to get drunk or get laid or both. She got both—drunk from a series of Rob Roys, laid by an equally-drunk Hispanic who called himself Chum, carried a disease-free card from the campus clinic, had the appropriate equipment for, as he put it, "stretching her leather," and didn't care about her name.

The intoxication was quick, the trip to the motel through snow that was just beginning as she grasped the wheel of her car while following Chum's jeep was quick, the lay was quick. By two in the morning Chum was gone — not knowing who the hell's leather he'd just stretched — and she was driving back to her apartment in a blizzard.

The coffee tasted terrible, but she drank it anyhow. Then she went into the bathroom and looked in the mirror. Her eyes were bloodshot, her face pale. Her hair was stringy and she remembered how Chum kept pulling it and pulling it after he'd turned her over to, "ride the red pony," as he so eloquently put it. She remembered imagining, during this ride, that she was Jamie Carter, drunk on vodka, being taken by the third Cossack that night. Indeed, Chum had felt like three guys.

As she stared in the mirror she became aware of the reflection of the bathtub. She turned and looked at the tub. Even though the tub in her apartment was a Jacuzzi and much larger than the tub in the bathroom outside her upstairs room at the Olympia Fields estate, she still thought of her father whenever she looked at it or sat in it. Last night after returning from the motel, she had soaked in the tub for a long time with the Jacuzzi jets on full blast. And now she recalled that, to keep from thinking of her father, she'd had crazy thoughts about extraterrestrials and how she might interview them. Then, when people like Jamie and Arkady and their asinine relatives claimed that wasn't any big deal because they'd been talking with them all along, she imagined pulling out a gun and shooting them.

She'd fallen asleep in the tub, the timer for the Jacuzzi jets shutting off and her head slipping beneath the water. She awoke, gasping and coughing, not dead. Not yet.

☢ ☢ ☢

"Dad? Can you hear me?"

"Yes, it's cleared up some."

"I don't know what else to say except, Wow!"

"I know, Jamie. Mom and I had the same reaction when we saw you on the news. But quit giving me credit."

"Why not, Dad? The ideas I've been talking about are yours."

"Not mine. You have ideas. Arkady has ideas. A lot of people have ideas. But you've put them into words. You've said the right things at the right times in the right places. That takes judgment, Jamie. And I'd say you've shown just about the best judgment of anyone I know. By the way, how old do you have to be to run for the Senate?"

"What Senate?"

"State, national, take your pick because you'd probably win hands down."

"All I've been doing lately is blushing, Dad. I am right . . . right now! Can you hear me?"

"Barely!"

"I'd . . . I'd talk to . . . Dad?"

"I hear you, Jamie!"

"I'd talk to Mom but the connection has some kind of interference . . . "

"Okay, Jamie. We love you!"

"I love both of you, too!"

Paul put the phone down slowly and looked across to Judy sitting in the recliner on the other side of the end table. Her head was wrapped in the white turban she'd been wearing since the chemotherapy had caused her total loss of hair. It was the second time Judy had lost her hair. The first time was after her mastectomy when she'd had chemotherapy because of the cancer remaining in her lymph nodes. This time the chemotherapy was because of inoperable pancreatic and liver cancer that had been discovered shortly after Jamie left for Moscow.

"Do you still think not telling her is the right decision?" asked Paul.

"Yes," said Judy. "There's nothing she can do about it and I don't want to upset her life now."

"We'll have to tell her eventually."

"I know."

"It's a good thing the bastard responsible for this is dead. If he wasn't . . . "

Judy raised her hand slightly to stop him. "Paul, no more. It's not as if Harold Ducain personally dumped those drums out in that field to hurt people. What's done is done." She shook her head and tears came into her eyes. "There's no sense being bitter about it."

Paul stood and went to her. He sat on the arm of the chair and held her. "I'm sorry."

"Don't be sorry. But do promise me one thing."

"What?"

"Promise me that whatever happens you won't give up your dreams."

"Nothing will happen."

"Paul, be realistic! I'm getting chemo once a month, for a week after I puke my guts out despite the drugs, and my hair is gone! If I go, I go! All I'm trying to say is that there are other people in the world besides me, other reasons to go on!"

Judy began crying and held him very tightly, her body shaking violently. "Oh, Paul! Jesus, Paul! Why me?"

He did not answer. Instead he held her and imagined Jamie's view that things were just fine back home was the true view of the world.

After a few seconds Judy broke away and went into the bathroom while Paul stood and looked out the window. Outside, the snow was coming down steadily. In the distance he could barely see Joe Siebert's ice fishing shack in the middle of the lake. Behind him he heard Judy begin throwing up in the bathroom. He left the window and went into the bathroom to hold her by her shoulders, to steady her as he always did, as he would always do.

CHAPTER 10

DURING THE SNOWS OF JANUARY, Jamie had been aware of the frequent delays of international and domestic flights in and out of Moscow's three airports. Information about flight delays had not only come from reports in the press, but also from public officials and foreign diplomats who missed meetings, were late for appointments, and did not hold back when it came to complaining about air travel to and from Moscow that winter. So, in February, when she finally arranged time off from her studies and her recent work as the United States representative on a United Nations environmental committee based in Moscow, Jamie took the train to Kiev instead of flying.

She bought a second class ticket, called "hard class" in Russian. The only difference between second and first class was that the berths in second class had thin cushions, while first class — called "soft seat" compartments — had thick upholstered berths. The compartment sizes were the same with four berths in each and she didn't find out until she boarded that the compartments were unisex. At first she was greatly relieved to see a man and wife in the compartment along with the old man in the berth below hers. But later, when she realized that Russian train passengers generally look out for one another as if their compartment mates are family members, she decided it would not have mattered if she had shared the compartment with three men. Soon after the train pulled out of the station at midnight, each of her compartment mates made a trip to the washroom at the end of the car — the old man coming back wearing his red nightshirt instead of changing in the berth like the others — curtains were pulled, the lights went out and the gentle rocking of the train put her to sleep.

In the morning, near the borders of Russia, Byelorussia, and the Ukraine, Jamie sat at the small table in the compartment drinking a glass of hot lemon tea that she had gotten from the conductor's *samovar* at the end of the car opposite the washroom. The old man from the lower berth sat across from her sipping his tea and staring out the window.

The old man was perhaps seventy, with sunken blue eyes. He was bald on top but had thick gray hair — cowlicked from sleep — at the sides. He had changed from his red nightshirt back into the suit he wore the night before. It seemed in Russia old men she saw in markets or on the streets or in buses or trains wore a suit, white shirt, tie. Younger men — she hadn't decided where the cutoff was, perhaps age sixty or so — dressed much more casually.

The other man in the compartment and his wife were about fifty. The man had emerged from his berth wearing blue jeans and a yellow turtleneck sweater. His wife had emerged wearing what looked like a ski outfit. The couple had gone to another car, the woman frowning at her husband when she said, "So the chimney can smoke."

The landscape outside the window was flat and covered with snow. Occasionally she saw telephone poles and fence posts, more rarely a group of houses and farm buildings. The land looked paralyzed, and just when she began to think of the land as being abandoned, she saw a group of a dozen or so children being picked up by a school bus. Back home all school buses were yellow. This one was green and had a flat front with an expansive windshield through which she could see the woman driver in a blue uniform.

The old man turned from the window and spoke slowly and deliberately as he had last evening when he found out she was American.

"Now you see why they call it White Russia." He pointed out the window.

"Yes," she said. "It makes one more aware of color."

"White is a deceptive color," he said. "Within it all colors are hidden. For example, beneath that snow there is still much danger for the people who live here."

"Radiation?"

"Very good. You have read your history."

"Chernobyl wasn't that long ago."

"Almost three decades already," he said. "You must not have been born when it happened."

"I was born the year after."

"No, I thought you were much younger than that. You can't be more than twenty."

The old man smiled at her, his blue eyes twinkling. Jamie could feel the warmth of a blush on her cheeks. It was a cozy feeling to have warm cheeks in this compartment sipping hot lemon tea with this old man while it snowed outside and the condensation dripping from the metal sill of the window jiggled with the motion of the train.

"Why are you going to Kiev?" asked the old man.

"To visit a friend."

"A boy?"

"Yes."

The old man smiled again, his eyes open wide. "I knew it. If I had one wish I would wish that I were that boy."

As she felt another blush and looked at the man, Jamie could see that not only did the old man have blue eyes, but he had sea blue eyes. Sea blue and serious like Brian's eyes. She remembered her departure, four months earlier, from the Champaign station on the train to the airport in Chicago. She had expected to be alone at departure when suddenly, on the platform, Brian had been there staring at her with his sea blue eyes, saying he wished her luck, saying he'd see her again when she returned, saying all those things that made her feel guilty at having rebuffed him so many times. She and Brian had dated off and on for two years before she'd met Arkady. And while she and Arkady dated, Brian had left her alone, staying friends but keeping his distance. Not only did the old man's eyes remind her of Brian's eyes, but the old man's smile reminded her of Brian's smile. It was the smile of someone who has only his thoughts and imaginings to console him. It was a sad smile, and for a moment she felt homesick for the States, and for Brian.

After sipping his tea and staring out the window for a moment, the old man turned back to her. "Tell me what it is like to live in America."

"For a student it's really not so different from living here."

"Yes," said the old man, "it would be similar for students. But what about after one's studies? What about business and the accumulation of wealth? Here there are some who have made themselves comfortable since the changes. But in America I understand it is commonplace to be prosperous."

Jamie looked out the window at a cemetery where only the tips of the stones peeked through the snow. "Wealth is a relative thing. For example, my country, like others, has a large national debt that must be repaid some day. Unfortunately the system in my country has problems dealing with this reality. We are a nation who has figured out how to borrow from future generations. We do this economically and environmentally. Naturally, at the time a proposal to consume more of these borrowed resources is made, we fully intend to pay back the debt. But, so far, our record is very poor."

The old man reached across the table and touched her hand briefly. "So, my friend from America, how are we to solve the problems of the world?"

"Which problems should we solve first?"

The old man considered for a moment, putting his hand on his chin. "From my perspective it is the land that holds everything for us. Farmers understand that. I think the rest need to understand it. I'm not simply referring to the use of fields for crops, but all the land, farmland and non-farmland. The Earth, if you like. How will we save the Earth?"

Jamie took a sip of tea, put her glass down and stared at the old man, at his sad eyes so much like Brian's eyes. Brian who was probably on a Sierra Club outing thinking about the very questions the old man was asking. How many other people were there, scattered throughout the world, asking questions about the environment and future generations, but unable to do anything? Unless they had someone to speak for them . . .

"Well?" asked the old man.

"Saving the environment is a large issue," she said. "Saving the environment, and therefore our species, will take *all* resources. In order for those resources to be mustered, political and ethnic and religious unrest must eventually end. And they will end one way or another. I think the way to begin is to assign economic value to social and environmental well-being. Of course, business, as practiced in the past, will try to cash in, will create a kind of black market. But ultimately, I think it is the only way. If, for example, a factory puts a certain amount of emissions into the air or water, it must pay for that privilege and those funds must be used to eliminate similar emissions. I don't mean the more profitable companies simply paying for the privilege of polluting. I mean they should pay for the research and equipment to lessen the pollution of all industry. And if technology exists in one country to curb emissions, the technology must be given to countries just beginning to industrialize."

"This solution sounds very complicated," said the old man. "It sounds similar to suggested solutions I've heard for the problem of terrorists."

"I know," said Jamie, looking back out the window. "I know."

☢ ☢ ☢

When Jamie's train arrived later that morning in Kiev, Arkady was waiting for her on the platform. Unfortunately, two men stood between her and Arkady. One man held out an identification card that showed him to be a reporter for *Pravda Ukrainy*, while the other man held out a microphone connected to a tape recorder he held in his other hand. Arkady stood directly behind the two men, smiled, shrugged, and waited as if standing in line for his turn to meet her.

"Miss Carter," said the reporter who had shown his identification, "we've read about your activities in Moscow and want to ask about your visit to Kiev."

"I'm here to visit a friend."

"We thought perhaps you would visit our famous gerontology institute or perhaps go on to see some of our homes for pensioners at the Black Sea."

"I don't know what to say. I'm honored that you want to talk to me, but really, I'm simply visiting a friend."

Behind the two men she could see Arkady standing on his toes and peeking at her between the heads of the two. Arkady made a cross-eyed face and when she laughed the man holding the recorder glanced back toward Arkady and sneered. The reporter continued.

"We've heard, Miss Carter, of your recent comments concerning the short-sighted orientation of government, not just your government and the governments of Russia and the Ukraine, but all governments. Perhaps you can give us an example of this so-called short-sightedness."

"Very well. In my country the passenger railroad system declined greatly at the end of the last century. Tracks were torn up and some railroad track beds leveled. A few were turned into walking and bicycling paths. But now, with passenger railroads apparently becoming popular and economical again, the bicycle paths are being turned back into railroad lines. My point is, it was unfortunate that no one had the forethought to save all of the track beds."

"I see," said the reporter. "And today, since you just came from the north by train, and since you yourself were an innocent victim of a manmade disaster, please tell us your thoughts."

"My thoughts?"

"Yes, about the Chernobyl disaster. In April it will be twenty-nine years since the disaster and many of our people are still suffering the consequences of shoddy technology."

"I don't know about the quality of the technology," said Jamie. "But as I crossed the northern Ukraine on the train this morning, I did have some thoughts I can share with you."

"Please do," said the reporter, seeming a bit too excited now so that Jamie thought he was putting on a show for her.

"Very well. From the train I saw power lines looping across the landscape. The lines were connected to huge steel towers that looked like stick men marching across the snow. It made me think of two other men who used to walk together every morning. This was in the state of Illinois where I live. One section of the path that the two men walked on paralleled the railroad tracks. Three mornings a week the men stopped to watch a train that still travels those tracks. One of the men was my father who has since moved to the state of Michigan with my mother. The other man, a veteran of our infamous Vietnam War, is dead now. But the train is still alive, still travels across Illinois into Indiana three mornings a week. The people along the route call it the Dawn Patrol. The train carries nuclear waste from a power plant to a disposal site."

The reporter looked somewhat puzzled, but Jamie figured she

had nothing to lose, and she also figured an involved statement might get rid of these two and she would be alone with Arkady, so she continued.

"What made me think of the Dawn Patrol this morning is that last week I sat in on a committee meeting in which two scientists — one Russian, one Ukrainian — proposed several possible solutions for the nuclear waste produced by power plants. Their proposals involve much safer disposal techniques that can actually take place at the site where the waste is created. My wish this morning on the train from Moscow was that the scientists of all countries would join together to provide positive solutions that will help everyone instead of working independently as if all activities in this life are some kind of contest."

She thought this would satisfy the reporter, but he continued, asking now about the fear of terror in the world.

"Poverty is at the root of the problem. Poverty creates environments that not only encourage unrest, but attracts those who cause unrest. Perhaps I'll be criticized for saying this, but I believe the terrorists are among us because of the impoverished state of affairs. Terrorists are leeches. Poverty is what they feed upon. We've got to eliminate poverty so the leeches will die off or look for something else to do. And I don't mean that terrorists should all die. I mean their organizations will die when the members leave of their own accord. In my country the economic system rewards poverty. Poverty is maintained by the system in order to have places to dispose of the lower class so there are more resources to share among the wealthy. I'm not a socialist, but we've got to come up with systems that get people out of poverty rather than maintaining them in poverty. Poverty, not religion, is the mother of terror."

The reporter seemed satisfied with this, thanked her profusely, left with his sound man and, finally, she ran to Arkady and hugged him.

☢ ☢ ☢

"I feel privileged."

"What are you talking about?"

"A famous political personality has not only granted me a visit to my humble student quarters, but now she lies in bed with me."

"Please, let's keep politics and my private life separate. Besides, I'm not famous. Somebody at Moscow University probably called ahead to have them meet me as a joke."

"No, they were for real. And you, my dear sweet innocent Jamie, answered them like a professional."

"A professional what? Lady body builder?"

"No, a professional politician."

Arkady had been on his back looking up at the ceiling and now he turned, propped himself up on his elbow and looked down at her. "Lady body builder?"

"It was all I could think of when you said professional."

Arkady bent and kissed her. "I don't think you have anything to build up. You have the correct parts and plenty of stamina. We just proved that, didn't we?"

Jamie lifted her head from the pillow and kissed Arkady back. "Yes, we did."

There was a thumping sound on the wall next to the bed and Arkady raised his arm to look at his watch. "Sergei is right on time."

"Who's Sergei?"

"My next door neighbor. The walls in these rooms are quite thin. The sound was his bed being shoved against the wall as he got up."

"I see," said Jamie. "Is he alone?"

"Oh, yes," said Arkady. "If he had company in bed we would have heard them. He sleeps late today because he has only evening classes."

"He sleeps until three in the afternoon?"

"He had to. This morning I heard him come in at dawn and he was groaning. Too much to drink, the stomach gets upset, he lies in bed and groans."

"Do you think he heard us?"

Arkady shrugged his shoulders and smiled. "Does it matter?"

"Not to us," said Jamie. "I was concerned that poor Sergei would have trouble concentrating in his classes tonight." Jamie tickled Arkady.

Arkady tickled Jamie back.

They had a tickling contest which eventually resulted in both of them falling to the floor.

There was a muffled shout from behind the wall. "Arkady!"

Arkady shouted back. "Yes, Sergei!"

"Who's in there with you?"

"That belly dancer from the *Club Raj*!"

"Be serious!"

"I am!"

Arkady held his finger to his lips and whispered. "Now we've got him. Listen, hear that rustling against the wall?"

"What's he doing?" whispered Jamie.

"He has his ear to the wall, trying to hear us."

"What should we do?"

"I don't know," whispered Arkady. "What kind of sound would a belly dancer make?"

Jamie knelt up on the floor, made a fist and held it to her mouth. Then she tried making a sound like a snake charmer blowing his pipe. It sounded pretty good, except that every few seconds she couldn't help laughing and had to start over. Finally she couldn't stop laughing. It was infectious and soon they were both laughing.

"You're crazy!" shouted Sergei through the wall. "Both of you!" Then a door opened and closed and she heard Sergei march down the hall, apparently wearing loose-fitting slippers that slapped against the floor.

"He's gone to the washroom," said Arkady.

Jamie stood up, made the snake charmer pipe sound again, this time gyrating her hips in a slow circular motion.

Arkady got up from the floor and sat on the edge of the bed. He was no longer laughing as he stared at her with his dark eyes.

She danced a little faster, humming the tune and snapping her fingers with her arms outstretched. She spun around a few times, then danced closer to Arkady. When she stopped dancing, Arkady continued to stare at her, his eyes open wide, his smile boyish and evil.

"Don't belly dancers usually get tips when they finish?" she asked.

"Yes," said Arkady.

He reached out and pulled her close. He spread his legs so she could stand directly in front of his face. He kissed her belly once, twice, three times. Then he rose slowly, kissing her midriff, her breasts, her neck, her lips.

☢ ☢ ☢

During the next two days, Arkady took her on a tour of Kiev. The weather had improved, the drizzle that had fallen in Kiev, while Moscow got its snow, ending so that the days became brilliant and crisp.

Kiev is a city of cathedrals and museums and Jamie was certain they visited all of them. They traveled about the city on the metro, on buses, and even on a funicular that traversed the hill from the lower city to the upper city. They saw old women lighting candles in the Monastery of the Caves. They saw eighteenth century rural life re-enacted in a play at the Ukrainian Drama Theater. They visited the museum dedicated to the poet Taras Shevchenko. Arkady wanted to take her on a boat ride on the Dnieper River, but the tourist boats did not run in January.

On Thursday night in bed Arkady held her tightly and asked, "What do you think of marriage?"

"I don't know. Where would we live?"

"Here or there," said Arkady. "It doesn't matter to me as long as we are together."

"Is that why we're going to visit your family over the weekend? So they can give their blessing?"

"No, they've been expecting me for a long time. I thought you wanted to get a close look at life in a resettlement village."

"I do, Arkady. But I didn't expect you to bring up marriage."

"And now I have brought it up," said Arkady.

"Yes, you have."

"Do you want me to ask more directly?"

"No, Arkady. I don't . . . I don't know what to do. It's too soon. Maybe not too soon for others, but I've got things to do."

"Your career."

"I don't look upon what I want to do as a career. It's something else. It has to do with what happened in Easthaven and what happened at Chernobyl. I feel that life is short and we should enjoy ourselves, but I also feel this pressure to do what I can while I can, and sometimes I hate myself for it."

"Don't hate yourself."

"Why shouldn't I when the most beautiful man in the world has just proposed to me?"

"I didn't want you to think I didn't care. That's why I asked. If I had not asked, both of us would have kept wondering. If you had asked me instead of the other way around, I think I would have also had doubts."

"Arkady?"

"Yes."

"Instead of me saying no, or you saying no, let's leave it up in the air for a while. Can we do that?"

"Yes, I like that idea." Arkady smiled. "And if someone in my family asks, we'll say we have not yet made up our minds whether to fall from our up-in-the-air position."

"We'll be telling the truth," said Jamie.

Arkady kissed her, stroked her hair. "We should take advantage of this night because tomorrow night at my parents' house in Svyezhl we won't have any privacy at all."

As Arkady kissed her, Jamie wondered if, by the end of the weekend, after meeting his family, she might change her mind, tell Arkady she *would* marry him. After all, her career wasn't *that* important. Then, suddenly, she thought of Brian seeing her off for her trip to Moscow, Brian writing that he looked forward to the day she returned to the states, Brian saying he'd wait for her, Brian with eyes as sad as the eyes of the old man on the train. Sea blue eyes and dark brown eyes. Brian and Arkady. Life and . . .

Arkady held her tightly and trembled. "Jamie?"

"Yes."

"It's not your career that stands in the way, is it."

"No."

"It's us. It's what is in us. You don't want to get married because eventually one of us will be struck down. You don't want to hurt me and I don't want to hurt you."

"But I do love you, Arkady."

"Yes, love is a strange thing. It seems to have a life of its own."

☢ ☢ ☢

Arkady's mother was red-cheeked and round-faced and buxom. She seemed to have limitless energy as she rushed about in the small house keeping things orderly and efficient and convenient and even comfortable despite the number of people in the house. Arkady's father was short and thin with sunken eyes, and she was again reminded of both Brian and the old man in her compartment on the train from Moscow.

Both Arkady's parents were much older than Jamie's parents.

Arkady's two sisters were also older than Jamie thought they would be — one forty-one, the other forty-three. Arkady had never mentioned ages, just that he was the youngest child.

Arkady's oldest sibling, Lev, had died of cancer at the turn of the decade, fourteen years after the Chernobyl disaster. Arkady's father, who recounted the events surrounding the disaster in detail while most of those in the house, except for the children, got drunk, said that Lev had driven a truck far north of the old village the morning of the explosion to pick up a cultivator that was being repaired. During the trip he passed very near the plant where, according to Arkady's father, "The fools at the reactor, who most likely still had their mothers' milk on their lips, hadn't even bothered to have the road closed." According to Arkady's father, Lev had not gotten a bad enough dose to go to a Moscow clinic. "Just bad enough to kill him fourteen years later," said Arkady's father, weeping.

The recounting of the days following the disaster, as well as the months moving from temporary camps and housing at other collectives and the eventual move to Svyezhl, took place on Saturday night. To Jamie it seemed they had done nothing on Saturday after their arrival except eat and drink and exchange bear hugs. Besides Arkady's parents and sisters, there were the husbands, the children, several aunts and uncles and a few cousins thrown in for good measure. It seemed even more crowded because the house was tiny — a combination living room-dining room, a galley kitchen, a bathroom and one small bedroom. As the evening wore on and the heads of the adults began to nod, Jamie thought everyone would simply drop where they sat or stood, and sleeping people would be lying all over the place.

But that's not what happened. At midnight, Arkady's mother began collecting glasses and plates, asked for Jamie's help, began rousing the others, made tea and practically forced everyone to have a cup. Then she gently escorted one or two at a time out the door while at the same time offering cheery goodnights that the others returned. Within a half hour of asking for Jamie's help, Arkady's mother had emptied the house. Even Arkady seemed surprised.

Jamie and Arkady slept on the daybed in the living room. Throughout the night she could hear Arkady's father snoring. It was a strange night full of doubt and confusion about her values in life. What was more important? A career that ultimately might help a few people, touch a few lives? Or an immediate grasping-touching-holding of the ones you love?

In the morning, after breakfast, Arkady's father asked Arkady to accompany him to the other side of the village to see the new farm buildings and the farm equipment that had just been delivered for use in the spring. To Jamie the excursion seemed contrived. Soon she would experience the Ukrainian version of the mother-to-possible-future-daughter-in-law talk. But it wasn't that way at all.

They sat across the dining room table from one another, the sunlight from the window behind Arkady's mother making the wisps of gray hair sticking out of her babushka glow like filaments.

"Years ago we were forced to learn Russian. Now, because of the children, and despite the breakup of the Union so long ago, it remains our primary language. Your Russian is very good, Jamie. More clear and precise than we Ukrainians speak it."

"Thank you. My high school offered Russian courses. When I started college, our countries were cooperating more and more and

I thought it would be good to continue studying Russian."

"You made a wise decision. I heard your name mentioned on Radio Kiev last week."

"Really?"

"Yes. They said that, as a student in Moscow, you are doing much more to foster cooperation between nations than most politicians."

"You're making me blush."

"Blushing is a good thing. It keeps your cheeks rosy. Look at mine, they are rosy all the time now because when I was a young woman I blushed constantly. Arkady's father used to say I would blush when I saw two birds sitting on the same branch."

Arkady's mother reached across the table and squeezed Jamie's hand. "Tell me, Jamie Carter, why do we human beings seem to require tragedy to guide our lives?"

"I'm not sure I know what you mean."

"It's quite simple. You were involved in a tragic disaster. Arkady was involved in a tragic disaster. And so, because of shared tragedy you met and thereafter fell in love. Am I right?"

"Yes."

"Good. And now look around you. Hasn't the tragedy called Chernobyl guided my life and the lives of those near me?"

"It has, but you seem to have bounced back quite well."

"Bounced?"

"Sorry, an American idiom. Bounced like a ball. It means you recovered and put things back to normal in a rapid manner."

"Yes, I suppose it appears that way. I remember when we first came to this village. When we got off the bus we must have stood dumbstruck for a long time as we stared at row upon row of identical boxes. The minister for reconstruction and other officials in attendance at the opening of the village had to use a loudspeaker to tell us to go ahead and inspect our new homes. The houses were numbered, you see, and a head of each family grasped a slip of paper with the matching number in his or her hand."

"The houses don't look like identical boxes now," said Jamie.

Arkady's mother nodded. "The changes began as soon as we moved in. A window box here, a garden there. Then sheds and different colors of paint and shutters and awnings. It was interesting to observe that many houses took on characteristics of the original house the family had been forced to abandon after Chernobyl. We are creatures of habit in need of a great deal of security, I suppose. If possible, some of us would probably gather our infant blankets and hug a favorite doll or stuffed animal to our bosoms as we head off to jobs or the farm fields."

After waiting a moment to be certain Arkady's mother was finished with the thought, Jamie spoke. "One thing I've noticed since I've been here in your country is that elderly citizens seem to remain more attached to their families than they do in my country."

"It's because the pensioners in my country fulfill a need."

"What need is that?" asked Jamie.

"They take care of the children. I don't mean simply what you call baby-sitting. It has been true for generations that the children are more important to us than anything else. The wars did that I think. All those people killed in the wars, massacred. What can one do? Nothing except replace them. Have children and give the children everything you can to prepare them for life."

Arkady's mother turned and looked out the window, her profile determined. "The old people here don't expect much. They require minimal comforts. But they do enjoy laughter, to feel good inside at least for a moment or two. Children do that. Children make the old feel good. The old take care of the children. A bargain has been struck. An old person should never live alone, even if one has no family. For example, many people choose not to have children or cannot, like my Arkady. But that does not mean they should live alone when they are old. I think if old people have no one else, they should move in with one another. Men with men, women with women, men and women together. It doesn't matter as long as someone is there to keep one company."

Arkady's mother turned back toward Jamie and smiled. "At my age — you can believe this or not, as you wish — there is a definite reduction in the sexual urge." She held her hand to the side of her mouth as if telling a secret. "Especially when he blows off the roof with his snoring."

Jamie laughed, but Arkady's mother remained serious and continued.

"That's why I say formalities such as marriage should be done away with when people reach a certain age. They should simply be allowed to live together and take care of one another instead of being pressured by these societies ruled by religions and governments, which seem to have a strong need to remain in control at all times."

Arkady's mother stood and went to the kitchen sink where she filled the *samovar* with water for tea. "When we found out about the radiation from Chernobyl we immediately took Arkady to the clinic for an iodine treatment. Then we sent him with relatives to a Black Sea camp with the other children."

When the *samovar* was filled and lit, Arkady's mother came back to the table and smiled. "I hope you and Arkady live long and happy lives. And whether you remain together or live apart from one another, you will remain together in my heart."

Jamie stood. They hugged. Outside, a group of children screaming as they played ran past the door.

CHAPTER 11

READING THE NEWS HAD BECOME Heather's specialty. Knowing when to provide nuance or inflection, knowing when to smile or raise her eyebrows as if impressed, knowing that she must read each story slowly and thoughtfully. Especially this story. Heather felt she had performed professionally as she read the story of Jamie Carter's return to Moscow, along with a brief profile of Jamie handed her at the last minute.

But the story, on this particular evening, disturbed Heather. It was bring-daughters-to-work day, and perhaps the camera operator's daughter, the little girl sitting behind the camera staring at her, had done it. It was the first time Heather had been unable to temporarily erase the memory of her father from her mind. He was there in the studio as she read the story. Telling her how to succeed in her career by using Jamie's career as an example. How clever it had been for the little girl, called Chemical Jamie by schoolyard bullies, to greedily take full advantage of the Easthaven chemical spill.

The conclusion of the story was especially sickening. Heather could tell it had been written by the new writer, Thom — Thom instead of Tom, the asshole who tried to make a date with her his first week on the job even though she knew by the look on his face that someone in the office had disclosed her reputation as a man-hater or a ball-cutter or whatever they called her behind closed doors or in e-mails. If Thom had been available at the news desk she felt she could strangle the bastard. Thoughts of her father and Thom and the little girl with short brown hair sitting there staring at her teamed up to create a feather in her throat as she read.

"If this spokeswoman for my generation were running for public office — as we're certain she will some day soon — it seems environmental issues will be her specialty." At this point Heather swallowed hard to get rid of the feather. "Future polluters take notice."

The story had started out with Jamie's mention of the Dawn Patrol still shipping nuclear waste from the old Iroquois Power Plant to the Tri-State disposal facility. Apparently Jamie had mentioned the Dawn Patrol when reporters at the Kiev Central Railroad Station asked her opinion about the Chernobyl Nuclear Power Plant disaster. Following the quotes from Jamie's statement was a summary of ideas she had expressed to various student groups and government committees while in Russia attending Moscow University.

A representative of the Russian President had taken the occasion of Jamie's return to Moscow to summarize these various ideas concerning the world environment, poverty in cities as well as developing countries, how national and world economies relate to these problems, and an emphasis on creativity in the scientific world. This overt praise from the Russian President's representative, apparently

quoted directly from the translation and not smoothed-out by the
foreign news writer, was followed by a brief profile of Jamie Carter
— how she was a graduate political science major at U of I currently
studying in Moscow, how she had spent summers working as a
Senate page in Washington, how this past summer she had served
as an aide to Senator Jim Hansen of Illinois, how for several years
she had served, and still held a seat, on the U of I student senate.

Before its sickening conclusion, the story went on to say that
Jamie had just returned from visiting the family of a friend at one of
the Chernobyl resettlement villages, apparently using the occasion
to act as goodwill ambassador during her visit to some of the unfortunate victims who were still suffering from the disaster that took
place almost three decades earlier.

After the broadcast, Leslie Gale met Heather in the hallway and
asked her to come to her office.

"Is something wrong tonight, Heather? You seemed . . . off."

"I thought I did fine. Did I misread something?"

"No, but I gathered you were forcing it. I hope I'm not being
overly critical, Heather. Please take it as constructive criticism from
someone who's interested in your career. It just seemed you didn't
have your heart in it, or you didn't believe what you were saying.
Especially that story about Jamie Carter."

"I . . . my stomach was a little sour from dinner, I should have
done better. Your point is well-taken."

Leslie walked around her desk and touched Heather's shoulder.
"A professional knows how to learn from her mistakes as well as her
successes. Better get something for your stomach. And later maybe
you'd like to join us at Campus Charlie's for pizza. Russ is bringing

his daughter who thinks the world of you."

"His daughter?"

"Yes. She was in the studio."

"Oh. Thanks, but I think I'll just go home."

"Well, if you change your mind . . . "

"Thanks."

☢ ☢ ☢

Heather stared at her face in the bathroom mirror for a long, long time. It was a beautiful face, made up just right for the lights and cameras.

She took the hair clips she held in her hand and used them to pin her hair back from her face. Then she bent over the sink, splashed warm water on her face, took a washrag and soap and scrubbed her face. She looked in the mirror as she distorted her face into variations of childhood bogeymen while she scrubbed.

When she was finished washing and drying her face, she reached for the makeup case next to the sink on the counter. After using base on her skin, she curled her lashes, used eyebrow pencil and liner, mascara, dark blush. Everything was dark, even the lipliner and lipstick.

She stared at her face in the mirror. It was a beautiful face, the contrasts of color exaggerated as if for a stage play, or as if for attracting schoolyard bullies beneath a mercury vapor light on a warm summer evening. It was the face of a survivor.

She took the pins out of her hair and let it down. She brushed the television camera hairdo out, brushed the long amber curls straight like men always say they like it when asked what kind of hair they like on a woman. *Long. Real long so I can touch it and it touches me. Yeah, long, just the way Daddy likes it.*

She went into her bedroom, took off her bra and put on a red blouse with a very low-cut sweetheart neckline. She pulled on a pair of tight blue jeans and leather, calf-high, heeled boots. She went to the closet, unzipped a garment bag, took out her fox jacket and put it on. She took two hundred dollars in cash and her keys from her purse and put the money and keys in the inside pocket of the jacket. She paused at the full-length mirror on the back of her closet door.

Beautiful. Yeah, built like a brick shithouse.

The doll in the mirror turned to leave, to escape, to go someplace where Leslie and the crew and the writers and the little girl and the guys always trying to put the make on her wouldn't find her no matter how hard they tried.

☢ ☢ ☢

The bar was thirty-five miles north of Champaign in an unincorporated area near a truck stop just off Interstate 57. While she was still an intern the station had done a story about the bar and she remembered reading it. A survivor. One of the few bars in central Illinois able to maintain its open smoking policy because of its obscure location and questionable county jurisdiction. Maybe she'd do a follow-up on the bar. Write something of her own instead of simply reading what others had written. She parked her car at the truck stop and walked to the bar. As she crossed the parking lot, a trucker in a cowboy hat paused while climbing into his rig and whistled at her.

It was dark in the bar and the smoke burned her eyes. The last time she remembered being somewhere this smoky was years earlier when she was a little girl and her father briefly took her into a board of directors meeting to show them his "precious bundle of molecules." The men at the meeting — flabby-faced and smoking cigars — had laughed at this. Thinking they were laughing at her, she had begun crying and her father had carried her from the room where their chauffeur had taken her from her father and driven her home. She'd been wearing gloves and a ribboned cartwheel hat that day, just the way Mom always dressed little Jennifer when she was going somewhere special, like to church to sit between her mother and father and listen to a meaningless sermon, or to the courthouse to watch four men and eight women steal glances at her as her father's head attorney pleaded for mercy from the court.

The music coming from the jukebox at the back of the bar was country and western. A song had just ended as she walked in, slide guitar twanging up in pitch as she stood inside the door. During the silence between songs she saw heads at tables and at the bar turn. Mostly men, a couple of worn-looking women. Most of the patrons older than her. Several young men with eyes still capable of opening a few notches wider when a woman walks in. The patrons did not turn their heads completely, but showed cheeky profiles as they stared at her, apparently from the corners of their eyes. One young man wore a cowboy hat; some were hatless; many wore baseball caps. The men with baseball caps were older, heavier, the years of beer having piled up on their belts.

As she walked toward the bar, an old Patsy Cline song started on the jukebox. The song was called "I Fall to Pieces," and as she strolled confidently to the bar and Patsy Cline wailed from the jukebox, Heather imagined everyone else in the place but her was falling to pieces. Yeah, every single asshole in the place a loser except her. And they all knew it.

There was an empty seat at the bar, the bartender standing in front of it wiping a spot for her elbows. Before she got to the seat a guy slid over, offered the stool he'd been sitting on. Two hatless men had opened a spot for her between them, leaning away and studying her as she mounted the stool, leaning back closer than before after she was settled.

The bartender was bald and wore thick glasses. She ordered a Bloody Mary and watched as the bartender made it in a practiced rush of motion in which only his arms and hands moved. The glass was huge, the celery stalk almost a foot long. As the bartender slid the drink across to her he said, "Ladies' night double bloody." The ten dollar bill she'd put on the bar disappeared, more arm movements at the cash register, and the change appeared.

"Ladies' night?" she said.

"Yeah," said the bartender, moving away. "Every night's ladies' night in this place."

"He's celebrating the end of life on this planet as we know it," said the man to her right, the man who had changed seats.

He was in his 20s, high cheek bones, black hair spiked on top, slicked back at the sides. He smiled a half-smile while the other half of his mouth held a thin short cigar.

She took the celery stick from her drink, sucked the end so it wouldn't drip, held the celery stick like a big fat cigar, took a sip of the Bloody Mary — strong, not very red, bloodless — and said, "So why is life going to end on this planet?"

He smiled, stared at the cigar he held between his fingers. "It's all this here pollution."

"Haven't you heard the news?" she said.

"What's that?"

"Smoking is bad for your health and the health of those around you. I believe it was somewhere in the middle of the last century they found out."

"When I was a kid my dad smoked five dollar cigars." It was the man to the left of her. He looked a couple years older than his partner, thinner, bushy sand-colored hair.

"When I was a kid," she said, "my dad smoked twenty dollar cigars and had his chauffeur drive me to kindergarten."

"She's got you beat, Danny," said the guy to her right. "By the way, my name's Kenny."

"I kept hoping some day I'd have a chauffeur," said Danny. "But I guess my days of having my own chauffeur have passed me by."

"Funny you should mention hope," she said, leaning forward and glancing first to Kenny then to Danny, "because my name's Hope."

Kenny nodded. "Well, like I said, I've had a lot of hope during my lifetime. But you're the first real Hope I've met."

Kenny raised his glass and all three drank to this.

"I didn't think anyone's folks ever named their kid Hope anymore," said Danny.

"Mine didn't," said Heather. "Daddy used to call me his 'precious bundle of molecules,' but it wouldn't fit on the name card at kindergarten so I changed it to Hope."

"You should've shortened it to Precious," said Kenny, smashing his cigar out in an ashtray. He smiled a full-mouthed, leering smile.

"Here's to Hope," said Danny, holding up his glass.

They drank again. Even a few others along the bar who had overheard drank to this. So much for introductions. A few seconds later, after another swig of the bloodless Bloody Mary, she felt Kenny's left knee push against her right knee, and Danny's right knee push against her left knee.

Danny said, "Let's get back to the fact that there's not much time left for this old Earth."

"Why not?" asked Kenny.

"Yeah, so what do you think?"

"No," said Kenny. "I mean why do you want to waste time talking about the environment and all that when we got other important things to do?"

"What important things?" asked Danny.

They both smiled at Heather, their thighs squeezing in closer.

Heather put the remainder of the stringy celery stalk down on the bar and took a sip of her Bloody Mary. "I'd say the environment is pretty important. For example, what are you two doing about global warming?"

A slight easing of thighs against hers.

Danny said, "We're doing a lot, aren't we, Kenny old boy?"

"Yeah," said Kenny. "We got a place where we live off the land."

"Oh, really," said Heather.

"Yeah, really," said Danny. "Normally we don't talk about our plans for the future with others, but since you brought it up . . . "

"Of course," said Kenny, "if you wanted to see our place . . . "

"What's so special about your place?" asked Heather.

"Self-sufficiency," said Danny. "Pure and simple."

"You have solar panels and all that?" asked Heather.

"A few," said Danny. "And other things."

"Like what?" asked Heather.

"Like ways to protect what we have," interrupted Kenny.

"Oh," said Heather. "Survivalists."

"Something wrong with that?" asked Danny.

"Not at all," said Heather. "I'm a survivalist myself."

"You live in the woods?" asked Kenny.

"Not in the woods," said Heather. "I'm what you'd call an urban survivalist."

"How's that work?" asked Danny.

Heather thought back to earlier in the evening, keeping her composure while reading the story about Jamie, the little girl watching, the world watching, everyone thinking they know who Heather West is, but not knowing a damn thing about her. The world not knowing that she changed her name and changed her life so that some day . . .

"Yeah," said Kenny, leaning in closer, "how's this urban survivalist thing work? By urban you mean Urbana?"

All three laughed at this, drank their drinks, thighs pressing in again.

"So," said Heather softly. "Do you guys have guns?"

☢ ☢ ☢

The motel was across the street from the bar. The air outside was thick with diesel fumes from the truck stop. It was cold and windy and they half-ran, Danny and Kenny giggling and already playing grabass. They acted like schoolboys on their first date until they got into the room. Then they raped her. Not at all like Pete in the park pavilion. Rougher, much rougher.

Not that she hadn't asked for it. What she hadn't asked for was to be turned over, pulled up by her hair and taken by both at the same time.

At first she protested, but they were strong and wiry and even though they kept giggling and joking about "high hopes" and "precious cargo" and "dinner time in a tropical forest," it was obvious they would have their way. So, she gave in and they filled her.

☢ ☢ ☢

She was on the bed. Her head ached at the back where her hair had been tugged. She felt slick and oily and could still smell the rubbery odor of the condoms they had used. As if taking a commercial break from a rape scene in a movie, they had paused, one holding her down while the other opened the foil packets. When they were finished, she had pulled the sheet up over her and pretended to sleep. Now she slowly lowered the sheet and peeked up over it.

Danny sat in the chair near the door lacing his work boots. Kenny stood with his back to her. Both were dressed. Something dangled from Kenny's side — a snaky wire — and she realized he was on a cell phone with the charging wire attached. She listened.

"I *said* she was hot, man. We didn't slip her nothin'. Make you a deal. A cool hundred and she's yours. No, man, just you. Any others and it's fifty more apiece. You will when you see her."

She turned away from him slowly. She reached down to the

side of the bed and found her jeans. She saw that her jacket was still hanging on a hook outside the bathroom door where she'd left it. She yawned and sat up, stretching. She took her jeans and went into the bathroom, staggering to simulate the effects of the pill she'd managed to spit over the side of the bed after it had been slipped beneath her tongue.

The face in the mirror was not beautiful. Its makeup was smeared, its eyes red-rimmed. Below the face was a red neck where redneck stubble had rubbed. She'd conjured up a darker face, the truck stop hooker they'd done a story on recently — hardened, streetwise — but her face glowed white in the overly-bright bathroom.

She pulled on her jeans, then looked around the bathroom for something she could use as a weapon. She tried pulling loose the shower rod and the towel bars, but they were screwed tightly to the walls. She considered the lid on the back of the toilet, but it was too bulky to lift and swing.

Then she looked down at her faded denim jeans. She took a washrag, soaked it and repeatedly blotted the washrag on her jeans until her jeans were wet and dark at the crotch and halfway down the thighs.

She stood at the door and took several deep breaths. Then she opened the door and ran out screaming, "My God! I'm bleeding! I'm hemorrhaging!"

She grabbed her jacket, put it on, and ran to the door. One of them shouted, "Hey!" and they both started toward her. But she paralyzed them both by screaming again that she was bleeding, unlocked the door, and ran barefoot across the road toward the truck stop. As she ran she checked the inside pocket of her jacket and found her keys. Even her money was still there.

So now who was the survivor? Goddamn them! Goddamn them all!

☢ ☢ ☢

It wasn't until the following week at the St. Anne home that she was able to tell someone the story of what had happened to her. Because her mother had a private room, she was able to keep the story between her and her mother. After she finished telling about the rape and her close brush with a gang-bang, her mother stared down at her hands and nodded just as she had all through the telling of the story, just as she always did when anyone spoke to her.

When her mother first entered the home, Heather had hoped she might improve. But somewhere a door had closed, the psychologists at the home saying that it was her mother's way of blocking out the past.

"Imagine going to a bar for a friendly drink and getting raped. I should carry a gun to protect myself. You think I should apply for a permit, Mom?"

Nod.

"Me, too. It wasn't like I was asking for it. When I got home I sat in the tub for hours. Imagine me sitting in a bathtub that long after what happened to Daddy . . .

"One thing's for sure, Mom. I've learned the hard way how it feels to be violated. But who knows? The experience might toughen me up. You used to say I needed to toughen myself up. Remember? So, maybe I'm toughened up now. Leslie says I'm back on track at the station. Have you been watching me every night?"

Nod.

"That's good. It's nice to know there's someone out there who appreciates a survivor. If Daddy were alive he'd watch. Remember how he used to call me his 'precious bundle of molecules?' At the bar the two men called me Precious. Maybe that's why I didn't fight back any more than I did. Calling me Precious reminded me of Daddy . . ."

Nod.

"I never told you this, Mom." She reached out and lifted her mother's chin, looked into her mother's eyes. "Mom, remember when Daddy used to give me a bath? Listen to me, Mom." She spoke more loudly. "Do you remember when Daddy gave me baths?"

When she let her mother's chin down, her mother stared at her hands.

"Come on, Mom! I tell you something so personal I can hardly stand it and all you can do . . .!

"Look, Mom. Even though he did it, and even though we'll never know whether I needed the abortion because of Pete or because of him, I still loved him. Maybe I shouldn't have loved him, but I did. That's why when I found him . . ."

Her mother nodded again and Heather felt tears in her eyes. For a moment she thought she'd join her mother, go nuts, let the analysts have at her. When they asked her name, she'd say Jenny. Or maybe she'd slur the name and it would come out Jamie. She'd say she never thought she'd be able to tell anyone about the guilt and shame she's felt over the years . . .

But she did not join her mother or change her name to Jenny or

Jamie. Instead, she took a tissue from the bedside table, dabbed her eyes so as not to smear her eye makeup, straightened her hair using the metal mirror screwed to the wall, and walked out of the room, past the mulatto guard, Latoya, and into the sun. In an hour she was due back at the station.

CHAPTER 12

IN THE SPRING OF THAT year, shortly after the anniversary of the Chernobyl disaster in the northern Ukraine, there was a nuclear accident in the United States that caused great public outcry, not so much because the amount of radiation released was extensive — it wasn't — but because the previous winter an American political science student studying in Moscow and visiting Kiev had as much as predicted it.

Unlike the Chernobyl disaster, the radiation release was not airborne. The accident took place near the small Indiana town of Wheatfield. On a curve, after passing through Wheatfield, one of the cars of the train called the Dawn Patrol jumped track after a wheel apparently locked up. In all, three cars derailed before the train came to a stop. A resident of Wheatfield said the train had come through town faster than usual that morning.

Even though Nuclear Regulatory Commission personnel who rushed to the scene declared the spill "minuscule" and that cleanup would be completed in a few days, the town of Wheatfield was evacuated as a precaution while the area was cleaned up, the cars were put back on the tracks, and the Dawn Patrol resumed its journey at lowered speed.

While it was morning in the United States when news of the Dawn Patrol's derailment began to break, it was already evening in Russia. In the library of Moscow University, a political science undergraduate student named Viktor ran between the stacks in the government and politics section calling out, "Jamie! Jamie Carter!"

When Jamie heard her name being called, she put back the volume she had been referencing and ran out into the main aisle.

"Viktor, what is it?"

"Hurry!" said Viktor, grabbing her arm and pulling her toward the door.

"But my books," she said.

"Leave the books!"

On their way past the study desk she had been using, she snatched up her notebooks and satchel.

"Hurry," said Viktor, his hands out as if pleading, "before it's over."

Viktor managed to get Jamie across the square and into the student cafeteria in time to hear only the tail end of the story of the Dawn Patrol that was being broadcast on a television in one of the cafeteria's lounges. But the tail end of the story had quite an impact on Jamie because the commentator referred to an interview with her the past winter in Kiev when she'd criticized the movement of nuclear waste by rail and suggested that scientists worldwide join together to find solutions to the growing world nuclear waste dilemma.

"What did I miss, Viktor?"

"Everything. When the story began, I thought it would be one of those short ones, so I watched for a while. Then, when they brought on a couple of scientists and a spokesman from the Atomic Energy Committee and these three started talking about fission versus fusion and reusable fuels and the problems involved with putting another sarcophagus on top of the existing Chernobyl sarcophagus and all that, I assumed it would turn into one of those hour-long discussions. That's when I decided to find you."

"Did they mention me at the beginning of the story, too?"

"Yes, and one of the scientists said you should be commended for your constructive suggestions."

"Wow."

"Yes," said Viktor. "Wow. And now that I've gone through all the trouble to find you and give you the good news, perhaps you can help me with my project for Foreign Relations History."

"Of course I'll help you, Viktor. That's what a graduate assistant is supposed to do."

"Yes, I know. But I thought by being the bearer of good news I might get *extra* help."

Jamie stared at Viktor and couldn't help smiling when he smiled. "Okay, what's the topic of your project?"

"It's called, 'Reagan and Gorbachev, Comrades or Actors on a Stage.'"

"Catchy title, Viktor."

As Jamie read Viktor's overview of his project outline — which included a compilation of instances of joking and good-natured ribbing between the two leaders — she could not help letting her mind wander. She wondered what Arkady would think when he heard the news, and what Brian would think, and what effect the news might have on what she now referred to as her "future political career back home." But most of all, her mind wandered because, on the one hand, she was very homesick for the States, and for Brian, and on the other hand, she wondered if, after she returned home, she would ever see Arkady again.

She loved Arkady. But if she were honest with herself, she had to admit she also loved Brian. If Arkady were here in Moscow instead of in the Ukraine, and if he could read her mind, he would wink at her with his dark brown eyes. He would say he understood. If Brian were here and could read her mind, he'd stare at her and also say he understood. Arkady and Brian. Perhaps that is why she loved them both. Brian, who once told her, when she said his eyes were the color of the sea, that the seas would rise and that his eyes would then be full of tears. Arkady, who told her during her visit to the Ukraine, that his eyes were the color of the soil beneath the farm fields, the soil in which he would eventually be buried.

☢ ☢ ☢

Late that evening, just before going to bed, Jamie received a long distance call from Senator Jim Hansen of Illinois.

"Where are you calling from, Jim?"

"Washington. Listen, Jamie. In politics things often happen very slowly, but once in a while everything speeds up. This Dawn Patrol accident could be a godsend for your career."

"I wondered what effect it might have. This summer, after I graduate, I figured I'll learn more about what direction to take while working for you."

"I'd love to have you as an assistant again. But with this derailment and something else that's happened recently, you should reconsider."

"What else has happened?"

"I assumed you wouldn't have gotten the local news over there yet. You remember Barbara Lynn, the Illinois congresswoman from the U of I district?"

"Nothing's happened to her, has it?"

"No. But last weekend she announced she would retire after this term. That's your district, Jamie. Officially you're a resident there even though you've been away this school year."

"My God, the Illinois Congress? I'm still in school."

"So what? You meet the age requirement, and I, for one, can vouch for your qualifications. You've got strong views that people identify with. I've heard and seen it. People refer to you in conversation. People ask me when you're coming back to the states. Why not take a shot at it, Jamie? You'll have plenty of time to work on your campaign before the elections. And if it falls through at nomination, I'm sure we can find something for you to do here in Washington again. You've got to strike while the iron's hot. If you agree to announce your intention to run as soon as you land at the Champaign airport, I'll make sure the media is tipped off and waiting for you. By the way, exactly when do you come back?"

"Four weeks."

"Good. That'll give you some time to think about it. Just make sure you give me at least a week's notice before you tell anyone else. We need to work on the best way to announce. If you still have doubts, Jamie, keep in mind that there's a new political atmosphere brewing in the Midwest. It's becoming a lot like California in the 1960s. The power brokers are out and a more freewheeling, experimental mood is in the air. So, unless you've got a dozen or so skeletons in the closet . . . "

"I . . . I just like to keep my private life separate."

"Nothing wrong with that unless you're sensitive about the media crowding you, which it will from time to time."

"I don't know what to say, Jim."

"Say good-bye for now. These calls to Moscow cost a fortune and the eagle eyes are watching the bills."

"Thanks, Jim."

"Hey, what are friends for? I just wish you could get into office here in Washington sooner. We could use an environmental spokeswoman with a following like yours."

"And all because of a coincidence."

"I like to call it fate," said Senator Hansen.

Unfortunately, fate did not allow Jamie to reach her decision and make the call to Senator Hansen to have the media waiting. Her stay at Moscow University was cut short when she received the phone call from her father in the middle of the night. Her mother was in the hospital and quite ill. Her father said he and her mother had hoped the situation would improve so they could tell Jamie the news after her return from Moscow. But fate does not work that way. Jamie's mother, after a relapse of cancer that had gone on for many weeks, was in the hospital in Traverse City. Doctors said she did not have long to live.

☢ ☢ ☢

As Jamie's plane made its descent into Traverse City and crossed over the Lake Michigan shoreline, she looked down trying to follow roads so she could see Wylie Lake. But Wylie Lake was too far south in the county, and instead of seeing Wylie Lake she saw larger lakes and huge Grand Traverse Bay with its West Arm and East Arm. It was twilight and the twinkling lights of Traverse City outlining the shimmering bottom tips of the twin bays made her think of a mother's milk-swollen breasts.

She had been traveling over half a day and this was the fourth plane she'd been on. When the flight from Chicago landed at Traverse City — a direct flight from New York would have arrived later than the connecting flight from Chicago — she knew there would be no one waiting for her. Her father would be at the hospital. The last time she had talked to him was when she called from New York. At that time she found out her mother had slipped into a coma earlier in the day and the doctors had been unable to revive her.

In the cab to the hospital she felt suddenly very weak, as if she might pass out. It was one of those moments when she thought illness and death might have caught up with *her*. She wondered if she could go on. She lowered the cab window and breathed deeply. There was a cool north breeze and she could smell the bay. She took a couple more nourishing breaths, thought of her father waiting anxiously all day for her arrival, and felt strong again.

☢ ☢ ☢

Her mother's eyes were closed, but not tightly. Jamie could see

159

moisture between the lids and she took this as a bad sign. It seemed as if the effort needed to close her eyes completely had eluded her mother.

Air tubes were in both nostrils, her mouth on the verge of opening as if the skin around it was already drying, pulling back, withering. Her lips were no longer full and were the color of the rest of her face, as if someone had stretched a fine gauze over her skin to turn it ashen. She was very thin and the sheet over her chest did not hide the fact that, not only was she breastless, but now, near death, seemed sunken in.

Jamie kissed her mother, said, "Hi, Mom. It's me, Jamie. I'm home. Anything to eat around here?"

In the hallway she hugged her father and they both wept.

"With all these damn cancer research breakthroughs they keep harping about on the news, you'd think they'd have something to at least stop its progress. And not that damn chemotherapy and radiation. They might just as well have dipped her in acid. I don't know what's killing her, the cancer or the treatments she's had to endure all these years."

They were in an alcove lounge at the side of the hall a few doors down from her mother's room. Jamie was letting her father talk without interruption because that was what he seemed to need.

"My emotions are all screwed up, Jamie. Here you are back in the states after all that time away, and what are we doing? Sitting in a hospital, waiting. We should be at the cottage, all three of us. We could have sat on the porch and watched the sunset. It was a beautiful sunset tonight." He pointed to the far end of the hall. "I saw it out the window. Reminded me of an evening we all sat on the porch last spring . . . no, the spring before last. God, time sure is a bastard, can't stop for anything. Anyway, I remember you and Arkady there with us. Bianca was also there. You remember Bianca?"

"Of course."

"Bianca was here a couple days ago when your mom was still talking. I'd stayed the night before and was pretty worn out. I must have looked terrible because your mom and Bianca sent me home. Probably because I needed a shower and shave."

He smiled when he said it and this made Jamie feel a sudden wave of hope. Everything would be all right now. They'd go back into the room and Mom would be awake, trying to sit up, complaining about the service in the hospital, pulling out the breathing tubes and itching her nose with the back of her hand, asking for a tissue, asking for a hairbrush.

"Later that evening, after sleeping almost the entire day, I drove back and found that Bianca was still here. She'd stayed with your mom all day. She'd done your mom's hair and nails, even her toenails. She'd put on makeup." He smiled again, another wave of hope. "She was beautiful."

He paused, rubbed his eyes, looked down the hall in the direction of the room. "After Bianca left, your mother said some strange things."

Jamie waited, when he did not continue, asked, "What did she say?"

"She started talking about society and tribal cultures, how my ideas for Wylie Lake were sacred things and that we should pursue them. She mentioned the projects me and Bill Cochran and Joe Siebert and the others had started."

He turned to Jamie. "I forgot, you've been gone. A few of us around the lake have gotten together and made some plans. Bill's got a wind generator partially completed — he's waiting for parts — and Joe's got a pretty good compost setup going for yard waste and food scraps. A few of us are thinking of selling our cars and all going in on a van that we'll share."

Jamie's father paused several seconds, staring at her before he continued. "Anyway, she talked about all these crazy ideas and plans as if they were the most important things in the world. I told her the most important thing in the world was that she get well and come back home. But she disagreed. She said future generations were much more important than her. She said the tribal things we're doing at Wylie Lake aren't just for us but for future genera-tions. Then she said she loved you and loved me but that there were a lot of others who hadn't even been born who needed love. She said Wylie Lake was for people who haven't been born yet and we should do what we can while we're here. She said she wondered if, when people died, their love stayed on and took their place."

Her father seemed to wait for a reaction to what he'd just said. Then he looked down at his folded hands and continued.

"After that was the strangest part. You have to realize, Jamie, that Bianca had been here all day. You have to realize *that* probably had a lot to do with the things your mother said."

"What did she say, Dad?"

He continued staring down. "She said Bianca offered friendship and needed friendship in return. She said if Hiram were alive and needed a friend, she would be Hiram's friend. When I said she *had been* Hiram's friend, she shook her head and looked at me and said that I should know what she was talking about and that she shouldn't have to spell it out for me. She said it wouldn't matter what people thought or said. She said it wouldn't matter because, eventually, we all blend into one another after . . . after we're gone."

The hallway was very quiet. But in the distance, there was a tinkling sound like someone jiggling a huge set of keys. The sound was rhythmic and got louder and louder. Then, just as it became apparent that it was not a set of keys, a thin young male nurse dressed in white with a trim beard and short hair pushed a cart containing trays of medications around the corner.

The nurse went into the room next to her mother's and Jamie could hear mumbling and a high-pitched voice saying, "Yuck!" in a good-natured way. The nurse came out, pushed the cart to her mother's door, picked up something from the cart and went into the room whistling a song.

"What song is that?" she asked her father. "It sounds familiar but I can't think of the name."

Her father looked up and smiled. "You remember. It's called "Angel of the Morning.""

☢ ☢ ☢

In the morning, just before dawn when, statistically, the largest number of natural deaths occur, Judy Carter died and the body was taken down to the hospital holding area until the family made arrangements. Before noon the body was transported to a nearby

funeral home for a visitation by family and close friends that evening. The next day the body was cremated.

In the car on the way back to Wylie Lake with the ashes, Jamie
said, "When I visited Arkady's family, his mother said mothers take
care of the world."

"Your mother would have disagreed," said her father. "She
would have said we all take care of the world."

As her father drove south toward Wylie Lake, Jamie thought
about the things her mother had said to her father before her death,
especially the part about a person's love staying on after they are
gone. Yes, she could feel it. A horrible pain of loss, yet on the other
side of the pain, there was something rhythmic and mysterious, as
if the strength of love needed for a woman and a man to survive in
society had stayed on long after it was needed. Some day, even if she
could not have children of her own, perhaps, like her mother, she
might also leave part of herself behind for future generations.

That evening it was calm on Wylie Lake, not a ripple to be seen
except those trailing off an aluminum rowboat rowed by a man
whose passenger on the stern seat, a young woman, held a small
container out toward the sunset before spilling its contents into the
dark, still water.

CHAPTER 13

IT WAS VERY QUIET AT the cottage that day. On other days, during the two months following Judy's death, there had been plenty of activity. Jamie had stayed on for two weeks before returning to U of I to prepare the presentation of her doctoral thesis to the graduate committee. After Jamie left it seemed every day he had visitors. Bill and Joe and Bianca and so many others came over at such odd hours of the day, he imagined a sign-up sheet circulating around the lake so that each resident would drop in for a while, bring cookies or bran muffins or preserves for him to sample, and generally keep an eye on poor old Paul Carter who acted so damned despondent and, by God, had to be pulled out of it for their sake if not for his.

It was hard to believe two months had gone by. June already and activity on the lake had picked up. More people fishing and an occasional speedboat dropped in at the public access so water skiers or tube riders could be skimmed around the small lake in mad circles, the buzzing boats putting out wakes that slapped the shore like the thump-thump-thump of a drum, or like a waterlogged heart so slow it sounded near death. He and some other Wylie Lake residents had been pushing for the DNR to allow only electric motors on the lake, but now he figured, the hell with it.

Some of the extra people on the lake were locals from town, others were guests — usually sons and daughters, grandsons and granddaughters — of lake residents. Perhaps that was why the visitations to his cottage had slackened off in the past few days. The additional guests were keeping his friends busy. No preserves or muffins or cookies for at least a week. Maybe he'd starve to death.

And then, added to all this, was his guilt.

After she had been back at U of I for a month, Jamie had called to ask him to visit. The occasion was the awarding of her doctorate. Of course, because she had left Moscow early and had delayed going back to school to stay with him after Judy's death, Jamie finished school too late in the spring for the official ceremony. But Jamie had asked him to come visit her and celebrate with her before she left for Washington to work for Senator Hansen.

The guilt he felt now was not only because he had refused, but also because of the reason he'd given. He had told Jamie that she had her career and that was more important than drinking a toast to a scroll of paper. He had told Jamie that she needed to break away, to start fresh on her own, to not look back so much and try to figure out why life had dealt some pretty vicious blows. He had fooled himself into believing he meant it in the most positive way at the time. Jamie had been calling him every night and he had been concerned that she might never get over her mother's death if she kept checking back to see how he was every night . . . every night.

But his attempt at the old shove-out-of-the-nest had backfired because between the lines he knew he was implying that he thought Jamie might have put politics and career ahead of family. Now, whenever he heard news of evil in the world — whether it was violence in Chicago or Los Angeles or Detroit or New York, or a terrorist attack far away in a developing country, or a food riot caused by the encroachment of desert into the home of Bianca's ancestors — he identified with the evil. *He* was the evil. *He* was a terrorist. *He* was the embodiment of men who enslaved, men who destroyed the women seeking some semblance of justice, enough to at least topple the altars on which tribal warriors sacrificed the women who bore their children.

Perhaps he was simply going crazy. After all, Jamie showed no anger toward him. She still called him every week and said that now that she was in Washington he should take advantage of that, visit her there, stay at her apartment and see the sights. But she also said she would not pressure him. No, Jamie had bounced back just fine and apparently had not needed that shove. His use of trite phrases like, "I'm just not ready to leave here yet," and "I'd rather stick it out here for a while until I get over your mom's death," sounded foolish now. The guilt, he had decided, was the result of having lied. Instead of saying he feared Jamie might become obsessed with her mother's death, he acted like he needed more time to reflect, more time to, as he put it, "deal with it in my own mind." Indeed, he was the one obsessed.

One evening, after turning down another of Jamie's invitations, he had climbed the hill behind the cottage to watch the sunset. It was a beautiful sunset, and afterward the sky turned crimson. That evening, as he sat in the clearing on the hill long after sunset watching the line between treetops and sky fade, he recalled the week in spring, over a year earlier, when Jamie and Arkady had stayed at the cottage. He recalled fishing with Arkady and sailing with Jamie. He recalled the storm, the lightning strike on the mast, the trip to the doctor anyway after finding out Arkady had simply been knocked down and was not injured. He recalled the evenings playing Scrabble and working puzzles. And he recalled the bicycle ride to the beach where Jamie helped two little girls build a sand castle.

On the hill that evening, he had decided that the week shared with Judy and Jamie and Arkady had been the happiest week of his life, and that no week, day, hour, minute, or second for the remainder of his life would ever come close. As someone once said, "It's all downhill from here." He remembered thinking those exact maudlin words as he trudged back to the cottage that night, the steep slope of the hill making him walk faster than he wanted.

And so here he was on this very quiet night in June sitting in the darkened living room. He didn't want to go to bed because he had trouble falling asleep and, during the past few days, when he did fall asleep, the dream about the leaking drums at Ducain Chemical came back, complete with flashing lights and Jamie with the Ducain girl at the backyard pool and one-armed Hiram reaching up for them. What was most frightening about the dream now was that when he came awake he expected Judy to be there.

Paul?

Come on, Paul. You're dreaming. And you're sweating like hell again.

He dreamed this part, too, so that when he did wake up to the reality that Judy was not there, he was terrified.

He had tried alcohol, a few stiff brandies before bed so he could not remember going to bed. But this simply delayed the dream until early morning when he was sober. And the following day he was so sick he thought perhaps the amount of brandy he had taken might have been a drunken suicide attempt.

He stood and walked out of the darkened living room. He left the house by the back door and went into the garage. He closed the garage door behind him. He felt his way toward the car and touched its hood. It was cool. It had not been run in several days. He stood for a long time with one hand on the hood of the car and the other hand in his pocket clutching the car key which he had, automatically, singled out from the other keys because of its plastic keygrip and its double-sided serrations.

As he stood there he heard something behind him, a kind of intermittent buzzing. At first he thought a large moth was fluttering against the side of the garage. But then, when the buzz sounded a third time, he could tell by its duration that it was the ringing of the telephone coming through the walls of the house, through the space between, and finally into the garage.

"Dad, how are you? You sound out of breath."

"I just ran in from the garage."

"Besides being winded, how is everything?"

He felt like a child who had done something extremely evil. He felt like a fool. He wondered why Jamie had not asked what he was doing in the garage in the dead of night until he turned on the kitchen light and saw that it was only nine-thirty.

"Dad?"

"Yeah, I was just getting the light. I was out tinkering in the garage so long it got dark outside."

"Did it rain today? The weather channel showed clouds over Michigan."

"No, but it was cloudy and dismal all day. Got dark early. So, what's up with you? I've been thinking about you a lot."

"That's nice of you to say, Dad."

"I'm not just saying it. In fact, maybe I will come out and visit you one of these days, let you take me on a tour of all those Washington monuments."

"You'd better hurry."

"Why?"

"Because I might not be here too much longer. But don't worry. It's good news. I didn't tell you about it when I was there in April, but there's been this move to . . . God, this is exciting!"

"What?"

"The party wants me to run for Illinois State Congress. It's all happened quite fast and I don't suppose you get any local Champaign, Illinois, news up there. Anyway, the petitions are signed, I'll definitely be on the ballot, Senator Hansen is backing me and, who knows, in a year or so people might be calling me Miss Congresswoman. Well? What do you think?"

"I don't know what to say. Ha! Wow! That's great!"

"That's what I said!"

They were both laughing now. When they stopped laughing, Jamie said, "I wish Mom were here."

"Me, too."

"You really miss her, don't you?"

"Yes, more than you can guess."

"I'll need you out there rooting for me, Dad. Even though you can't vote for me."

"Maybe I should take up residence in Champaign."

"Not enough time to be eligible before the election. Anyway, you've got work to do there."

"Work?"

"Yes. How can I become an active spokeswoman for the environment if I can't say that my dad taught me everything I know?"

"You get more of the mom and pop votes that way?"

Jamie laughed. "Spoken like a true father of the politician."

"So, when do you go back to Illinois?"

"I'll visit to sign things but won't set up housekeeping for a few weeks. In the meantime I'm going on a Middle East tour with Jim Hansen. I was going to call you about that, but then this Illinois Congress thing came up. Anyway, next week I'll leave to go along with Jim as an aide to gather information. It's a great chance to get some Middle East experience."

"Sounds like the Illinois Congress is simply a stepping stone. I remember when Arkady was here he said women would take over. I can't remember his exact words, but he meant it in the most positive way. You know that Arkady . . . Now I've said too much, put my foot in my mouth again."

Jamie laughed and Paul began laughing with her. It was the first time he had laughed in months.

☢ ☢ ☢

It was quiet and dark again and he sat, as he had earlier, in the living room looking out at the lake where a few reflected lights shimmered on the water. After Jamie's call he had turned out the kitchen light. He had wanted the good news from Jamie to take the darkness away. Sitting in the dark now, after his turmoil earlier in the evening, was an experiment. He recalled the jobs he'd had as a computer programmer and imagined that, as in a programming language, he could, with a simple command, choose to delete lines of code or data that had ceased to be useful. Yes, perhaps somewhere a programmer using a software package called FATE would delete him.

He sat and stared and wondered if, when he slept that night, he would have the dream again. Jamie and the Ducain girl together at the pool as if they'd been childhood friends. He thought again of the letter from Ducain's daughter after the suicide, the letter blaming him for her father's death, the letter signed, "Miss J. Ducain," in childish penmanship. He tried to imagine the little girl's thoughts at that moment of signing the letter.

Don't put on my first name. He can't call me that. Only Daddy called me that.

As Paul remembered, Ducain's daughter was about Jamie's age at the time. And, like Jamie, she would now be a woman in her late 20s. He wondered what she was doing now, and if she still thought him a murderer.

Something made a popping sound out by the road, tires on gravel, a car turning around in his driveway. But then he heard the engine rev slightly before it stopped.

He sat very still, listening. He heard a door slam, and shortly afterward heard footsteps on the sidewalk alongside the garage. They were the short, sharp footsteps of a woman, a woman walking quickly as if determined about something. The footsteps paused. He could tell that the woman was not yet to the back door. She was at the garage door, the door he had left open as he ran into the house to answer the phone.

It couldn't be Jamie looking into the garage for him. Jamie was in Washington.

It was silent and he felt very cold. Perhaps it had been his imagination. No car, no footsteps. Perhaps he was conjuring up a dream he wanted to dream instead of the nightmare. Perhaps the woman in the dream would be wearing gloves and a cartwheel hat . . .

The footsteps began again, coming closer, traversing the distance between garage and back door. And then what? Through the door? Through the kitchen? Coming up behind him in the dark? His head turning to look, neck twisted to one side as if forced down upon a cold stone altar.

He felt frozen in his chair. But the knock at the door made him leap out of the chair so fast he bumped the coffee table and his empty coffee cup toppled and rolled off, hitting the carpeted floor with a thud.

Another series of knocks sounded as he felt his way through the kitchen. In the darkness between the house and garage he could see a shape, a woman's figure in pants and blouse. *Judy.* But the woman had an enlarged head, too much hair, someone else.

"Paul?"

He reached to the wall switch, turned on the light and the huge head became a natural sized head surrounded by tightly curled hair. "My God, Bianca! You scared the crap out of me!"

"That's okay because you've been scaring the crap out of me!"

"You?"

"Yes, me. I'm damn tired of looking out across that lake night after night wishing you'd turn on a light. The others said leave you alone, you'll get over it. I say, bullshit!"

He stared at her, wondering if it was some kind of joke. The other Wylie Lake residents would jump out of the bushes or out from behind the wood pile, try to cheer him up with an idiotic surprise party. But for what? It wasn't his birthday for another month.

"I don't know what to say, Bianca."

"Try, 'Please come in.' "

She wore black slacks and a beige blouse. Her hair was cut a little shorter than the last time he'd seen her, but not as short as Judy wore hers before . . .

Bianca's skin seemed a shade lighter — a shade toward bronze — perhaps because, as he led her into the living room, he turned on every light in the place.

"That's better," she said, sitting down on the sofa.

He picked up his coffee cup from where it had dropped to the floor and sat across from her in his chair. He stared at her remembering the morning he'd seen her in her cottage window while on his morning walk around the lake shortly after Hiram's death. He remembered thinking what a waste it was for her to be alone. He remembered telling this to Judy and how Judy responded by inviting Bianca over and visiting her and sending him to her cottage with . . . yes, cookies, muffins, preserves. He remembered once, after having rowed across the lake to deliver the goods, watching Bianca wave from the shoreline as he rowed back and thinking, *God, she's a beautiful woman.* And finally, he remembered telling this to

Judy and Judy saying black was beautiful.

It was all too much for him. Judy telling him over and over that Bianca was a good friend, his trip to the garage — even though he didn't think he would have done it — and now Bianca here sitting across from him. It was all too much, like a pressure cooker at the limit. And so it all came out in a rush.

He told Bianca everything that had gone through his mind during the quiet, dismal day and the terrifying evening. He told her how Jamie's call had brought him joy to relieve the sadness, but had also intensified his guilt at having tried to distance himself. Then he told her about the fear and terror inside his mind. He spoke of the trial and the letter from Ducain's daughter. He spoke of the dream, even Hiram's cameo appearance as the backyard swimming pool troll. Finally, after reliving the horrible dream again, he paused, then told Bianca that during the last two months, the thought even crossed his mind that perhaps marrying Judy had been a selfish thing, she'd been an environmental activist and his courting her had been nothing more than an attempt to show his rebelliousness, his power. And if that were true, then he was the most evil person in the world.

"I'm pretty damn religious," said Bianca. "Always have been. And believe me, you're no Satan. Evil's everywhere. Especially in the minds and souls of terrorists. All we can do is go on. All we can do is try and not be part of it. That's *all* we can do in this life. That's *all*."

Bianca stood and went into the kitchen. He heard the refrigerator open.

"You've got two beers in here. You want one?"

"No. Help yourself."

She sat across from him again, took a couple of swigs from the bottle, put it down and said, "Are you as uncomfortable about this situation as I am?"

"Yes, I am."

"Good."

"Why good?"

She took another swig of beer, plumped up the throw pillow in the corner of the sofa, kicked off her shoes and lay down, her head cocked to the side looking at him.

"Because," she said, "I'm spending the night here to keep an eye out for trolls and you're going to bed."

CHAPTER 14

ALTHOUGH THERE WERE THREE CAMERAS in the studio, only two camera operators were on duty; the third had called in to say he was taking his wife to the hospital. Because the absent operator's wife was going to have a baby, the studio crew was cheerful and took the lack of one camera operator in stride. To record the interview with three cameras — giving the director her choice of closeups of both participants, plus long shots — one of the operators simply handled two cameras, occasionally walking quickly across the set to the other camera when the shot needed adjustment. Initially this worked fine. But as the interview went on, Heather became on edge, kept shifting in her seat, and generally, as the director put it in the control room, "acting like a Mexican jumping bean."

"How come we didn't put an earpiece on her?" asked the director, tugging at her earring. "I'd like to tell her to sit still."

"Because it's just a one-on-one," said the engineer, his huge, hairy hands hovering over the slides.

"I can't interrupt because Leslie insists on spontaneity," said the director. "If I interrupt now she'll see the gap and it'll be my ass."

"You've got a beautiful ass," said the engineer.

"Shut up, Charles. Just shut up."

Out on the floor, both camera operators smiled up toward the booth.

"Okay, boys," said the director, "eyeballs where they belong. Alex, number three is off again. Maybe I'll put camera one on for a while and you can run up and tell Miss Heather Hopper to sit still. Nuts. Stay there. Someone's got to itch her nose. Wait. Not now. Aw, forget it. Just back off the long shot and leave it. Who knows, maybe it'll be effective this way. Makes it look like Heather's more interested than she really is."

And so, without interruption, the interview of the candidate for the Illinois congressional district continued.

"Miss Carter, there's something in the past, an event I'm certain our older viewers will recall, that may have influenced your environmental concerns. Can you tell us about it?"

"Yes. I won't go into much detail, but when I was two years old, my parents and I lived in the town of Easthaven. It was about fifty miles from Chicago. I'm sure many recall the name. Briefly, there was a chemical dump near our neighborhood in which barrels of toxins were found to be leaking. The leakage was severe and had, for some time, been spread by runoff and even car and foot traffic once the toxins washed onto the roads and sidewalks. Unfortunately, routine monitoring was not done, and by the time the leakage was discovered, the entire neighborhood — virtually all of Easthaven — was found to be dangerously contaminated. We all had to move, and, as with Times Beach and Love Canal, Easthaven became a ghost town."

"Were you or members of your family contaminated?"

"Everyone in the neighborhood showed traces, a few had larger amounts. Not long ago I received a call from a woman who lived in the neighborhood. Her son, who had been my age during the incident, now has bone cancer. But their house was much closer to the dump site than our house."

"Was your health affected, or will it be affected?"

"I'd rather keep my private life and my political life separate."

"I'm afraid that's impossible," said Heather, leaning forward for emphasis. "You're in the public eye, at least for the duration of the campaign. I'm sure viewers will agree that the health of our representatives is quite important."

"Very well. The doctors aren't certain if my health will be affected by Easthaven. The toxins are carcinogens. Everyone is exposed to carcinogens in varying degrees. Put simply, the statistical probability that carcinoma will occur is greater for former residents of Easthaven."

"I understand there were birth defects among Easthaven women who subsequently had children."

"As you know, the eggs in a woman's ovaries are vulnerable to genetic damage from the moment they are produced. Therefore an egg affected by toxins can result in a deformed birth at any subsequent date."

"I'm sorry to have to ask another personal question, Miss Carter, but does that risk affect you?"

"Based on tests made when I was younger, I've made an informed decision that it would be best that I not have children."

"What chances do the doctors give you?"

"The probability of my giving birth to a deformed child is fifty-fifty."

"That must have been quite a blow when you found out."

"It still is. But knowing that I can have an effect in the world keeps me going. After all, *I* don't have a birth defect."

Camera one caught Jamie Carter's smile. Not a contemptuous or bitter smile, not a humorous smile, but the kind of smile meant to exit an uncomfortable moment with grace and dignity.

When the director switched to camera two, Heather was also smiling. At first it seemed a knowing smile meant to say, "Yes, I understand." But very slowly and very subtly the smile altered, becoming supercilious, but also seeming to say, "I'm glad it happened to you and not me." The director viewed Heather's uncomfortable stilted smile, and the pause that went with it, as an externalized facial reaction resulting from Heather trying to figure out what to say next, so the director quickly switched to the long shot on camera three. The director thought Heather would change the subject now, but she did not.

"One more thing concerning the so-called Easthaven chemical spill, Miss Carter. If you were to look back on it now and point out a single tragic figure from that terrible episode in your past, who would it be?"

"There was a boy in the neighborhood who climbed the fence at the dump site on numerous occasions prior to the discovery of the leaking barrels. Some blamed him for spreading a large amount of toxins. He died within weeks of the discovery. His name was Ricky Wade."

"Yes, that *is* tragic. But I'm surprised you didn't mention your mother. I understand she died of cancer only a few months ago."

"She did. But there's no definitive proof the chemical spill had anything to do with it. As I said earlier, carcinogens operate on the principles of statistical probability. You asked about a tragic character at Easthaven. Ricky Wade died of toxic poisoning, not cancer."

In the control room the director tugged at her earring and said, "God, this is getting morbid."

The engineer said, "Bring out the tissues before I get electrocuted from all of Miss Sensitivity's tears."

The director sneered at the engineer but said nothing that might be picked up by the camera operators and make them smile at her again.

"Yes," said Heather finally. "That is a tragic story. But now, since life must go on, please tell us some of your environmental ideas."

"Do you have a specific area or topic in mind?"

"What about our nation's continued heavy use of fossil fuels?"

"Okay. Although methods to improve efficiency and progress in fuel cell implementation have grown since the Middle East crises of the last decades, many feel we still must face the fact that the freedom to travel by private automobile at our discretion may eventually be at risk. To offset public fears — I look at it as a kind of national cabin fever — I'd like to strongly support some of the recent moves in the area of public transportation.

"For example, some time ago a friend and I had the pleasure of traveling between Wisconsin and Michigan on a ferry across Lake Michigan. Having researched the cargo and passenger capacity versus fuel consumed, it seems to be an economically and environmentally sound method of travel. Although much slower than air travel, one major advantage of traveling on a ferry is that it's fun. Ferry services on the Great Lakes are expanding and we need to encourage this. Another relatively recent move has been a shift back to passenger railroads. This is another less hectic form of travel that should be encouraged.

"My point in all this is to encourage environmentally sound energy use in travel and in all other usage areas, not by piling restriction upon restriction, but by offering economically sound alternatives that are taken by choice rather than being mandated."

Heather chuckled. "I don't think you can pry me out of *my* car. And I'm sure a lot of others feel the same way."

"You're probably right. But imagine for a moment that you want to travel west, say, to the mountains. Not just outside Denver, you want to visit various places — The Black Hills, Devil's Tower, Yellowstone, The Tetons, Rocky Mountain National Park. You certainly wouldn't fly. But instead of driving, suppose a series of interconnected rail lines could take you on such a trip. Suppose you had a private compartment or a shared compartment with private berths at a reasonable cost and the food rivaled the quality of the finest restaurants. No tedious driving, no searching for motels. Suppose, as it should be if the railroads learn to become more efficient, that the trip by rail is cheaper than the trip by car. Would that pry you out?"

In the control room the director said, "Say yes," switched to camera two, caught Heather smiling wryly as if she thought someone was trying to trick her, then switched quickly back to camera one because it seemed Miss Carter would speak again.

The engineer yawned in an exaggerated way and said, "Wake me when someone starts talking again."

Finally, after a long pause, Heather said, "I see your point."

"I realize it's a simple example," said Miss Carter. "But it's an example of an attitude, a way of life we need to adopt if we, as a species, plan to enjoy our short time on the planet. True environmentalists don't want to stop people from doing things. True environmentalists seek *better* ways to do things."

"I've heard you might have inherited some of these concerns from your father. I understand he's involved in some kind of self-sustaining community in Michigan. Is this community akin to the Gray Panthers?"

"They're not protesters, if that's what you mean."

"What are they?"

"I don't like to label people or organized groups of people. My father and the others in his community do things like experiment with solar power and compost their own yard waste and kitchen scraps. Some of their achievements could be considered models for other such communities. They've profited from careers in the modern world, now they work to give something back."

"Killing two birds with one stone?" asked Heather.

Jamie smiled. "I'd rather not put it that way. But I do see their community offering some solutions for our aging population and our prematurely aging planet."

"What about ethnic strife in other parts of the world?"

"What a transition," said the director, switching back to Miss Carter on camera one for her answer.

"That's an awfully general question."

"Yes, but I think it's a question the constituency is interested in even if you *are* running for local office."

"All right. I think ethnic groups on the other side of the world need to be treated the way we treat more familiar ethnic groups and nations. For example, in a border dispute we should consider what we would do if a similar situation occurred between, say, the United States and Canada."

"Not very likely."

"No, but that's exactly why a Middle East conflict or an African conflict or a South American conflict or an Eastern European conflict should be considered in light of how we would view a conflict involving us directly. When handling international issues in the future, our nation needs to be much more objective and much less nationalistic."

"You've been accused of being an idealist."

"I admit it. I *am* an idealist. But I also level with people. If taxes need to be raised, we should say so. I've always hated it when politicians try to kill issues by complicating them in order to put a slightly more positive-sounding spin on them. Domestically we've got problems in our cities and there are too many poor people out there. We need to economically reward getting people *out* of poverty, not maintaining them in poverty."

Heather leaned forward. "I'll play devil's advocate and say, aren't some people just lazy? Don't some people choose poverty?"

"It may seem that way," said Jamie. "But I don't think anyone chooses a life devoid of fulfillment. To lessen poverty — we have to admit we can never completely eliminate it — we have to find ways to nurture fulfillment. It might take another New Deal like that of the 1930s to do it. We might have to set up organized youth corps. A lot of things we should consider might rankle some nerves because of the memories they bring up. All I'm saying is that we can't simply continue with an economically-induced dog-eat-dog system. If we do, we might as well throw philosophy and ethics and dignity and love out the window, because then we'd be just another animal species in the jungle on the verge of extinction."

"I wonder," said Heather, "what kind of philosophy of life drives you, since you apparently are not a religious person."

"Maybe I'm going out on a limb," said Jamie, "but I'm not going to do just-arrived-at-Sunday-church-meeting sound bytes simply because I'm running for office. My parents were never religious in a formal sense, but they had strong ethical beliefs and passed those beliefs on to me. A friend of mine once said everyone should have some strong beliefs but, at the same time, should always bear in mind that their beliefs could be flawed. That way, the strengths of various beliefs work together instead of simply causing one conflict after another."

Heather did not react after Jamie spoke, and the next question, asked in the same tone of voice as the previous questions, seemed bizarre.

"Tell me something, Miss Carter. People have asked about your past, about your teenaged years — boys, dates, all that. Any skeletons in the closet you'd like to bring out now that would come out later anyhow?"

Jamie stared at Heather without answering for a moment, then said, "I already opened the closet when I told you about my reason for not being able to have a child."

"Very well," said Heather, glancing toward the side table at her notes. "What about business and its relation to the environment?"

"Business," said Jamie, "needs to get off its short-term binge. Attention to short-term profits has put thousands of companies out of business. Businesses that put the local and global environment at the top of their list of priorities will be making long-term plans and will reap the economic benefits. Businesses that allow culture to guide us into the future will hang in there to enjoy that future. In short, businesses that demonstrate a desire to stay around well into the twenty-first century will be taking advantage of the strongest marketing tool devised."

Heather glanced toward her notes again, hesitated before she spoke. "Yes . . . and speaking of business, let's get to specific local issues. What exactly can you do for Champaign and Urbana?"

And so the interview went, Heather asking questions implying that, since Miss Carter established her residency while a student of U of I, she might be more interested in university affairs than in working people. And Miss Carter countering those questions with detailed suggestions involving area jobs, roads, neighborhoods, secondary schools, and a health preservation plan she wanted to bring to the floor of the state house.

"She's been doing her homework," said the director during the last part of the interview.

"If she didn't," said the engineer, "she wouldn't get no supper."

"I don't know about Heather, though. She looks like she's getting messages from outer space."

"I didn't mean to be hard on you."

"You weren't hard on me."

"My director said she thought it came off very impromptu, the way our station manager likes it."

"Knowing the cameras are on sure makes a difference. Remember the mock debates we used to have at the grad house?"

"Yes, I remember."

After leaving the studio, Jamie and Heather had gone to a restaurant on campus for dinner. They had eaten and now sipped coffee as they spoke. It was after eight, and the restaurant, a little pricey for students, was almost empty.

"Have you heard from Arkady recently?" asked Heather.

"We e-mail one another every couple of weeks. Hard to believe it's been over six months since I've seen him."

"Is his health okay?"

"As far as I know."

"Please don't think I'm trying to pry," said Heather. "I'm asking all the questions I couldn't ask when I had my confrontational hat on."

"What hat do you have on now?"

"My friendship hat," said Heather. "And as a friend, I've got to tell you that one of the interns at the U of I station tipped me off that you might be seeing Brian Jones again."

"Brian's an old friend and supporter," said Jamie. "He wants to work for my campaign."

"And if you're elected?"

"If I'm elected he'll probably stay on as an aide, maybe even get a few bucks out of the congressional budget."

When Heather did not comment on this, Jamie said, "Look, he was a talented political science major and now he's had experience lobbying on environmental issues. We do things like this in politics. You know, like hire qualified people. And if we become friends, then the working relationship is all that much better."

Heather pointed to her head. "Friendship hat, remember?"

"Sure," said Jamie. "I'm a little sensitive about those things. Brian did his undergraduate work at the University of Alabama and his graduate work here at U of I. We dated a couple years back and recently we've been out a few times. He knows about Arkady. Brian's a nice guy and I like him."

"And Arkady's on the other side of the world," said Heather.

"Right. Arkady's on the other side of the world."

"Do you wish he was here?"

"Yes, I do. But I guess none of us can have everything we want."

Heather stared past Jamie for a moment as if seeing those things or that single thing she wanted but could not have. Then she sipped her coffee again, looked at Jamie and changed the subject.

"How has your dad taken the loss of your mother?"

"It was pretty rough for a while. I wasn't sure what was going on in his head and I couldn't get through to him. But he has a friend now. Her husband's dead and they support one another."

"Hard to believe that just a few years ago you were telling me about how your parents were environmental activists back in the '70s."

When Heather said this, Jamie thought she noticed a wry smile, the kind of smile Heather had used on the air. This made her think of the time, as undergrads, she and Heather had smoked pot in one of the guy's rooms in the dorm, and how everyone, including her, had admitted that their parents had at least tried it. She also remembered telling about the time her father had been slipped acid in his beer, and the time both her parents had been arrested for protesting at the Iroquois Nuclear Power Plant.

"A lot of people today consider themselves environmental activists. My parents were simply ahead of the times."

"Right on," said Heather, smiling her wry smile. "So, tell me about your father and his friend. Any marriage plans?"

"I didn't ask."

"Do they live together?"

"They've each got a cottage on the lake."

"But it's beyond dating?"

"The word 'dating' doesn't quite seem to fit," said Jamie, putting her hand over her cup as the waiter strolled past again with steaming regular and decaf. "But, yes, they've been seeing one another on a regular basis. What about you, Heather? Anyone on your horizon?"

"I was hoping you'd ask," said Heather. "His name's Jack. He's a vice president at the network in New York. We met a few weeks ago when he visited the station. We've gone out a couple times and he's arranged a New York trip for me next month. My station manager's not too happy about it, but what the hell. Only problem is, he's in his 50s."

"Why is that a problem?"

Heather cocked her head to one side and looked somewhat annoyed. "Right, life expectancy has gone pretty high, and with all the breakthroughs in genetically-engineered drugs and biotechnology, we might be able to make old Jack into a teenager with raging hormones who'll . . . "

When Heather paused and stared at her, Jamie said, "I just asked."

"I'm the interviewer, remember? Like in the old days, one of our grad house debates."

"Okay. Ask a question."

"How about this?" said Heather. "Assume you get elected to the Illinois Congress. Then, assume your career buzzes along and next thing you know, *Voilà*, you're elected governor."

"Quite a set of assumptions," said Jamie.

"Just assume," said Heather, putting artificial sweetener in her coffee.

"Okay, I'll assume. What's the question?"

"You're on a talk show and the interviewer asks, 'Now that the votes are counted and you're on your way to the mansion in Springfield, what impact do you think the 1989 Easthaven chemical disaster had on your career?'"

"I'm surprised you didn't try to warm me up by asking how it will be to live in the mansion all by myself."

Heather had that wry smile again. "I suppose it was simply an accident that you chose to be an environmentalist."

"You're right, Heather. Easthaven had a lot to do with where my interests lie. But I don't think Easthaven will get me elected to Congress, or to any other office."

"Jim Hansen's support and the incumbent's support sure won't hurt."

"You think they'd back someone solely because when she was little she got a dose of DBCP?"

"You said it, not me."

"Listen, Heather. If there's something on your mind, let's have it."

Heather stared at Jamie. Her lips were held tightly closed, and soon a tear appeared and ran down her cheek.

Jamie reached out and touched her hand. "Heather, what's wrong?"

"Nothing you can help me with."

"But I can listen. If you need a listener . . . "

Heather pulled her hand away and waved it. "No. It's easy for you to want to keep your private life separate from your career because in *your* private life at least a few good things have happened. Some of us keep our private lives secret because we have to, because we're ashamed!"

Heather began weeping, pulling tissues from her purse, blowing her nose. Jamie remained silent and waited.

"When you were talking about your father . . . " Heather stopped, blew her nose again. "When you were talking about your father the way you always did in school in such glowing terms . . . "

Heather stared at Jamie, her eyes suddenly seeming older, harder. She continued in a lowered voice, deeper, as if from someone other than Heather.

"He was in the bathtub and I was standing next to the tub. I was just a little girl and he wanted me to take baths with him. Mom was always gone, but she knew. She must have known because after the problem with Peter she never looked at me again. We lived in the same house and she never looked at me because . . . "

Heather did not continue. Instead she began sobbing.

Jamie stood, walked around the table and held Heather's shoulder. Heather leaned toward her for a moment, letting Jamie hold her. But then Heather pulled away, stood, and went toward the ladies' room. Jamie left the tab plus tip on the table and walked to the ladies' room after her.

Just before Jamie opened the door, Heather came out, smiled a seemingly unpretentious smile and, handing Jamie a fifty dollar bill, said, "It was my treat, remember? Come on, it's almost ten." She straightened her hair as she walked through the restaurant. "Got to get home in time to see this precious mug on the tube."

As Heather drove Jamie back to the motel she temporarily called home, she did not mention her father or mother and spoke incessantly of trivialities concerning the world of broadcast journalism. While Heather spoke, Jamie tried to remember if Heather had ever before mentioned, or hinted at, incest. Perhaps Heather's seemingly shallow personality over the years was part of her defense mechanism, her way of blocking out the past. Jamie even considered the possibility that, during their off-and-on friendship, Heather had been attempting to transfer her past to Jamie. Perhaps that was the reason Heather had always shown an interest in the details of Easthaven and now showed interest in her father and Bianca even though she'd never met Bianca.

When they arrived at the motel, Heather was still talking and only stopped when Jamie interrupted.

"Heather, let me ask you something."

"Go ahead."

"What you said earlier about your relationship with your parents . . . have you ever spoken to anyone else about it?"

"What are you talking about?"

"I just wondered if talking about it helped, and if it did, then perhaps . . . "

"Get out! Get the fuck out!"

In the darkness of the car she could not see Heather's face. The car's engine revved when she opened the door and jumped out. She watched the car speed off, fishtailing as it left the motel parking lot.

It was over. Not just friendship, something else. As Jamie walked up the outside stairway to her room on the second level of the motel, she could hear the sounds of the campus in the distance — a motor scooter here and there, the shout of a male student — and suddenly she felt a whole hell of a lot older.

Back in her apartment, her face smiled at her from the far end of the room. On the large screen television, the face was twice its actual size. Because it was a high-definition television, any blemish or flaw on her skin, any fleck of perspiration, any speck of dandruff would have shown. But there were no flaws. Her face was perfect.

But that pose, that closeup of her at the beginning of the interview when she introduced Jamie, was the end of the perfection she had hoped for. Her performance during the interview was worse than the performance of the second-string weekend anchor who had introduced her. Not that she stumbled over her words or asked the wrong questions. It was the way she asked questions, the way she responded, the way she kept fidgeting and, most of all, the horrible camera work and direction that brought out the worst of the most uncomfortable interview she had ever done.

Instead of switching between closeups at the appropriate times, the director had seemed to try to anticipate who would speak next. And when there was a long shot, it was so far back that her nervous movements in her seat stood out when compared with Jamie who sat stone still, prim and proper with hands folded demurely, just so, on her knees.

As she watched the interview, Heather saw that at one point, even though the director knew she hated it, camera two showed her profile for a full five seconds. She looked like a nodding robot, or like a rookie doing a canned reaction shot in the field for the first time. Maybe she could blame the whole rotten interview on the horrible camera work. Maybe Leslie would take her side. When she couldn't stand watching any longer, Heather turned the sound up and went into her bedroom.

As she took off her clothes and put on her robe, the sound of her own voice calling Jamie "Miss Carter" made her feel ill. And, even though she was not watching the picture, she remembered that Jamie had scrutinized her like a professor lecturing a student who couldn't quite get it, or like her mother used to scrutinize her before she found out, before she went crazy. Maybe Jamie would go crazy. Or, like her father, maybe Jamie would be in her room some day and casually walk to the dresser and pull open the drawer and push aside her underwear and, like her father . . .

Without realizing it, Heather had gone to the dresser. The top drawer was open, her hand holding her stacked precious underwear aside to reveal . . .

It was the gun she had bought after the two survivalist rednecks she'd met in the truck stop bar raped her. Danny and Kenny. Why would she remember their names now? Why did she think she needed protection when, after all, she had asked for it? She reached into the drawer and touched the gun to be certain it was real. Outside the room a voice boomed through the wall.

"The probability of my giving birth to a deformed child is fifty-fifty."

Heather slammed the drawer shut, ran out into the living room and shut off the television.

New York. The interview was local and would not be shown in New York.

She sat on the sofa, curled her feet beneath her robe, picked up the phone and placed a call to New York.

"Jack, honey."

"Hey, Heather. I was hoping it would be you."

"Were you?"

"Of course. Sorry I didn't call. Premiers this week. That's why I'm at the office late. Watch any of the new shows?"

"No, sorry. Too busy."

"Yeah, the both of us."

"Jack?"

"Yeah."

"What you said when you were here last time."

"You mean the answer to my question?"

"Yes, Jack. Please ask it again. I . . . I need to hear it."

"Okay. If I divorce my wife, will you marry me?"

Heather held the phone in both hands, hugging it to her face as she whispered, "Yes."

CHAPTER 15

AFTER CLEANING THE FISH AT *a wooden table at the side of the cottage, the old woman wraps the fish in newspaper and hands the bundle to the young man. She leads the young man to the front door and once inside goes to the window in the living room. The sun is higher now, brilliantly lighting up the far shore. The old woman points out another cottage across the lake.*

"I used to live over there with Hiram, my first husband. This cottage here belonged to my second husband, Jamie's father."

The young man leans forward and looks north along the shore. "My uncle's cottage is over there. You can barely see it through the trees."

"Joe Siebert?" asks the old woman.

"Yes, how did you know?"

"I see a resemblance. Especially in your profile. Joe used to fish a lot out on the lake. Sometimes in the morning he'd fish in close along the shore here. I'd see him in profile. He had an old wooden rowboat back then. It leaked and he used to keep patching it. Paul told Joe many times he needed to get a new boat, but Joe insisted on using his old wooden boat."

"The old boat is still there," says the young man. "It's alongside the south side of the cottage with flowers planted in it."

"Daffs," says the old woman.

"Daffs?" asks the young man, puzzled.

"Daffodils," says the old woman. "I gave Joe's wife the bulbs way back when. Dug them up from the side of my old cottage across the lake. Hiram used to call them daffs. We had so many around the old cottage Hiram said in spring the place looked like it was marked for a Huey landing. See, he served in the Vietnam War a long time ago. Huey was the name of a helicopter. Anyway, funny how people are dead and gone but the bulbs keep coming back no matter what." She shakes her head. "It sure has been a long, long time."

After staring out the window for a moment more, the old woman turns and points to the newspaper-wrapped bundle of fish the young man is holding. "Anyway, come on, let's get those critters in the pan."

While the old woman works in the kitchen, the young man sits at the kitchen table and listens as she begins telling about the years, several decades earlier, during which the effects of global warming began to take hold and about an Earth Day speech in the year 2018.

☢ ☢ ☢

During the century's second decade, a feeling grew throughout the world that political, social, economic, and environmental affairs would begin to change rapidly. For some, rapid changes were alarming, causing many to speak of Armageddon. But for others, rapid changes were cause for hope, especially when considering the many environmental dilemmas that could now be rapidly solved through ingenuity and the concerted efforts of all nations.

Although terrorists had changed the world, death was the great leveler. Not only had political leaders belonging to the old order begun to die away, but so had terrorist leaders. The world found itself positioned in an interlude of relative peace. The MIT professor who was first to decipher messages from extraterrestrials mentioned during an interview that perhaps knowledge that we had company in the universe had taken hold. But most world leaders said the outbreak of peace was due to the extent of global challenges facing all nations.

Unlike the "Star Wars" predictions of the twentieth century, in which the Earth would be surrounded by killer satellites and technological shields, space, during the early twenty-first century, became a place from which Homo sapiens could view the borderless fragility of the planet. Enhanced views from space stations broadcast to all parts of the globe began to have psychological impacts stronger than any weapons systems. Basically, if one were allowed to repeatedly view the Earth from space and to see the effects of its inhabitants upon it, then one could readily grasp the necessity to cooperate in the global lifesaving efforts at hand.

Temperature-enhanced views from space proved global warming a reality to even its most vocal critics; shoreline changes of island nations, as well as coastal continental shifts due to erosion, were clearly visible. Color-enhanced views showed the effects of acid rain, depleted rain forests, and dark palls of haze over third-world industrial areas. On every continent, non-technical citizens had begun to make the connection between the global environment and continuation of their cultures and their families. Citizens who had once been manipulated by government and business now protested the destruction of their Earth.

After decades of research, wind and solar power were being used to some extent on every continent. Not that solar and wind power were cheap. What had happened was that monetary values of energy had risen high enough to make virtually all modes efficient in their own way. Renewable energy alternatives had finally come into their own.

In April of the year 2018, to help celebrate the forty-eighth anniversary of Earth Day in the United States, an Illinois State congresswoman spoke at a gathering outside the site of an Illinois town abandoned in 1989 because of the discovery of a highly-toxic chemical dump. In the 1990s, houses nearest the dump had been leveled, storm sewers plugged, and a ventilated cap of clay, plastic, dirt, and grass constructed over the site to keep ground water from moving and spreading the contamination farther. The site was behind a high chainlink fence with signs posted every few yards that said, "DANGER, HAZARDOUS WASTE AREA, UNAUTHORIZED PERSONS KEEP OUT."

The Illinois State congresswoman spoke eloquently on that Earth Day of the reduction of world arms expenditures, relating the decrease of defense budgets to recent economic recoveries. She spoke of the relationships between conservation, economic stability, and world peace. She spoke of individual responsibility and the need for adults to have additional concerns for children. Because the woman had, during her years as a state congresswoman, gone outside her district and established national and international acclaim, the speech was carried on news broadcasts worldwide.

The congresswoman's speech was of special interest to the youth of the world, especially the youth of America's cities who identified strongly with her because of her idea to creatively harness the apparent need to form urban gangs. She told the story of a friend of her father, a Vietnam veteran who had once been a gang member in Chicago. She told the story of another friend, the wife of the Vietnam veteran — how a younger brother had been killed in a drive-by shooting years earlier in Los Angeles. She challenged gangs to come out into the open, to show the courage of brothers and sisters who protested against segregation and war in the 1960s.

On that Earth Day of 2018, the Illinois congresswoman used the phrase "caretaker culture" to label what must happen throughout the world if a global environmental cataclysm were to be avoided. She spoke of the burning of the rain forests and the appetite for the fossil fuels that took the Earth millions of years to create. She spoke of major environmental disasters in recent times — Bhopal, Chernobyl, Love Canal, Hanford, Times Beach, Three-Mile Island, Easthaven, the Middle East oil fields.

What made the congresswoman's speech most moving, and more convincing to many viewers, was her eloquent concluding statement. She spoke of the struggles of America's forebears and their various escapes to a new land at various times in history. She spoke of the tearing apart of African ancestral families and the dark age of slavery. She spoke of this once new land as having offered the only hope, the land sacrificing itself for those who lived upon it. Then she revealed that she had once been a little girl in the abandoned town behind her. She said that because of the effects of toxic exposure she would never be able to have children. Although tears streamed down her cheeks during this part of her speech, she maintained her composure and her voice did not falter. Her name was Congresswoman Jamie Carter. The town was called Easthaven. Both names, as well as her concept of a global caretaker culture, were repeated around the globe on the vast communications networks.

☢ ☢ ☢

After the Earth Day speech, Jamie took the Illinois Central to Chicago where she would speak the following day to the Chicago City Council. When she got out of the cab that took her from the train station to the Intercontinental Hotel, reporters from two Chicago television stations were waiting for her at the entrance. She answered questions about Easthaven by detailing the story yet again. She answered questions about future political plans by saying she was too busy in her current position to think about it. She answered questions about her health by repeating again that she would never be able to have children.

Apparently satisfied that she had answered all their questions, the reporters finally abandoned her in the hotel lobby. She registered and took the elevator to her floor, a bellboy met her at her door with her luggage, and when she opened the door and stepped inside Brian came to her.

"I hope y'all weren't planning on an evening alone," he said, holding both her hands.

"Not when I can spend it with you."

The bellboy brought her luggage in from the hallway, the three of them exchanged nods and smiles, Brian provided the tip, then the bellboy left and they were alone.

"I watched your speech on television," said Brian as they hugged.

"Did you like it?"

"Very much."

"How did you get in here?"

"I talked them into giving me the adjacent room, and the bell captain's a friend of mine."

"Let's put on disguises."

Brian held her at arm's length. "Disguises?"

"So we can go out on the town without being interrupted. I'm starving."

Brian didn't need to be disguised, but he went along with her plan. She took off her makeup, brushed her hair straight, put on baggy sweats and running shoes, and topped it off with a Chicago Cubs baseball cap. Brian wore jeans, a sweatshirt, and a Sierra Club baseball cap. The sun was low in the west, hidden by the buildings, when they walked out of the hotel and headed south on Michigan Avenue.

Brian grasped her hand as she pulled him along. "Where are we headed?"

"Buckingham Fountain."

"I thought you were hungry."

"I am."

Although the sun was down by the time they reached the fountain, the bright orange of the sky coming through the fountain's mist managed to paint a rainbow on the city's shadowed skyline. Traffic on Columbus Drive and Lake Shore Drive ebbed and flowed according to the timing of traffic lights. Mostly fossil-fuel driven vehicles, but here and there a hybrid car or bus, and even a couple of electrics that Brian pointed out. A breeze was at their backs, coming off Lake

Michigan, so that the spray blew in toward the skyline. The smell of steaming Chicago red hots from a nearby concession wagon drifted in the air. As they stared at the fountain, a group of children ran past screeching like gulls being fed. Within the fountain, fish and nymphs and gargoyles gone green with algae regurgitated streams of water.

They ate two Chicago red hots apiece while they sat on a park bench.

To the east, beyond Lake Shore Drive, the lake was the color of slate beneath the evening sky. To the west, the sky was losing its orange and deepening. Brian stared at the fountain as he chewed. In profile, and in the gathering darkness, she could not see the color of his eyes. But because of the bright street lights that had come on along Columbus Drive, and because the breeze had shifted and the fountain's mist was hitting their faces, she could see that droplets from the mist had settled on Brian's lashes, making them sparkle.

They finished their red hots, threw their trash into a receptacle, bought cups of steaming coffee at the concession wagon, and found another bench, this one farther back from the fountain. The bench faced west, and as the evening sky went dark, the city sparkled.

Jamie leaned against Brian and he put his arm around her.

"Beautiful night," she said.

"It is," said Brian. "Too bad there are still some fossil fuels being used for all those lights."

"I thought Chicago was a hundred percent nuclear," said Jamie.

"Sometimes it is. Depends on grid conditions. This time of day I'm sure coal is in the mix."

"At least it's low sulfur coal."

"That's true."

"Brian?"

"Yes."

"I want you to know the invitation is still open. We've got a lot of environmental work to do in Springfield, and if you want . . . "

Brian turned to her and smiled. "Don't get me wrong, I'd love to work for you. But every time I think I'm about to take your offer seriously, things come up."

"Things in Washington?"

"Right. The Club lobbyists need more research done, more position papers. They keep telling me I'm the only one who can provide what they need when they need it."

"It sounds like you're indispensable."

Brian laughed. "I wouldn't put it that way."

"Well, anyway, my committee in Springfield could use someone like you. The other committee members keep asking if you're available. I want you to know, Brian, that I don't bring it up lightly, or because of our relationship."

Brian turned her to him, kissed her quickly. "Thanks."

She stood, pulled him by the hand. "Come on."

"Where are we going?"

"I want to listen to waves."

Jamie let go of Brian's hand and ran ahead of him down the steps that led away from the fountain. She stopped at the bottom where other couples and families headed out onto the crosswalk that went across Lake Shore Drive. She turned around and saw Brian taking his time, walking slowly down the steps. "Come on, before the 'Walk' light changes!"

He walked even more slowly, turning his Sierra Club cap backwards and doing a kind of Charlie Chaplin slow motion walk on each step before taking a step down. Behind her on Lake Shore Drive there was a screech of tires and a horn sounded. She turned and saw that a car had come up fast on the stopped traffic and had barely been able to stop, skidding sideways, its nose pointing toward her, and almost plowing into the stopped cars. When she turned back to Brian she saw him running down the stairs two at a time toward her.

Brian put his arm around her and pulled her back from the curb. "Jamie, don't stand so close! What if that car had skidded this way?"

The "Walk" light had gone out and they stood together back from the curb. As the traffic accelerated past she had to speak up to be heard.

"I'm sorry!"

"Don't be sorry!" shouted Brian, turning his Sierra Club cap forward on his head. After the bulk of traffic had moved off, he stared at her seriously. "Be careful."

It was quieter when they got across Lake Shore Drive and headed down the incline toward the bicycle path and the lake. They waited to cross the path as a young couple rode slowly past on their bicycles. They exchanged greetings with the couple and continued down toward the lakeshore.

"You still owe me one," said Brian.

"What?"

"That bicycle ride we were supposed to take across the country."

"Are you serious?"

"Of course I'm serious.

"If I ride across the entire country on a bicycle, won't my butt fall off?"

Brian laughed. "I'll be sure to pick it up."

"I didn't say anything when we went on that ride along the Mississippi, but that was the worst part."

"And the best part?"

"Being with you. Being able to tell someone I love about Easthaven."

Brian stopped, took both her hands in his. "That's a first."

"Telling you about Easthaven before anyone else? You knew that."

"I mean that other word. The four-letter one."

They were close enough to hear small waves slapping gently against the pilings. Brian pulled her closer and they kissed.

When they continued walking along the lakeshore, Jamie said, "That was nice. Maybe I should tell you about Easthaven again if that's the result. Just think, if you were the victim of an environmental disaster . . . " She stopped herself, looked out toward lake. "I'm sorry, Brian. I didn't know what I was saying."

"Don't worry," said Brian. "Some day we'll all be victims of environmental disaster. All we have to do is wait."

"Come on," she said, as she began climbing the embankment, pulling Brian behind her.

"Where are we going?" he asked, as they stood waiting for traffic to stop and the "Walk" light to come on.

"Back to the hotel."

Once across Lake Shore Drive they ran hand-in-hand up the stairs taking them two at a time.

"I'm going to have to make a note on my calendar!" shouted Brian.

"About what?"

"To make sure I'm around for your next Earth Day speech, wherever that might be!"

☢ ☢ ☢

When Jamie gave the 2018 Earth Day speech outside the fence of the abandoned town of Easthaven, she had been the Illinois congresswoman for the Champaign district for three years and would represent the district for three more years. During those three years she had sponsored model legislation to make environmental programs economically rewarding. And, despite the fact that she was a state congresswoman, she had become a national spokeswoman for the environment, using her position to demonstrate to the nation and the world that the temporary reversal of global warming caused by the Mount Pinatubo volcano decades earlier was just that — temporary.

Three years later, in 2021, just before the end of her term at the age of thirty-four, Jamie was asked by the President of the United States to fill the Russian ambassadorship being vacated by Ambassador George Denison who had made a decision to retire and return to the States with his family. Jamie spent three years as ambassador to Russia. During those three years she made many friends and contacts in all of the countries of eastern and western Europe. She also played key roles in world Eastern European, Middle East, Asian, and African Alliance talks by acting as liaison between Russian and United States officials who had co-sponsored the talks.

Although most of her time was spent in Moscow during those years, she also visited cities in many of the surrounding countries of this new Europe.

While in Kiev meeting with the United States Ambassador to the Ukraine, Jamie was able to take a side trip to the village of Svyezhl where Arkady managed a settlement of pensioners from various parts of the Ukraine. The pensioners at Arkady's settlement cared for physically and mentally disabled Chernobyl survivors, and also for children who had no homes or relatives as a result of a series of earthquakes in the Caucasus Mountain region.

The visit was an emotional turning point for both Jamie and Arkady, not only because of the years that had passed since they last saw one another — they were now both in their mid-30s — but because of the realization that the separate paths their lives had taken made the possibility of marriage, once considered and delayed, out of the question.

When Jamie returned to Moscow after the visit, she felt as if a vital part of her life had ended, as if everything she had done up until then had been in preparation for that visit. Even the Russian ambassadorship seemed meaningless until she was asked to meet with Russian environmentalists and represent the United States at the next world environmental conference. Soon after the appointment, she received an e-mail from Arkady saying that the world and its children needed her to participate. Then, shortly after she received Arkady's e-mail, and as if he could read her mind, Brian called her from Washington, where he had recently become the Sierra Club's lead environmental lobbyist. Brian told her he was happy she was "officially" working for the environment and hoped that, when she returned to the states, they could work together. As Jamie listened to Brian's voice during the phone call, she closed her eyes and could imagine Brian staring at her with his blue eyes.

It seemed strangely comical at first. A guy with sea blue eyes calling her from across the sea, Arkady helping Chernobyl survivors, and here she sits in Moscow. Arkady, Brian, and her like bugs crawling about on a world biding its time.

For several days she became quite depressed and was unable to keep her mind on her work. Finally, she did get busy and the depression changed to melancholy. After a week of feeling sorry for herself, she realized the only solution to her melancholy was to immerse herself in her work. And so she became deeply involved in planning the upcoming environmental conference hosted by Moscow.

During the following year, Jamie expressed an interest in more than the planning and coordinating role of the ambassadorship. She wanted to once more take part in making laws as she had done in the Illinois Congress. While speaking with Senator Jim Hansen during a visit back to the States, Jamie found out that Jim's colleague Barbara O'Neil, the other United States Senator from Illinois, had confided to Jim that she would be retiring in three years. In several conversations with Jamie, Senator Hansen suggested that if she wanted to run for the spot she might want to get back into Illinois politics as soon as possible.

And so, in 2023, when the newly-nominated shoe-in candidate for Illinois governor from her party asked Jamie to run with him as lieutenant governor, she accepted, despite objections from conservative economic and business critics, and called the President to resign her post in Moscow. When she made that call, Jamie remembered wondering if she would ever return to Moscow or Kiev or Svyezhl again.

But, three years later, in the summer of 2026, while Lieutenant Governor of Illinois and candidate for the United States Senate, Jamie did return.

Unfortunately, the reason for her return was not good.

CHAPTER 16

"JAMIE, THIS IS A HELL of a time to be leaving the country. The campaign is short enough as it is. And with all these new campaign rules, it's hard to get any exposure."

"It can't be helped."

"The numbers show Emerson gaining in the polls after being stagnant for over a month. You used to complain about television crowding you. If you keep this up you won't have to worry about that. The election's only three months away and you and Emerson are dead-even. What do I say to the media when they ask where you've gone?"

"You're the campaign manager, Brian."

"You want me to make something up?"

"No, sorry, I've got a lot on my mind. Of course you'll have to tell them the truth."

"You sure know how to hurt a guy."

"I know. Sometimes I wonder if that's why friendship was invented."

"The hurting part?"

"Yes."

"On second thought, why should I be hurt? Working as a lobbyist while you were in Moscow made me into one tough cookie." Brian pointed to his head. "I'm so tough, even my hair is having trouble growing through this skull of mine."

Jamie paused at the door to her office and turned to Brian. "All right, what's this about your hair?"

"It's falling out."

"No, it isn't. It's thinning. You look more distinguished. More like a campaign manager."

"My hair used to be thick. Maybe if I grow it long like I used to wear it."

"I don't think so," said Jamie. "I saved a photograph of you with long hair and that photograph was taken a long time ago. Did I ever tell you I carry it with me wherever I go?"

"You carry my long-haired photo with you?"

"Yes. It's tucked into my luggage. So now let me out of here before I miss my flight."

"Okay. You'd better get going. But, back to what we were discussing. Are you sure you want me to say you've gone to the Ukraine to visit a friend who's dying?"

"You're right. I guess it would be better to simply say he's ill. I don't want anyone thinking I'm trying to use the situation to get votes. Although, politics being what it is, I'm sure that will pop up somewhere."

"Should I tell them he has leukemia and give the whole gruesome story of your involvement at Easthaven and his at Chernobyl?"

"I say don't volunteer any details. Only answer the questions."

"You're sure you want to go alone?"

"Yes. And I'd like my itinerary kept quiet."

"Shall I tell the reporters Arkady is a close personal friend?"

"Yes."

"Would you consider me a close personal friend?"

"Jesus, Brian. Sometimes I feel you're my only friend."

"Okay, sweetheart, I'll do the dirty work. But only because I love you."

"Brian, I . . . Never mind. I'll see you when I get back."

"Have a kiss for me?"

"Of course. But you didn't have to ask."

☢ ☢ ☢

Since it was time for her quarterly bank of tests at the University of Chicago Medical Center, and since there was an Illinois Central Station near the center, Jamie decided to take the train and, after her tests, take a cab to the airport. Although her opponent's supporters derided her use of public transportation when a limousine was available to the lieutenant governor's office, riding the train to Chicago had become a matter of principle with Jamie. This was especially true because of her past efforts to improve this north-south Illinois run, making both increased speed and more trains possible because of the seamless track installed during her congressional term in Springfield and because of the new hydrogen-powered locomotives. As lieutenant governor she had continued her role as advocate for the railroads and other modes of mass transportation by using her first-hand knowledge of the efficiency and popularity of railroads in Europe and Asia. One of her recent successes in Illinois was a proposed link-up of train stations in outlying areas to bicycle and walking path systems. This encouraged commuters to ride or walk to stations rather than drive.

As Jamie rode north in one of the new quiet coaches, a reporter from the *Chicago Tribune* who had joined her on the train asked about the trip. The reporter's name was Sarah, also a U of I alumnus, class of 2017. Sarah was dark-skinned, young, and attractive, making Jamie aware of her thirty-eight years, and making her think of the past. So much had happened since that hot afternoon on campus when she first met Arkady and they found out what they had in common was the possibility of death at a young age. So now Arkady had leukemia and here she was plugging along, acting the part of the up-and-coming energetic politician, although sometimes she didn't feel up-and-coming or energetic at all, especially when faced with a reporter who was a baby when she and Arkady were at U of I tickling one another in bed and imagining a world away from doctors and questionable test results.

"How did you find out about the trip, Sarah?"

Sarah opened the briefcase on her lap, revealing her portable workstation. "My partner Tom called. He's also the one who was lurking in the bushes and saw you leave by the back door. We flipped a coin to see who would follow and who would stay for your campaign manager's press conference."

"Very clever. I left my workstation and phone behind. They're not compatible with all overseas systems. And being without a phone gives me time to think without constantly being interrupted."

"Now," said Sarah, "tell me about your relationship with Arkady Lyashko."

"We met in graduate school. After his stint at U of I, he went back to Kiev. While I was a student in Moscow I visited him in Kiev. After that we didn't see one another for almost ten years. The last time I saw him was three years ago when I was ambassador in Moscow. Other than those brief visits, we've corresponded on a regular basis."

"You've remained true to one another all these years?"

"As I've said, we've remained close friends despite the geographical distance. That doesn't mean we don't have other friends."

As soon as she said this Jamie thought of how she and Brian had parted. And she also thought about how Brian being her campaign manager had strained their relationship. But why should their relationship be strained? Her fault. It was all her fault. She'd be sure to call Brian from the medical center or from airport and . . .

"Was marriage ever in the picture between you and Arkady?" asked Sarah.

"We discussed it years ago and decided it wasn't for us."

"Can I ask why?"

"Sorry, that's getting personal."

"Okay. By the way, I am sorry about the reason for your trip. Did he just find out he has leukemia?"

"No, he'd already been through a year of treatment before he told me."

"Is he bitter about Chernobyl?"

"No. That's one of the many reasons I value him as a friend."

During part of the train trip, Jamie and Sarah talked about their days at U of I, about environmental issues, about women in politics, about the ongoing controversy concerning abortion. When the train passed the first of many commuter stations ringing the Chicago metropolitan area, Sarah commented on the number of cars parked in the commuter station's parking lot.

"At least they weren't driven all the way downtown," said Jamie.

"But even using the train wastes fuel," said Sarah. "I come from the Chicago suburbs and I've seen the traffic jams when the trains come in. Most people sit in their cars with engines idling waiting to get out of the lots. In summer, every one of those cars has its air-conditioner running."

"Yes," said Jamie, staring out at row after row of cars in the commuter station lot. "There's still more to be done."

"Like what?" asked Sarah.

Jamie turned to Sarah. "We've got to use our imaginations. My father calls it random thinking. It means dreaming up possible solutions without shooting holes in them."

"Please elaborate," said Sarah.

"You say to yourself, 'How about if I try this or that solution?' and before you start shooting holes in the idea by thinking about its application, you think up another idea, and another. The point is to get all your ideas about the subject on the table, no matter how ridiculous they may seem, and especially before thinking about the problems involved in applying them."

"Okay," said Sarah, "give me some crazy ideas about parking lots full of cars heating up in the sun."

"Well," said Jamie, "we might cover the lot. That way the cars wouldn't be so hot when the train comes in."

"Covering the lot costs money, uses resources. What's the pay-back?"

Jamie stared at Sarah a moment without answering. Then Sarah said, "Sorry, I ruined the idea by trying to apply it. I didn't let you finish."

"That's okay," said Jamie, looking outside again. "Suppose the covering over the parking lot is a roof constructed of photovoltaic cells. And suppose the cells are connected through a charging system to electric cars or hybrid cars. Or even better, suppose the chargers are available for those new electric bicycles. You've seen them. You can pedal them, but they also have a battery pack and an electric motor. Anyway, if the solar panels shading the lot are used for charging batteries, you kill two birds with one stone. You keep cars or bicycles out of the rain and sun, and you encourage commuters to use either electric cars or, better yet, electric bicycles which get them home much faster on the bicycle path system anyhow."

Sarah nodded and smiled. "You had this in mind when you pushed for the bicycle path tie-in with commuter stations, didn't you?"

"Maybe I did," said Jamie. "Maybe way back in everyone's head there are crazy ideas that aren't so crazy after all. Maybe that's my point."

Sarah paused as a man in business attire passed in the aisle, then continued. "What can you say to the coalition of business people who apparently think you're too idealistic?"

"I say I was being idealistic when I proposed the Illinois Health Preservation System back when I was in the Illinois Congress and that system's not doing all that badly."

"Okay," continued Sarah, "how about the criticism that your

'caretaker culture' concentrates on everyone except the Illinois constituency?'"

"I say that because of mass communication and the tearing down of old walls, we now have a world culture. I say it's time to involve Illinoisans in that world culture by taking the lead in health care and housing and jobs. We need a worldwide new deal for young people, a system that provides opportunity for everyone to contribute. One thing I learned while in Russia was a specific concept its elderly citizens miss about communism. They contend that the new freedom is good but that they wish there was a way to make everyone feel needed. They feel that, for a time, everyone felt something was expected of them, and that was good. We live in a world economy. Everyone *should* feel something is expected of them. For that reason alone it's obvious to me we need the carbon tax and I'm certain it will be passed at the next summit."

Jamie looked out the window at small patches of dry lawn amid piles of trash behind a row of run-down city houses. Then she continued. "Perhaps good old Mother Earth is the key to all of us feeling needed, the key to all of us feeling that something is expected of us. Wouldn't it be great if we had a kind of 1930s style CCC-like project for kids in the cities? Not out in the woods somewhere, I mean right in the cities."

As the train neared the University of Chicago station, Jamie was tempted to excuse herself without telling Sarah she was getting off there rather than going on directly to the airport. But this seemed a childish thing to do, so she told Sarah about the stop at the medical center for her usual tests.

"You go there every three months?"

"Yes."

"Funny I never heard about it."

"I don't like to publicize internal exams or blood and urine tests."

"You'd rather I leave it out of my story?"

"Yes."

Sarah smiled. "Okay."

In the taxi from the medical center to the airport, the driver recognized Jamie and went on at length about air pollution and the measures his cab company was taking to reduce their emissions. At one point he gestured toward a button pinned to the sun visor on the passenger side.

"See that? It's an award for low fuel consumption. They take down our mileage and fill the tanks when we go off duty. We get a bonus if we're low enough. Best average for a week gets an extra bonus and a button."

"What's the button say? I can't read it from here."

" 'Slow burn artist.' Maybe you should mention us to the press."

"I will."

At last, in the plane on the overnight flight to Moscow, she was alone. The seat beside her was empty. She ate dinner and slept, feeling much better after calling Brian and hearing his voice.

When the flight attendant awakened her well ahead of arrival so she could prepare for her connecting flight to Kiev, she realized she had been dreaming.

In the dream she was in a rowboat that rocked back and forth rhythmically so that she was frightened she might become sick. She was rowing the boat and it was surrounded by darkness. She could not even see the water in which the boat floated. Occasionally, she was aware of someone sitting behind her on the bow seat. Yes, someone was there, but for whatever reason, the dream world kept the identity of the person from her. However she did have the feeling it was a woman with hands clasped — no, manacled — the woman looking down at her hands and feet in chains. But then, as Jamie came awake, the chains and manacles were gone and she had the feeling it was her mother sitting behind her in the boat. Perhaps the very gentle tapping of the flight attendant's hand on her shoulder had done that. Yes, perhaps that.

☢ ☢ ☢

It was afternoon when Jamie arrived in Moscow, early evening when she arrived in Kiev, and after dark when she got off the metro shuttle at Svyezhl Station. The platform was deserted except for a lone figure standing in the shadows beneath the sign for Svyezhl. Someone was to meet her, she had been told, someone to drive her to the new location, just outside town, of the recently expanded pensioners' home and orphanage that Arkady ran. She approached the figure, a thin bald man. She wondered if he was one of the Chernobyl victims housed at the home, perhaps a thin young man who had been a child when the reactor blew up, a child relishing in the drama of the disaster only to one day be picking up visitors to the home to which he has been sent to die. It wasn't until she was within twenty feet of him, and he stepped forward beneath a dim overhead light, that she realized it was Arkady.

When she hugged him she could feel his bones. When she kissed him she could taste tears, tears cooling in the night where the only sounds were the whine of the departing metro and the quickness of their breathing.

As they walked through the small empty station where the light was better, Arkady said, "I thought you would have looked more like a politician. I thought you would have looked . . . how can I put it? . . . more uncompromising." He stopped, put down her suitcase and turned her toward him. "But you look like something else, something one would naturally wish for on a night like this."

"What did you wish for?"

"A lover."

When Arkady opened the station door and she walked into a graveled parking area, something taller than her shuffled its feet on the gravel and snorted, making her stop suddenly so that Arkady bumped her with the suitcase.

"Don't be frightened. We call him Lyagushka." Arkady led her around the horse to the buggy. "Lyagushka means frog. The children named him for the croaking sound he makes when he trots."

The buggy was a four-wheeler with a partially covered wooden compartment open at the front for driver and passenger, and an open box behind. Arkady put her suitcase in the box and helped her up. Then he took out matches and lit two lanterns hung on hooks at the sides of the box. Except for the horse and buggy, the parking area was empty. The only light, besides the yellowish glow of the lanterns, came from the station. When Arkady took the reins and kissed the air quickly three times to start the horse, it became very dark, and soon the paved road became a dirt road. Ahead of them Lyagushka croaked gently, and his scent, mixed with the cool air of night, reminded Jamie of visits to farms and circuses when she was very small and had to be carried by her father.

"I feel as though I'm in an old movie, Arkady. Any moment I expect to see Gypsies camped at the side of the road."

"Perhaps you *will* see Gypsies. Perhaps time will back up, and instead of sleeping in old buses and vans and trailers, the Gypsies will be asleep beneath the stars."

Jamie leaned forward and looked up. "I saw stars before we landed in Kiev, but I don't see any now."

"It's been cloudy all day here. Look, up ahead."

"What?"

"Fog."

And indeed, Lyagushka carried them into a thick patch of ground fog that oozed from a ravine at the side of the road.

"Now I feel as though I'm being kidnapped."

"Perhaps I *have* kidnapped you," said Arkady.

"Where are we going?"

"To another world where no one knows us."

Jamie moved closer to Arkady. "Good."

As Lyagushka croaked ahead in the fog, Arkady put his arm around Jamie and held her tightly while she reached up and touched his bald head.

"Your head is cold. You should wear a hat."

"I'm experimenting to see if damp evening air promotes hair growth."

"It's so smooth. I didn't think chemotherapy did such a thorough job. I was away the times my mother had it."

"I cheated," said Arkady. "I've been shaving every other day in order not to resemble a dog with mange."

"Do you use an electric razor?"

"Yes, why?"

"I just wondered, with the horse and buggy and all."

When they came out of the fog, Jamie saw lights to the left. The lights came from the windows of small houses. Some of the lights flickered in unison, and she realized this was the flicker of televisions in the houses.

"The village has a new addition," said Arkady as they came upon a satellite dish mounted to the top of a small shed. "Now they get channels from everywhere. My mother would have enjoyed it. She watched a lot of television during her last months. I've witnessed a lot of people staring at the television just before they die. It's as if a parallel world lacking the causes of death beckons from behind the screen."

Jamie felt suddenly cold when she recognized the village she had visited so long ago. She held Arkady more tightly.

"I never told you about my mother's death because I knew you were fond of her. Every time I tried to write about her death, the words sounded superficial. She died shortly after the home moved to its new location outside town. I've often wondered whether my moving that small distance from her had something to do with it. When the home was in the village where you last visited, my mother was close enough so that she often walked over to see us when the weather was pleasant."

"Your father? And your sisters?"

"Everyone else is fine. My father is probably there now in his chair in front of the television. He likes to watch sports. It's very strange, isn't it?"

"What?"

"Driving a horse and buggy past houses where the victims of botched technology are, as you would say, glued to the screen. Riding in the buggy, especially at night, always makes me wonder about the logic of our world."

"Last time I was here you had a car. Is this your sole means of transportation now?"

Arkady laughed. "No, I only use Lyagushka when the weather is right and because the station is only a few miles away. Otherwise we have a couple of old buses and a new electric van." Arkady tickled her ribs. "I hope I haven't disappointed you. I know you wished for travel backward in time."

When Jamie tickled Arkady's fleshless ribs, his laughter made Lyagushka trot faster, and soon the porch lights of what resembled a large mansion from the old American south loomed up out of the fog.

"We're here!" shouted Arkady, and soon several children ran to them from the brightly lit porch, some shouting, "Lyagushka! Lyagushka!" while an old man walking arm-in-arm with a heavyset woman followed.

As Arkady helped Jamie down from the buggy, the old man steadied Lyagushka while the woman held hands with two little girls who stared at Jamie and twisted and bit their lips in childlike embarrassment.

"Tea and cake are ready," said the old woman.

The children ran ahead to the house cheering. Behind them, as she and Arkady and the old woman walked up the porch steps, Jamie could hear Lyagushka croaking gently as the old man whispered his name again and again while leading him to a huge dark barn in the distance.

☢ ☢ ☢

Arkady was so thin as she held him in her arms that night. So thin that she felt she must never let go. If she did, he might slip away into the night and never return. His mother having died without her knowing might have had something to do with how she felt that night. His mother lighting the *samovar* and, as if it were a ritual to which a wish could be attached, saying that, together or apart, she and Arkady would always remain together in her heart.

She held Arkady tightly that night and, although it filled her eyes with tears, she thought of her own mother — the loss of weight, the powdery ashes floating on the surface of the lake for a moment before sinking. She also thought of her father and Bianca and Hiram and how, although few persons had been close to her during her life, it seemed many were being taken away. She thought of Brian and how unfair she had been to him. She wondered if depression would overcome her as it had for nearly a month following her last visit to Arkady. Or would three more years of maturity have made her . . . made her what? Colder?

"Perhaps, dear Jamie, you've grown allergic to me."

"Why do you say that?"

"Because your eyes are wet and I can taste your salt."

"Seeing you without hair made me sad."

"Ahh, but a bald head should make you happy."

"Why?"

"When I rub you with it like this — and like this — how does it feel?"

"It feels good."

"See? Everything that happens has its good side."

"And earlier, when you had that pain?"

"Simply my liver. The doctors say it is a bit enlarged. See how simple? It takes up too much space, you press against it, I say ouch. By the way, where is your liver? Is it here? Or here? Perhaps here?"

"I don't think so."

Arkady kissed her. "You know what I would do if I were starting out in school again?"

"What?"

"I'd be a doctor."

"So you could examine all the young ladies?"

"Yes, but only ladies as beautiful as you. I must draw the line somewhere."

☢ ☢ ☢

In the middle of the night, as she lay awake listening to Arkady's labored breathing, Jamie heard a dog howling in the distance. It seemed farther away than the outbuildings of the pensioners' home and orphanage, but she could not be certain because her arrival in the dark had given no clue to the size of the grounds. The only things she had seen when she arrived were the large barn, the columned front porch of the main house, the kitchen, complete with *samovar*, and Arkady's room on the main floor, the room in which she now lay, the room in which the first thing she'd noticed was her photograph on the bedside table. In the dark she could just see the rectangular outline of the frame and she wondered if the photograph was always here beside Arkady's bed or if it had recently been removed from a drawer.

As if he had read her mind, Arkady suddenly took a deep, rattling breath and turned toward her. "Jamie?"

"I thought you were asleep."

"Perhaps I should go to another room."

"Why?"

"Noisy lungs."

"But they work okay?"

"Of course. Do I have to prove it again?"

"Maybe you should rest."

Arkady sat up on the edge of the bed, coughed several times. "Yes, perhaps after . . . after I rest up."

Arkady went into the hall and she heard the bathroom door close. He was gone a long time and she heard coughing. When he came back he fell asleep quickly, his breathing becoming deep and steady. Outside, the dog had stopped howling and dawn began to creep up the curtains.

She was in another world, a world of weariness and despair and letting-go. She fell asleep.

☢☢   ☢☢   ☢☢

When she awoke, the sun was high and bright, the window was open wide, Arkady was doing deep knee bends while breathing in the late morning air, and the despair that often comes in the early hours of morning was gone.

Breakfast consisted of cornmeal pancakes — which Yelena, the plump woman who had welcomed them the night before, called Transylvanian pancakes — stewed prunes, chilled fresh cherries, and lemon tea. After breakfast Arkady and Jamie went on the grand tour.

The home, which was called *Svyezhl Ozero* (Fresh Lake), was actually a varied mix of buildings that had been a collective farm in the previous century before democratization. The main house was the oldest building, an old hunting lodge that had somehow survived two wars and was recently refurbished. Most of the pensioners and children lived in the smaller houses and cottages that were once part of the collective. The farm buildings were used for livestock and there was a cherry orchard, a plum orchard, and vegetable gardens.

A small lake — Fresh Lake — bordered the orchards. When Jamie saw the lake, with its single wooden pier and two wooden rowboats, she immediately compared it to Wylie Lake in Michigan. She imagined this was how Wylie Lake must have looked in the late 1800s after loggers had gone through and before the first summer cottages had been built.

The living arrangements at the home were relatively simple.

When a pensioned couple arrived, they would be given a cottage and one or two orphaned children to care for. When single pensioners arrived, they would occupy rooms in segregated cottages until, and if, they found a partner of the same or opposite sex with whom they felt comfortable. If so, the new couple would decide whether to take on children to care for. Because of the reputation of the home, this pairing of elderly men and women, and the subsequent responsibility for one or more children, was the normal progression for pensioners who came to live there.

And so, the children were given a life closer to that which a family would provide, and the pensioners were given a sense of purpose — the "generativity" Arkady referred to as he took Jamie on tour.

The adjacent town of Svyezhl, which could be seen from a hilltop on the other side of the lake, provided the schooling and other community services. When she and Arkady sat on the grassy hill to rest after their walk around the lake, Jamie could see across the lake where the horse from the night before and a few cattle grazed. In the distance she could also see the satellite dish at the village and, farther away, the metro tracks, straight as Illinois Central tracks, traversing the steppes of the Ukraine.

"I keep waiting for you to mention Thoreau," said Arkady.

"*Walden* was subtitled, *Life in the Woods*," said Jamie. "There are no woods here, and your lake is much larger than Walden Pond."

"Have you seen Walden Pond?"

"Yes, but it wasn't what I'd expected. Through the years it's been surrounded by housing developments."

"From what you've seen here, do you think the effort has been worth it?"

Jamie turned to Arkady. "You shouldn't have to ask that. You have a wonderful atmosphere of community and cooperation here."

"I remember," said Arkady, "that wonderful spring long ago when we went to visit your parents at their cottage. I remember your father asking about the collective system and his hope that some of the advantages might have remained as the government in my country went through its changes. Perhaps what he said then had an effect on my planning here."

"That's very kind of you to say, Arkady. I'll tell him when I see him."

"With all the campaigning, I suppose you don't see him often."

"No."

"You are famous for much more than the normal fifteen minutes," said Arkady. "It started when you were still a student in Moscow. However, what some call your claim to fame was heightened greatly when you gave your Earth Day speech. Do you sometimes wish you were not so well-known, that you had more privacy?"

"I try to keep my private life separate from my public life. But, yes, I do sometimes wish I had more privacy. Often, when I think about privacy, I long for those days when we were in school together. There'll be hard times ahead for me. I know it, but I accept it."

"Everyone has hard times ahead," said Arkady. "But very few admit it."

"Do you wish you were back in school, knowing what's ahead for you?"

"I'm not sure," said Arkady, shaking his head. "Lately, when I think of all the effort of youth spent studying in school, and all the work I've put into this place, I become tired. Perhaps that is also the reason I sometimes wonder whether it has been worth the effort."

"The home?"

"Yes. One part of the project has disappointed me greatly."

"What part?"

"The children from Chernobyl." Arkady had pulled a thick, shiny blade of meadow grass and was twisting it about his finger. "See this grass?"

"Yes."

"It's called Chernobyl grass. Not from the disaster, but from the original meaning of the term *Chernobyl.*"

"The biblical legend? The star that was supposed to have come down and leveled everything?"

"Yes. That's why this grass has always been called Chernobyl grass. According to the legend, it was the only thing tough enough to survive." Arkady turned to her. "My disappointment here has been that few who were children at the time of Chernobyl have survived. Two who were boys — in their 50s now — are cared for in the main house. But soon they'll go the way of the rest. Soon we won't be able to care for them and we'll have to send them to hospital. They usually don't last long after that."

"You were a child at the time . . . "

"Yes, but I was an infant, one of the lucky ones sent away to relatives shortly after the accident. I didn't get the full dose like the others."

Arkady tore the blade of Chernobyl grass into several pieces, tossed the pieces aside, looked at her and smiled. "Anyway, do you think Fresh Lake demonstrates the kind of simplicity needed to solve problems?"

"Yes."

"Will you tell your father about Fresh Lake when you see him?"

"I will."

Arkady placed his hand on hers. "Good."

"Arkady?"

"Yes."

"You've seen news about me running for the Senate and you know it takes a lot of work and help from others."

"Yes."

Jamie looked at Arkady's eyes. Arkady's dark brown eyes were somewhat sunken, and with his bald head and loss of weight, his presence seemed suddenly more cerebral than physical, as if the physicalness taken away by the leukemia had left a kind of enlightenment behind.

She said, "You know what I'm going to say, don't you?"

"You're going to bring up two things we must discuss during this visit."

"All right, guru and sage, what are they?"

Arkady stared toward the horizon where the high-pitched whistle of a metro train leaving the station sounded in the distance. "Number one, being in a high political position will occupy most of your time so that we will not see one another very often, at least not in this lifetime."

The approaching metro train sped from the station making a thin silver line like a pen pushed across green paper. Jamie remembered the train to Kiev on her first visit to the Ukraine, remembered the old man on the train, the old man with blue eyes like Brian's eyes, the old man saying he wished he were the young man waiting at the platform for her. She remembered the reporters at the platform in Kiev. Arkady, then with a full head of black hair, jumping up and down behind the reporters as she told about the Dawn Patrol. She remembered the train trip from Champaign to Chicago with Arkady on their way to Wylie Lake that beautiful spring when her mother was still alive. But she also remembered a bus trip. Her and Brian on the way back from a bicycle trip along the Mississippi River. Her and Brian agreeing to remain friends while they pursued their careers.

When the metro finally disappeared beyond the village, Jamie asked, "What is the second thing I was going to say?"

"You were going to say what I, too, must say. You were going to say that, during the years that have passed, there have been others." He turned and stared at her. "Or one other. You were going to say that our lives are moving faster than the relationship we've had. I'm not certain how you might have put it, but you were going to say something that would make us both very sad but would set our hearts free."

"Is there someone now?" she asked.

"No. But there has been. And you?"

"Yes. But I've kept him at a distance."

Arkady stood, took her hand and helped her up. "Now you don't have to keep him at a distance. What's his name?"

"Brian."

"A very good name. This is the same Brian you've spoken of in the past?"

"Yes."

Arkady smiled and kissed her. They embraced. Then they

separated and walked down the hill close together but not touching, not physically.

CHAPTER 17

A SIREN, HIGH-PITCHED, INTERRUPTED the night. He held his breath, kept his eyes tightly closed. The siren recalled stroboscopic dream images of emergency lights illuminating aluminum siding and a fence surrounding a backyard swimming pool.

He took a deep breath, held it again and listened.

After the lowered tones of the receding siren diminished to danger somewhere else for someone else, he heard a gust of wind in the trees. Raindrops, gathered on thousands of oak leaves, drummed the roof and the dream faded. He exhaled, took another deep breath, felt a rattle in his throat as if God would have the final word, sat up, coughed.

"Paul?"

"Okay . . . I'm okay."

"It was a siren on the road. Here, lie back down. Better?"

"Sure. Better."

"The dream again?"

"Yeah."

"Jamie and the other girl in it? Hiram in it?"

"Don't remember. The siren woke me. One of those split-second-coming-awake dreams. Acid trip coming back. Damn thing'll follow me to the grave."

"Turn. Let me rub your shoulders. Better?"

"Yeah."

"Getting old is bullshit when you've got extra baggage on your mind. We should get hold of that Ducain girl's address, write her a letter, ask how it feels to be getting on close to forty. Ask how she feels now about the old man poisoning a town full of folks minding their own business."

"Her feeling guilty won't do any good now, Bianca."

"Sometimes I wonder."

"Ouch, don't rub so hard."

"Better?"

"Yeah."

"How about down here?"

"You're a she-wolf."

"What I always wanted to be."

"I love you."

"We agreed not to talk that kind of bullshit. Reminds us of those who aren't here, and sometimes it's better to forget, at least for a while."

"All right. What should we talk about?"

"I don't know. But if you lay down I talk much better."

"Lie down, baby, so I can talk to you?"

"Yeah. And after that we'll walk, rain or no rain."

☢ ☢ ☢

The overnight rain had freshened the air. Deep in the woods, pines growing sparse but tall amid oaks and maples scented the air. Except where roots and rocks had surfaced, needles and leaves atop sandy soil gave the path a feel like carpet. As the path neared the shore on the far side of the lake, the pine smell was replaced by the faint bittersweet smell of the uncoiled white bark on birches growing amid poplars along the bank.

When Paul and Bianca left the cottage there had been a purplish pre-dawn light in the sky, a few trailing clouds following the rain system away to the south. Now the sky was clear, brightening to the east as the sun made ready to rise.

At the far side of the lake opposite Paul's cottage, they paused in front of Bianca's cottage to watch the sunrise. The varnished pine bench, built by Hiram during his short stay at the cottage before his death, faced the lake in front of the cottage. Droplets of rainwater beaded the bench and Bianca went into her cottage for a towel.

As Paul stood looking out across the lake, he squinted and was barely able to see the painted surface of his cottage on the far shore. Beyond the cottage, the hill above which the sun would rise was in dark shadow because of the contrast against the pink sky. The shape of the hill was oblong and it seemed to Paul a casket-shaped hole in the horizon.

It had been eleven years since Judy's death. Whenever he was alone and thought about that day in the hospital in Traverse City, he wondered when he would die. He was seventy-four. The last time he went to the doctor he was told that, barring an accident or an unforeseen genetic or toxic event in his system, he would eventually join the millions of Americans in the century club. He wondered if in twenty-six years he'd be standing here celebrating his one-hundredth birthday watching yet another sunrise. Or perhaps he'd be sitting, not on Hiram's bench, but wheeled here by Bianca.

Paul turned when he heard the cottage door slam and watched Bianca walk down the porch steps. She wore blue jeans and a white sweatshirt. Her curly hair — salt and pepper now — still reminded him of black power posters from the previous century. There was a slight flattening at the back of Bianca's head where she had pressed into the pillow beneath him shortly before they dressed for their morning walk. As she bent to wipe rainwater from the bench, her hips widened and he could feel her again. He could feel himself within her, a throbbing jungle heat, a continent, Africa. When he sat down on the bench beside Bianca and glanced toward the oblong hole in the horizon — growing even darker because of the sun's approach behind it — he again experienced the overwhelming feeling of not deserving what he had been given following Judy's death. Bianca was at his side. They were living a life he had always dreamed of living with Judy. His daughter was Lieutenant Governor of Illinois, running for the United States Senate. No. He didn't deserve any of it.

"Are you still nervous about today's interview?" asked Bianca.

"Knowing millions of people will see it, and my gut feeling that what we have here isn't all that special, makes it hard not to be nervous."

"Try to think about Bill. They'll be talking to him and he's had a stroke. At least we won't be fumbling for words." Bianca held his hand. "I'll be there. When they ask a stupid question, just remember I'll be thinking *bullshit* while I'm saying all those syrupy things."

"Why can't we be left alone? Other people retire and don't have to put up with this."

Bianca touched his cheek, turned his face so he would look at her. "You're the one who always went on about commitment, Paul. You're the one who invited the rest of us up here to live this so-called self-sufficient life of yours. Don't start this *why me?* bullshit again."

"Why not? Where is it written that you and I aren't allowed privacy?"

"I suppose we didn't have privacy this morning. I suppose they've got cameras poking through the knotty pine. Maybe they'll use a recording of us to sell mattresses or some of those so-called enhancement pills. When will you stop feeling sorry for yourself, Paul? Sometimes you're like a goddamn little kid!"

Paul stood, spun around to face Bianca. "Damn it! I don't feel *sorry* for myself!"

"What do you feel?"

"What I feel is . . . is that I don't deserve any of this! Not the cottage or the lake or the damn sunrise or Jamie . . . or you!"

Bianca stood, took both his hands in hers. She stared at him for a moment. Then she smiled and spoke softly. "You're right. But it's not just you. I also have those feelings. Why do you suppose I haven't sold the cottage? We keep fooling ourselves by saying it's a good investment, that because of global warming the land up here to the east of Lake Michigan will skyrocket. But that's so much more bullshit. Sure, it's a good investment, but for who?"

Bianca stared at him, her eyes wet and pinkish from the coming sunrise. "You know the real reason I don't sell this place is because of Hiram. Hiram's dead, but he's still here. Everything we've done, everyone we've met or kissed or made love to will always be around to poke us in the ribs. Admit it. If Judy were here you'd still complain about the interview today."

"I know," said Paul. "She'd say I brought it on myself, spouting off about how I think others should live their lives and make a few sacrifices."

"And," said Bianca, "she'd say it's your turn."

Bianca looked over Paul's shoulder, her brown skin aglow, the gray in her hair turning orange. She put her hand on his shoulder, turned him around and they sat to watch the sunrise over Wylie Lake.

☢ ☢ ☢

The interviewer for the *20/20* spot that would be aired the following week was a young man with thick black hair and mustache. During a tour of the east side of Wylie Lake, Bianca whispered to Paul that the young man looked like a teenager. Although the young man was not a teenager, he was young for a *20/20* interviewer. His name was Anwar, one of the first well-known television personalities of Arab ancestry on United States network television. Anwar was born at the turn of the century. Although his parents, second-generation Arab-Americans, named Anwar after assassinated Egyptian President Anwar el-Sadat, Anwar had called himself Andy during the years of Middle-East terror, until being assigned by the network to *20/20* when he reverted to his given name.

The tour started at Paul's cottage. Paul showed Anwar his catalytic-converter wood stove, his solar-augmented water heater, his new geothermal furnace, and his pedal boat with its alternate solar-charged battery power.

After touring Paul's cottage, the crew, Anwar, Paul, and Bianca moved on to Bill Cochran's cottage where they viewed Bill's 12-volt solar-powered lighting system, his experimental septic system methane gas producer, the hot water heater fueled by the methane, and the Wylie Lake electric van stored in Bill's garage.

Bill conducted the tour from his wheelchair, not talking much, but gesturing enthusiastically while his wife or Paul or Bianca did the talking for him. They finished up the tour at the edge of Bill's property where the composting unit for residents on the east side of the lake was maintained.

While at the composting unit, Bill blurted out something about peanut butter and jelly, then looked down and shook his head sadly. Bill's wife, who was standing beside his wheelchair, said, "Because of the stroke, Bill gets words mixed around. But I know what he means."

"What does he mean?" asked Anwar.

"Peanut butter and jelly are foods that do well together. Our composter mixes all kinds of foods and leaves and things and does the environment a good turn. I've been reading the research on strokes. Lots of folks still think strokes make a person stupid. But that isn't true at all." She placed her hand on Bill's shoulder. "Bill's still smarter than most folks. Only now he doesn't have to mess with meaningless how-do-you-do words when peanut butter and jelly says it all."

Following the tour, Anwar interviewed Paul and Bianca at the lakeshore in front of Paul's cottage. They sat at Paul's picnic table near the foot of the dock where the rowboat and pedal boat were tied. Paul and Bianca sat on one side of the bench, Anwar sat on the other side. The cameraman stood at the end of the bench, using the lake as a backdrop.

"Tell us about your trip three years ago in the electric van," said Anwar.

"We went west," said Paul. "That was before Bill's stroke. We went with Bill and his wife. GM sponsored it. There weren't many recharging stations then. Had to follow a kind of zigzag route."

"I understand you took a ferry across Lake Michigan to start."

"Yes. It was the opening run of a new schedule from Ludington to Chicago. Back in the early 1900s there were lots of ferries and cruise ships on the Great Lakes. By the 1970s and 80s most of the old coal-powered lines had been discontinued, not because of the use of coal, but because it was faster and cheaper to travel by car. I'm glad to say things have changed now."

"A lot of people say community groups like the one here at Wylie Lake help bring those changes about," said Anwar. "What do you think about that?"

"I don't think we do anything special."

Anwar turned to Bianca. "What do you think, Bianca?"

"I think everything we do in life has an effect on those around us."

"Can you give an example from your own life?"

"My husband was in Vietnam," said Bianca. "The war affected the rest of his life and the things he said about the war affected everyone he met."

"In what way?"

"He let them know that war is a hell of a thing. He showed them — without having to be there — that a place where there's war is a place you don't want to be."

"Since you brought up your husband, Bianca . . . and Paul, since we spoke earlier about your wife, there's something you know I must bring up."

"Yes," said Paul, "go ahead."

"All right," said Anwar. "Both of you have lived during a time when segregation was still fairly common in this country. Tell me, either one of you, how you happened to get together and how your relationship with one another has affected those around you."

Neither answered for a moment, the cameraman alternating with face-on shots of them both. Then Bianca spoke.

"It's like this. Paul and my husband were friends for many years. The fact that Paul and I are the color we are, and happen to live together, isn't as important these days as the fact that we live together and no one particularly cares. It's like you being on *20/20*. After the terrorist attacks and war at the beginning of the century, I don't think *20/20* would have hired an Anwar no matter how good he was. Things are different now. What's important today is that Paul and I being together doesn't make people want to throw sheets over their heads."

Anwar turned to Paul. "Anything you'd like to add?"

"Bianca doesn't bullshit around."

"We might edit that," said Anwar smiling.

"I hope so," said Paul. "That way Bianca will have the last word."

Eventually Paul did answer more questions because he was the only one who could. The questions were about Jamie's rapid rise in politics over the past several years. After he answered the traditional how-does-it-feel-to-have-a-daughter question, which Paul answered by saying he was very proud, Anwar asked about Jamie's critics.

"Paul, your daughter has some rather outspoken critics, especially in the business community. They say she emphasizes domestic problems only because she was out of the country for so long when she was Russian ambassador. They say she isn't really interested in Illinois or its people, but simply wants to use the United States Senate to pursue her international environmental agenda. How do you answer those critics?"

Paul turned to look out at the lake for a moment, then looked back to Anwar. "I'd say, look, the world's gotten a hell of a lot smaller so that state and local officials need to be interested in global affairs, especially when it comes to the environment. But I'd also point out that my daughter has some damn good ideas to help people back home."

"Can you be specific?" asked Anwar.

"Well, she did a lot for that IHPS thing they have in Illinois."

Anwar elaborated. "The Illinois Health Preservation System for health care?"

"Right. And she's got some good ideas to help people get out of poverty. Not simply handouts, a new system where getting people back into the mainstream is rewarded all around, where that goal is built into the system. Is that specific enough?"

"Sure," said Anwar.

Before the interview was over, Paul got in a plug for a friend of his named Eric Shaw who had retired to Florida. Eric had been a programmer with Hiram and Paul for many years and had contacted

Paul after the publicity following the electric van trip. Eric headed a volunteer group of retirees who traveled around the Miami area tracking down old refrigerators and air-conditioners in order to safely bleed and neutralize CFCs that would otherwise eventually escape and affect the Earth's ozone layer.

When Paul finished his spiel about Eric's work in Florida, Anwar promised he would use it on the show. "Like I said earlier," added Bianca, "everything we do makes a difference."

"Yes, ma'am," said Anwar, looking out across the lake.

☢ ☢ ☢

That evening after dinner, while they watched news about Jamie's arrival back from her visit to the Ukraine, Paul said, "I wonder if something that happened here might have caused Arkady's leukemia."

"Why would you wonder that?" asked Bianca.

"Because of the time he came out to help when Jamie and I capsized the sailboat in the storm. What if the lightning strike, in combination with the dose of radiation he got at Chernobyl, was the trigger that made a DNA molecule throw that one cell off?"

"Or," said Bianca, "what if the lightning delayed a DNA molecule from acting for a few more years? What if the lightning was from heaven to give Arkady the chance to help all those old folks and orphans over there?"

"We'll never know."

"Not in this place."

While the news commentator mentioned Jamie's rise in the polls for the United States Senate race, the screen showed Jamie at a train platform in Chicago.

"It sure is unfair what happened to those two," said Bianca. "Imagine being young like they were and not even being able to consider marriage because one doesn't want to hurt the other."

When the news switched to another story, Paul stood and went to the window. "Not too long and the sun will be down."

"Want to go on up the hill?" asked Bianca. "Make it last longer?"

"It's already been a long day," said Paul.

"So what?" said Bianca.

The climb seemed longer and slower than usual, Paul pulling Bianca along, then Bianca pulling Paul along. They made the top of the hill just as the sun touched the treetops on the far side of the lake. They turned toward the sun and sat on the weathered, barkless log they had been using for the past few years when watching sunsets from the hill.

When the sun was almost gone, Paul said, "Should we get married?"

Bianca took a deep breath and said, "I don't want a ceremony, Paul. I don't want reminders. No bullshit. Just us."

When the sun had disappeared and the cool of night began to creep in, Paul stood and helped Bianca up. "Time to go."

"Besides," said Bianca, slapping Paul's behind, "I like doing it and not being married."

"Why?"

"Because this way folks are always left guessing and it makes for real juicy gossip."

CHAPTER 18

THE *20/20* EDITING STAFF COMPLETED the final cut of the Wylie Lake story three days before the show would air. Heather West was given access to the cut to help her prepare for a final commentary in her five-part series, "Senior Settlements, Baby Boomers Grow Old." The series dealt with several settlements in the country where retirees lived together in cooperatives reminiscent of the communes of their youth. Heather's final commentary in the series was timed to be on the newscast following the broadcast of the Wylie Lake interview on *20/20*. The tie-in with the *20/20* show, along with teasers during commercials, was expected to substantially increase the audience share on that evening's network news.

The first four parts in Heather's series had covered the social and community services performed by the senior settlements. The final part of the series was to take a look at senior settlements claiming to be self-sufficient and environmentally neutral — thus the tie-in with the Wylie Lake spot on *20/20*.

During the first part of this last commentary in the series, Heather summarized positive activities at many of the settlements and praised the seniors for their unselfish generosity. After the praise, however, Heather said that, as a responsible journalist, she was required to bring up what she called, "a dark side of old age." She said she did not mean death. What she meant was an isolationism and complacency some of the settlements had demonstrated. She used the Wylie Lake settlement as an example.

Where *20/20* had contended that the Wylie Lake settlement was one of several serving as models for the eventual development of nationwide, and perhaps worldwide, environmentally neutral communities, Heather criticized Wylie Lake residents for being naïve, for trying to sell the American public on that naïveté, and for being unashamedly socialistic. She questioned whether, rather than actively seeking ways to help fellow citizens, the retirees at Wylie Lake had simply found a way to withdraw from reality.

Then, after a brief description of the Fresh Lake Compound in the village of Svyezhl in the Ukraine — a description in which Heather stressed the cohabitation of unmarried seniors — she claimed that what she'd seen of the Wylie Lake settlement reminded her of an old brand of communism not only because of its emphasis on all members sharing the goods despite their work or lack thereof, but because of what she called a "denigration of the moral values of their members."

At the conclusion of the commentary Heather said that, like anyone else, seniors had the right to choose their partners and friends and to live their lives as they wished. What Heather objected to was, "the lifestyle of one group of elders being held up as a moral model for the rest of us."

When Heather left the studio after recording the commentary that would be aired that night, the director in the control room — the same woman who had directed the interview with then Illinois State congressional candidate Jamie Carter over ten years earlier — turned to the sound engineer and said, "I'd say Heather came off as a right-wing bitch on this one."

"Who knows," said the sound engineer, taking off his earphones. "Maybe she'll come out looking objective and cop a Pulitzer."

"I hope not. If she gets promoted I might have to work for her."

"I wouldn't mind working for her."

"How come?"

The engineer smiled a leering smile and said, "Because, unlike you, I'd *like* to kiss her ass."

☢ ☢ ☢

In the plane on the flight to New York, Heather hoped the seat next to her in first class would remain empty. But before the cabin door was closed, a young man rushed on board and plopped down next to her. The man had ridiculously long hair and a bushy mustache. He wore a loose tie-dyed shirt and looked like a throwback to the previous century. After he caught his breath he began talking incessantly.

"Good thing they have that seventy-five-percent-full rule otherwise I don't think they would have waited. In the old days they used to fly half empty. Name's Connie, short for Conrad. Conrad's my stage name. I'm in that musical, *Dead Heads*. Heard of it?"

Heather nodded.

"Great nostalgia for the old folks. When you look at the old farts now it's hard to imagine them as fans back then. I wasn't even born until 2001, right after the attacks in New York. We open tomorrow night for another month. So far so good. You look familiar . . . "

"Heather West."

"Hey, yeah, on the news. Cool."

"You've picked up the slang of the times, I see."

"Slang?"

"Yes. Cool."

"Yeah. Heavy."

Conrad talked during taxi and takeoff. But then, perhaps because she was very "cool" toward him, his eyes became "heavy." When he finally fell asleep she relished the hypnotic whine of the engines.

After the plane climbed through the clouds, Heather could see only blackness below and a starry moonless sky above. Flying, when no one was talking next to her, made her feel quite alone. She liked that, being alone. Perhaps it was in her genes. Perhaps that was why her mother had chosen complete isolation from the world. She knew her mother could not be faking, not after the things she'd told her, especially when she told how Peter might not have been the one who got little Jennifer pregnant.

Alone. She imagined flying west instead of east, heading to her mountain hideaway. If she were telekinetic she could will the plane to turn about. She'd glance to the side and, presto, the seat next to her would be empty. Everyone going to New York on another plane. She, alone, headed to the mountain cabin. Perhaps she'd parachute into the mountains instead of renting a car in Denver.

She turned toward the seat next to her, saw Conrad sleeping with his mouth agape like a fur-lined tunnel, and caught herself chuckling aloud. She'd tell Jack about this Dead Head from the past and how ridiculous it was to waste time on the past when everything that meant anything was in the future.

To Jack, the future meant a life together hopping between condominiums located in countries of semi-tropical climate. For Jack, to enter retirement with a lovely and successful woman twenty years younger than himself at his side was to be his dream come true. But to her, the future was something completely different.

Whenever Heather tried to imagine her real future — not the fictitious one Jack painted — she visualized herself alone at the mountain cabin. Alone, yet knowing she's had an effect on the world. *That* was a future worth working for.

Last year on their wedding anniversary, Jack gave her a hundred thousand dollars. She'd used part of the money to pay off the remainder she owed on the cabin. The rest she spent on clothing and jewelry, partially because she wanted them, partially to continue the cover-up of the cabin she'd secretly been making payments on through a Denver broker. Now the cabin, and the acreage surrounding it, was hers. Although she'd been there only three times, she carried her recollection of its serenity and isolation with her.

At the cabin she was a different woman, able to turn the past on its head. Standing proudly beside her father in the courtroom instead of lurking in the rear with her older brother while her father stares guiltily down at his hands folded on the defense table. Or feeling sorry for her friend Jamie who just might have had a disturbing past in which she's been abused by a family member. Or having parents — good parents — with guts enough to stick it out in this shitty world instead of . . .

As the plane began its descent and the lights of Manhattan came into view, Heather looked at her watch, saw it was after eleven Eastern time and the news would be on. She wondered if Jamie would see her final commentary in the series. Perhaps, later tonight, Jamie would call to congratulate her.

No, Jamie would not call. Jamie would never call again, not since that last call when she told Jamie they had nothing in common, that their friendship was over.

When the plane touched down, Conrad woke from the dead and began babbling again about his part in the musical. While he spoke, Heather stared at his mustache and imagined the mustache aflame in the fiery crash. But, as usual, the plane landed safely.

The penthouse overlooked Central Park. When Heather walked down the hall into the living room, she saw Jack standing at the window in his robe. Jack's gray hair was thickened from being blow-dried, and when he turned from the view of the park, he smiled and sipped his drink.

Heather put her bag down on the sofa and walked past Jack to look out the window. Jack came close behind her and caressed her shoulder.

"I've been saving it for you," he said.

"What's that?" asked Heather.

"The view. I told them to keep it just the way it was so it would be perfect for your arrival."

Heather continued staring out the window. "Your mating signals are quite consistent."

He moved his hand from her shoulder to her neck, caressing the back of her neck at the hairline. "Which mating signals?"

She turned slowly so that his hand, remaining where it was, ended up at the open vee of her blouse. She looked down as he moved his hand lower, reaching into her blouse like a boy reaching for cookies.

"Robe, drink, view," she said. "Those are your mating signals."

"You don't approve?"

She backed away slowly as Jack held his hand limply in the air, staring at it sadly as if it were an injured bird. Then he looked at her.

"Where are you going?" asked Jack.

"To the bedroom," said Heather.

"Not out here?"

"Not this time. I was on the air tonight and the ratings were probably pretty damn good with the tie-in."

"I thought you liked being recognized."

"Not through thick lenses."

Jack put down his drink and followed her to the bedroom. While she undressed, Heather asked Jack what he thought of her final commentary, but he did not answer. Instead he took off his robe, helped her finish undressing and insisted they talk about it later.

☢ ☢ ☢

"Jack?"

"Yes?"

"You said you'd tell me what you thought."

"It was lovely as usual, my dear."

"The commentary, Jack."

"Very well. If I must. You see, darling, I'm afraid the news isn't quite as good as you expected. Too late to do anything about it now, but Shelby from marketing called. It seems a representative from Ford called to say your timing with such a negative viewpoint on a newscast with a story featuring the announcement of a new Ford electric van left something to be desired. The actual quote, I'm sorry to say, was, 'Is she from the Middle Ages, or what?' "

When Heather did not comment on this, Jack touched her arm. "Don't concern yourself, lover. It's not the end of the world. I told Shelby you haven't been feeling well lately. I said you'd be taking a few weeks off. By then it will blow over. These things always do."

Heather opened her eyes wider, trying to see in the dark. She turned toward Jack but could see only his outline against the lights of the city coming through the drapes at the balcony door. She pulled her arm away.

"Heather, darling, it's all right. No one in the network knows you and Jamie Carter were once friends. Although I can't for the life of me understand why you would go after her father."

"I didn't go after anybody!"

"Please don't tell me picking on her father was a coincidence. Please don't tell me you really meant those things you said, because I don't know if I can believe that."

She turned away from Jack and got out of bed. She went into the bathroom, closed the door, turned on the light and looked into the mirror. The two age lines that had appeared at the outside corners of her eyes when she hit thirty-five were lengthening as she approached forty. She held her fingertips to her face, squeezed the skin to elongate the lines.

She let go of her face and the lines shortened, the distortion of the pinching, that had made a scary face like a child trying to create a monster, was gone. She was still a beautiful woman, a woman who most likely made millions of guest appearances in nightly wet dreams throughout the country. Jack had joked about that. "When you're on the air some time," he'd said, "imagine all the adolescent wet dreams you'll be in that night. Try it. I think it will give you a wonderful smile."

Jack was also the one who suggested cosmetic surgery. Only if she wanted it, he had said. Not that she really needed it. Not yet. But cosmetic surgery didn't fit in with her long-term plans. A survivor didn't need cosmetic surgery. All a survivor needed was . . .

"Heather?" It was Jack outside the door. "Come on, Heather. What is this thing with you and Jamie Carter? You haven't spoken to her in years, yet you bear this ridiculous grudge."

"I told you. I just don't care for her."

"But there's got to be a reason, Heather. Look, imagine you're in the confessional and I'm the priest. You can't see me, I can't see you, and I don't know who you are. You've said your bless-me-Fathers and we're ready for the naked truth. So tell me, young lady, why is it you have committed the sin of enmity against this other woman?"

The face in the mirror smiled back at her. She couldn't help it. Jack was crazy and his craziness always made her smile.

"Come, come, young lady. The confessional is a place for cleansing. Tell Father Confessor the truth and he'll come right in there and wash away your sins. He'll put you into the tub and wash you. Or, better yet, Father Confessor will remove his robes and get into the tub with you. Perhaps, in a Christ-like way of course, he'll let you eat of his flesh. Purely Christ-like, mind you. It's the least Father can do to save your soul."

The face in the mirror was no longer smiling. It was a face full of fear and loathing. She turned, opened the door and fell into Jack's arms as she sobbed.

"It's okay, Heather. You'll be okay."

"I . . . I didn't mean it."

"I know. I understand."

"She . . . she doesn't deserve what she has. She's never deserved it. Where's it written I have to hold in all this shit about someone . . . about someone who might be a goddamn senator. Someone whose parents were drug dealers. Someone who goes into bars and invites men back to her motel room."

Jack held her at arms length and stared at her. "Drug dealers?"

"They used drugs. Her father experimented with acid. But that other thing, the men in the bar, the motel . . . My God, she told me about it years ago and I've never been able to make myself forget. Especially the abortion. I'll never forget how matter-of-fact she was when she told me about the abortion. And now, imagine a senator with the hang-ups she must have . . . "

Jack stared at her, a momentary look of shock on his face before he answered. "Heather, there's nothing you can do. My advice is to stay clear of her. You can't prove a damn thing and there's no forum for proving anything. You were both children. She made up the escapade for shock effect . . . "

"But she was hemorrhaging! I saw it! I saw the blood when she came out of the motel!"

☢ ☢ ☢

After Jack had fallen asleep, Heather went through the bathroom to her room and put on a sweatsuit and running shoes. The top of the sweatsuit had deep pockets and she went to her dresser drawer, dug beneath her underwear, took out her pistol and put it into her right pocket.

After she got off the elevator, she ran through the lobby where the doorman smiled and said, "Have a safe run."

It was peaceful in the park, but she was not alone. There were other runners and walkers and a bicycle or two. Then, of course, there were the Park Angels in their yellow sweatshirts and caps. Every time she passed an Angel, he or she gave her a chest level salute that seemed a throwback to an ancient dictatorship.

Although Heather was not alone in the park no matter what time of night she ran, she still felt a sense of isolation. Perhaps it was the exertion that split her off onto a side track so that she was able to look at her life more objectively. Yes, running was a cleansing ritual, much as the rape in the motel north of Champaign had been a cleansing ritual. But it was still no good, still not cleansing enough. The only thing that would be truly cleansing would be total and complete physical isolation.

On her way back to the building, Heather saw a light halfway up and to the right and knew it was the light on the balcony outside Jack's bedroom. The light had not been on when she left and she knew Jack would be there when she got back, his binoculars in hand and him repeating again that, no matter how many Park Angels were out, he wished she wouldn't run in the middle of the night.

Poor Jack. What would he do when she disappeared?

CHAPTER 19

THE SMELL OF FRYING FISH quickly fills the cottage, permeating every room, even closets. A closet in one of the bedrooms is open. A man's shirts and slacks and sweatshirts neatly arranged on hangers absorb the smells from the kitchen. The bedroom is small, its double bed made up but obviously sagging from years of use. A single nightstand contains a framed photograph of a young couple in bathing suits standing at the lakeshore. They stand on either side of a small sailboat pulled up onto the shore. The sailboat leans toward the young man and he reaches out with one hand holding onto the mast of the sailboat. The young woman holds both hands out toward the man as if making a presentation for the benefit of the camera of the man holding the sailboat mast. Behind them the lake is calm, the sky cloudless.

Tucked into a lower corner of the frame, directly below the image of the young man holding the sailboat mast is a funeral card. Below an ornate crucifix at the top of the card is the name Arkady Lyashko. The remainder of the card is printed in small Cyrillic type.

The cottage's kitchen window above the sink faces east and the morning sun shines onto the floor between the table and the stove. The young man sitting at the table watching the old woman frying fish is not the young man in the photograph in the bedroom. Although they both have dark hair, the young man in the photograph in the bedroom is much thinner with a prominent nose and bushy eyebrows. The man in the kitchen has a small nose and his complexion is darkened by the short stubble of thick facial hair.

The table is set for two; salads, bread, and two glasses of water await the fried fish.

"You know who I am," says the old woman, her back to the young man as she continues frying the fish.

"Yes," says the young man. "Your name is Bianca. My uncle's family told me. My name is Joe. I was named after my uncle. We're the only two Joes in the family."

Bianca finishes putting the last of the fried fish on a plate and walks slowly into the sunlight coming through the window as she brings the plate to the table. Joe stands, pulls a chair out for her and Bianca sighs as she sits down.

When Joe returns to his chair, Bianca begins dishing up the fish, and also begins recalling the Presidential election of the year 2032.

☢ ☢ ☢

It was spring, the Presidential election of 2032 rapidly approaching. Although the party conventions were still months off, the major parties seemed to have already reached a consensus during the primaries. Because the outgoing Republican President was finishing his second term, it seemed the young Vice President was a shoe-in for his party's nomination. The Worker's Independent Party offered yet another Texan to woo votes away from the Republicans and

Democrats. And on the Democratic side, the elder senator from Illinois, who had declined nomination for years, had succumbed to pressure and agreed to run, much to the relief of his party. Senator Jim Hansen announced his intention to run during an informal celebration of his sixty-ninth birthday hosted by his Illinois colleague, Senator Jamie Carter.

The Republican's front runner, who was from California, was being called a traditionalistic. Senator Hansen was being called a progressive. The Independent's candidate had been dubbed a libertarian. All three candidates said they wanted to maintain peace in the world while fighting terrorism; all three said they were strong on the environment; all three said they planned to deal with the national and world economic situation.

In 2032 it was obvious the environment and the world economy were forever linked. Previous Earth summits had been hampered by delaying tactics and even by terrorist disruptions. This had helped neither the world economy nor the environment. The huge costs of converting from fossil fuels to hydrogen, solar, wind, and nuclear in the developed nations carried the burden of blame for the world's problems. The recent London Environmental Protocol threatened to be a repeat of past failures. The reason for potential failure was the ongoing reluctance of developed countries to subsidize underdeveloped countries to enable them to skip the period of fossil fuel dependency that the developed countries went through in the twentieth century. Many said there was no choice. If underdeveloped countries were left to their own resources, they would evolve through the fossil fuel stages of their forebears, adding substantially to global warming in their efforts to feed their starving people. And so, according to most world leaders, the new technologies *must* be handed over. It was a matter of world survival. As one member of the London Protocol Committee stated, "Given the choice between a decade of economic depression and the world disaster that would result from a one-meter rise in sea level, I'll take the depression every time."

Although, at the time of the London Protocol, the mean temperature increase on Earth since the beginning of the century was less than two degrees Celsius, and average ocean rise was still being measured in centimeters, the projections were not good. According to robotic ocean temperature measurements, the Earth continued absorbing much more energy from the sun than it radiated into space because of the still increasing greenhouse effect. And, according to computer models generated at research centers throughout the world, the mean temperature would keep rising at an alarming rate until mid-century despite measures in effect or to be taken in the future. The result would be oceans a half meter higher than present levels, even with the stringent worldwide "anti-warming" efforts already in effect and already planned. A terrorist group in the Middle East that had specialized in setting oil wells and refineries on fire during the previous decades went so far as to accept responsibility for the projected rise in sea levels and indicated there was more to come.

On the positive side, the majority in all countries refused to take the predictions lying down. Throughout the world, local regulations regarding near shore development were in place and coastal cities were beginning to "build-back." Because of these regulations, it was determined that by mid-century, damage to coastal cities would be greatly reduced.

To minimize the amount of greenhouse gases, many imaginative ideas were already being tried. At a solar generating farm in Kansas, an experiment was being performed in the shade beneath the solar collection panels. Here, a quarter-mile long row of mesh-like CFC catalytic converter curtains had been hung from the bottoms of the solar collectors like laundry out to dry. The experiment had recently been proven quite successful in eliminating ninety percent of the lower atmosphere CFCs passing through. Because of the success of the experiment, funding to construct much higher-volume converters had already been passed by both houses of Congress. The President, under pressure from the growing environmental concerns, had signed the bill.

Another successful experiment was the artificial stimulation of plankton growth near the poles by adding tons of minerals to the sea. The theory was that increased plankton population would absorb more atmospheric carbon dioxide into the seas. Critics claimed the solution was short-term and must be watched carefully so as not to upset the Earth's carbon cycle or upset the flow of ocean currents that had survived for centuries. Nevertheless, all agreed that the plankton stimulation go forward, at least for the time being.

In several unique parts of the world, where the location of land mass relative to the seas made it possible, tidal-electric generating plants had been built and many others were being planned. The areas so far included the Baltic Sea, the North Sea, the Sea of Japan, and the Panama Canal.

Closer to home, billions of trees planted after the turn of the century in selected sites across the United States were now more than twenty years old and their absorption of carbon dioxide was beginning to appear on the charts. The absorption was small but noteworthy.

The most significant contribution to weaning the nation away from heavy dependence on fossil fuels had been developments in efficiency through economic incentives and the development of renewable energy sources. Some experts claimed that the only long-term solution was a hydrogen-based economy centered around the new recyclable-fuel reactor. Others claimed there was still a lot to be done with solar. What was most important was that the pioneer spirit in the United States had found a cause around which to rally.

An example of this pioneer spirit was demonstrated by senior citizens throughout the country who had begun establishing commune-like settlements in which they performed various environmental and community services. The rallying cry for many of these settlements was aimed toward widows and widowers who needed a new commitment — a new life — after the loss of their spouses. The theory was that senior citizens should not live alone but should join others and become creative to the extent of their abilities. The phenomenon of seniors leaving homes they had lived in for decades in order to join so-called "caretaker" settlements had been dubbed the "Grand Traverse Movement" by the media.

The name Grand Traverse was first used in the context of senior settlements by the *20/20* television program years earlier. The name had been chosen as story title because the commentator who interviewed Paul Carter and Bianca Davis commented, in his final statements, that Wylie Lake was located in southern Grand Traverse County in Michigan, and that the county name seemed an appropriate footnote to this story about seniors who had found a cause to work for rather than withdrawing into the isolation of old age.

☢ ☢ ☢

During her marriage to Jack, Heather escaped to her secret cabin whenever she could, usually when Jack was out of the country selling the rights to network reruns to broadcasters serving the Orient and even the Middle East and Africa. She accompanied Jack on one of these month-long trips but begged off on the others saying she did not like being out of the country. Perhaps Jack would add fear of travel to the list of phobias he attributed to her occasionally strange behavior. But it didn't matter what Jack thought. What mattered was that soon she would escape from him and all the other bastards in the world.

Away from the bastards at the New York station to which she'd been transferred to do straight news after upsetting the network brass with her commentaries. Away from the bastards who most likely still talk about her breakdown on the air the night Jamie Carter was elected senator from Illinois. Away from New York with its idealists bent on rejuvenation and revitalization and so-called equality of life, as if equality were possible in this melting pot. Away from Central Park with its trees trimmed to skeletons and its Park Angels who, from her balcony, could become so many yellow fish in a green sea should the oceans rise high enough. Away from a stagnant life where control has replaced anticipation, where Park Angels work for the city, where guns are banned unless you're a cop. Away from floor-to-ceiling mirrors that so vividly display the aging process. Away from the constant din of news about a Pollyanna world in which Senator Jamie Carter has become the so-called "spokesperson for the environment."

As she stood on the balcony looking down at the horse-drawn carriages and swimming schools of Park Angels, Heather visualized the inside of her mountain cabin with its cupboards and shelves, its wood stove, its steep stairway to the sleeping loft, its carpet in the main room beneath which was the trap door leading to the cellar where the water pump and valves, along with several months of provisions, remained unfrozen throughout the long winter.

Whenever she thought of the stacks of provisions beneath the cabin, she recalled one of the first stories she'd read on the air back when she was an up-and-coming, built-like-a-brick-shithouse intern at the U of I station. She remembered reading about survivalists at a hideaway in the Wisconsin northwoods. The survivalists' warning about terrorist threats and civil upheavals. She recalled that the survivalists shown on the recording accompanying the story had worn ski masks. One of the survivalists had been a young woman with long amber hair streaming out beneath the mask.

"Was that you in the mask, Heather?" her co-anchor at the U of I station had asked after the recording played.

"Of course it was," she'd answered. "When the conflagration comes they'll need doctors and nurses and anchorwomen in their camp."

She remembered watching the recording after the show that night. It was her second week on the air and she had been so clever, so young. Now, older and wiser, she hoped she was at least still clever. Clever enough to know when to escape. Except for Jack, she had no strings attached. Her mother was dead, her brother was retired and out of the country, Ducain Chemical's meager assets had been bought up by Dow after the final bankruptcy hearing.

Heather leaned out over the balcony and looked down to the street. From the seventeenth floor, the scene reminded her of the view from a Hong Kong hotel room during a trip she'd taken with Jack. Instead of full-size cabs and police cars and personal cars, the street crawled with pedal and electric bicycles, miniature electric cars, and those damned three-wheeled cabs that looked, from above, like rickshaws.

As she stared down she saw one of the rickshaw-like cabs pull up to the curb in front of the building. The driver flipped open the front canopy and jumped out. When the driver opened the rear door, a man with gray hair got out and paid the driver. She could tell it was Jack because of his cane and his pronounced limp. Jack back from the coast not knowing he had just flown over her cabin in the mountains. Jack arriving with something in gold and diamonds to add to her collection.

Jack would strip, climb into the whirlpool and sigh with relief. Then, after a Scotch to further drown the pain, to bed. She would assume the superior role, listening to his arthritic moans as she manipulated carefully above his fragile bones.

She turned and walked into the apartment. She closed the sliding door, cutting off the incessant sounds of bicycle bells and pneumatic side horns that had come into fashion. She went into the bathroom and began running the water to fill the whirlpool.

☢ ☢ ☢

As Paul neared eighty he wondered how much longer he could

keep up the pace. He and Bianca had traveled extensively in the four-state region of Michigan, Indiana, Illinois, and Wisconsin. They had given talks at community centers and homes for the elderly, encouraging others to be socially and environmentally active. They had even gotten a Michigan State University grant for travel expenses.

Paul hated giving speeches. He was a tinkerer and, whenever away from Wylie Lake for more than a few hours, wanted to hurry back. Bianca loved giving speeches. At least it seemed so to Paul. The only part of being away from Wylie Lake and appearing in front of groups Paul enjoyed was watching Bianca. He always spoke first for this reason, so he could enjoy watching and listening to her without suffering from those damned butterflies. Bianca never stood behind podiums, never sat at a front desk. Instead she walked back and forth on stage or in the front of the room as she spoke.

Sometimes she would have her hands on her hips. Sometimes she would wag her finger at the audience and bend slightly forward as if scolding children. The audiences ate it up. And sometimes, when Paul glanced at the faces, he thought he could see a glow in the eyes of old men like him as Bianca strolled across the stage like a beauty contest winner who *knew* she deserved it. Proud. Yes, he was proud of her, and he loved her.

☢ ☢ ☢

At an elderly community that cared for orphans in the Ukraine village of Svyezhl, what remained of the Lyashko family mourned the death, several days before yet another anniversary of the Chernobyl disaster, of Arkady Lyashko. Arkady was survived by his two sisters and their families. His father had died several years earlier at the *Svyezhl Ozero* (Fresh Lake) home for pensioners at which Arkady was supervisor.

In the United States, news of Arkady's death was carried as part of the coverage of the Chernobyl anniversary. Arkady was said to be one of countless adults who had died in recent years because of radiation received from Chernobyl. His brave fight against leukemia lasted many years.

Jamie was in New York when news of Arkady's death aired. One of the other senators on the Environment and Public Works Committee called her in her hotel room early in the morning and told her to turn on the news. Ironically, when Jamie turned on the television she saw Heather West read of Chernobyl and of Arkady's death. Heather read the news professionally and without apparent emotion. But at the end of the story, when Heather glanced up from the page from which she read, Jamie noticed a slight movement of Heather's mouth, an upturn at the corner, one of those characteristics a person doesn't forget. Despite the aging of Heather's face, Jamie realized this was the same facial expression she had seen on Heather's face years earlier when Heather interviewed her during the Illinois congressional race. It was as if Heather knew she was watching. It was as if, with that expression, Heather wished to twist the knife.

Jamie shut off the television and took a tissue from her robe pocket. But it was only an automatic response. She was not crying and she put the tissue back. She went to the hotel window and looked out. The window faced east. It was after dawn but the sunrise was obscured by thick clouds.

Arkady was dead. He had suffered enough and he was dead. She had done her weeping a week earlier when she spoke with Arkady's sister on the phone. She had done her weeping when she found out Arkady was in a coma and realized she would never even hear his voice again.

"Why are you up so early? The solid waste plant isn't until ten."

Jamie turned. Brian stood in the bedroom doorway in his shorts, his sandy hair disheveled, a corny look on his face, trying to be funny, trying to make her laugh until he saw the look on her face. "Hey. What's wrong?"

"Arkady's dead."

Brian came to her, held her. She thought she wouldn't cry, but now, as Brian held her, she cried and held on as if to let go of Brian would be to slip from the surface of the Earth.

☢ ☢ ☢

The terrorist attack in Paris killed 183 people. Apparently several suitcase bombs had exploded simultaneously in various locations within the Intercontinental-Paris Hotel. The hotel was the site of a conference examining the latest research concerning the ongoing cryptic messages being received from extraterrestrials. Two terrorist groups claimed responsibility for the attack. Polar opposites, one was an old Islamic organization, while the other was an American-born survivalist group. Speculation as to the reason for the attack included evidence being put forth by several researchers that the extraterrestrial messages sent from thousands of light years away contained allusions to collaboration amongst enemies as the only means to survival.

After watching the latest report about the Paris attack, Brian turned off the news and went across the hall to Jamie's hotel room. He knocked and when she let him in he saw that she had also watched the same broadcast. She was wearing a robe. He closed the door and hugged her.

"There's too much enmity in this world is what they're telling us," said Brian.

Jamie turned and walked to the sofa, picked up the remote and turned off the television. "There's always been enmity, Brian. Digging into people's lives and making them public is another form of it."

"No one saw me come across the hall. We'll have breakfast sent in. Anyway, what's wrong with the Chairwoman of the Senate Environment and Public Works Committee having a breakfast meeting with the Committee Staff Director?"

"Nothing's wrong with that. What *is* wrong is that we should never have kept our relationship secret . . . I know, don't say it. There's no conflict of interest, we're consenting adults, neither of us has ever been married . . . Damn it, Brian! I understand all that!"

"Then, why worry about it?"

"Because when we do bring it out, no matter how open and honest we are, someone somewhere will say, 'Hey, she's a senator. What the hell is she doing shacking up with her former campaign manager?' "

"I know why you're upset. And I understand."

Jamie sat on the sofa. Brian joined her.

"Maybe if you talk about Arkady, say whatever comes to mind."

"Get it off my chest? Therapy?"

"Yes."

"Except what's strange about it is Arkady's dead and now here I am thinking about Heather West."

"Why her?"

"I'm not sure . . . "

And so she sat there like a patient and said her thoughts aloud as if to a shrink.

"I remember years ago at U of I when Arkady and I first met. In retrospect such innocent times. Two weirdoes brought together by environmental tragedy. A bad play. And then there was Heather. I remember the time she tried to seduce Arkady. It seemed funny then, the way Arkady told it, until the next time we saw Heather. It was in the basement of the grad house. They'd sent us there because a tornado had been sighted. Heather looked terrible, like she'd been dragged down the stairs. Weirdoes attract weirdoes I guess.

"A few years later, when Heather interviewed me during the Illinois Congress run, things she said made me wonder if she had really been hurt back then. Made me wonder if she had genuine feelings for Arkady and I screwed it up. Like that time she used her commentary to criticize Dad's and Bianca's efforts at Wylie Lake. And then again, tonight . . . something about her face, something . . .

"It's the way she looks when she talks about anything remotely related to me. Sometimes I've even wondered if she might blurt out that my parents smoked pot or got arrested for a sit-in. I'm not sure why she'd do it. I'm not sure of anything.

"Damn, I wish I would have found out about Arkady from anyone but her!

"I remember how those old people and children at the home

loved Arkady. I remember talking to his mother and thinking, at the time, 'So this is where Arkady learned respect for his fellow human beings.' I remember Arkady listening while I told about the families at Easthaven who'd been closer to the dump site, the people who got bone tumors, that little girl whose damn teeth calcified and fell out. He listened when I told how lucky I was. He listened when I told how unlucky I was. He listened when I told about my tests in Chicago, he listened when I said that perhaps, for us, marriage just wasn't in the cards."

Jamie turned and looked at Brian. "So, you see? Arkady was just like you in a lot of ways. And now, knowing that I've loved two men and one is gone, I feel like I've lost both of you."

"Why?"

"I don't know."

Brian hugged her, she hugged back.

She recalled years earlier, her mother asking if she loved Arkady. She remembered thinking then about both Brian and Arkady and telling her mother that, yes, she did love Arkady. Now, as Brian held her tightly, she knew that if her mother were here now, if her mother were alive, she would admit to her that today there was only one man alive on Earth that she truly loved. And that man was Brian Jones.

Jamie stood up from the sofa and walked to the bedroom of the suite. Brian followed.

☢ ☢ ☢

When they were both dressed for the day's activities and room-service breakfast arrived, Jamie sat across from Brian.

"Listen," said Brian. "I grew up in Birmingham, Alabama, and graduated from a university whose old fart alumni probably hung blacks for kicks on Saturday night. And now, here I am, a forty-four-year-old descendent of Johnny Reb sitting across the breakfast table from a liberal senator who I've just been in bed with. And frankly, my dear, I *do* give a damn."

"You're funny."

"I try to be."

"Maybe you should run for office."

"Why should I? Appointments are much easier. Anyhow, I couldn't take the pace of a campaign."

"Except behind the scenes."

"Right. Managing your campaign was right up my alley. When you run again, I'll be there."

"*If* I run again."

"You'll run. It's in your blood."

After breakfast, Brian stopped Jamie at the door, held her in his arms. "I'm sorry about Arkady. I feel I knew him."

"Thanks. It's over. Can't look back." When she said this, Jamie had a sudden image of Arkady's tiny room at the university in Kiev. Arkady was sitting on the bed, her moving toward him, wiggling as she hummed a snake-charmer ditty for the benefit of Arkady's neighbor on the other side of the wall who thought she was a belly dancer from the *Club Raj*.

"What's wrong?" asked Brian.

"Nothing. Let's go. We've got lives to live and work to do."

And so the Chairwoman of the Senate Environment and Public Works Committee and the Committee Staff Director left to tour

New York's new solid waste disposal facility designed to finally eliminate ocean dumping and meet the last extension date allowed by Congress.

CHAPTER 20

THE TELEVISION REPORTER WAS A young man. He wore sunglasses, a paisley shirt, bright green tie, and khaki slacks. He pointed behind and to his left across a field of corn interrupted by the narrow band of an erosion-control tree line in the distance.

"Five miles from where I'm standing, over there to the southwest, is the site of one of the first nuclear reactors used to generate electricity in this country."

The reporter began walking slowly and the camera panned to follow him, the microphone picking up the sounds of his shoes crunching the gravel of the road on which he walked.

"Construction on the reactor started in the late 1950s and the plant went on line in the early 1960s. If you were born in the Chicago area, chances are at least part of the electricity powering the lights in your delivery room was generated by that plant."

The reporter stopped walking.

"The plant has been shut down since the turn of the century, but its years of reliable service, and its use as a storage site for other plants, have left behind tons of radioactive waste."

The reporter pointed to his right across more corn fields interrupted by erosion-control tree lines.

"Over this way, just beyond that nearest tree line, a set of railroad tracks crosses this rich farm country into equally-rich Indiana farm country. The tracks pass through several towns along the way and, until recently, a train called the Dawn Patrol used those tracks three mornings a week to take radioactive waste material from the nuclear plant site to a nuclear waste disposal facility near the Indiana-Michigan border. Back in the spring of 2015, an accident on the line caused the residents of the town of Wheatfield, Indiana, to evacuate their homes for several days while crews cleaned up the spill."

The reporter began walking toward the camera.

"But today, technology has caught up to the Dawn Patrol and it's made its last run. In fact, technology has now made what we used to call radioactive waste into radioactive fuel."

The camera panned right to follow as the reporter stepped up onto the concrete platform of a commuter train station and walked along the tracks.

"We're in the small but growing town of Iroquois, Illinois. Not long ago the townspeople of Iroquois received news that the old Iroquois Power Plant was going to be rebuilt. At first, many residents protested. But when they found out the rebuilt reactor would not only be safer and more reliable than its predecessor, but would also be using the remaining waste stored there as fuel, the residents of Iroquois became supporters of the project."

The reporter stopped at the end of the platform where "Iroquois" was ornately painted on a sign board hung by eye hooks from the platform shelter. The sign board swung gently in the wind.

"The citizens of Iroquois have reason to trust technology because the plan to build the new waste-recyclable power plant at the old site comes on the heels of a very successful project right here at the Iroquois commuter station. It's one of several commuter projects recently completed throughout the country. The project was originally proposed by the United States Senate Environment and Public Works Committee."

The reporter stepped off the platform and walked across the tracks toward three long shelters with slanted roofs held up by metal supports. The roofs of the shelters glistened in the sun as if wet. Beneath the shelters were hundreds of bicycles and electric motor scooters.

"For some time Iroquois has had one of the finest bicycle path systems of any town in the state. A few years ago someone came up with the idea to connect the bicycle path network to several paths that lead here to the commuter station, and to provide safe, sheltered bicycle parking. The parking is also secure because senior citizens in the area serve as volunteer observers to notify the police if vandals are sighted."

The camera switched to two old men in straw hats sitting on a bench. One of the men held up a portable phone and smiled. Then the camera switched back to the reporter.

"As you can see, the seniors are on duty."

The camera switched to a close shot of one of the shelters.

"Earlier this year, something else began to happen at the station.

As the mayor of Iroquois put it, 'Solar technicians literally crawled all over the place.' In a matter of days they installed photovoltaic cells on the roofs of the shelters and connected them to battery charging systems. And so, as I speak, hundreds of electric motor scooters and bicycles fitted with auxiliary electric motors are having their batteries charged while their owners are at work."

The camera showed a closeup of a polished aluminum panel with card slots for payment above a row of three-prong receptacles, several of which had plugs in them.

"The cost to plug in is less than the cost to park a car at the nearby lot. And if you need exercise, as we all do, you can still park your human-powered bicycle free of charge."

The camera showed a closeup of the reporter.

"That's it for Technology Today. I'm Larry Van Horn at the train station in Iroquois, Illinois."

In the studio, the young woman news reporter, whose bangs-and-kiss-curl hair style had been made popular a year earlier by songstress Tammy Saint Vincent, said, "Thanks Larry. As a side note, our own Senator Jamie Carter, who chairs the Senate Environment and Public Works Committee, was guest of honor at the dedication of the Iroquois station earlier this week. In her dedication speech, Senator Carter congratulated the environmentally-conscious business organizations that helped make the project possible, and she also reminded all Illinoisans to keep planting trees wherever you can, so long as their growth will not block somebody's solar collectors."

As station manager Leslie Gale watched the monitor in her office at the Champaign, Illinois, ABC affiliate, she was proud of her two young reporters. Both were recent graduates of the University of Illinois School of Broadcast Journalism. Their success meant a lot because their careers were probably the last ones Leslie would be able to launch before her upcoming retirement.

Leslie watched with pride as the young woman segued into the next story, which concerned the Democratic Convention in Chicago. The story began with blurry, low-definition footage from another Chicago convention that took place over six decades earlier. On the screen, billy club wielding policemen pushed young men and women into tall, boxy police patrol wagons while others shouted, "The whole world is watching!" with fists raised.

At sunset, the lake outside the cottage window twinkled orange as if thousands of electric filaments floated on the surface of the water.

"Landing in Traverse City will probably be like landing in a corn field compared to all the places she's been lately," said Paul.

"How long has it been?"

"Since she's been here or since we saw her?"

"Since she's been here."

"Last Christmas," said Paul.

"We're her only family," said Bianca. "Everyone needs to be with family sometimes."

"Right. She can't always be tough, even if she is a senator."

"We should get going," said Bianca, standing and looking out across the lake where the sun was disappearing behind the distant treeline. "We promised we'd drop those people off at the Interlochen concert on the way."

"Will the concert be over by the time we're ready to come back?" asked Paul, taking off his glasses and holding them up to the fading light to inspect them for smudges.

"Yes, we're leaving early for them. They'll have to wait for us on the way back." Bianca turned toward him, her face in shadows. "I should drive because it's after sunset."

Paul put his glasses back on and stood. A pain shot from his hip into his abdomen and he rubbed it as he walked bent over toward the hallway.

"You all right?" asked Bianca.

"No, I'm not all right," said Paul. "I'm eighty years old."

"Touchy-touchy," said Bianca, following him to the door.

When the plane descended above the twin tips of Traverse Bay, Jamie thought, as she had once before, about a mother's breasts, about her mother, about her own breasts. So far so good, according to her last mammogram. And, according to her new doctor at the University of Chicago Medical Center earlier that day, her health in general appeared to be normal.

The Democratic convention was in session in Chicago but, so far during her career, she had managed to stay away from conventions. Her speeches and appearances during her campaign for United States Senate had taken place in schools and hotels and community centers and auditoriums and, especially, at sites of various environmental projects she had sponsored before and after becoming senator. She hoped she would never be asked to make a convention appearance. She couldn't imagine herself bellowing at the podium and then smiling like a Cheshire cat while waiting for the raucous convention-style cheers and applause to die down.

At the airport in Chicago, a reporter had asked whether, since one of the men seeking the Presidential candidacy had been her mentor and was currently her colleague in the Senate, she would be able to support any candidate chosen by the party. Like a loyal party member, she had said yes. Although she added that Senator Jim Hansen of Illinois had the most experience and was the best person for the job. The reporter had wanted more specifics but the plane was about to leave and she quickly boarded the flight to Traverse City.

As she often did, and always did when visiting Wylie Lake, she traveled alone. It seemed, during the last few years, that half her life had been taken up with travel, while the other half had been spent on the Senate floor. During the last two years alone she had been to South America to attend a tropical forest conference, to Europe to confer about reforestation that had taken place there since the acid rain reductions, to Africa to study environmentally self-sufficient village systems, to the Middle East to talk with Saudi officials about using solar there despite the economic pressures of oil, to Japan regarding successes there in tidal-electric power, to China to attend a population control conference, to Australia to attend a southern hemisphere environmental protocol, and finally to Antarctica where she saw a sky not quite as blue as in the last century because of the hole in the ozone layer.

The last time she'd been to the Ukraine was when Arkady's

health had taken a turn for the worse. She'd gone to see Arkady after a Moscow conference. Arkady had been shriveled and gaunt, but smiled from his bed, proud of his newly-grown head of hair. When she hugged Arkady, he had moaned in pain.

"I remember when you came back from that trip you said you felt Arkady was near death," Brian had said before she left Washington for Wylie Lake earlier that morning. "And I also remember that he bounced back for quite a while afterward."

"What are you getting at?" She had been on her way out the door, in a hurry as usual, and now she wished she had not been in such a hurry.

"What I'm getting at is that you're not very good at predictions."

"I didn't think I was trying to predict his death back then. I was simply commenting on how terrible he looked. What are you trying to say, Brian? I've got a plane to catch."

"What I'm trying to say, Jamie, is that I feel like crap not being able to go with you on this trip. What I'm trying to say is that we never discuss marriage and, deep inside, I feel that you've already discounted it because you have this idiotic notion ingrained in you that you don't deserve to follow your emotions because something horrible will come of it."

"I'm sorry, Brian. What can I say? It's not that I don't love you."

"Just say you'll think about it."

"Marriage?"

"Yes, damn it!"

☢ ☢ ☢

When the plane landed, her father and Bianca were there to meet her. She sat in the back of the van while Bianca drove and her father sat next to Bianca. Her father's profile against the lights of Traverse City made him appear much older than when she'd last seen him. And there was another change. Instead of Bianca doing most of the talking as she had during past visits, Jamie's father talked incessantly, often repeating himself.

He told about the van they were in, how it was methane-powered and how a new ex-engineer had moved to Wylie Lake and taken over Bill Cochran's septic system methane producer. He talked about the increased use of bicycles and motor scooters and buses in Traverse City. He pointed out one of the new Ford minicars that ran on hydrogen. He re-told about last year's drowning of a teenaged boy at the public access site at Wylie Lake, describing the drowning in detail as if it had happened within the last week. Finally, he told about his and Bianca's recent trip to Wisconsin on the ferry and their appearances at homes for senior citizens in Green Bay and Manitowoc and Oshkosh.

"I wish you talked this much when we visited those homes," said Bianca.

On the way to Wylie Lake they picked up a retired couple and their granddaughter at the Interlochen Music Camp. The little girl, whose name was Tina, sat next to Jamie. Tina was nine years old, was staying with her grandparents during the concert season. She had played the flute in that night's concert and told about her hours and hours of practice, saying she didn't like practice at home that much but that it was especially nice to practice on the shore of Wylie Lake where the notes echoed back to her after being played. Tina said that since Jamie would be at the cottage the next day she might hear her flute early in the morning just after sunrise.

As Tina spoke about her flute and her dream of a career in music, Jamie realized that when she was Tina's age she had been caught up in the seemingly endless legal battles surrounding the Easthaven disaster. Whereas Jamie felt that her entire life would be ruled by legal machinations, Tina, at nine years old, had a musical career ahead of her — the solitude of practice, the art of creating the music, the freedom from an invasion of chemicals that might or might not kill her some day, and, during the litigation, the invasion of attorneys into her parents' living room each evening.

As Tina continued talking, Jamie wondered if, given a choice, she would do it over again, starting out as another little girl with another mother and father, another college girl getting a break from Jim Hansen and meeting someone other than Arkady, a woman with a family, a mother of a child like Tina by the time someone like Brian comes along. No, there was no choice. She was who she was.

Outside the van, the woods were dark and seemed suddenly ominous. And ahead, when she leaned to the center and looked between the seats, she could see the reflection of the headlights in the eyes of a small creature — a muskrat or raccoon — as it darted from the road because of the van's approach.

☢ ☢ ☢

It was very quiet in the cottage. She remembered Arkady saying it was quiet years earlier in this very guest room on this same squeaky sunken bed. She wondered if she would ever bring Brian here. And if she did, she wondered if he would also comment on how quiet it was.

A gentle knock on the door startled her and she turned on the light.

Bianca came in, sat on the edge of the bed, one hand deep in the pocket of her robe, the other pointing to her curlers. "When I was a girl my mother gave me permanents to straighten my hair. Now that I'm older it straightens on its own so I use curlers. Your father likes it curly. Something about a '60s black power poster. Anyway, no need to wait until morning to find out who's nominated. I put on the earphones after you and Paul went to bed."

"Did Jim Hansen get it?"

"Yes," said Bianca, smiling. "And there's something else I thought shouldn't wait until morning."

"What?"

"The reporters grabbed hold of his campaign manager and I don't know if he was supposed to do it or if they're sending out feelers or what." Bianca touched her arm. "Your name was mentioned, Jamie. When they asked if Hansen had any Vice Presidential candidates in mind, you were one of them."

"No. He can't. We're from the same state and, as far as I know, no one's done a background check on me. The campaign manager did it to get a reaction. If he wants a woman he'll pick Betty Kole from California or Trish Porter from Texas. No, he'd never pick me. It's suicide to go with someone from your own state. Even if he did ask me, I don't know if I'd accept."

"Why not?"

"I don't think I'm ready."

286

Bianca moved closer, lifted Jamie's chin and stared at her. "When will you be ready?"

"I don't know."

Bianca continued staring. "You've got someone else to think about, don't you? You can't fool me, sugar. You've got someone. I've known it since last Christmas so you might as well tell me."

And so she told Bianca about Brian — how they met at U of I; how he worked for her first campaign; how she eventually took him on as an aide; how, despite her love for Arkady, she fell in love with Brian when he became her campaign manager for the United States Senate race; how, on his own merits and his credentials as a Sierra Club environmental lobbyist, he convinced the Environment and Public Works Committee to make him Staff Director before she became Committee Chairwoman.

"Why haven't you told anyone?" asked Bianca.

"I'm not sure. When Arkady was alive, I felt that my being in the public eye, and news traveling the way it does these days . . . "

"You thought you'd hurt Arkady."

"Yes, but more than that I didn't feel I should make anything official out of my relationship with Brian until . . . "

"Jamie, you weren't married to Arkady."

"But we had a bond between us. I know it sounds gruesome, but ever since we met there's been a kind of unwritten law chiseled in stone that we'd wait around to see who died first. We never said it to one another, but we felt it. In a lot of ways it's like we were the same person."

"And now that he's gone?"

"Now that he's gone, part of me is gone."

Bianca touched Jamie's cheek. "And so, dear Jamie, what's left?"

"Me. I'm still here. That's what makes it so sad. It took Arkady's death to make me realize how much I love Brian."

"Brian's a lucky guy," said Bianca. "Good looking, too. At least he was last time I saw him on television."

"Yes, except now that I've managed to keep my private life so damn private, I'm worried Brian will get hurt."

"How?"

"I'm not sure."

Things happened very fast the next day when Paul woke up. He had expected a relaxing day, perhaps a morning boat ride with Jamie, the lake calm and serene, the little girl's flute across the water. Instead, no sooner was he told about the announcement of Jamie's name as a possible Vice Presidential candidate, and the phone rang.

It was Jim Hansen's campaign manager asking Jamie a pile of questions and Jamie telling the campaign manager about someone named Brian Jones and about Bianca living with her father — him — at Wylie Lake and even about his and Judy's arrest for marching in an environmental rally and about them marching in anti-segregation rallies and him smoking pot and being slipped some acid once.

"Shit!" he said while Jamie was still on the phone. "I knew that goddamn acid would bite me in the ass some day!"

Bianca shushed him, then Jamie was off the phone telling about it all — how Jim Hansen's backers felt that the weakness of a ticket consisting of senators from the same state was offset by Jamie's strength in international politics and her role in the growing national and international environmental movements; how everyone in Hansen's campaign felt that the time was right for an environmentalist on the ticket.

A few minutes later the campaign manager was back on the phone again. By noon they were out the door with Jamie driving back to Traverse City.

In the van Paul couldn't help himself despite the pain in his hips and abdomen. He laughed out loud and said, "Damn, my own little girl running for Vice President!"

CHAPTER 21

BECAUSE OF A CAMPAIGN ADVERTISING guideline initiative that came about after several brutal campaigns at the beginning of the century, the ads for the Presidential election of 2032 were written with great care. This was true not only because of spending limits put on media advertising, but because each ad, according to the initiative, was, "to represent the candidate's detailed views on at least one key campaign issue," and was, "to avoid stating or implying any opponent's views on the issue." The initiative provided that a campaign advertising committee of representatives of all parties be convened during the campaign to judge whether ads stayed within the guidelines. If an ad was judged to be outside the guidelines, ad time was granted the opposing candidate or candidates with the purpose of providing time for rebuttal.

In ads for her campaign, Vice Presidential candidate Jamie Carter, the Senator from Illinois, had chosen issues detailing how elected officials should relate to events beyond their terms of office, indeed, beyond their lifetimes. She spoke of a move from territorial loyalties to global loyalties. According to many commentators, Jamie Carter was eloquent and specific on ways to change what she called the "short-sighted orientation of the past." She agreed with the new election guidelines, saying that recent effects of a media hard-wired to the emotions of the electorate had collided head-on with the electoral process created by the founding fathers.

Critics of this view stated that the electoral process worked just fine, not in spite of instantaneous communication and minute-by-minute punditry, but because of them. According to these critics, many office holders were voted out because of unkept promises. But Senator Carter, in her ads on this issue, contended that long-term relationships between officials and the welfare of the people needed to be established. Not long-term in the sense of monarchy, but long-term in the sense of an ancestral bond with the future.

According to a CNN analyst, who had originally been critical of Governor Hansen's choice of running mate, Senator Carter's "ancestral bond" issue was not only an honest implementation of her views on social and environmental concerns, but also served as an educational forum for voters.

"Indeed," said the analyst, "Senator Carter's ideas may be the philosophical change we need. Whether or not you agree with her proposals for welfare system overhaul by putting people of all ages to work in the so-called Youth Corps or Junior Corps or Middle Corps or Senior Corps — whether or not you agree with her proposals to overhaul the nation's health care system by modeling it after the IHPS system in Illinois — whether or not you agree with her proposals for world summits on all issues, not only environment, but economy, nuclear and chemical arms, ethnic strife, and religious differences — and, finally, whether or not you agree with her radical proposal for upping the carbon tax, you have to agree that this American woman truly believes in what she has dubbed the 'caretaker culture' of the twenty-first century."

When the *Election 2032* news special ended, Heather reached out to the coffee table, stabbing at the "Off" button on the remote and at the same time taking a gulp from the glass of single malt Scotch whiskey to which she had recently taken a liking. The news special had been relentless in its praise of Jamie Carter. How politically clever Jamie Carter had been to reveal past and present details of her private life so far ahead of the election, details including her relationship with Arkady Lyashko, now deceased, and her current relationship with Brian Jones, her former campaign manager and Staff Director of the Senate Environment and Public Works Committee.

Heather took another gulp of Scotch. *Snow White, that's what she was, fucking Snow White.* As Heather had said to Jack the other night, "Given half a chance she'd probably fuck every one of those seven dwarfs and still have some left over for her other friends in the woods!"

"I don't understand this deep-seated hatred of yours," Jack had said. "I hope this is something you'd say only to me . . . "

"Oh, fuck it! You never saw what a double-sided cunt she was! Miss Prim on one side, truck stop whore on the other side!"

Heather had consumed quite enough Scotch that night, too. But not so much that she was unaware that Jack, instead of coming to her and holding her as he had in the past, had only stared at her and said, "My, aren't *we* a bitch tonight."

That was three nights ago and Jack hadn't been home since. He wasn't out of town. It was September, the new shows were premiering, and Jack sometimes stayed in the office suite for days at a time during premiers. But still, he hadn't called. The least he could have done was called.

Heather put down her Scotch, stood, waited for the dizziness to ease, then walked toward the window where her reflection wobbled unsteadily against the night sky. She wore a black silk gown with a plunging neckline. Despite tonight's internal raving, and the raving at Jack the other night, she felt that she looked halfway decent, a mature woman in control. She folded her arms beneath her breasts.

A mother's breasts. Several weeks earlier, when she'd taken a much needed trip to her mountain retreat, the young man working to renovate the old ski-tow had suckled her breasts like a baby.

She'd been on a hike when she came across him. On previous hikes she'd thought the old ski-tow off the gravel road permanently abandoned and beyond repair. But there he was, muscled and shirtless with long hair and sunglasses held onto his head with a strap so that she never once had to look into his eyes.

They spoke little, she telling him she'd driven to the spot from Denver that very morning — she hadn't wanted him to know about her cabin hidden less than a mile away in the woods — him telling her about the use of old car wheels as pulleys for the ski-tow He spoke quickly because he was obviously nervous and didn't know what to make of this woman emerging from the woods. Speaking with a little too much drawl like he was faking a southern accent.

He was perhaps eighteen, not much older than Pete at the park pavilion so long ago. She made the first move by reaching out and touching his rippled, taut stomach.

She reached out now, as she had then, and touched her image on the window, fingertips to fingertips. She stood there for several minutes reliving the incident, feeling the heat of the sun on her head, the cool mountain air on her skin, feeling the nervous, skittering search of her flesh, feeling the coarse, pine-needled forest floor on her back, feeling him inside her. And helping him, helping him do it again even though he didn't think it possible.

Although the sunglasses hid his eyes, Heather imagined he must have had blue eyes. Blue eyes because his facial features and his long hair resembled those of a much younger Brian Jones. Brian Jones during his first week at the University of Illinois. The same Brian Jones who, at the time, gave her the brush-off, saying he was already spoken for. Already dating someone else.

And what is that someone else's name?

Jamie Carter. She says she knows you. She speaks well of you.

I bet she does, Mr. Brian Jones, who's apparently too good for us Northern ladies.

Even after Jamie met Arkady, Mr. Brian Jones was too good for her. Always talking about the environment and going on Sierra Club outings. Starting a new Sierra Club branch on campus, ignoring her even when she tried to show interest.

When Heather opened her eyes she was still standing at the window, her outstretched fingertips still touching the fingertips of the lovely mature woman in the image. Beyond the woman, the lights illuminating the paths in Central Park flickered as a windy September shower began to flex the trees. On the window, the image became spattered and she felt a wave of disgust as she recalled a scene from a gang-bang video she had found hidden in Jack's collection shortly after their marriage. Probably the same kind of collection most men have hidden away. Even bastards like Brian Jones. All those bastards out there waiting for a climactic scene like the one she'd seen on Jack's video. Yes, a climactic scene indeed as a redheaded woman who looked surprisingly like her lay sprawled at the feet of no less than a dozen masturbating black men.

She walked quickly from the window and sat on the sofa again. She picked up her glass and gulped the remaining Scotch. Then she picked up the phone and placed a call to a number she had memorized several days earlier.

"Hi, this is Leslie Gale. I'm unable to answer either my stationary or portable phone right now, so please leave a brief message. Thanks."

Heather was about to hang up, but instead she brought the phone back to her face and said, "Leslie. This is Heather . . . Heather West. Everything here's okay . . . as well as can be expected I guess. Jack's fine and all that, but I hardly see him. Premier week. I say everything's as well as can be expected because . . . well, it's really not. I mean, I'm okay, although I do hate reading news at the fucking crack of dawn. It's this old friend of mine who's got me down. She's in the public eye and a long time ago she got herself into some pretty bad scrapes that would really hurt if they were made public. The other night she told me she wished she could go back to the good old 2000s and start over. Hey, who hasn't thought about doing that?

Sometimes I wish I could be back there at good old Channel 10 in Champaign. Anyway, I hope this friend of mine doesn't do something stupid. One time back then she got herself drunk, drunker than I am now, and was so depressed she got herself gang-banged. She thought if she could get some guys to give her a little loving . . . Dumb little shit. Falling to pieces, like the old song says. Oh well, you know my number. Later . . . "

Heather hung up the phone, stood, almost fell, then held onto the walls as she made her way down the hall to her bedroom. She went to her closet and retrieved a box from the top shelf. She sat at her dressing table, opened the box, took out a straw cartwheel hat and put it on her head. She stared at her image in the dressing table mirror, a puzzled look on her face as she tried to recall the details of the message she had left Leslie Gale. She opened a drawer in her dressing table, got out a pair of evening gloves and put them on. Finally, she opened a lower drawer in the dressing table — the drawer where she used to keep her pistol before the bastards upped the ante on the city handgun law — and took out a plastic pill bottle. She carried the bottle into the bathroom, filled a glass with water, opened the pill bottle, dumped all of the pills into her mouth, downed them with several gulps of water.

As she stood at the sink, the image of the woman in cartwheel hat and gloves swam in the mirror, smiling at her. The face had aged significantly. Those lines. Those goddamn lines.

She held the water glass up and toasted her reflection. "Happy thirteenth annivers . . . an' happy forty-fifth . . . "

☢ ☢ ☢

In the hospital she did not watch television, she did not access the computer information retrieval library, she did not listen to the radio, she did not read newspapers or magazines. As if already at her secret mountain retreat, she isolated herself. The only people she saw were the doctors and the private nurses and Jack.

The morning after the stomach pumping, that had resulted in temporary laryngitis caused by the tube shoved down her throat, Jack had told her about the frantic call to his office from Leslie Gale. Jack had tried to console her — the usual crap, anything he did or said? anything he could do to help? — and he told her of his success in keeping the incident out of the news.

Heather was surprised at how successfully she had dramatized her fear of hearing or reading about the attempted suicide. But, after a few days, her excuse for self-imposed isolation was wearing thin. And after a week in the hospital, and her obvious lack of co-operation with three shrinks sent to speak with her, it was obvious Jack and the doctors and nurses and the rest of the world were wait-ing for her to suddenly start shrieking and tearing up the bedsheets and pounding her fists on the walls.

And then this morning that damn nurse coming on duty had to stand just outside the door and tell the night nurse going off duty how Jamie Carter was, as she put it, "such a simply super-excellent woman who's got my vote, sister, and all the votes I can drum up."

"She's got mine, too," said the night nurse who really wasn't the other's sister. "I say it's about time we got off our backs and squatted on top where we belong."

Both nurses had laughed then, and Heather had clutched her top sheet, indeed, had even tried to tear it. But when the chattering had finally stopped and the morning nurse came into the room, Heather was able to appear quite calm because she saw that the nurse held in her hand the paper bag containing the clothing for which she had received a substantial fee from Heather the day before.

And so, with jeans, blouse, jacket, and shoes in the bag, and with her "great escape" cash that had been in a safety deposit box for over a year at a nearby bank — a bank Jack did not do business with — Heather was ready to make the "great escape" to her cabin a mile in the sky. But there was one more thing to do before she left the hospital.

After lunch, wearing the street clothes and telling the nurse how therapeutic it was to be dressed like a normal person, Heather sat in the chair at the side of the bed and waited for the nurse to put on her earphones as she always did in the afternoon. Then Heather waited until she could see, by the slight head movements, that the nurse was immersed in the music.

The escape began with the phone call Heather had planned all week. After dialing the number, she watched the nurse carefully to make sure the nurse could not hear her.

"Hello, is this Bobbie?" she asked in a sexy voice.

"Quite so," said a man with a high-pitched voice.

"Bobbie, you don't know me but I read your paper all the time. When I don't have time to pick it up at the market, I access it on the web."

"That's grand. Who is this? Or, if you don't want to say who you are, which it seems you don't, at least tell me where you're calling from."

"New Jersey. I live in New Jersey by the shore."

"Ah, the shore is wonderful this time of year."

"Yes, it is. Anyway, I've got some important things to tell you."

"Okay, shoot."

"It's a bunch of little things I know for a fact, but they add up to a lot."

"Go on."

"I'm talking about Miss Untouchable. I'm talking about Carter."

"Jamie Carter?"

"Yes."

"What do you know about Jamie Carter and why should I be listening to you?"

"First, we went to school together, second, I have reliable sources, third, I'd appreciate it if you didn't speak down to me."

After a pause, Heather turned toward the wall, lowering her voice and concealing the phone in case the nurse looked up. The nurse in the chair near the window did not look up, but continued bobbing her head to the music on her earphones.

When Heather finally hung up, she wondered for a moment if Bobbie had caller-ID, or if he was a cheap bastard who didn't care, or didn't want to know who was on the other end. No matter. She knew he'd be unable to contact all the sources she'd given because half of them didn't exist. Besides, if he did have caller-ID and called back, she'd soon be two-thousand miles west and over a mile high. If she had to she could always drive down from the cabin into Denver and call again. And if Bobbie didn't start the old allegation ball rolling, there were others she could call. For now she'd wait and see what happened to her seeds. After all, there were still two months to go before the election.

Heather stood and went into the bathroom, making a detour near the nurse to be certain she'd be seen. Once inside the bathroom Heather peeked back out. Then, very quickly like an endangered mountain cat, she left the bathroom, slid along the wall and slipped out the partially open door into the hallway.

In the room the nurse sat looking out the window, her head bobbing to the music.

CHAPTER 22

"HI, DAD, IT'S ME."

"Where are you calling from?"

"Washington. Came back to vote on the budget."

"How are you doing?"

"Physically, I'm okay. Emotionally, I'm really tired."

"Are you going to take some time off?"

"Yes. That's why I called. Jim suggested I get out from under the lights over the weekend. I thought I'd come out there, visit you and Bianca for a while, throw a line in the water and see what other kind of monsters I can pull out."

"It's a bunch of goddamn lies and everybody knows it."

"But it has it's humorous side. Jim's campaign manager is calling me Hester Prynne."

"Who?"

"Hester Prynne from *The Scarlet Letter.* Anyway, Jim asked me to take the weekend to think it over."

"Jesus, Jamie, not that."

"Yes. He's leaving it up to me. I feel like shit, Dad."

"I know. It'll be okay once you're here."

"Right. Everything will be okay if Jim wins. But if he loses . . . "

"It wouldn't be your fault if he lost."

"Yes, it would. If I stay on and he loses, it'll be my fault. If I toss it in and he loses, it'll be my fault . . . "

"You're being too hard on yourself."

"Maybe I should be. That's the way it is with us prostitutes with brain damage. Sounds like a daytime talk show. Prostitutes with brain damage. Stay tuned . . . "

"Well, I sure didn't help back in the '70s blowin' grass and waving my damn signs."

"None of this is your fault, Dad."

"Sure, I'm the one who dropped acid so I'd have X-ray vision like Superman."

"Wait a minute, Dad! You were slipped some acid once and had a bad trip! Pretending you did it on purpose doesn't help at all!"

"Yes, I . . . I'm sorry. I was just trying to help."

"I know. I'm sorry for blowing up."

"Anyway, Jamie, the things they're saying aren't that bad. I remember years ago how they used to sling mud around, and after the election was over they acted like old buddy-buddies."

"The only reason there haven't been smear ads is because of the campaign guidelines and because Brian's out there taking the heat. It doesn't matter. It's in the news and if it's going to do me in, it'll do me in."

"But people should think about the future like you always say."

"They are thinking about the future, Dad. They're wondering if the future will be better or worse if I'm Vice President. What's come out has to enter into their decision and I can't blame them for that."

"But you've got to tell them it's all lies. They'll believe you, Jamie. Damn it! They've got to believe you! Does Jim believe you?"

"Of course he does, Dad. This whole thing is really hard on him because he's viewed as having been my mentor. Any doubts people might have about my credibility go on his back."

"What about Brian?"

"If you mean does Brian believe any of this crap, the answer is no."

"I wondered what he might have said about me, not knowing me and all."

"Dad, this is very hard to talk about, especially on the phone. I'll be leaving for the airport in a few minutes and I'll be there tonight."

"Is Brian coming with you?"

"No, Jim asked him to spend the weekend trying to put out fires. He'll be my official repudiator for a couple days. They feel it will be better not to have me up there saying that the rumors are ridiculous lies. I guess one of my weaknesses is that I don't show outrage in public well enough."

"Should we meet you at the airport?"

"No, Dad. The Secret Service is already there to pick me up. They'll also be around while I'm at the lake. So if you want to call any neighbors and let them know why there's so many cars parked in the driveway . . . "

"Jamie?"

303

"Yes."

"I forgot to say I love you. Bianca reminded me. She loves you, too."

"I love you both, Dad. See you later."

☢ ☢ ☢

Wylie Lake was very calm that Saturday morning, but it was overcast and dreary. Instead of the sunrise lighting up the trees across the lake, the dawn simply brightened a little, then stopped as if a huge hand had reached out to stop the Earth's rotation. At the north end of the lake the girl played her flute for a while, but she stopped in mid-song as if someone had grabbed her from behind. There was only one other boat on the lake, the small green fishing boat that Paul recognized as belonging to Joe Siebert. Every minute or so Paul could see movement in the distant boat as Joe either cast out his line or bailed water from the bottom of his leaky old boat.

Jamie sat next to Paul in the pedal boat. They had left the dock using the electric motor, but Jamie had said she wanted to pedal. Because the sun wasn't out, the small meter mounted beneath the photovoltaic canopy showed only a minuscule trickle of charging current.

"E equals I times R," said Paul, pointing to the meter.

"What?" asked Jamie.

"Voltage equals current times resistance. Ohm's law. If one thing changes, they all change."

When they did not speak, the only sound was the sloshing of the paddles beneath the center hump of the boat. Although Paul was used to pedaling the boat and he thought his legs fairly strong, he could feel the energy of Jamie's pedaling on his pedals. He was not used to pedaling quite so fast and first one knee, then his hips and back began to ache.

"We're in the middle," he said. "Let's stop for a while."

After they stopped pedaling, Paul cranked the rudder hard-a-port and they circled around facing back toward the cottage. On shore Paul saw two men in blue nylon jackets. Both had binoculars. One man sat at the picnic bench looking out over the lake, the other stood down on the bank alternately scanning the north and south shorelines.

"A month and a half to go," said Jamie.

"Huh?"

"Jim has only a month and a half to get voters used to a new running mate if I decide to withdraw."

"Bianca's right," said Paul. "Withdrawing is bullshit."

"Maybe everything is bullshit."

"Well, that may be true."

"I wonder what those guys on shore would do if I jumped overboard."

"They've got the rowboat. I suppose they'd be out here pretty quick."

"Think they teach them how to row at Secret Service school?" said Jamie.

"Probably do. Probably teach them how to fish, too. Saw one out here yesterday scoping the place out."

"The extent to which they watch the family of a Vice Presidential candidate is discretionary. They'll probably stay on after I leave because of all the uproar in the news."

The pedal boat had done a slow full circle as they drifted and now they faced the far side of the lake where Joe was alternately bailing out his boat and casting. Paul stared at Joe's boat as he spoke.

"I wonder why those damn reporters haven't been out here."

"If I decide not to withdraw I'm sure they'll be here. They might come even if I do decide to withdraw."

"When they come I'll tell them a thing or two. No one has the right to say things like that. No one has the right to imply that a father and daughter . . . "

"I know, Dad. But it doesn't do any good to accuse any one individual in the media or the press. I'm sure a lot of them are uncomfortable about the stories, too. They're just doing their jobs, following through. A lot of them are friends of mine."

"Some friends. Is that ex-classmate of yours reporting this bullshit?"

"Heather? I don't know. I haven't had contact with her in a long time. The last time I saw her on the air she was reading the early morning news in New York. Her career kind of petered out a while back."

"Maybe *she* started all this."

"Dad, why would she do that?"

"I don't know. I just figured if she knew you in school and told someone and they started gossiping and making things up . . . "

Jamie shook her head. "No, the accusations are too detailed to have come from gossip. Everyone on staff thinks they originated with someone who has a political ax to grind."

Paul reached over the side and put his hand in the cool water. "If your mother were here this would break her heart."

"I know, Dad. Everyone I'm close to feels bad. Brian said for me to tell you that he's thinking of you and Bianca and wants to get to know you better no matter how this turns out."

"Is he like Arkady? I mean is he intelligent and sensible like Arkady?"

"I think he is."

"Good."

"Sometimes when we're alone, Brian tries to talk in this phony southern drawl. Back in school, before I met Arkady, I remember Brian trying to get the woman behind the counter in the dorm cafeteria to fill his plate with black-eyed peas . . . the way he said it made the poor woman laugh like hell."

They both laughed at this. Then Jamie said, "To this day he can't stand black-eyed peas." And they laughed again.

"Why are we laughing?" asked Paul.

"I guess we needed it," said Jamie. "I guess we were looking for something to start us off."

The boat completed another half circle and now Paul could see Bianca sitting on the swing in front of the porch.

"I'm glad I'm older than Bianca."

"Why?" asked Jamie.

"Because I wouldn't want her to die before me."

"Good thing we have such a common name," said Jamie. "Don't have to worry about not being able to carry it on."

Paul turned to Jamie and saw that she was staring at him. "You've already made up your mind, haven't you?"

Jamie nodded. "Yes."

"You figure we haven't got much to lose because there won't be a future generation to disgrace if anyone is stupid enough to believe the crap that's being shoveled."

Jamie nodded again. "We think alike."

"I was telling Bianca before you got here last night that none of this bullshit will hurt us. Of course she disagreed as she often does."

"She did?"

"Yeah. She said sometimes bullshit *does* hurt, but just because it hurts doesn't mean we can't take it. Come on, let's start pedaling."

"Where to?" asked Jamie.

"I want to get back and tell Bianca the good news."

CHAPTER 23

THE PRESS CONFERENCE WAS SCHEDULED for the following Wednesday. Jim Hansen had wanted to hold it in Chicago, but his campaign manager convinced him to hold it in Washington to give the event more national emphasis.

When Jamie called her father late Monday afternoon to tell him about the conference, he wished her luck and said he and Bianca would be watching. Then, fifteen minutes after she hung up, Jamie's father called her back.

"It was Bianca's idea. I have to admit she's right. It scares the crap out of me to even think about it."

"What are you talking about, Dad?"

"I should be there. I mean just in case anyone wants to ask me questions. Not that they will, but I should at least be there to give you moral support. I'll leave it up to your guys. I don't know. Maybe they'll think it's a stupid idea. Too sentimental or something."

"Dad, I want you to come. Even if you don't answer any

questions, I want you to come."

"Then I will."

"Dad . . . that's great . . . I . . . "

"Wonderful, we're already getting sentimental. We better not blubber at this thing."

"We won't blubber. I've learned to get my tears out ahead of time."

"Like now?"

"Yes, like now."

"I feel bad that I've never been with you during campaigns. If your Mom had been here she wouldn't have let me get away with it. She would have dragged me to all the speeches and dinners and rallies. I haven't been a very good father since she died."

"Dad!"

"No, let me finish. I want to tell you something. It was a bad time for me when your mom died, but I had no right crawling into my shell like that. Remember when you graduated and I didn't even show up?"

"That was so long ago, Dad. And there wasn't an official ceremony. I graduated mid-year."

"Yes, but you asked me to come celebrate with you and I said no. I've felt guilty about that all these years . . . "

"But . . . "

"No. There's more. Deep inside I think I was jealous of you. You'd inherited the best your mom had to offer and ran away with it. Then I got depressed, so depressed I even thought . . . I even thought of killing myself. But two people came along and saved me."

"Who? What happened?"

"You happened, Jamie. You called me that night. I was in the garage. I remember standing there with one hand on the hood of the car and my other hand in my pocket holding the car key. I thought I was the loneliest person on Earth. Then the phone rang and I ran into the house and it was you . . . "

"I never knew. But you said two people helped you."

"That same night Bianca showed up. She said she'd gotten tired of looking across the lake and seeing the cottage dark at night."

"I was worried," said Bianca in the background. "I knew what he was going through and I was worried."

"Will Bianca be coming with you?"

"Of course I will," said Bianca, closer now, the phone rustling as Jamie pictured them sharing the receiver.

Jamie stood up from her desk and turned to look out the window. Her office was on the Delaware Avenue side of the Russell building facing northwest. It was on the same side of the building as Jim Hansen's office, and many senators had said from the start of the campaign that this was a good omen for Jim because the offices on the Delaware side had windows facing the direction of the White House. Although Jamie could not see the White House from her window, she could, if she leaned close to the window, see the Capital dome to her left. The sun was setting and, although she could see only the orange-purple sunset glow in the sky above the buildings to the northwest, she was able to see the glint of the sun's setting as a bright orange radius reflecting off the Capital dome.

"Dad? Bianca?"

"We're still here," said her father.

"I'll have someone call you about the flight time. By the way, the sun's almost down here and it's a beautiful sunset. I'll send it your way."

☢ ☢ ☢

At the press conference six chairs were set up behind the podium. Senator Jim Hansen's campaign manager stood at the podium and asked for quiet so the conference could begin, introduced Hansen, then sat in his chair.

Jim Hansen started with humor. "In 1980, Ronald Reagan was sixty-nine years old when he was elected President. I'm seventy and I guess if I'm elected you'll all have to put up with Jim Hansen's brand of nostalgia. But I promise not to mention anything about winning one for the Gipper."

The laughter was polite.

"Of course, maybe sometimes it's good to look back. Sometimes — miracle of miracles — we even learn from our mistakes. I've looked back to previous political aspirants who were dashed on the rocks by rumor and innuendo, but none of those situations seems to fit. No, I had to go a long, long way back in history to find a situation similar to ours here today. The situation I'm referring to isn't even part of our political past. It's part of our literary past and something you should all be familiar with. The situation is portrayed in a classic tale of fiction. Even though the story comes from fiction, I think it truly fits.

"Her name was Hester Prynne. She was ostracized from her community and forced to wear a scarlet letter A on her breast. She suffered because she was not able to defend herself, was not able to point out to the people of her community the cause of her so-called shame.

"Imagine how it was back in those days when having a baby

could be made into such a shameful thing. I guess the abortion issue would have really been a hot topic back then."

More polite laughter.

"My point in all this is to remind everyone of the effect of time in regard to accusation. Throughout the ages persons have been convicted of crimes and later found to be innocent. Throughout the ages persons have been the subject of rumor and gossip and have been vindicated days, months, or even years later when the vindication comes too late to do them any good. As a colleague of mine who had been blackballed said to me, 'Okay, I'm innocent of all charges. Now where do I go to get back my reputation?'

"Ladies and gentlemen, we have only a month and a half until the election. I can only hope and pray that rumor and gossip of the tabloid variety do not once again enter into the decision-making process of our electorate."

Before introducing Jamie, Jim Hansen answered a few questions. The significant component of his wording in answering those questions was his use of phrases like "our opponents" and "our views" and "our proposals." Obviously, he was committed to fighting side by side with Jamie.

When Jamie came to the podium she said she would be as brief as possible and that sometimes she might even seem terse. "I know of no other way to say things I never thought I would have to say than to be perfectly blunt."

She looked down at her prepared notes. "I've numbered the items so that both you and I can better keep track of them in case there are questions."

As she read from the list, Jamie looked down at her notes, studied each item until she was sure of the exact wording, then made eye contact with a different member of the audience during the reading of each item.

"Number one, regarding past sexual relationships. There have been only two persons with whom I've been intimate in my life. Both were men. I met Arkady Lyashko, a Ukrainian exchange student, when we were in graduate school at the University of Illinois. We had a close relationship for almost a year until he returned home. Over the past twenty or so years I visited him several times in the Ukraine. The last time I saw him was a year ago. He died this year after a long battle with leukemia.

"I first met Brian Jones, my current campaign manager, when I was an undergrad at the University of Illinois. When I became a member of the Illinois Congress, I asked Brian to serve as a state congressional aide. He went on to be a United States congressional aide, an environmental lobbyist, my campaign manager when I ran for Senate, and, while he is my campaign manager again, he is on leave from his position of Staff Supervisor of the Senate Environment and Public Works Committee. He is also active in the Sierra Club. Brian and I have had an ongoing relationship for many years.

"As a teen I dated but never became serious with any individual boy. If, as some rumors have suggested, I had an abortion resulting from youthful promiscuity, it would have caused terrible hurt and pain for my parents and myself. Although I can deny the allegation, I do not have a video recording of every moment of my past to play back for you. I don't think any of us would want such a replaying of lives, because if that were possible we would diminish the need for honesty and sincerity in this world."

Jamie looked down, studied her notes and looked up again.

"Number two, regarding past counseling I have received. All of the residents of Easthaven, Illinois, went through a period of several months of counseling to help them deal with the trauma of suddenly having to flee their homes and being told they might some day suffer the effects of their contact with toxic chemicals. In my case, although I was only two years old at the time of the disaster, I believe I was more affected later because of media attention at the trial of the president of the chemical company. The reason for this is that my father was the plaintiff at that trial."

A quick glance at her notes this time.

"Number three, regarding the possibility of brain damage resulting from exposure to toxins at Easthaven. Any damage sustained by me will not affect my brain cells. The damage is to the eggs in my ovaries and therefore would show up only in my children. Consequently, long ago I made the decision to never become pregnant."

Another glance.

"Number four, regarding the examination program I am involved in at the University of Chicago Medical Center. I agreed to this testing years ago for two reasons. First, the tests are a good way for me to feel confident I will know of any possible ill effect of toxins in time to do something about it. The most significant ill effect from a long-ago-banned pesticide called DBCP, to which I was exposed, is cancer. The second reason I agreed to the testing program, along with other children from Easthaven, is because it provides vital information in ongoing cancer research. As you all know, although many breakthroughs in cancer research have been made in recent years, there is still much to be done."

The notes again.

"Number five, regarding my parents' use of drugs. Like many of your parents, mine occasionally smoked marijuana in the early 1970s while they were college students. Other than that, my father was once given a dose of the hallucinogen lysergic acid diethylamide, commonly known as LSD, or acid. This occurred at a party when the LSD was slipped into his beer. My father has agreed to come here today. Later, after I'm finished, you can ask him about the details of the incident if you wish."

This time Jamie glanced at her notes for quite some time. When she started speaking again, her voice wavered slightly before she composed herself.

"Number . . . six, regarding my . . . relationship with my father. No one . . . I repeat . . . no one could have a better relationship with their parents than I've had. When my mother died, my father doubled his support of my goals in life to make up for the loss. Any good parent does this through love of their children. Today, I think of my father's friend Bianca Davis as my second mother. Ladies and gentlemen, to comment further on unfounded rumors of incest would be repulsive and hateful."

Jamie put aside her notes.

"A long time ago when I was visiting my friend Arkady Lyashko in the Ukraine, I had an opportunity to have a long talk with his mother. The Lyashkos lived in one of the villages newly constructed near the end of the last century for victims of the Chernobyl disaster. Mrs. Lyashko, instead of being bitter about losing her home and, at that time, one son to the disaster, spoke at length about what she called the endless life cycle. She spoke of a bargain struck between the very young and the very old. The best way I can describe it is like a relay race in which one runner is finished and another takes over. Have you ever watched them? No matter how tired and spent the runner who hands off the baton may be, that runner always takes time to look ahead and be certain the one handed the baton has gotten a good sendoff.

"Look, we've got to start something new here. We've got to get off this media image kick and buzzword kick and communicate more directly. Because of the problems we face in our world today, we need government officials like relay runners. We need government officials who are not satisfied simply with the immediacy of their images, but who instead take a long-distance view beyond their terms and beyond their lifetimes."

There were only two questions after Jamie's statement. The first came from a veteran reporter up front.

"Senator Carter, since you didn't mention the incidents, what about the arrest of your parents in the 1970s during a demonstration at the Iroquois Nuclear Power Plant and their participation in anti-segregation rallies?"

"In the first incident, the charges against my parents, and hundreds of other demonstrators, were dropped. Therefore, according to our legal system, none of the protesters released without being charged were shown to be guilty of a crime. As far as anti-segregation rallies are concerned, my parents participated with thousands of other anti-segregation protesters and were never arrested."

The second question came from a young man at the back of the room whom Jamie did not recognize.

"I agree that the rumors involving you are deplorable. However, I must ask two obvious questions. Why should we believe you? And why should we not assume you are using the misfortunes in life for your own gains?"

"I have no idea why you should believe me, and I have no idea why you should not believe me. Each of us has our own private thought life. The only way anyone could know anyone else's true rationale for their words and deeds would be to somehow share their thought life. And, so far, I don't think anyone has been able to do this."

After Jamie introduced her father, she hugged him quickly before returning to her seat. As she sat down, Brian, Bianca, and Jim Hansen smiled at her while Brian clutched her hand briefly. Hansen's campaign manager, who had been dead-set against repeating the rumors at the conference, was the only one who did not smile, and Jamie thought, *It's over. It's all over.*

When Jamie's father got to the podium he did not make a statement first. Instead, he said, "Anything you folks want to ask?" This made Hansen's campaign manager look down and shake his head slowly.

A question boomed out from the audience, a woman's voice. "What about these innuendoes about your relationship with your daughter? Was it child abuse?"

Many in the audience turned to the questioner with looks of disgust while Jamie's father coughed and fumbled nervously with his notes and his glasses. Jamie started to get up to take over, but Bianca touched her arm and she waited with the others while her father, looking frail as he stood at the podium hanging onto it, alternately stared at his notes and stared, with an obvious look of contempt she could see in the monitor, in the direction of the woman who had asked the question.

"Right now . . . " said her father, taking off his glasses and clearing his throat before continuing. "Right now, I feel worse than that time someone slipped acid into my beer at the Sigma-Alpha-whatever fraternity house party. I didn't belong to the fraternity and it doesn't matter now who did it. But it was a bad trip. They had to take me to the campus hospital. I remember, when I finally came out of it, thinking I had X-ray vision. Even later in life I've had experiences from that one damn trip where I think I can see into things. I can't, of course, but you know how the brain can play tricks.

"Anyway, the only other so-called drug I did back then was pot. I did that on my own along with just about everyone else. I can't say I did it in Vietnam because I got deferred — first school, then my job. My friend Hiram wasn't so lucky. He went over when he was just a kid, nineteen, I think. Anyway, Judy and I dated and we were activists and got arrested at least once that I can recall. We were hauled in and, like Jamie said, we were released early in the morning after a few hours in the can. We were never charged. I guess they didn't have room for all of us in court that day. The arrest was back in the 1970s or 80s, before Judy and I were married. I can't even remember what decade it was in. Anyway, Jamie wasn't around then so you can't blame her."

There were a few chuckles in the audience.

"Judy and I, we quit going to marches after we were married and Jamie was born. Somewhere in the late 1980s I got a traffic ticket for too fast for conditions in a fender-bender in a snowstorm. In this century I got a ticket for speeding in Michigan where I live now."

Out of the corner of her eye Jamie could see Jim's campaign manager lean toward Jim to whisper something. Jim glanced toward her with a closed-lip smile as if to say, *Well, we did our best.*

"Does that answer your question?" said her father.

"No," said the woman in the audience.

"But, I just told you everything I've ever done in my life that could get me in trouble with the law. So, you see, I *have* answered your question."

There were a few smiles and nods in the audience, then a few more. It seemed infectious. The looks of shared embarrassment and discomfort were replaced by more smiles. Jim Hansen turned to Jamie again, this time smiling more naturally as if to say, *Okay, so it's not over.*

"Before you ask any more questions," said her father, "let me say a few things I've prepared."

He put on his glasses and looked down at his notes. He mumbled, "When you're in your 80s your short-term memory sucks."

After the laughter subsided, her father read his prepared statement.

"Love is a learned emotion that starts with a person's mother. Sure, fathers can also teach love, but a mother's love is the basic thing. A mother's love comes from something that's planted deep inside every woman when she's born. I don't know how it gets there. I don't even want to speculate about God and infinity and us being grains of sand and all that. The important thing is my belief that women are the carriers of love from generation to generation."

Jamie's father took off his glasses and looked out at the audience. "Ever since she was only two years old, after the first tests at the

University of Chicago, we knew Jamie would never have children. My wife Judy was the one who had to tell Jamie about it when she got older and I know it was really hard on both of them. It was something a man can understand in one way, but not the way a woman can understand it. So Jamie will never have children. But damn it, motherly love is still there. And maybe if she's Vice President she'll be able to share it with more people. I don't mind. There's plenty left for me. Like my wife Judy said before she died, 'There are a lot of others who haven't even been born yet who need love.' "

After reading his prepared text, Jamie's father asked again if there were questions and he was asked about his memories of the Easthaven disaster. So he told all about it. He told it as he'd seen it in his nightmares, complete with flashing lights in the middle of the night, the swimming pool contaminated by Ricky Wade, the resettlement in temporary housing, the horrible days of waiting for test results while some whose homes were closer to the site were discovered to have bone tumors and nerve damage and cancers. Finally, he told about his role in the lawsuit against Ducain Chemical and about the settlement that, after years of distress, had allowed Easthaven residents to finally go on with their lives. He told about Harold Ducain's suicide after the settlement, and the letter from Ducain's daughter, the letter that he said had haunted him all these years, the letter that said by singling out Harold Ducain for blame, he had killed Harold Ducain.

When Paul finished answering detailed questions about the disaster, he paused, looked uncomfortable, gave a kind of wave, and said, "Well, guess that's it," and went back to his chair.

Someone in the audience applauded, a few others joined in, and when she looked at her father, Jamie could see that he was happy. The smile — wide-eyed and genuine — made him look younger. The last time she remembered him looking so happy and relieved was the time Arkady was struck by lightning in the sailboat and they found out, when they got ashore, that he was all right. No matter what happened in the election or what happened during the rest of her life, the one thing that was most important at that moment was that her father was truly happy.

The following week, a Senate-directed investigation found a link between what was being called the Jamie Carter smear campaign and a print and web-based tabloid in Pittsburgh called *The Eagle*. Bobbie Tracy, editor of *The Eagle*, admitted that he received the information during a series of anonymous phone calls and passed the information on to friends at other tabloids in order to lend the story credibility. Further investigation of subpoenaed telephone computer data found that the first of the anonymous calls originated from the hospital room of Heather West, an employee of ABC in New York and a college classmate of Jamie Carter. Heather West's husband, a New York network executive, and her only known relative, told Senate investigators that his wife disappeared from her hospital room on the day of the phone call and had not been heard from since.

CHAPTER 24

AFTER BIANCA AND JOE FINISH their breakfast of salad and fried fish, they stare at one another in the silence of the kitchen until Bianca suddenly pushes back her chair.

"My goodness. We didn't have anything to drink except water. Can I make coffee or tea?"

"Whatever you prefer," says Joe.

"I usually have tea," says Bianca. "Jamie introduced me to hot lemon tea some time back. She says they drink it that way in the Ukraine."

"Hot lemon tea is fine."

The sun is higher now, shining down into the sink as Bianca fills the kettle. She stares out the window. "Too bad they had to clear that land."

Joe stands and comes to the sink. He sees that Bianca's hand is shaking and he takes the water-filled kettle from her. Bianca lets go of the kettle and continues staring out the window.

Joe looks toward where she is staring. "You mean the clearing up on the hill?"

Bianca points. "Yes, halfway up the hill. Paul and I used to climb up the *hill to watch the sun set on the other side of the lake. They put that damn thing in right where our path went up the hill."*

Joe squints towards the woods, barely able to make out the clearing in the distance. "It's not that bad, you can hardly see it from here."

Bianca turns, walks to the stove and turns it on. Joe puts the kettle on the stove. After Bianca puts out the teapot and tea and a lemon, they both return to the table and she begins speaking of hit songs from the previous decade.

In the year 2034, a musical genre called story songs became popular on computer networks and satellite radio. The songs were usually ballads having something to do with environmental issues. One such song told the story of a couple who get married, plan a honeymoon drive to the west coast, and stop for the night at a motel where solar power is stored during the day and used to charge the batteries of travelers' electric cars at night. The couple get stuck at the motel three days and nights because of cloudy weather. After three days, the young man, initially vigorous and amorous, attempts to pull up the nightshade. As in the old joke, he goes up with the shade while his bride watches. This story song, done in a modified Chicago blues style was titled "Three Day Charge."

In the year 2034, even music critics voiced their opinions when it came to environmental issues. One critic, in panning "Three Day Charge," mentioned the recently-opened coast-to-coast MLT (Magnetically-Levitated Train) as a fine alternative for the honeymooners.

The celebration of the completion of the MLT took place in Promontory, Utah, where the original golden spike for the Union

Pacific Railroad was driven in 1869. President Jim Hansen was at the celebration to flip the switch turning on the final section of superconducting magnet. A San Francisco musical group released a story song reminiscent of "Chattanooga Choo-Choo" based on the MLT, but it failed miserably.

At its beginning in 2030, the decade had been dubbed the "Decade of the Environment." Some of the major environmental activities and breakthroughs taking place in the United States during this decade included ultrasonic separation of waste for recycling, environmentally-neutral wetland sewage treatment systems, planting of varied forests rather than hybrids to regenerate virgin forests, planting of varied crop species to lessen agri-chemical dependency and, most significantly, a reduction of the United States share of total world energy usage.

Many environmental successes in the decade were attributed to policies of the Senate Environment and Public Works Committee. The committee not only made specific technological and economic recommendations, but educational ones as well. However, there were still potentially disastrous environmental blunders of the previous century to deal with.

One of these blunders began over a hundred years earlier when chemical weapons were first developed for World War I. Some were used, most were not. Throughout the twentieth century, chemical weapons were manufactured and stockpiled again and again by country after country using the argument of deterrence. True, atomic weapons had also been stockpiled, but these could be dismantled. The destruction that could be caused by nuclear warheads was potential, needing a sophisticated trigger to change the substances into deadly destruction and radioactivity. Chemical weapons, however, carried their full potential with them, making them highly sought after by terrorists. To release their destructive capability, chemical weapons did not require triggering, but simply exposure to the atmosphere. They could not be dismantled. They had to either be chemically neutralized in expensive processes unique to each, or be put into containment vessels that would need to be maintained and guarded forever.

One unique, but expensive, method for dealing with especially concentrated chemical weapons that had short-sightedly been sunk inside ships at sea was to put their deteriorating containers aboard space shuttles and launch them from an Earth station to permanent orbit around the Moon. The half dozen disposal satellites that were sent into orbit around the Moon might appear, to aliens coming across them in the future, as displays of graffiti. This was due to the signage of every known language and using every horrible facial expression that experts could dream up to warn potential trespassers. One expert in a moment of frivolity added, in English, the statement, "Get the fuck away! This stuff is like sliding down a banister that turns into a razor blade!"

In 2034, another environmental story song was a ballad called "Ripples" by a young woman whose voice was reminiscent of Patsy Cline. In "Ripples," a little boy and girl toss pebbles into a pond while dreaming of what they will become. When the ripples bounce off the far shore of the pond and return, the boy and girl are older and dreaming of what they can do to help future generations. The song was especially popular with senior citizens involved in what was called the Grand Traverse Movement at senior settlements across the country. Digital copies of "Ripples" sold fairly well, but not nearly as well as "Three Day Charge."

☢ ☢ ☢

"It *is* a beautiful city, isn't it, Brian?"

"Beautiful, yes. But that's not the main reason I'm glad I came with you."

"Hard to believe St. Sophia's cathedral is almost a thousand years old."

"Not all of it, sweetheart. The guidebook says the tower was finished in 1852. Of course, if you're looking for *Ripley's Believe It or Not* numbers from the past, the tower took over one-hundred years to build. They started work on the foundation in 1744."

"That tickles."

"Is this better?"

"Hmm, better. Anyway, I wonder if the cathedral will be around as long as the Chernobyl Sarcophagus."

"I doubt it. They'll have to keep piling more concrete on that thing. The cathedral will weather away eventually."

"Sort of like us?"

"Just like us, Jamie."

"You know, when we were at Chernobyl today I couldn't talk because of all the media people, but I got to read some of the graffiti. Most of it was in Ukrainian, but a lot was in Russian."

"What did it say?"

"The one I remember said, 'At last, a safe nuclear reactor. And we did it first.' It was signed, 'An old and loyal party member.'"

"That's not very funny."

"Not to you, but having been exposed to Russian and Ukrainian humor, and not being able to laugh because of the serious ceremony, I had to bite my lip."

"Next time I'll bite your lip for you."

"Right. When we get back home the tabloids will have us secretly married again. And now, since the Sierra Club voted you their president, the headline will read, 'President secretly weds Vice President.' "

Jamie and Brian were in their room at the Hotel Dnieper in Kiev. It was night and outside the window the tower of St. Sophia's Cathedral was brightly lit. That morning they had toured the Chernobyl facility where a new fuel recycling reactor, which would burn old Chernobyl waste, had recently been dedicated. Afterwards they had viewed the Sarcophagus covering the site of the damaged reactor and Jamie had laid a wreath there to honor the victims of the disaster. In the afternoon they visited the home for pensioners at Svyezhl and were served a late lunch.

During her two years as Vice President, this was the only time Brian had accompanied her on a trip. Besides keeping his position as Staff Director at the Senate Environment and Public Works Committee, Brian's responsibilities at the Sierra Club had increased.

Originally, when Jamie became Vice President, she considered appointing Brian to the new staff position of Executive Assistant for the Environment, but both of them agreed that, although it was unlikely in the current environmental mood in the country, conflict of interest might be construed some day. They also agreed to have separate careers because they felt it would enhance their relationship.

Although she did not like leaving her chair as Senate President for these trips, Jamie took on the role Jim Hansen had asked of her. During the last two years she had traveled throughout the world trying to live up to what Jim called, "a catalyst for change in the world environment." During her travels, one conclusion she had come to was that no single technological or economic or sociological or political idea or breakthrough would solve the Earth's problems. As she had stated just that day in front of the Sarcophagus, it would take all of the solutions of all peoples operating together for the Earth to make its Grand Traverse into the next century.

She had begun using the term "Grand Traverse" widely to represent all aspects of the forward-looking emphasis she wanted to portray. Part of the purpose of that day's visit to the pensioner's home Arkady had started was to carry a message and gifts from the Wylie Lake settlement in Grand Traverse County, Michigan.

The message taken to the *Svyezhl Ozero* pensioner's home was to the effect that senior citizens of the world would one day meet on the other side in another place and look back with great pride on the legacy they left behind. Many of the current generation of interpreters of the extraterrestrial messages that continued to be received contended that this was pretty much the gist of the messages from light years away.

The gifts taken to the *Svyezhl Ozero* pensioner's home consisted of the components for a methane-producing septic system and several wind generators. Also as gifts, her father had sent along solar-powered personal cooling fans he'd constructed in his garage workshop, and Bianca had sent along potted oak tree seedlings she'd grown from acorns. Her father and Bianca might have made the visit personally had it not been for the discovery of spinal cancer in her father and the subsequent surgery and ongoing treatment. Although many breakthroughs had been made in cancer research, and most victims' lives were at least extended beyond what they might have expected in the past, cancer of a major organ — blood, bones, liver, spinal chord — was generally fatal.

It was late evening. They had just returned from a dinner hosted by Kiev and Ukraine officials. Lucy, Jamie's Chief of Staff, had just left Jamie's room. Except for a brief moment or two during the flight to Kiev, this was the first time she had been alone with Brian during the trip.

The light in the room went out and Brian joined her at the window. He stood behind her and put his arms around her. He unbuttoned her blouse and slid one hand inside.

"Your hand is warm."

"I keep that one in my pocket at all times for just this purpose."

"There's something I wanted to tell you during this trip but I haven't had a chance until now."

"Can't it wait?"

"It won't take long."

"Relatively speaking, I'm getting closer and closer to your age. And when a guy gets older he starts to worry about how long he can keep it up."

Jamie laughed. "It won't take that long."

"Okay. What is it?"

"Jim says he won't run for a second term."

"Really?"

"Yes. He said he'll announce next month and I should be ready before he announces. He wants me to run. He's giving me a month for it to grow on me before he makes his decision public. He suggested I wait a year until just before the one year campaign-fund deadline to make it official, but not to deny it. When I asked him what I should do during that year he said I should keep doing what I've been doing. He also pointed out what he claimed was my main weakness. He said I was a lot like my namesake, Jimmy Carter, and that I should learn from past mistakes. According to Jim I'm not supposed to try to understand everything, and not try to give everyone my code of ethics. He said not only does the public need this extra time to get used to the idea of me as President, but I can use the time to figure out who I really am and how I should handle the Presidency."

"That's incredible! How do you feel about it?"

"Scared as hell."

"But you'll do it."

"Have I got a choice?"

"No. I always thought Jim had it in the back of his mind to help put you into the oval office. But I thought it would be in 2040, not in 2036."

"I'll be forty-nine."

"And I'll be forty-seven."

"During the campaign there'll be even more pressure to get married than there is now."

Brian turned her toward him and kissed her. Then he whispered in her ear. "Okay. Will you marry me?"

"Let's go to bed."

"Lie down baby, so I can talk to you?"

"Yes."

CHAPTER 25

THERE WAS A SNOWSTORM IN the mountains. In town the snow had melted on the streets. On the main road out of town it had formed an inch-thick layer of slush that sprayed into the wheel wells of her truck, sounding like drum rolls. On the gravel road the snow had been several inches deep. Now, on the logging trail that led to the cabin, she had to put the truck into four-wheel drive because of the layer of snow atop a base of mud churned up by her trip out from the cabin in the rain that morning.

It was November. Because of the predicted snowstorm she had gone into town that morning for her winter supplies. The previous winter she had been snowed in from mid-December through early March. She had not expected a snowstorm in November and had put off her trip for supplies. Outside, the snow whipped into the logging trail's narrow canyon through the trees. The snow was heavier now, drifts a foot deep. The truck was weighed down with bottled and canned goods, five-gallon containers of kerosene for her backup heater and gasoline for her chain saw. The four-wheel drive worked well considering the extra weight. As long as she kept her forward momentum, the truck would make it to the cabin with its precious cargo just fine.

It had taken the morning and part of the afternoon to make the rounds of various stores collecting her goods. She had stopped at the bank for cash first, taking five-thousand dollars in fifty-dollar bills from the safe-deposit box she had rented three years earlier under the name Jenny Ducain. Two years ago, when she permanently moved here, she had sold all her jewelry and added that cash to her personal savings. She had put the cash totaling almost two million dollars into safe-deposit boxes in several banks north of Denver. Today, after visiting one of those banks, she had gone to four grocery stores, two hardware stores, a gun shop, a ski shop, a clothing store, a gas station, and a liquor store.

She was beginning to see her signs now, nailed to trees along both sides of the narrowing trail. After purchasing the cabin years earlier she had put up a variety of Keep-Out, No-Trespassing, Private-Property, Beware-of-Dog signs along the trail and completely surrounding the property. The cabin had never been broken into during her long absences when she was still Heather West. The final sign along the trail, made from a bumper sticker that said "Protected by Smith & Wesson," must have conjured up images of a bitter old man sitting with a twelve-gauge across his lap and his vicious dog by his side at the end of the trail.

The truck slipped sideways at the bend in the trail and she had to fight the steering wheel as the front tires banged against tree roots hidden by snow and mud. Cans and bottles clattered and rattled in the back of the truck.

When she passed the Smith & Wesson sign she recalled a gun control commentary she had done years earlier. She had cleverly berated an Illinois congressman who was in favor of gun control for conflicting statements he'd made regarding his right to protect his family. She remembered Leslie Gale being very proud of her on that one. It was one of the many commentaries she did at Channel 10 in Champaign to which Leslie responded by disagreeing with the message while praising the method. One of the commentaries she recalled often these days was one involving an Illinois survivalist group. In the commentary she had given details of an outing taken by the group to the Wisconsin Northwoods. Her colleagues later told her that after all the sordid details of beer-drinking and shooting the bark off trees they had expected her to condemn the survivalists. Instead, she had compared the survivalist outing to the antics at tailgate parties at the university. An innocent blowing off of steam. Leslie had almost agreed with her on that one. Neither Leslie nor her colleagues at the station had any idea that Heather West was a survivalist at heart. No one knew. Of all the advantages of escaping to her cabin, the part she enjoyed most, even after two years in hiding, was that no one knew where she was, or even if she still existed. Perhaps the extraterrestrials, cleverly having sent messages ahead to keep the eggheads busy, had been kidnapping the brightest and the best from the face of the Earth all along.

She could see her stacks of firewood now, row upon row of logs she had cut from fallen trees in the forest, hauled in her truck, and split by hand. She felt a sense of pride as she viewed the stacks with their curving caps of snow. She remembered the slivers and cuts and bruises and blisters that, after a few weeks, had turned to calluses. She had felt like a pioneer woman in the new world, a woman who had no need for men.

She was forty-eight years old. The last time she had been with a man was over two years earlier with Jack. Now her sexual encounters were only in her mind, encounters drawing upon her experiences. But not with Jack. The experiences she drew upon now were the one-night stands when she was younger, the night at the truck stop motel, the summer she stumbled across the young man working on the ski-tow.

She saw the cabin's chimney first — no smoke so she knew she'd have to rebuild the fire — then she saw the roof line rounded smooth with snow, the window to the sleeping loft, the porch. She skidded to a stop in front of the cabin, pulled on her watch cap, tightened the laces on her boots, and went out into the driving snowstorm.

She put away the kerosene and gasoline first, hauling the five-gallon containers to the shed. She had built the shed during her first full year living here. She had read books on carpentry, bought the tools she needed and hauled the materials here in the truck. No one had ever made a delivery here since she'd moved in. Here, she was completely and utterly alone.

As she stood for a moment in the shed looking out at the snowstorm, at her stacks of firewood, at her truck, at her cabin, she remembered a night not so long ago when she'd heard a noise out by the shed. At first she'd gotten out her pistol, then changed her mind and loaded the shotgun. When she cracked open the door she saw several deer run from behind the shed, their white tails aglow in moonlight as they leapt and darted about her wood piles seeking the safety of the woods. One of the deer had clearly been a large buck and this had set her mind racing as she imagined men instead of deer out in the moonlight. For several nights after that the gang-bangers in her fantasy world made their home in the shed and she went out with her sleeping bag to be with them.

She wiped the moisture of melting snow from her face with her jacket sleeve. Then, very suddenly, she was a little girl named Jennifer again. The motion of wiping her face with her sleeve, the feeling of wet snow on her face, the smell of her wet jacket, had recreated a snowy day in Illinois when she was a girl. She had been in the backyard trying to build a snowman. Her brother and his friends had thrown snowballs at her and she had run into the garage. Outside on the white lawn, her father, wearing no coat, had come from the house to defend her. The snowball fight lasted only a few minutes, the boys driven away by her father's superior aim. Now her father was coming to her, bending a little as he neared. He would pick her up. He would pick up his precious bundle of molecules and take her inside.

But he did not pick her up and when she opened her eyes she saw the snowstorm, her stacks of firewood, her truck, her cabin, and beyond it all the trees in the woods bending in the wind. She went out to the truck to begin taking her provisions into the cabin.

She took only one small box of canned goods on her first trip so she would have a free hand to unlock the door. Inside the cabin she put the box on the table and surveyed the inside as she always did when she'd been away any length of time. True, she always locked the door, but someone could get in through a window and she needed to be certain, to reaffirm in her mind this place of security, her only place of security in the world.

She checked each corner. She checked the sleeping loft. She checked the bathroom, sliding back the curtain on the shower quickly. Then she pulled back the rug in the main room and lifted the trap door to the cellar, leaned down, turned on the light and checked there, too.

All was in order and she spent the rest of the afternoon bringing in the provisions from her truck and neatly organizing and marking everything as she stored the provisions away for her winter hibernation.

☢ ☢ ☢

That evening, after dinner, she showered and put on her black nightgown. The fire in the wood stove had warmed the cabin up to eighty degrees. She made a drink, single malt scotch on ice. There were three cases of scotch in the cellar, plenty enough to go around.

She went to the large floor-to-ceiling cabinet on the windowless back wall of the cabin and opened it. Inside the cabinet was a television monitor, a satellite scanning receiver, the remote control for the dish antenna she had mounted herself to the back side of the cabin, an AM-FM radio, a control for the radio's directional antenna rotor, a short-wave receiver, an antenna tuner for the wire antenna strung between trees in the woods, a satellite receiver, audio and video recorders, and a computer, printer, and FAX.

Above the equipment, neatly organized on shelves, were media recordings she had made as they were broadcast, or made by accessing the remote access media historical file to which she'd subscribed. By accessing the web site of the media file service in Denver and putting in her password, she could view and record newspaper or magazine articles, she could watch television news and commentary, or she could listen to radio news and commentary stored on the system, all of it collected by the media service from over the past twenty or more years. The media coverage recordings she had saved were on minidisks. The minidisks were in boxes of ten and each was labeled. On the top shelf the labels read, "H. West" followed by a date and year. Even more boxes of minidisks were stored on the shelf below this. These were labeled, "J. Carter" followed by a date and year.

She turned on her computer and accessed the media service in Denver. The computer screen displayed a summary of the day's stories. But she already knew the summary. She had seen the headlines while in the grocery store and had heard people talking about the news. Yesterday, a full two years before the 2036 election, President Jim Hansen had announced that he would not run for a second term. And, shortly thereafter, Vice President Jamie Carter, when pressed, had not denied that she would run, and if she did run would wait until the right time to officially announce.

She clicked on the button for a detailed story and sat down to watch. When the computer screen went into high-resolution mode and began showing the news as first covered by each of the major networks in turn, she sipped from her glass of Scotch.

☢ ☢ ☢

Later that evening, after having watched all of the major coverage of the previous day's number one story, which included a mini-biography of the Vice President and probable future candidate, she put her glass down next to the half-empty Scotch bottle and went to the cabinet, hanging onto it for balance. She typed, "J. Carter, Wylie Lake," into the media search program, pressed Enter, and stumbled back to her chair.

As the screen showed details of the Wylie Lake settlement, including interviews with Paul Carter and Bianca Davis, and including a brief historical account of Paul Carter's role in the lawsuit "Easthaven versus Ducain," she lifted the now iceless glass of Scotch to her lips again and again.

When the coverage on Wylie Lake ended, she shut off the computer and closed the cabinet. She stumbled and nearly fell but made it to the sleeping loft stairway. The climb to the loft was difficult and she had to stop halfway above the spinning main room to rest. When she finally made it up the stairs she took her pistol from her dresser and fell backwards across the bed holding the pistol near her breast. But she did not point the pistol at herself.

No. She would never point it at herself the way her father did. She would not even point it at the gang-bangers when they came. The pistol was for someone else.

As the early November snowstorm raged outside, closing the cabin in for winter, she slept.

CHAPTER 26

ALTHOUGH THE BEGINNING OF WINTER was unseasonably cold and significant snowfall had occurred across the United States, the winter finished off quite mild. Whereas, in November and December of 2034, there had been speculation that perhaps global warming had begun to reverse, by February and March of 2035, the speculation had taken an about-face, with polls taken throughout the country predicting that most citizens felt the worst was yet to come.

In the summer of 2035 — a hot one, especially in the Midwest — it was announced that the world sea levels had, on average, gone up another four centimeters. This, along with the heat wave, did not help the mood in the country. Even the optimistic scientific findings released at the most recent protocol of the Intergovernmental Panel for Climate Change held that year in New York did not help.

The findings of the most recent protocol, gathered from scientific working groups throughout the world, showed that, although the Earth's atmosphere was still warming up, the trend of slowing down the rise, begun several years earlier, was having some effect. The best evidence now showed that a decade or so after mid-century the rise in average atmospheric temperature would top out and begin to fall at much the same rate as it had risen. As for the rise in sea levels, scientists said that the best computer models showed that the effects of temperature on sea levels would follow the same curve but that the increase in level would, because of the huge heat storage capability of the seas, top out at least another decade later. This was devastating news for island nations already hard hit earlier in the century.

As far as the current heat wave in the United States was concerned, this was said to be a cyclical anomaly. Although the summers until mid-century would have average temperatures hotter than summers of the previous century, it was not necessarily true that all summers would now be as hot or hotter than the summer of 2035.

The economic working groups who met that summer at the New York Protocol were more optimistic. According to data they had gathered, the developing countries in the world had, on average, made significant strides toward renewable-based economies. This had been done with huge expense to the developed countries. But the economists were quick to point out that, had the developed nations not provided this aid, there would now be many countries hooked so strongly to fossil fuel economies that, not only would the scientific findings have been very grim, but local skirmishes, increased terrorist attacks and, perhaps, major war might have been the result. Although many developing countries were not as prosperous as they might have wanted to be, they were at least following a new path toward prosperity, one that, as the economic protocol statement read, ". . . does not rely on burning all their bridges behind them as happened in the two centuries following the industrial revolution of 1800."

The sociological working groups were the pessimists. The reasons for their pessimism were the effects observed in various societies across the globe when it was announced that global warming would continue beyond mid-century. Even though scientists and political leaders and the world media went into great detail explaining that the temperature increases would be less and less each year as the turning point approached, the psychological effects of knowing that the peak year was decades into the future, and that many people would never even live to see that infamous year, were devastating. Indeed, reported the sociological working groups, "If we are to survive to witness the year of the turning point, the way of life on our planet will be forced to change a great deal more than it has already changed in the last decade." An optimistic footnote given by the report of the sociological working groups stated simply that, "Working together as a world nation, perhaps we can find our way through to the other side."

☢ ☢ ☢

In the United States, during the summer of 2035, use of fossil fuel in personal vehicles was at an all time low because the internal combustion engine had finally been replaced by fuel cells in most new vehicles. As for mass transportation, an extensive variety of more efficient options of travel, including van pools, traditional rail, MLT, and organized flight tours, also helped reduce consumption. Some, however, were not going to give up their gas guzzlers. Even though the expense was outrageous, die-hards insisted on the freedom to travel where they wanted, when they wanted, and as fast as they wanted by a route chosen by them. Of course, with many gas stations closing along cross-country interstates, the die-hards often had to plan hundreds of miles ahead so as not to be stuck in the middle of nowhere.

In the mountains, on the communications devices connecting her to the outside world, the woman who once called herself Heather West had been made aware of this problem with gasoline and had prepared ahead. If she was going to make a long journey in her truck in the fall, she could not afford to run out of gas. And so, during the summer, she had stocked up, purchasing extra gasoline containers, filling them and securing them in the back of her truck. According to her calculations she had increased the range of her truck to almost two-thousand miles, more than enough to reach her destination. And, assuming she was still able to purchase some gasoline along the way, she would most likely have more than enough to make the return trip once her goal was accomplished.

She sat in a wooden chair on the porch of her cabin. She wore tattered jeans, a plaid shirt, and work boots. Her hair, stringy and wild when she first sat down, was smoother and straighter now because of the brush she pulled through the amber rat's nest again and again. If she was going to travel and be seen outside the small town where she bought supplies, she needed to look more presentable.

She stood and walked to the truck, bent to look at her reflection in the side mirror. Her hair looked fine, just fine. As far as her face was concerned, she no longer cared because she hadn't bothered with makeup for many months. Last winter, during her hibernation, she proved that she no longer cared about wrinkles and age lines when she took all the mirrors out of the cabin and broke them to pieces behind the shed.

After inspecting her hair in the truck's side mirror, and noting that her face was nicely-bronzed from its daily exposure to the bright mountain sun, she went back to the porch and sat in her chair in the shade. Once seated, she picked up a bottle of Scotch from the floor next to the chair and took a swallow.

Her truck was ready. She was ready. But it was still summer. Perhaps she would leave in October. Yes, October thirty-first. Halloween. Trick-or-treat, y'all.

☢ ☢ ☢

It had been a long summer for Vice President Jamie Carter. During the first half of the Senate's summer recess she toured the nation making appearances to push for social and environmental legislation. Then she attended the New York Protocol where she was chairperson. Then a trip to Africa and the Middle East to meet with leaders about the possibility of a reduction in aid from the United States. While in Africa, she spoke to African leaders about a hunger summit slated for 2036.

In October, the Vice President was in Washington overseeing the Senate where, among other bills, a new budget was hammered out. In early November, as planned, she officially announced her candidacy for President in the election of 2036. After announcing, instead of hitting the campaign trail, she flew to the Orient for a trip planned over a year earlier in which she was to meet with business leaders in China and Japan and Korea on trade issues.

When she flew back from Japan after the November meetings, Jamie thought she would immediately be able to get on the campaign trail. It was one year before the election and, because of initial higher-than-expected showings by the other party's front-runner in national polls, she wanted to start her run for the year-off election as soon as possible. Doing the job of Vice President might be enough for nomination, but it wasn't enough for the Presidency. She needed to convince the public she was a serious candidate. She had convictions and she needed to tell people what those convictions were and what they meant for America. As many media pundits put it, she needed to show that she was Presidential material. But during the press session following the final meeting in Japan, Jamie's campaign plans were put on hold when her Chief of Staff brought news that her father's cancer had reached a critical stage and he was in the hospital in Traverse City.

☢ ☢ ☢

The pain in his chest and back and shoulders told him he would never again be able to sit up under his own power. Above him, where the ceiling met the far wall, a story on television — young man once paralyzed but now able to walk with the aid of an electronic nerve stimulator — mocked him. He struggled to press the remote button placed beneath his right hand by Bianca before she left the room. He had wanted the television left on — much better than death-like silence — but he had not expected a story of a young man's struggles to affect him so deeply.

When he finally managed to switch the station, he saw a ghostly image. It was a blurred photograph of a woman in a cartwheel hat. A woman being held by her gloved hand by a man whose body had been cropped out of the photo. As he stared at the photo, a male narrator told of the unsolved disappearance of Heather West, how she walked out of a New York hospital three years earlier and was never seen again.

As he stared at the photograph, something about the woman made him tremble, something about the way the corner of her mouth turned upward. But more than that, he stared at the area just below the brim of the woman's hat. That hair — reddish, amber — took him back in time to a little girl staring at him from the back of a courtroom, a little girl being led by an older boy from the court-room, a little girl almost seeming to smile at him despite the gravity of the situation. A smile that seemed to imply . . .

He struggled, groping for the call button on the remote control. Soon after he pushed it, the nurse's face and Bianca's face came be-tween him and the story being told on television. He tried to speak, but could not. He tried to point, but his arm felt as if it had already been drained of blood by the mortician. He tried to get Bianca to ask questions so he could nod or shake his head in order to tell her what he knew, in order to tell her that Heather West — Jamie's friend from years earlier, the same Heather West who tried to turn public opinion against Jamie — was really Jennifer Ducain. But he failed. And soon, with the effort, tears filled his eyes and he could not see.

He tried one more desperate attempt to sit up, but the pain

crushed him and the world went black.

☢ ☢ ☢

When Air Force Two landed for a stopover at three in the morning in San Francisco, Brian Jones, who had been supervising a Sierra Club working group at Yosemite National Park, came on board after driving from Yosemite while Jamie's plane flew from Japan. During the stopover, and before the plane took off for Traverse City, Jamie's Chief of Staff and her Executive Assistant for Special Projects left her and Brian alone.

"Do you know anything more about your father?"

"Just that he's in a lot of pain. Bianca says I should see him before they sedate him further. Your eyes are red. How was the drive from Yosemite?"

"Snow in the mountains, then rain all the way to Stockton. First I had to put up with flakes the size of moths in my headlights, then smeary windshield wiper blades. With the lights and wipers on I was afraid the batteries wouldn't hold out."

"I slept on the flight here. You must be tired as hell."

"I am. I'll try to sleep when we take off."

"Brian?"

"Yes."

"That part of the message you gave to Lucy when she called you, that part about needing to talk about something important before we arrive at Traverse City . . . is it what I think?"

"Yes, I think instead of waiting until Christmas to announce our engagement, we should do it now."

"Because of my father?"

"Yes, if his health is failing . . . "

Jamie put her arm around Brian, rubbed his neck. "Then we'll tell him when we get there and make it public afterward?"

"Sure," said Brian, moving his lips along the top of her head the way he'd been doing lately, her hair rubbing along his lips like the silky edge of a baby blanket. "Unless you think there's something special your campaign manager would like to time it with. And of course you'll have to tell your staff so they don't get blind-sided."

"What would you do if you were still my campaign manager?"

"I'd make the announcement from Wylie Lake. After you visit your father I'd tell you and your handsome and virile fiancee to go to Wylie Lake for a night on a squeaky old bed, send out a press release from there, and go into Traverse City the next day to visit some jewelry stores and make it official."

"You're a sweet guy, Brian."

"I know."

"I have mixed feelings right now. I'm anxious to let everyone know about us, and at the same time I'm worried as hell about Dad."

"Are you afraid to be worried and happy at the same time?"

"Yes."

"I'll help you."

Brian kissed her and held her tightly, then they lay down on the cushioned day bed against the plane's curved bulkhead across from the conference table.

"I hope no one walks in," said Jamie.

"Aren't they supposed to knock?"

"If I tell them. I told my staff we needed some privacy and they won't be back until just before takeoff, but the crew . . . "

"Ah, the crew," said Brian. "Then we'll keep our clothes on for a dry hump."

"I've noticed you're using more sexually-oriented slang as the election nears."

"Yes, my dream come true. Ultimately, I want to be able to walk naked into the White House boudoir and say, 'Okay, enough of this running the country shit. Let's fuck.' "

"Is that the only reason you want to marry me?"

"No, I like rubbing my lips on your hair."

"And that's it?"

"Your smile's okay, too."

"Am I smiling?"

"Yes, finally. And now, as long as you are smiling, there's one other thing I need to ask."

"What's that?"

"After this is over, win or lose, will you go on a trip with me?"

"A trip?"

"Yes, remember? You still owe me that bicycle ride across the country."

"I do remember. It's the trip that will make my butt fall off so that you'll have to be there to pick it up."

"That's the one."

They lay in one anothers' arms for several minutes until Brian fell asleep. Then Jamie carefully left the daybed, got a blanket from an overhead and covered Brian. The blanket had a silky edge that she positioned gently between his lips. He smiled, but kept his eyes closed.

When the plane took off for Traverse City at five in the morning, she went to the other compartment for a bite to eat with her staff. Everyone agreed that the jet lag had them all screwed up and that it felt like dinner time. They seemed tired until she told them the news about her and Brian. After that, it was all she could do to keep them from raiding the compartment where Brian slept.

☢ ☢ ☢

As they made their approach to the Traverse City airport at eleven in the morning Michigan time, Jamie whispered to Brian that for years, every time she flew over the twin arms of the bay, she thought the bay resembled a woman's breasts.

"Even more so at night because of the lights lining the shore. I especially remember the night I flew here to see my mother before she died."

Brian turned to her and smiled sadly. The moist blue of his eyes resembled the blue sheen of the water glistening outside the plane's window in the late morning sun. He blinked his eyes several times as the plane flew through low clouds and shadows from the windows across the aisle flickered on his face.

Brian took her hands in his and looked at her seriously. "I'm really sorry about your father and your mother and Arkady and all the rotten things that happened before I met you. But I want you to know that no matter what your past might have been like, and no matter what your name or position was, I would have fallen for you."

She kissed him quickly. "That's the kind of thing I need to hear on a day like this. I guess you're getting to know me."

☢ ☢ ☢

It was a bright, sunny morning and she wore sunglasses. There were reporters gathered in front of the terminal at a podium near the moveable stairway. If she were dressed differently and had a recorder and long-distance microphone she could blend in with them. But posing as a reporter, although she'd had experience at it, would have been a mistake. She was certain they had all gone through a thorough search in the terminal before coming outside.

She was not dressed as a reporter and she had not come through the terminal. She had come onto the field hours earlier while it was still dark by riding the back end of a truck that had driven through a service gate. Although the Secret Service in their nylon jackets were all over the place, she had been able to outmaneuver them. The one at the gate she had fooled by jumping off the far side of the truck and running quickly along its blind side being careful to stay behind its large rear wheels. After that, she had found a place among luggage carts to hide until morning.

She was dressed as an airport ground crew employee. She had been watching the workings of the ground crew personnel from the woods outside the fence through binoculars for several weeks. She had seen three women working at the airport, one of the women about her age and build. Last week she had stolen the uniform from a laundry truck parked at the airport. Early this morning, when she heard the news that the Vice President would be coming to Traverse City to see her father, she had put the uniform on over jeans and a sweatshirt and walked the mile or so from the State Park campground to the gate in the airport fence.

When she first arrived in Traverse City, she had considered going to Wylie Lake, but she knew it would be well-guarded there, and staying on the outskirts of the city, at the State Park campground, would be best.

When she heard news that he was in the hospital, she had considered going there. But she felt there would be too much confinement in the hospital, too many obstacles to her escape back to the cabin.

No. There was nothing to be done at the hospital. What she had to do must be done here.

She walked confidently across the tarmac, approaching the rolling stairway. She put on the sound-deadening ear cups and when the young man in a uniform just like hers looked puzzled and said something, she pointed to one ear, shrugged her shoulders, grasped one edge of the rolling stairway and stood ready to help the young man move it into position the way she'd watched others do it during the previous weeks.

The plane was approaching, its engines sending heat ripples into a blue sky dotted with low clouds. The plane taxied toward the gathered crowd of reporters. Her pistol was in the deep pocket of the uniform. She was ready.

☢ ☢ ☢

As suggested by Jamie's campaign manager, Brian would leave the plane well after her, just ahead of her staff as if he were one of them. Soon, very soon, that would not be so. Soon, he would accompany her as she exited and entered airplanes. Prior to the landing, Brian had made a joke about changing his name to Adam since very soon people would be calling him, "the first man."

As the plane landed, Jamie stared out the window and recalled the celebration that had taken place a few minutes earlier. If only her father and her mother could have been here. If only Arkady could have been here. How ironic to have a celebration at a time like this. All three of them would have insisted on celebrating with her and Brian and her staff despite the reason for the trip. All three of them would have admired the youth and energy of her staff, and would have had positive things to say about future generations. The only reason *she* hadn't said anything about the future was because the exuberance of her staff had made her weep.

Not long ago, before the seatbelt light came on, Jamie's staff had laughed like crazy and continued Brian's Adam and Eve joke, someone saying they'd have to avoid mentioning that the President used to be nothing but a rib from the first man. Someone else saying they'd have to keep an eye on her to make sure she didn't "serve up forbidden fruit at official dinners."

Jamie's campaign manager had said, "Dignitaries from the Middle East might understand the forbidden fruit business. But they'll have a hell of a time with the rest of the Adam and Eve story, especially the rib business."

Lucy, her chief of staff, had broken out a bottle of champagne and glasses. "To the future first couple. May their happiness be complete and lasting."

Her campaign manager had given another toast. "Both of you will always be in our hearts."

After the toasts, Jamie had broken into tears, and so had everyone else. "Come on, you're only crying because I am."

They had all denied it, saying they were crying because they had to.

But now the tears were dried, and as Brian held her arm and the plane taxied, Jamie had a brief image of a nation rejuvenated by the energy of youth. The energy of these beautiful people and so many others who were out there. Young people who care more for the future than the present. Young people who will take charge when she and her father and Bianca and Brian are gone. Despite the reason for the trip, it was time for her to become Presidential. Her staff and the voters expected it.

She and Brian stood when the seat belt light went out, they held hands in the aisle for a moment, kissed quickly, and she turned toward the forward exit.

After the plane's engines shut down, a young man in a ground-crew cap peeked in at the window and the cabin door was opened. As always, she waited long enough for Secret Service and ground crew personnel to clear the stairway, then she stepped outside and waved.

She did not pause to wave very long but went down the stairs quickly, heading for the podium to make the brief statement that she was here to visit her father whose illness had taken a turn for the worse. She imagined the questions she'd be asked as she descended the stairs. She imagined her answers.

I won't know how serious until I speak with his doctor.

Yes, apparently it's the cancer.

No, I haven't spoken to him on the phone.

Yes, Bianca is with him.

It was bright and sunny with only a few errant clouds in the sky. Jamie paused at the bottom of the stairway shading her eyes. The mayor of Traverse City, whom she recognized from a previous visit, stood at a distance waiting to greet her. She had asked Lucy to phone ahead that she wanted to make her brief statement first, answer a couple of questions, greet the mayor, then get the hell to the hospital.

Jamie was just about to walk to the podium when she noticed the woman in ground crew uniform standing off to the side. The woman wore sunglasses and looked about her age. The woman looked tough, her cheeks weathered and tanned. There was something familiar about the woman, something that conjured up memories of a softer face, a younger face. The woman wore a cap and had on ear protectors even though the plane's engines were off. She could see curls of amber hair coming out from behind the woman's ear protectors, amber hair aglow in the sunlight.

Jamie started walking forward to the podium. There were a few handclaps. Someone shouted, "Miss Vice President!" But she did not look at the shouter. She turned back to look at the woman who stared at her strangely and . . .

The woman took off her sunglasses quickly and dropped them to the ground. Then she smiled a wry smile that made Jamie turn and raise her arm to point.

But it was too late. Brian was standing in the doorway, his sandy hair blowing in the wind, then he was coming down the stairs and the gun was there and the explosions and smoke were there and suddenly he was shot in the face and chest and was falling and she was pushed down and saw the woman running. Running!

She screamed, trying to say the name. But all she could scream was, "Brian! . . . Brian!"

When she stopped screaming, two agents were carrying her, running with her, her feet dragging, trying to stop them so she could go to Brian.

In the distance, above shouts and sounds of running feet and a plane landing out on a runway, a woman in the crowd screamed over and over in a high-pitched voice, "Someone save us! Someone save us! Someone please save us!"

☢ ☢ ☢

The pain continued to squeeze him as if he were being molded by vast mechanisms into various shapes like a man of red-hot steel. He tried again to concentrate, tried to remember if the image of Heather West in a cartwheel hat was real or not. He tried to tell himself that the pain was not something that would kill him, not yet. He tried again to convince himself that the pain he felt was in his mind, was simply the result of electrical impulses sent to the brain and that, since the impulses were not of lethal voltage or current, they would not hurt him. The pain alone would not kill him, and he would be able to get at the truth.

A hand touched his arm and he tried not to grimace before opening his eyes. He did not want Bianca to look sad because hers was a face that should never look sad again.

But when he opened his eyes he did not see Bianca.

Jamie!

She looked much older than when he'd last seen her. And her eyes were red as if she'd been weeping. He wondered if the end was closer than he had thought. He wondered if he'd been out for days or weeks and they had resuscitated him for the final moment. But no, the pain was too strong. He was still fighting the damn pain.

Bianca was also there, behind Jamie, both of their faces floating above him.

Jamie touched his cheek. "Don't try to talk, Dad. I'll do the talking."

But she did not talk. Instead, her eyes squinted and her smile faded and one tear, then another, ran down her cheeks. She leaned forward and kissed him on the cheek. Despite the pain he tried to reach out to her. Her face was at the side of his, her breath wet and fast in his ear.

"Dad," she whispered. "Dad."

Jamie's sobs made him feel a sudden strength. He saw Bianca's face at the side of Jamie's head and reached out for her. Somehow he managed to move his arm and they all three hugged and wept.

Something was very wrong.

CHAPTER 27

NOVEMBER ENDED WITH A COLD snap, which again reversed the volatile convictions of many regarding whether global warming would continue or not. Perhaps the cold weather would continue. Perhaps this winter would be a signal sent back from the future that the dreaded greenhouse effect had been thwarted and the ice caps would once more begin to add to their bulk. Perhaps the reversal of global warming would somehow affect the brain of the species. Through a kind of evolutionary jump into the new future, the human species sharing Earth with so many other species would become a docile, peace-loving creature, a protector of the Earth and all its creatures instead of a cold-blooded killer.

The event that took place earlier in November at the airport in Traverse City, Michigan, when it was unseasonably warm throughout the country, had made many wish for this change of weather. Yes, at least it was a change. At least something had changed and everyone could go on with their lives.

On Thanksgiving weekend it snowed in Traverse City, it snowed in Chicago, it even snowed as far south as the University of Illinois in Champaign-Urbana. It was considered quite a cold snap when it hit this hard, this far south, this early in the season in this century of global warming.

The local weather forecast had just ended, confirming the fact that it was snowing outside her apartment window in Champaign. Leslie Gale turned up the volume of the television because now, Larry Van Horn, one of Leslie's protégés, and of whom she was quite proud, was making his commentary debut on the network nationwide.

Larry was the last commentator of merit Leslie had trained before her retirement and she felt warm inside as she remembered his fledgling days at Channel 10. Imagine mispronouncing Chernobyl by sounding the Y as if it were a long I. He had done that reading a story about one of Vice President Carter's visits to the Ukraine. But then he was young, his birth still decades away when the Chernobyl disaster occurred in 1986. So, who could blame him?

Larry Van Horn had black hair and brown eyes. He had a prominent chin and high cheekbones. His mother was Cherokee Indian, his father's lineage was mixed — Dutch, French, German, Hungarian, Polish — and he would have had to trace back several generations before he found a branch in his family tree that originated outside the United States. The mispronunciation of Chernobyl was a fluke. He had read widely and even knew details of the incident. But, as he told Leslie following that early broadcast at the start of his career, he could not remember hearing someone else pronounce it.

When Larry finally appeared on the screen, Leslie leaned

forward in her chair to watch and listen carefully.

"As I'm sure you've heard by now, Paul Carter, the father of Vice President Jamie Carter, died this past Monday in Traverse City, Michigan, after a year-long battle with cancer. He was eighty-four years old. In the obituary printed in the Traverse City paper it says that he is survived by his daughter and his friend Bianca Davis and by all of his other friends at Wylie Lake.

"As you know, Paul Carter, because of his work establishing the Wylie Lake settlement, was considered a leader in the Grand Traverse Movement. But Paul Carter was socially active at other times in his life. In the 1960s and 70s, for example, he joined many other Americans protesting the Vietnam War. And in the late 1980s and early 1990s, after the Easthaven chemical disaster forced him, his wife Judy, and their daughter Jamie from their home, Paul Carter became the key figure in a lawsuit against the Ducain Chemical Company. That lawsuit resulted in not only helping the financially strapped victims of the disaster, but also set a legal precedent that changed the way chemical companies did business in our country. Unfortunately, the lawsuit was also the apparent cause of the suicide of Harold Ducain, then president of Ducain Chemical Company.

"Last Wednesday, the day before Thanksgiving, Paul Carter's ashes were spread on the surface of Wylie Lake in front of his cottage at sunset by his daughter Jamie and his friend Bianca Davis."

During the initial part of his commentary, Leslie noticed that Larry had glanced occasionally at his notes. Now he stared directly at the camera, which zoomed in ever-so-slightly.

"Paul Carter died of cancer two weeks after the shooting at the Traverse City airport in which Brian Jones, a close friend of the Vice

President, was killed while accompanying her to the hospital where her father lay critically ill.

"Personally, I will never forget the images on the news that day. I will never forget the scene at the emergency entrance to the hospital when Vice President Carter broke away from the two Secret Servicemen holding her by the arms and ran ahead to accompany the gurney on which Brian Jones lay with a bloodied bandage covering his face. I will never forget the look on the Vice President's face caught by the camera at the emergency entrance doorway as she ran alongside the gurney.

"As she ran into the entrance alongside the gurney, the Vice President glanced at the camera. Her face was wet with tears. It is a scene that will remain in the memories of everyone who saw it for a long, long time. Especially memorable to me was the impression that her face at that moment in time portrayed what millions of words could not portray. Her face portrayed fear and sorrow and suffering. But the look on her face also showed anger and release. To me, the moment captured the innate violence of the past, present, and future of our species. It captured a personal reaction to violence and caused, in me, a realization that we are still, and will always be, at the water hole brandishing our newly-discovered clubs and sharpened stones."

When Larry paused, Leslie noticed that the camera zoomed back slowly and Larry again referred to his notes. Yes, she thought, no matter how refined the prompters, using printed notes is still effective.

"If you've been following the news this week I'm sure you're aware of the findings of the various investigative organizations regarding the shooting at the Traverse City airport. I'm sure you've seen the footage of the four-wheel drive truck with Colorado license plate at the Traverse City campground. I'm sure you noticed the bedding and gasoline containers in the back of the truck, and the evidence that someone had been camped at the site for some time. I'm sure you also heard the news that the truck was registered to the Colorado woman who allegedly killed Brian Jones.

"Today, over two weeks after the shooting, the identity of the woman, which had been kept confidential pending a thorough nationwide investigation, was finally revealed. We now know that Heather West's original name was Jennifer Ducain, that she was the daughter of Harold Ducain, the former president of the Ducain Chemical Company that once had a facility in Easthaven, Illinois, and that, for at least the past three years, Ms. Ducain had lived alone in a cabin deep in the woods in the Colorado Rockies.

"There's been a lot of speculation concerning motive. Perhaps it has to do with what separates our species from the other species on our planet. Sadly, to do harm to a fellow human being, an attacker need not necessarily attack that person, but rather someone close to the person. We are privileged as a species to be granted the gift of emotion. This incident, unfortunately, demonstrates the dark side, an attack on a loved one."

The camera zoomed forward again and Larry abandoned his notes.

"Like me, Heather West graduated with a degree in broadcast journalism from the University of Illinois. Like me, she interned at the campus television station. She even worked for my former boss, Leslie Gale, at the Channel 10 affiliate in Champaign after graduation. Eventually Heather West came here to New York and made broadcasts from this very studio.

"I hope I can do better than Heather did. I hope I can do my part to contribute to peace and survival on our planet."

There was a longer pause as the camera zoomed back farther than before and Leslie could tell Larry was wrapping up.

"The Presidential election of 2036 is less than a year away. Today, Vice President Jamie Carter said that she hopes the events that took place in Traverse City do not affect the decision of the voting public. She said she hopes everyone votes on her record and not on her personal affairs.

"But the moment has flashed before us and we know everything affects everything. If I had not followed the same course of studies and career path that one of my predecessors did two decades before me, perhaps I would not have been given the opportunity to be here tonight. It is, after all, a matter of being in the right place at the right time.

"My name is Larry Van Horn. Good night and Happy Thanksgiving."

Leslie shut off the television and went to the window. The snow was heavier now with at least two inches on the ground, and she thought, how surprised and delighted her granddaughter will be to see this beautiful snowfall when she gets off the train tonight at the Illinois Central Station with her grandfather and father and mother as they arrive home from their fishing trip in the Ozarks.

Leslie picked up the phone on the table near the window and placed a call to New York to congratulate Larry.

CHAPTER 28

AFTER THE PRESIDENTIAL INAUGURATION IN January of 2037, work was begun on a helicopter pad on a hill near Wylie Lake in Michigan. The hill overlooked the cottage retreat of the new President. The cottage was maintained by the President's friend Bianca Davis. Work was also being done on the garage adjacent to the cottage. This would serve as a command post for the Secret Service when the President was in residence. Beyond the cottage, which the President had insisted did not need refurbishing or work of any kind, was the lake.

The lake was frozen that year, much more solidly than it had been during the past few warm winters, and there was one ice fishing shanty on it. The shanty belonged to Joe Siebert, named after his uncle, Joe Siebert, who had been one of the original Wylie Lake residents. The younger Joe had worked undercover for the Secret Service for several years and was now assigned permanently to Wylie Lake. Fishing was good that January and tests by the Michigan

Department of Natural Resources showed that contamination levels were down. Like his uncle, the younger Joe fished the lake more for peace and quiet than for the catch. If he did manage to catch something, he usually released it.

In February of 2037, Heather West — a.k.a. Jennifer Ducain — was sent to Leavenworth, Kansas, where she was incarcerated in the women's section of the Facility for the Mentally Ill. Although the staff assigned to the section did their best to bring Heather out of her silent world, the only time she uttered a sound was when she was in the section's stainless steel whirlpool bath. The guard assigned to watch Heather in the whirlpool room reported that, when she came close behind Heather and listened, she could hear Heather repeating over and over, "There, there, Precious. There, there," as she stared down into the churning water.

In April of 2037, to mark the anniversary of Arkady Lyashko's death, his two sisters and their families placed a wreath in his honor at the site of the Chernobyl Sarcophagus. During the laying of the wreath, nearby construction crews, who were reinforcing the sarcophagus, shut off their equipment and took off their hats to show respect.

In the summer of 2037, at the Rio de Janeiro Protocol in Brazil, scientific working groups from around the world revealed that their findings showed that the average rise in ocean levels would not, as had been expected, peak at mid-century, but would instead peak perhaps another ten centimeters higher between twenty and thirty years later. Although this meant more losses for island nations and coastal areas, the scientists said they were now absolutely certain that the decade of the 2070s was the magic decade; the average rise would peak out and begin to fall no later than 2080.

The sociological working groups at the Rio Protocol, for the first time, officially recognized the importance of the Grand Traverse Movement of senior citizens worldwide. For this reason, representatives of the movement from participating countries were invited. Bianca Davis of the Wylie Lake settlement in Grand Traverse County, Michigan, represented the United States.

At the conclusion of the Rio Protocol, all members of the panel and all economic, sociological, and scientific working groups agreed that there was still much work to be done. The theoretical interpretations of ongoing extraterrestrial messages continued to include allusions to collaboration amongst former adversaries. This interpretation had become a protocol mantra. The protocol for the following year was scheduled to be held in Chicago, Illinois, The United States of America.

☢ ☢ ☢

In December of 2037, an old song from the 1980s made a comeback. Several artists recorded the song and the original was digitized and appeared on the computer networks. The song's popularity was attributed to the President, who told the media, after her surgery in the fall to remove a lump from her breast, that she sang the song in the shower every morning to cheer herself up. The song was called, "Angel of the Morning."

THE END

Don't Miss Michael Beres'
Next Exciting Novel

THE
PRESIDENT'S
NEMESIS

MICHAEL BERES

ISBN#1932815732

Platinum

$24.95

Political Thriller

September 2006

MEN OF BRONZE

scott oden

" Sing, O Goddess, of the ruin of Egypt..."

It is 526 B.C. and the empire of the Pharaohs is dying, crushed by the weight of its own antiquity. Decay riddles its cities, infects its aristocracy, and weakens its armies. While across the expanse of Sinai, like jackals drawn to carrion, the forces of the King of Persia watch . . . and wait.

Leading the fight to preserve the soul of Egypt is Hasdrabal Barca, Pharaoh's deadliest killer. Possessed of a rage few men can fathom and fewer can withstand, Barca struggles each day to preserve the last sliver of hi humanity. But, when one of Egypt's most celebrated generals, a Greek mercenary called Phanes, defects to the Persians, it triggers a savage war that will tax Barca's skills, and his humanity, to the limit. From the political wasteland of Palestine, to the searing deserts east of the Nile, to the streets of ancient Memphis, Barca and Phanes play a desperate game of cat-and-mouse — a game culminating in the bloodiest battle of Egypt's history.

Caught in the midst of this violence is Jauharah, a slave in the House of Life. She is Arabian, dark-haired and proud — a healer with gifts her blood, her station, and her gender overshadow. Though her hands tend to Barca's countless wounds, it is her spirit that heals and changes him. Once a fearsome demigod of war, Hasdrabal Barca becomes human again. A man now motivated as much by love as anger.

Nevertheless honor and duty have bound Barca to the fate of Egypt. A final conflict remains, a reckoning set to unfold in the dusty hills east of Pelusium. There, over the dead of two nations, Hasdrabal Barca will face the same choice as the heroes of old: Death and eternal fame . . .

Or obscurity and long life . . .

ISBN#193281518X
Platinum
$26.95
Historical Fiction
www.scottoden.com

The Keeners
Maura D. Shaw

The rough beauty of County Clare is seventeen-year-old Margaret Meehan's whole world, and it is nearly perfect. Her family is well and thriving, farming Ireland's staple crop. She expects to marry handsome Tom Riordan, raise their children, and live in a cottage across the lane from her best friend, Kitty Dooley. She has found her calling and is apprenticed to the old keener Nuala Lynch. Together they keen for the dead, wailing the grief and pain of the bereaved in hopes of healing their sorrow. Margaret's life is full of hope, full of purpose.

But the year is 1846. The potato blight has returned. Pitiful harvests rot overnight and the people are dying. Ireland is dying. And Margaret cannot keen for an entire country.

Out of devastation, Margaret Meehan's tale begins. Leaving her decimated family, the tragic Kitty, and the death of dreams behind, she flees with her husband, now a wanted man, to America. In Troy, New York, where pig iron, starched collars, and union banners herald the success of Irish immigrants, Margaret discovers something even more precious than a new life and modest prosperity. She finds the heart and soul of Ireland. And she finds it in the voice of . . . The Keeners . . .

ISBN# 1932815155
Platinum
$25.95
Historical Fiction
Available Now
w w w . m a u r a d s h a w . c o m

A FOREIGN POLICY

Richard Graham-Yooll

Guy Sinclair is an insurance agent. But not just any agent.

When the company director invites him to a restaurant to talk about his doubts concerning the firm's world renowned business partners, the last thing he expects to be is the target of a suicide bomber. Miraculously surviving, he flies to Saudi Arabia to investigate a routine claim that turns out to be anything but routine.

Accepting yet another invitation he should have turned down, Sinclair atends a party turned surreal. Witnessing a brutal murder, he finds himself the suspect. The penalty under Saudi law? Beheading. The only person who can possibly help him? The sister of the woman who blew herself, and his boss, to smithereens.

Can it get worse? Yes. It can. When the trail he follows leads close to home. And Sinclair's family becomes involved with him in a deadly . . . Foreign Policy.

ISBN#193281549X
Gold
$6.99
Political Thriller
September 2005

BLOOD TiES

LORi G. ARMsTRONG

What do they mean?
How far would someone go to sever . . . or protect them?

Julie Collins is stuck in a dead-end secretarial job with the Bear Butte County Sheriff's office, and still grieving over the unsolved murder of her Lakota half-brother. Lack of public interest in finding his murderer, or the killer of several other transient Native American men, has left Julie with a bone-deep cynicism she counters with tequila, cigarettes, and dangerous men. The one bright spot in her mundane life is the time she spends working part-time as a PI with her childhood friend, Kevin Wells.

When the body of a sixteen-year old white girl is discovered in nearby Rapid Creek, Julie believes this victim will receive the attention others were denied. Then she learns Kevin has been hired, mysteriously, to find out where the murdered girl spent her last few days. Julie finds herself drawn into the case against her better judgment, and discovers not only the ugly reality of the young girl's tragic life and brutal death, but ties to her and Kevin's past that she is increasingly reluctant to revisit.

On the surface the situation is eerily familiar. But the parallels end when Julie realizes some family secrets are best kept buried deep. Especially those serious enough to kill for.

ISBN#1932815325
Gold
$6.99
Mystery
Available Now
www.loriarmstrong.com

For more information

about other great titles from

Medallion Press, visit

www.medallionpress.com